"Thou Shalt Not Suffer A Witch to Live. . . ."

Drena's head fell to her chest and jerked back. She was dropping off into a luxurious, lethargic sleep. The smoke began to rise through the cracks in the floor. As the sea breeze fanned the flames up the open stairs, the curtains became torches.

She looked down onto the street where Chris Dixon sat in the old Church station wagon, calmly smoking a cigarette and watching the house burn. She waved, but Chris just gave her a fixed stare.

As the inferno of flames reached Drena's body, Chris switched on the ignition. He drove away slowly as the wail of a siren cut across the quiet afternoon . . .

WITCH

Katina Alexis

POCKET BOOKS

New York   London   Toronto   Sydney   Tokyo   Singapore

An *Original* Publication of POCKET BOOKS

POCKET BOOKS, a division of Simon & Schuster Inc.
1230 Avenue of the Americas, New York, NY 10020

ISBN: 0-671-67627-X

First Pocket Books printing November 1990

10 9 8 7 6 5 4 3 2 1

POCKET and colophon are registered trademarks of Simon & Schuster Inc.

Printed in the U.S.A.

*To Janet Wilkens Manus
who believed in me
when no one else did.*

• Prologue •

Chris Dixon groaned and shifted in the bed, squinting against the burst of sunlight. He struggled in the twisted sheets, fighting against the smell of vomit and stale liquor. Had she opened the curtains? Or had they been open all night?

The house was up an isolated dirt road, five miles from any other dwelling. It seemed secure from the revenge of civilization. Outside, birds sang in the dew-wet meadow bordered by a wall of dark coniferous trees. Faint tendrils of mist rose into the warming air.

Chris struggled upright in the bed, rubbed his eyes, and surveyed the interior of the rustic house with its big central living room and second-story gallery ringing the open space. The room was a wreckage of overturned furniture, shoes, clothing, guttered-out candles, and pentagram-decorated black cloth. A goat's head sat on the mantel staring with glassy eyes, a suspended trickle of blood oozing down the rough stonework. In the corner was the mutilated pig they had killed with a butcher's cleaver.

Chris fought a dazed nausea. It had been the Sabbath, the witches' Sabbath. A woman had lain there, the goat's head and candles on her naked body, an altar to Satan.

Chris had wanted to leave before it all began, but he didn't have the will. And once his clothes were off, he didn't want to be anywhere else. She had simply been too beautiful.

1

He sensed her presence before she came into the room. She was as tall and exquisitely naked as he remembered. Jet black hair. Perfect breasts. Eyes that held him hypnotized. Even now, her gaze burned him with a deep fire.

"I buried the girl where she will not be found," she said.

"What?" Chris stuttered, still dazed.

"She was dead. I had to bury her."

A sudden panic crept through Chris as he remembered the blood and the screams, the knife rising and falling. His hand . . . holding the dripping hilt! A funny twist adorned the corners of his mouth. "Hey, you're putting me on. It's all a gag, right? Witches' Sabbath. I mean, that's all it was, wasn't it?"

An indulgent smile played on her perfect red lips. "You're one of us now. A very special one because I have chosen you for my mate. I know your soul and all its secrets. You are my clay to be molded. You have done the sacred killing—the religious sacrifice. You may now draw the body's power and mingle it with your own."

Chris swung his feet out of the bed and onto the rough board floor. He felt the terror of an animal caught in a trap. "I—I've got to be going. I didn't mean to stay the night. Things just, uh, got out of hand. I . . . uhm . . . I think . . . I'm imagining things."

She put her hands on her hips, blood-red nails facing him. He felt hypnotized as she rolled her head. She smiled again. "Don't leave before I give you something."

"Oh, hey, uh, no . . ." protested Chris. "I mean, I don't accept gifts from women." Terror had him in its grip. He wanted to be back in his apartment in the village near the campus, away from everything this woman represented.

She looked back over her shoulder as she walked to the mantel and found the meat cleaver she had used earlier. With one smooth movement, she laid the ring finger of her left hand on the mantel surface and chopped down with the blade. It made a sickening crunch as the cleaver stood imbedded in the heavy wood.

She jerked her wounded hand away and bent at the knees, clutching her hand to her abdomen and then to her breasts.

Her face clenched in intense pain. The severed finger lay on the mantel.

When she straightened up and pointed her bleeding hand at him, blood smeared her body. "You will carry it with you as a sign," she pronounced, her words divided by gasps of pain.

Chris Dixon faltered on the brink of reason and then took the long slide down to unconsciousness.

• / •

Congreve, Georgia, sat on a peninsula at the confluence of two muddy rivers, the Elstree and the Carteret. Modern suburbs sprawled across both riverbanks and to the north. Historic Congreve, no larger than two miles deep and one mile wide, was filled with charming old houses, jutting gables, and walled gardens that held the secrets of families that had occupied the same plots of ground since the seventeenth century.

The Reverend Christopher Lawrence Dixon III stretched his strong limbs and breathed in the scents. The azaleas and dogwood were just starting to blossom in that brief, glorious beauty before the onslaught of the hot summer. Chris smiled. The lavish beauty of spring seemed to match the blossoming of his career; he appeared to be destined for a bishopric.

At age thirty-nine, he was the youngest rector in the two-hundred-year history of the prestigious St. Helen's Church in downtown Congreve. A prominent church that held fast to Anglican tradition, St. Helen's was squarely in the middle of Congreve society. The members all lived in the right part of Congreve—south of Main Street—and their lives were dictated by an ordered social calendar.

Strikingly handsome, blond, generous to a fault, the Reverend Dixon knew he was going places. With his mag-

5

netic personality, Chris had been drawn to the charismatic movement within the church, and he had injected a new vibrancy and leadership into his services.

On this bright day, Chris was supervising the clearing of the unhallowed ground closely. To all who asked him, he explained that the weed-tangled half acre inside the rusted iron fence across from the church on 1 Bayswater Street was being opened for additional grave space. The plot sat ringed by old brick walls on two sides and decorative iron on the other two, a weed-choked haunt for birds and burrowing animals in the middle of the historic city. There were no headstones, so tourists never poked inside looking for dates. The one structure within it, a tiny mausoleum of Italian marble, bore no name or designation and was obscured by yew trees. The old ghost tale of a weeping child being heard beside it on moonlit nights was not to be found in any books of Congreve lore.

From the congregation, Chris had learned that St. Helen's graveyard proper had been filled since before the Civil War. With the opening of the new ground, he would be able to inter a limited number of prominent church members right in the heart of the old city of Congreve. As with all change in the historic city, it was a controversial move. But many of the wealthier church members seemed almost eager to die so as to receive the final honor of resting beside their oldest ancestors.

Splendidly educated at St. Paul's School, Dartmouth College, and Christ Church College, Oxford, Chris Dixon had refinement, culture, and old money—the *sine qua non* of the ministry. His mother Faith, who lived with him in the rectory, was a lady of polish, and it was assumed that the Reverend would someday marry a woman of equally perfect background. Many Congreve women were seen as fine matches, but no one would have been surprised had he selected a woman from Tennessee, where he had had his first church, or even the Hudson River Valley, where he had been raised. Both locales seemed appropriate, places of heritage that kept themselves immune to the plastic outside world.

Chris leaned on his mattock and watched as the workmen chopped at the thick brush. He liked to present the appearance of pitching in with the laborers and wanted to be able to tell the congregation how he had worked with his own hands in common toil. That would strike a fine note in the Sunday sermon on humility.

Across the quiet street, the fine neoclassical structure of St. Helen's stood solid and proud. Built in 1698, the original simple frame structure had burned a year later. It had been rebuilt in stone in the Wren style with twin towers and a covered porch between. The nave of the church was long, with a baroque German organ in the choir, fine ornamentation, and dark marble. Gothic additions had been built in the nineteenth century to suit the taste of that era—to the right, as you faced the church, an arcaded cloister with a garden in the center, and to the right of that, a chapter house that housed the church administrative offices and a separate school building. The manse was several doors down among a row of Federalist houses.

Chris turned from admiring his church to the workers. He wanted to be present in case anything irregular happened. Even in history-conscious Congreve, few knew the truth about the history of the unhallowed ground, but Chris knew from Ryan Stafford, the former rector, that it had been a special plot for those of substance who were outside the blessing of the church. Too wealthy for potter's field, but with a doubtful future in the afterlife, they had been barred from sacred soil.

The workers hacked at a twisted wisteria vine with picks and axes. It was as thick as a man's waist and so deeply rooted in the soil that it could never be completely dug out. The main thing was to clear off the lot so it could be used for burial.

Chris ran his fingers along the cast-iron fence as he nodded to a passing tourist wagon drawn by a mule with blinders. Among the gravestones, the winged skull decorations leered at him through weeds and blackberry bushes. Sticking his shovel into the soft earth, he wandered over to the tiny mausoleum. Like an imitation of a Greek temple, its sloped roof sat on two tiny, scrolled columns.

Using work gloves to protect his fingers, Chris pried at the edge of the cast-iron door. It grated on a century of dirt and grime, but widened enough to let him enter the somber tomb. There was the smell of damp, dead leaves and cool stone. Snail shells scattered as he scuffed his foot against the uneven brick floor.

Stone sarcophagi lay against either wall, repositories against the wet. It took all Chris's strength to lift the plain, uncarved lid on one of the stone boxes and slide it, grating, to one side. It contained nothing. No bones. No fragments of wood or cloth. Only dust and cobwebs. He grunted as he worked the lid back into place, edging it into the grooves with a heavy thud.

Pausing to wipe sweat from his forehead with a shirt-sleeve, Chris leaned against the wall and caught his breath. He turned to the other sarcophagus and wrenched the lid free, sliding it toward the foot of the coffin. In the dim light, he could see a face. Fear clicked in his mind like a switchblade. Gritting his teeth, he shoved the lid farther down. She was encased in a clear bag of heavy plastic to keep the moisture out. She wore no clothing, and her body—it was uncanny, because he knew she had been dead for twenty years—her body was not decomposed. She might have been buried yesterday. He reached out to touch her flesh through the bag, but drew back in dread. The eyes were open, still blue against her deep brown hair. They glistened through the plastic, staring up at him knowingly.

Her hands were heavy-looking and folded as if in prayer. They were thick, oddly in contrast with the rest of the feminine form. Chris gripped the edge of the stone coffin to keep from shaking.

For nearly two decades he had tried to deny his bondage to this body—tried to deny its promise of power, so sweet and alluring despite his sin of murder. They hadn't meant to kill her. They hadn't really killed her at all. The witch had done it—the witch who still filled his nightmares.

Terrified tears filled his eyes. Why had he disturbed this ground? Why was he such a weak fool? He could cast off his bondage if he only had the strength!

Chris tried to pray for divine mercy, but a biblical Scripture flooded his mind with an ominous message. Involuntarily, he whispered it aloud:

"And there was war in heaven; Michael and his angels fought against the dragon and his evil angels; and the dragon and his angels.

"Prevailed not; neither was their place found anymore in heaven.

"And the great dragon was cast out, that old serpent, called the Devil, and Satan, which deceiveth the whole world; he was cast out into the earth;

"Woe to the inhabiters of the earth and of the sea! for the Devil is come down unto you, having great wrath, because he knoweth that he hath but a short time."

Chris heard the workmen calling his name but he didn't answer. He told himself they would figure he was taking care of church business. He stayed in the mausoleum, frozen with fear of what was about to begin!

• 2 •

Drena Wrenn threw open all the windows of her rambling house on Robinson's Island. The wind brought in the smell of salt air off the sea, coursing over the thickly foliaged sand. It disarrayed the curtains and the loose papers on the desk in the study. But Drena wanted a good draft.

As she felt the Valium working its calming effect, Drena hummed softly to herself. The tune was "Camptown Races." The first-grade class used to sing it so many years ago. How many? Well, it must have been . . . thirty-one years? Long time ago, yet the memories were still vivid.

Drena had always had a good memory, especially for the sensual things: tastes, colors, smells. The way wool or cotton felt against the skin. A leisurely bath on a hot summer's night. Bare feet on a rotting boat dock littered with fish scales and oyster shells. The touch of a man's lips on her breasts.

Drena had been in love with life. Not a great beauty, she had an air about her that drew the artistic types, the men with sensitivity, the men who could sense her contact with other worldly emotions. She had always been artsy, making her own paper dolls as a small child, progressing to pastels and paints in grammar school, and finally to poetry in her adolescence. In college, she had edited a series of poetry journals and women's movement newsletters, occasionally a slick art magazine that would last for a few issues and then go bust.

Sitting down heavily in an armchair, Drena dabbled her finger in a gin and tonic. How odd to think that this was the last drink, the last cool taste of lime.

Idly, she looked around the study. Its walls were covered with photos of her and her friends mugging for the camera. Women of every size and shape in every manner of clothing —Mother Hubbard dresses, tight black leotards, see-through nightgowns. Women who wrote plays or romance novels in secret moments or threw pots or took painting courses at civic centers. Women who were in touch with their emotions.

Drena stared the longest at the Hutton Hall class photo of herself looking so Arcadian and beautiful in a Grecian toga. Hutton Hall, an exclusive Congreve girls' school where Drena had been voted most artistic before she had gone off to Bennington College in Vermont, her suitcase filled with black wool stockings, berets, and volumes of T. S. Eliot and Ezra Pound.

Drena took a long drink as she watched the curtains flap in the breeze. Even though it had seemed like such a sensible course of action at the time, she should never have come back home nine months ago. It was just that she had broken up with Michael, her art professor boyfriend at the University of Pennsylvania, and she didn't have any savings. When Drena had learned that her poor grandmother had died and left her the lovely old Robinson's Island family home, she had looked forward to a return to the clean, hot sunlight of the island where she had been born, a retreat to old friends and a youthful renaissance.

Drena hadn't expected to meet Chris Dixon again. After all, he was a Yankee. He belonged up in New York, not in Congreve.

Drena had always had a gift for looking deeply into human nature. And when someone recognized it, she was flattered. But then there were the ones who recognized her gift and felt threatened by it. They were the dangerous ones. The men with unplumbed depths of black evil. The ones who had chosen the left-hand path. Like Chris Dixon.

Suddenly feeling stifled, Drena lurched to her feet and leaned on the windowsill. She couldn't see smoke yet. The fire she had set with gasoline and rags on the ground floor had barely begun. The flames would take time to mount, even in the dry wood of the century-old beach house.

She looked down at the street where Chris Dixon sat in the old church station wagon, calmly smoking a cigarette and watching the house. Not many people knew that Chris smoked, since it wasn't appropriate for his image in the church. But Drena knew. She knew lots of things about Chris. Drena waved, but Chris just gave her a fixed stare. Drena felt so giddy. The Valium and gin was perfect. She wasn't scared at all. Soon she would pass into the next world where Chris Dixon couldn't follow her.

Drena laughed as she stumbled back to the armchair. She was seeing double now and had trouble picking up the glass. How wonderful not to be afraid. There was nothing to fear. She had had glimpses into the next world all her life. Flashes of realization and insight. Certain knowledge of that diaphanous world where sensibilities flowed like a soothing river toward a beckoning light. Soon Drena would be a speck of water in that eternal river.

Her head fell to her chest and jerked back up. She was dropping off into a luxurious, lethargic sleep. She wouldn't be awake for the pain. Drena didn't like pain. It was the opposite of pleasure, after all, she mumbled to herself. Why couldn't Chris see that? Why was he so intent on pain? She wouldn't be a part of pain. That was why she had to die. The Scriptures were quite clear on that point.

"Thou shalt not suffer a witch to live."

This was the last coherent thought to go through her head as smoke began to rise through the cracks in the floor. As the sea breeze fanned the flames up the open stairs, the curtains became torches. Sparks popped and flew.

Drena was dead of smoke inhalation before the inferno of flames caught her body and turned her into an unrecognizable, charred mass.

Out in the street, Chris Dixon switched on the ignition and waited calmly until the battery light went off. He started the engine just as a neighbor woman ran through the screen of trees that surrounded the house, made panic-stricken hand movements, and then ran back to her own house to telephone. The small fire station on the island had already spotted the rising smoke, and the wail of the siren cut across the quiet afternoon.

Chris drove slowly away, looking back only once in the rearview mirror. The wind was moving the tree leaves. It was the wind of death.

● 3 ●

"Don't go out there, lady," warned the uniformed cop. "If that girl grabs hold of you and jumps, there's nothing we can do."

Morgana Stone looked at the rail of the middle span of the big Carteret River Bridge, speculating on how awkward it would be to climb over it. One of her students was on the other side, holding on with both hands, leaning out over the river two hundred feet below.

"That girl needs me," she said to the cop. She dodged around him.

"Come back here!" ordered the cop, taking a few steps toward her. Then he glimpsed the wild eyes of the girl beyond the railing and hesitated.

Morgana had found the suicide note an hour before in her faculty mailbox at Hutton College. Its disjointed, rambling message described a distraught mind fearful of being possessed by evil forces. As a volunteer counselor from the psychology department, Morgana had worked with Joan Scott since autumn, making little progress. Frequently, she had urged the girl to commit herself to the psychiatric wing of the hospital.

In the last month, Joan had begun to describe a dreamy wish to plunge off the high bridge onto an island below that was filled with scrubby trees and nesting birds. The girl said she often jogged over the bridge, stopping to gaze down at the clean white birds. Alarmed, Morgana had tried to initiate an involuntary commitment, but no one would cooperate.

The moment she read the good-bye note, Morgana had known where to find Joan. Borrowing a bicycle, she had ridden through the lanes of jammed traffic and pushed her way past the crowd of police, firemen, and spectators.

"Miss Stone," cried the girl, "I didn't want you to come."

Morgana moved slowly forward, trying to capture Joan's eyes with her own. "You knew I couldn't let you do this," she said calmly.

"Satan's inside me," said Joan plaintively. "I have to drive him out. There's only one way to save myself. I have to die."

Morgana knew that Joan Scott was the product of a fundamentalist Christian upbringing. As such, she had a vivid notion of Satan as an actual evil force that could take possession of people's souls.

"We'll do it together, Joan," she said. "We'll find a way to drive him out together."

Joan started to cry. "I want help, but I can't find it! Preachers tell me to pray for salvation. Doctors tell me I'm crazy. I'm not crazy! You know that! There really is a devil tearing at me, making me have evil thoughts!"

Morgana reached the railing. The girl's hands were within inches. "I know about evil, Joan. I know it's real. I know it can be beaten. You don't need to die. Now, climb back over that fence."

Joan's mouth quivered. "I . . . I want to come back. But I'm afraid!"

"Don't let go, Joan," Morgana said, moving closer. "I'm coming over to help you."

Morgana began to climb over the railing slowly. Down below, the island was a shimmering mass of green, tangled jungle. White ibis sailed in to settle among the tree limbs.

Joan looked down at the island and surrounding water and froze. Then her face twisted into weird contortions. Morgana was just over the fence when the girl grabbed her around the neck, pressed her face close, and mouthed:

"I've got you now! I knew you'd come! I'm going to take you with me!"

Morgana looked Joan squarely in the eyes and barked: "Let go of me this instant! Take hold of that fence and climb back over it!"

Joan wavered. Her face assumed a dull expression, and with first one hand and then the other, she let go of Morgana and took hold of the fence. Slowly, she began to climb back over to safety. Morgana gave her a final push. Then she followed her over.

Two cops rushed forward and grabbed Joan. A cheer went up from the crowd. The girl looked around as though waking from a dream. "I don't know what happened . . ." she said to no one in particular. "First there was a voice telling me to jump. A voice from nowhere. It wanted me to grab Miss Stone and drag her down. I had no control. Then when Miss Stone told me to let go, I just had to obey. Like I was torn between two wills and hers finally won out. And there was . . . like a blue light around her head. It wavered and danced. I saw it." Joan began to sob as they led her to a car.

"Hey, you're a magician, lady," a cop said to Morgana, obviously awed. "You really must have overpowered her mentally. You know what I mean?"

"I know all about what you mean," said Morgana. "It's what I study." Suddenly, the reporters were swarming around her, snapping pictures and shouting questions.

● 4 ●

The next day, Debra Mosley looked through the blinds for the fifth time since eight o'clock. It was nearly eight-thirty. The Military campus was quiet. Since her estranged husband, Wayne, had the kids for the weekend, Debra knew her cadet boyfriend, Beau, would come by to see her. Even though she had found someone she preferred to Beau, she didn't want to be alone tonight. She didn't want to think about Drena Wrenn burning to death. It gave her the creeps.

Poor Drena. She and Debra had been casual acquaintances many years ago when Drena had spent summers on the beach. Except that Drena was older and her family had been well off, living in the most exclusive part of Robinson's Island, while Debra's parents, who lived on the beach year-round, had struggled to make ends meet in a shack near the fire station. Debra's father had been a policeman and her mother didn't work. With five children, she didn't have much time for anything else. The last time Debra had seen her mother was when she was five years old. Her mother had kissed her a tearful good-bye as she left her husband and five children for a sailor. Looking back on it, Debra couldn't blame her.

Debra put another dab of perfume behind her ears and

slid her hands down into her underpants. Her jeans were positively slack on her, she had lost so much weight since meeting Beau. In the beginning, she had actually believed herself in love. Now she knew differently. The new minister was the man of her life, the man of her future.

She divided the blinds and looked out into the growing dark of The Military campus. Masked by moss-hung oaks like dark-eyelashed courtesans, white barracks buildings with turrets and crenellations backed up against the broad Elstree River. As a fourth-year cadet at a very strict military college, Beau had to be back in the barracks by eleven. Debra knew all about it from a lifetime of dating The Military cadets. She had started at fifteen while going to high school. Beau was the best one ever.

Debra straightened the wedding photo on the TV. How pretty she had been in her Victorian gown with Wayne in salt and pepper as they walked along the avenue of crossed swords. But once the kids had come, Debra had lost her physique. When Beau had first noticed her, he had made her realize that she could still be good-looking. In the five months of her affair with Beau, Debra had become a new woman. She had lost nearly fifty pounds, she exercised regularly, she had changed her hairdo. Even Chris Dixon, the minister at their church, had noticed, and that was what had sparked their first encounter.

Debra's father had never been religious until his wife left him, and then he became a Pentecostal Baptist. Since Debra never was much on religion, she hadn't minded when Wayne asked her to join his church, St. Helen's, an exclusive church in downtown Congreve. Her mother-in-law kept saying that it was more secure for the children if they weren't raised with their parents in different religions.

Debra had begun to enjoy going to church at St. Helen's from the first Sunday Christopher Dixon had come a year ago. She was fascinated by his preaching. He seemed to be in touch with a very special God. He had charisma. He didn't mind expressing his emotions and encouraged his congregation to do the same. And Debra found she could really talk to him.

She had started by telling him a little about her troubles with Wayne. Not much, just enough to see how she felt about confessing to him. In their second talk, she had found herself confessing her love affair with a cadet. Chris had told her about the completeness of God's redemption and forgiveness. It was so simple, the way he explained it. Just follow your natural urges and be open with yourself, and that would bring forgiveness.

By the time of their fourth talk, it had seemed the most natural thing in the world for him to kiss her. He was handsome and unmarried. She was clearly going to divorce her husband. An electricity seemed to pass between their lips.

Debra was a grown woman. She was attracted to a man in a true and deep way and felt the need to express it completely. They had made love in a hungry, hurried manner, naked, in his office. She almost giggled to think of his hunger. The poor man was so strong in some ways, yet so denied in his physical needs. What they did hardly seemed sinful; it was more naughty or kinky in an innocent way— like sneaking a look at your gifts under the Christmas tree before time to open them.

Chris had given Debra the strength to see that she had to make Wayne move out of the house so she could have time alone "to think things over." Debra smiled to herself. Wayne had been stunned, but he had done what Debra wanted. They traded the kids a week at a time. Wayne had moved into a small apartment in the neighborhood next to The Military, which allowed him to drive little Wayne to school and Donny to day-care every day. He came by so early that no one had noticed that he wasn't living with Debra anymore, especially since Wayne continued to work on campus. Debra knew that Wayne was keeping their arrangement a secret so they wouldn't lose The Military housing, since he expected her to get back together with him.

Debra rushed to the door as soon as she heard the footsteps on the walk. She opened the door a crack against the chain lock and peeped out. A shadowy form was in the yard. In an instant, Debra slid the lock off and whipped the door open so Beau could slip inside.

He was big and strong as he held her tight, and Debra felt girlish again, like a teenager, not a woman of twenty-nine. He gripped her waist with both hands. "God, you're tough," he whispered in a husky voice. "You've lost more weight."

"Health spa twice a week," she said. "I'm a living aerobics freak." She rubbed herself against him. She didn't love him. She loved Chris Dixon. But she needed human comfort, a body close to her, deep inside her to drive away the night and fears of old age and death. The image of Drena dying in fire kept scurrying in and out of her mind, making her tremble.

His mouth found hers and his tongue probed hungrily. "I . . . I love you, Debra!" he stammered, almost as if he had rehearsed it. "I've never known a woman like you. I never thought I could know such love!"

Debra's hands swept down his body and took hold of his belt buckle. "Don't talk," she protested. "Just kiss me."

Beau shoved his hands down the back of her jeans and gripped her buttocks tightly. "Whatever the lady says," he whispered as he led her to the bedroom.

● **5** ●

Morgana Stone started for the Central Correctional Institute in Reidsville in midafternoon two days later. She'd taught two classes, done still another interview with a television reporter, and visited Joan in the psychiatric ward at the hospital. She grabbed a yogurt at the student union on her way out. It should take her an hour to get to the maximum-security prison. With luck, she'd be there by four.

Climbing into her Honda Prelude and heading toward the interstate, she thought of the first time she'd visited Squirt

Crawford in jail. A convicted killer, he had been the subject of psychiatric comment because of his strength of will and an intense charisma that had allowed him to keep a disparate cult of people living under his rule in a shabby North Congreve neighborhood. There were also reports of parapsychology happenings Squirt had done, like bending spoons and shattering glasses just by concentrating. Morgana's expertise in the area of cults and parapsychology had led the *Journal of Parapsychology* to ask her to do an article on him.

A roofer by trade, Squirt had presided over a large family of drifters, prostitutes, and runaway teenagers. He had made them reform and work at honest jobs, give up dope and turning tricks. He had offered them security. Strict in all matters, he had ruled the clan like the chief of a primitive tribe, having sex with all the women and making all of the children his own.

Squirt was in prison for gunning down two members of a satanic cult who had made off with one of his adopted babies and sacrificed it in a sickening, psychotic ritual. Naturally, his action in taking vengeance had been viewed favorably by much of the community, and two juries were hung before a third finally convicted him. Squirt was in his eighth year of a twenty-year sentence.

Morgana parked close to the entrance. This would probably be her last interview with Crawford. She steeled herself before entering. As she traversed the broad corridors and passed through various iron-door checkpoints, prisoners stared lustfully and tried to brush up against her, calling out obscenities. Two guards joined her at the last checkpoint to escort her to Squirt.

Constant jeers, howls, and conversation followed them on their trek through the prison. Beyond wire-reinforced glass, two men shot basketball in the yard on the east side. On the west, they passed the dormitory wings. There were rows of beds, some surrounded by plants and footlockers painted with homilies from the Koran. Everywhere the prisoners milled around with nothing to do. Two of them struck matches and threw them at each other. A Muslim in slippers and prayer cap was reading to himself. Demented-looking, weasel-faced men with mouths hanging slack smiled, showing broken gaps in their teeth. Morgana knew that she was surrounded by convicted armed robbers, killers, rapists. She was among the most antisocial, uncontrollable element in the population of the State of Georgia.

Morgana was not intimidated by these inmates. She had long ago learned to divine the fine edge of danger; she knew almost instinctively just how far she could go. What risk there was, she saw as a professional hazard. Hidden inside these prisoners was the key to the human brain, and it fascinated her.

Morgana's solitary quest for knowledge had given her prominence in her field, and by the time she had become tenured at Columbia University in New York, she was regarded as the preeminent authority on cults and cult behavior in America. For the past couple of years she had been living in Congreve, teaching at Hutton College, brought back to her hometown by her ailing mother. Even though she missed New York, Morgana was popular with the students and gave a lot of volunteer time to counseling troubled youths. Her rescue of Joan from the Carteret River Bridge the day before had sent her stock soaring even higher with the students, who seldom left her alone when she was on campus. Not only had she become something of a local heroine, but Joan's statement about the blue light had been picked up by the TV news. So now Morgana had to explain about auras—different-colored haloes of light that were visible to some people who claimed to have psychic aptitude.

Morgana's characteristic energy had been dulled somewhat by the fiery death of Drena Wrenn, her best friend from high school days; Drena had died, Morgana later learned, the same day that Joan had tried to jump off the bridge. The tragedy was a brutal reminder of human fragility and how people could seem so indelible, yet be erased a second later.

"Close detention coming up," said one of the guards.

The three of them squeezed into a narrow entry room

one-third the size of an elevator car; it could only be passed by the first door being locked before the second was opened. Both guards grinned as they pressed against Morgana. At thirty-eight, she was shapely and beautiful, her face having no more lines than a teenager's. Her hair was honey blond, her clothes stylish. Morgana ignored their crude amusement. She was hardened to the low-lifes of the world. Hardened but unaccepting. Under her smooth exterior was a certitude that the havoc people wreaked could be prevented if the world would just show some courage.

The thing that startled Morgana each time she visited the most closely guarded section of the prison was how these cons didn't look as mean as all the others. It was as if the certainty of their convictions had given them a calm that had even improved their physical features. Yet most of them had committed horrible crimes. These were the outwardly normal people you had to converse with at length before you found signs of homicidal mania. Many of them wore such perfect masks that they were very nearly impenetrable. Squirt Crawford was one of them.

Morgana knew why he was here. The police had uncovered a mass grave filled with the bodies of people who at various times had been members of his family. Though there was no evidence linking their deaths to Squirt, and the rest of his family had scattered after his conviction for killing the two Satan worshipers, she knew it was totally within his psychiatric profile to have committed such killings. If they had defied him and his laws, he would have felt perfectly justified in killing them. As far as Morgana could tell, Squirt had what she called a patriarch complex. He was strict about rules and propriety. So strict that if you broke any of his rules or did something he considered improper, he'd warn you the first time, and kill you the second. Not that he had confessed to anything, not even the Satan worshiper killings.

The guards led Morgana down a narrow hall beneath a triple tier of cells into a small meeting room with a chalkboard and two plastic chairs. Squirt was there waiting.

On seeing Morgana, he jumped up and slicked down his hair.

It was hard to accept how small and insignificant Squirt Crawford looked. Fifty-two years of age. Pale white skin from being out of the sun. Five feet two inches tall. Hundred and twenty pounds. Thick, graying hair. Funny little mustache. Almost no chin. He was like the little guy who'd learned to be agreeable and make himself the butt of jokes to survive around the big boys. Except Squirt was quite probably a mass murderer, and everyone who came into contact with him felt the force of his will and his utter willingness to kill.

"Here . . . here, pull up a seat, Miss Morgana," he said with clumsy politeness, like the poor hick kid in the presence of a fine lady. That was the way he had treated all the women in his commune, and a fair number had fallen passionately in love with him. Squirt had a frenzied, almost manic energy that made many long to be around him. When he had been free, he had channeled his energy into roofing work. His work had always provided plenty of money, so his commune was well provided for. They lived in a house with proper food and clothes and the kids had gone to school. None of the Charles Manson naked-in-the-desert routine. Squirt subscribed to middle-class virtues.

"Well, now, I'm right excited," he said eagerly. "I've really got some right good news, and I reckon you'll be as happy about it as I am."

"Oh?" said Morgana. Squirt had a way of projecting his enthusiasm that won many over. Morgana figured he had had an answer from the governor on his proposal to have all the condemned prisoners shipped to a Devil's Island environment where they could live abandoned and cut off from society forever. An organizer like Squirt would thrive in such an environment. But his faith in such a daydream was evidence that Squirt was not totally in touch with reality.

"I'm being paroled."

It took the words several moments to reach Morgana's brain. "You're . . . you're being what?" she said finally.

Squirt gestured expansively. "That's right. Set free. I'm a free man. I get out soon's the paperwork's done. Warden told me so himself." Squirt's eyes glistened with bright excitement.

"But . . ." began Morgana cautiously. She wondered briefly if he was telling the truth.

Squirt laughed. "You think I've flipped out. But I ain't. I've been a model prisoner. The parole board reviewed my record. They questioned me at length on those two devil worshippers people say I killed. They figure I've paid my debt."

Morgana didn't say anything, but it all made a certain amount of sense, given the prison system. He had served more time than many convicted killers.

"That's what parole's for. To get out early, don't you see? I didn't really kill them people. Someone else did that."

The horror of the truth was starting to register in Morgana's brain. Squirt didn't seem to notice her silence. He just continued to talk.

"I didn't have nothing to do with that there grave of my people they found," he said. "I don't know how them people died, I swear. No, sir. I'm packing my bags." He laughed. "Come on, I'll walk you back out."

The guards followed Morgana and Squirt down the row of cells to his ground-floor one. He had draped the bars with black cloth for privacy and stuck illustrated envelopes to the walls as decorations. Squirt liked to draw on envelopes—innocent pictures of cute squirrels and birds and rabbits like something out of a how-to-do-animated-cartoons book.

A color TV sat on a rack at the foot of his cot. The news was on, but Morgana didn't hear anything. Her mind was spinning. The bodies of fifteen people had been dug up in a junkyard near Squirt's house. All of them had been members of his commune. She fixed on his small hands. The nails were long and yellow and horny. Like weapons. Like knives.

"Lots of folks believe in me, Miss Morgana. Like you. Those folks know I don't lie. I'm a good citizen. There's a real fine minister from Congreve who comes up here. Reverend Dixon. He works with prisoners and always believed in me, too. When I get out, Miss Morgana, I'm going to start a new life. I'll show you and the Rector that I'm a good person."

Morgana was barely listening. She walked to her car in a daze. Drena Wrenn was dead in a fire. Squirt Crawford had been paroled. It was as if some perverse, evil force had suddenly invaded the world.

● 6 ●

Byron Moss saw the girl in the Hindu gown standing beside the road on Highway 250 outside of Wheeling, West Virginia. She wasn't hitchhiking, just gazing at the traffic. He pulled off the road, leaned across the seat, flipped open the door, and offered her a ride.

"Yeh, thanks," she said in a dreamy voice, climbing up into the passenger side of the van.

She was beautiful. With incredibly long black hair and a perfect American beauty queen face, she couldn't have been more than nineteen. The long saffron-colored silk gown she wore made her look exotic. Byron recognized the look immediately; she was one of those Hare Krishna types. The kind who ate no meat and lived a pure life while singing the praises of their leader, Krishna, hundreds of times a day in order to transcend material life and merge with God. Byron knew a lot about different types of religions. He was a Pentecostal minister himself.

"I'm a follower of Hare Krishna," she said as she combed out her long hair with one hand. Her eyes didn't focus. They seemed locked on some inner world of her own making.

"Yeah, well, where're you headed?" Byron had planned on going to Georgia, but he'd already decided to detour if necessary. He wished he didn't look so grubby. He was wearing his wrinkled pea-green seersucker suit and he hadn't shaved in two days. On the backseat, his open suitcase was filled with all of his possessions, mainly wads of dirty underwear.

"I don't care where we go," she answered slowly. "Anywhere will do. I'm like the bear. You know . . . in the song. The bear went over the mountain."

Byron grinned as he ran a hand through his graying hair, smoothing it down, rubbing the grease off on his palm. "I'm in a state of temporary financial embarrassment," he explained. "But I'm headed south to a job with a minister pal of mine."

Byron was smug about the future. Chris Dixon had to set him up royally. Byron knew too much about Chris's last church in Tennessee and the woman who had died there.

"I would be happy to share my belongings with you," said the girl. "But I have no money. Women are not allowed to handle money in the commune of Bhaktipada. We turned all money over to him."

Byron had seen photos of the temple and commune in New Vrindaban, West Virginia, in news magazines. Gleaming, opulent gold roofs and buildings with reflecting pools. It all looked like something out of a fairy tale.

"Well, don't you worry, little lady," Byron said. "My old buddy Chris Dixon will treat us right. It's nice down there in Congreve, Georgia. Real old historic city with fancy houses and high-class people. This minister's real beholden to me."

Leaning back against the door, the girl turned sideways in the car. She tucked a knee up under her chin and stared at Byron with a sublime expression. "I've never really talked to anyone on the outside before," she began. "I was separated from my mother and father by Bhaktipada. When I was seventeen, I was married to a man selected by the great guru."

Byron was intrigued. The mind control that the guru exerted over his followers was incredible. Byron wished he had that kind of control over his own congregations. If he had, he wouldn't be in his current situation.

"He called me Sulocana," the girl said, "but my father called me Cerise."

"Getting to be about suppertime," Byron said finally. He

looked at his watch. "I could use some dinner. Maybe Salisbury steak and mashed potatoes. Or some fried chicken. Makes my mouth water just to think about it. How about you?"

"Meat is forbidden to us," the girl said. "But it does not matter." She began to chant in a low voice: "Hare Krishna, Hare Krishna, Krishna, Krishna, Hare, Hare."

"Yeah, well, uh," Byron said as he pulled the car to a stop outside a Pizza Hut, "maybe we can find you something you'll like in here."

The girl was incredibly docile, but she refused to eat or drink anything. As Byron pulled into a ten-dollar-a-night hotel, he got the distinct impression that he had a companion for the duration. The Reverend Dixon would be impressed.

● 7 ●

Chris Dixon picked up Squirt Crawford at the prison in the dead of night several days later. The late hour had been arranged with the warden so that no newspaper or TV reporters would be around. It was understood that a prominent minister would not want a charitable act of this nature to be known around the state.

Squirt got into the car and sat without a word while Chris drove out of Reidsville and down the interstate toward Congreve. Chris found himself glancing frequently at the little man, wondering how he could sit without moving a muscle. It was creepy, almost threatening. Finally Squirt spoke.

"It's mighty nice of you to give me a break, Reverend Dixon," he said.

"That's what ministers are for," Chris said, trying to make it a joke.

Squirt lapsed back into silence as the car ate up the miles.

The headlights cut through the avenue of trees along the unpopulated highway. An hour passed. Why doesn't he speak? Chris wondered. Make small talk. Mention the weather. Ask about the work that he'd be doing around the church. Anything. He had talked willingly enough in the prison. Always yacking away about his life and telling his outrageous lies of innocence in a cruel world.

The man was a cold-blooded murderer. The police and prosecutors knew that. The warden knew it. The other convicts knew it. He had the power to kill without hesitation, without remorse. Chris had to get inside his brain, learn what made him tick. He had to learn the secret of the power to kill.

Chris offered to stop for something to eat, but Squirt declined. He said he didn't want the Reverend spending money on him until he had started earning his keep. Chris began to feel more confident. The man was intimidated by Chris's position and authority. He wanted to be humble, to curry favor.

"I'm told," said Chris, "that you can shatter a glass just by concentrating on it. Tell me about this."

Squirt shook his head. "That ain't true at all," he said finally. "Just something a lawyer man made up to get attention. It brought psychologists to talk to me. A real pretty gal would visit me right often. It broke the routine."

For some time, Chris had speculated about driving Squirt by the junkyard where the graves had been found. Just drive in there and point-blank ask Squirt how many people he had killed. See what he'd reveal. Now that Squirt was being so subservient, the plan seemed very sound. The surprise of cross-examination by a minister might open him up. Particularly since Squirt depended upon Chris now. He wouldn't want his parole revoked.

Turning off at one of the North Congreve exits, Chris drove through the maze of strip developments, bumped the car over some old railroad tracks, and turned down a narrow street of tiny, cracker-box houses. He glanced at Squirt, looking for any sign of recognition. Squirt sat motionless.

They passed the tiny asbestos-shingle house where Squirt had lived with his clan, the waifs he had taken in and organized into a family. No one lived there now, and the windows were dark. Chris had come out to the neighborhood several times, talking to people, trying to learn anything he could about Squirt. No one would talk.

The road turned to dirt and meandered into a small patch of scrub oak. There were no houses, only litter and drainage ditches filled with stagnant water and the stunted trees. A rusted wire fence appeared in the headlights, and Chris drove through an open gate into a world of huge, dark mountains of metal. Piles of junked cars lay like slag heaps near a mine.

Chris stopped the car and shut off the engine and lights. A dim quarter moon barely illuminated the twisted shapes of dead cars, car seats, tires, and broken glass. In the silence, a scurrying of rats could be heard. "I want to help you, Squirt," Chris said almost fiercely.

Squirt turned his head slowly and fixed Chris's eyes with his own. "You've already helped me. A whole lot."

Chris was amazed at his own courage. He was at the scene of a horrible crime, facing the murderer. "I want to help your soul," he said intensely. "I want you to trust me and tell me your sins. I want you to tell me what it was like. Why you did it. You know you can trust me. I'm on your side."

Squirt knitted his brows as if puzzled. "Why I did what?"

"You know. Why you killed all those people."

"I ain't never killed nobody," Squirt said blandly. "Not even them two devil worshippers the cops said I killed. Mind you, I would have liked to have killed them. They deserved to die. But I didn't do it."

"They found the graves here, Squirt. They found fifteen bodies. All buried at different times. Why did you kill those people? Did they deserve to die?"

Squirt's voice became hard and low. "I said I didn't kill nobody. Not ever. And I don't like folks accusing me of it."

Suddenly feeling fear, Chris clutched at the brass cylinder on a chain beneath his shirt. The simple change in voice tone threw him into near-panic. It was as if the voice projected a power that he could sense. Squirt was lying. It was clear. But embedded in the lie was a threat if he pressed further. And Chris was alone with a mass murderer at the site where he'd buried his victims. Fear crawled through his body like an animal gnawing at him. Sweat broke out in his armpits and began to drip.

"I—I'm sorry," Chris stammered. "I didn't mean to accuse you. I'm just trying to help you be at peace. I'm just . . ." His voice and thoughts failed him.

Squirt looked around the blighted landscape thoughtfully. "I know about them bodies. I read all about it in the newspaper. They was found over near the back fence. One wasn't deep enough and dogs dug it up. Somebody must have been in a big hurry to bury a body so shallow. Particularly when it don't take long to go down six feet or so in soil as sandy as this."

Chris couldn't say anything. The voice seemed to be holding him by the throat, making it hard for him to breathe.

"Do you want to go look at them grave sites?" Squirt asked. "I reckon I could find them. From descriptions I read in the newspapers."

Squirt got out of the car and stood listening to the night. The interior light turned Chris's stricken face yellow. Chris stared at his own white, slim hands, feeling that they were made of paper. Frightened and unwilling, he nevertheless found himself following when Squirt beckoned.

Together they walked among the mountains of scrap metal. Rats squeaked and ran in front of their feet. Near the fence, Squirt stopped and pointed to some shallow depressions where holes had been filled in. One or two were still carved deep and brimming with standing water.

"Yep, somebody buried them all right about here," said Squirt. "They musta figured it was real quiet back here. Junkyard been closed for years. Nobody coming back here. Yeh, they probably figured it was the perfect place to hide a body."

Chris realized that Squirt was opening up to him, but he was suddenly afraid to hear it.

"Yeh," mused Squirt. "It would always be quiet back here. A man could bring people here on some excuse or other and just shoot them over a hole that had been dug some time before. And if the bullet went right into the heart, there wouldn't be no screams."

"Somebody would hear," Chris protested. "The houses aren't that far away."

"Not if the person who was doing the killing could like . . . overpower them with his mind. Make them just give up."

"You can't do that, can you, Squirt?"

"Some folks say they've seen me bend metal just by thinking about it. Me, I'm not sure."

Chris shifted his weight. "I . . . I think we should go," he said. He was so scared he thought he was going to throw up.

Squirt never smiled. "I figure I'll stay here a little bit and think things over. I used to live right up the road a piece. Maybe I'll wander around a bit and get the feel of being out of prison. You go on home. I'll be there first thing in the morning."

"Okay," Chris agreed hurriedly. Once out of sight around the first mountain of cars, he started to run. He fell twice, tripping on rubbish. Getting his car started, he raced down the winding dirt road, bouncing in the potholes. His trembling hands gripped the wheel. Sweat was running down his back. How could the man stand there so calmly where he had killed and buried so many people? How could he be so callous about it all? What was the source of his power?

● *8* ●

Brian Murchison drove toward the North Congreve City Court late in the afternoon for a bond hearing. Traffic jammed the ten-mile strip development that separated North Congreve from historic downtown Congreve.

Murchison was so upset about Drena's death that he had actually twisted it into a form of anger at her. They had grown up together and their families had spent summers on Robinson's Island. But Drena had had the courage to leave Congreve for a life of adventure. Though Murchison had lost touch with her, they had always been friends, and her death left him feeling oddly empty, alone, and abandoned.

"The sorry bitch," he said angrily. "She didn't have the guts to face life any longer." Yet deep down, he wondered if what she had done required more courage than what he was doing. He scowled at the bleak landscape.

The North Congreve Town Hall was on the fringe of a mall parking lot. Inside were the mayor's offices, council chambers, city court, and the police station. There was no shade in the treeless lot. Murchison parked his old Chevy convertible next to a drainage pond. Struggling out of the car, he adjusted his sunglasses. He had a hangover and felt lousy, but that was par for the course.

As Murchison walked into the building, he was approached by a horde of rough-looking blacks. He counted twelve men, ten women, and seven children. Most of the men had dreadlocks and wore shorts and sandals. The women wore veils and bed sheets cut and sewn like Arab djellabas. They all knew who he was. Murchison was their lawyer, and they wanted justice. One of the women waved an uprooted thorn apple plant and wailed, "Ja jove."

From what Murchison could gather, they were a religious group espousing a mix of plant worship, Rastafarianism, and Islam. Drifting through town, they had been living in an old school bus in a patch of pines close to Old South Mall. The local police had spotted them smoking marijuana during some sort of ritual. The whole thing was so ridiculous as to be almost funny.

Murchison rubbed at his bleary, hung-over eyes while he tried to get them to sit down and be quiet.

"Evil is a force of the air," one of the men asserted. "It enters man and makes him evil."

"Yeah, great," said Murchison. "So why are all you here for smoking reefer?"

"We were appeasing the evil forces," the man continued. "It was an act of self-defense. The evil forces must be placated."

Murchison turned off his ears as he shook four hundred dollars out of them for his fee, then went off with the municipal judge. Murchison was friends with him from way back, and they worked a deal where the group could post bond and leave town, forfeiting the bond as a fine for marijuana possession. Somehow, the notion of sending vagrants on their way seemed appropriate to Murchison.

Even though it was three o'clock by the time he had finished, the sun was blistering the parking lot when Murchison climbed back into his car. It was unseasonably hot even for May. Sweating, he sat in the convertible and ruminated on how his life had lost what little direction it had once had. Taking a pint of Old Crow out of the glove compartment, he downed a third of it and winced as the liquor struggled into his system, opening up the blood vessels and driving back a splitting headache.

Murchison was going to be forty in October, and his life seemed more pointless than ever. When he had been a football jock in college and later a sailor on the Mekong in Vietnam, the incongruities of life had made more sense. He'd drunk a lot, done some dope, but it had been more for the thrill then. Until he'd seen death up close. Then the drinking and dope smoking had become a crutch, something he needed so he wouldn't think about any of it.

Murchison had emerged from Vietnam determined to follow in his father's footsteps. His father had been a big-deal criminal lawyer who had always wanted Brian to practice law. But Murchison had decided to be patriotic once he'd gotten out of law school, and his old man had been dead when he got home. Now the sheer insanity of the criminal classes made all of civilization seem like a tasteless joke.

So much had changed since he was a kid. North Congreve had been one street with only a barbershop and a small grocery store. Now, a sign of exploding world population, the city sprawled like a hive of fire ants. The courts used to shut down in the heat of summer, but now killers plea-bargained their way through the system on a nonstop treadmill, a line of misfits who snuffed human life with the same cold and calculating instinct of developers slashing down trees and pouring concrete on their way to riches.

Murchison got off the interstate on Quaker Street and headed south. He passed black ghettos and seedy businesses on his way to the very tip of the peninsula where the rich spent their time keeping the beautiful eighteenth- and nineteenth-century houses intact. Swarmed over by tourists, mercilessly taxed by local government, they gritted their teeth, put their heads down, and bulled ahead in their quest for status.

Murchison's family had lived below Main Street for two centuries, and he still owned the house with the historic marker. Haunted by the ghosts of the past, he refused to live there, just left it vacant, with dustcovers over the furniture, mildew and rot slowly creeping in. His office was on Main Street, where lawyers' and realtors' offices were lined up like leeches on a blood vein.

Parking his car down by the old harbor wall, he breathed in the hot sea air and drank another third of the pint. He couldn't remember where he had been the night before, but there was nothing worth remembering, as far as he could tell. Putting the bourbon in his pocket, he climbed toward his office. Minutes later, he sat at his desk surveying a neatly marked folder, telling himself he had to sober up.

He had something important to do tonight. He had to defend Chris Dixon, the minister of St. Helen's Church. As far as Murchison was concerned, Dixon's predicament was like an allegory of the modern world. Here was a respectable man from a fine family with a fine education and reputation. But tonight would begin his nightmare. Dixon had been charged with ministerial misconduct by a parishioner at his previous church in Tennessee. According to the charges, under the guise of counseling a woman, Dixon had beaten her and subjected her to physical and sexual abuse. The whole thing had the aura of unreality. The woman had killed herself several months later, and her husband, having found a diary that outlined her supposed disgrace, was determined to see Dixon removed from the ministry. Apparently the Church Committee had tried to ignore the charges, but the husband had become vociferous, threatening to make his information public. Hoping to appease him, the church had ordered a hearing.

Chris Dixon had been sheepish and very embarrassed when he approached Murchison. But he did need a lawyer, and Brian knew ecclesiastical law since he had studied it at Oxford.

Looking over the charges, Murchison shook his head. The cruelty of fate. You could do everything right, always keep your nose clean, try to do nothing but good—and then along came a crazy to savage you.

They were the same age, Chris Dixon and Brian Murchison. Chris Dixon had taken the high road, while Brian Murchison had taken the low road. But still Murchison felt oddly protective toward Dixon. Murchison felt he had to protect him from the filth that sucks you down. It was a small gesture toward his own upbringing, a small return on his father's hopes.

Defending Chris Dixon was a duty. There had to be justice somewhere in this hateful world.

● *9* ●

Morgana Stone lived with her mother, Patricia, in a house on the Victorian end of Oglethorpe Street, one of the oldest streets in downtown Congreve. Designed in the style of the "single house," the Stone abode was white clapboard, two stories, one room wide, with the gallery porches referred to locally as "piazzas," positioned to catch the breezes off the harbor.

"So," said Patricia to her daughter as she dragged the garden hose around the yard, watering the lush growth of plants that was her pride. "Your killer is getting out of jail." In the excruciating midday heat, Patricia Stone wore a fiber sun helmet, work gloves, and an old cotton dress with twine in the pockets to tie up the climbing plants. She looked weathered and fierce.

Morgana cringed. There had been two columns of letters to the editor in the Congreve newspaper this morning debating the impending release of Squirt Crawford. "He's not my killer. I was doing a study."

"It's a modern conundrum," Patricia Stone continued. "Is it wrong to kill men who killed a baby?" She picked some dead geraniums off their stalks and threw them on the lawn.

"I don't have an answer to that," Morgana said quietly. "They seem to have thought that he was ready for parole. I have my doubts."

"Brian Murchison," Patricia mused under her breath. "He did quite a job defending Crawford. He had most of the town figuring those two monsters needed personal execution. It was quite a defense job for someone who drinks himself silly most of the time."

"Brian was Squirt Crawford's lawyer?" Morgana asked. "I didn't know that."

Patricia walked over to the bougainvillea that was climbing up the lamppost. "It was more than nine years ago that that trial happened. Brian seemed . . . well . . . a lot more in control of himself then. The Crawford murders were the talk of the town. I'm not sure how they got a jury to convict him."

Morgana fidgeted. Brian Murchison. She hadn't seen him in more than fifteen years. And she had read most of the newspaper accounts of Crawford's trial. Had she wanted to block Murchison out of her life so badly that she hadn't even noticed his name in the newspapers?

"I sometimes wonder if there's a God," Patricia continued. "Your father never had any doubts on the subject, but I'm becoming dubious with old age."

Thinking about her father made Morgana feel empty. Jack Stone had been a Congreve native with a lot of charisma. He was even-tempered, mannerly, loving. He had been forty-five when Morgana was born, and Patricia had been nearly forty. They had been quite a couple.

Morgana couldn't help but like her eccentric mother. Patricia Stone had personality. She found a reason to live in each day. And Morgana was glad that she had taken after her mother. Morgana didn't want a boring, humdrum life. She wanted to learn and study. And her name had inspired her to study psychology. Like many psychologists, Morgana believed that names help shape personalities. The Joes and Suzies of this world usually turned out stolid, but ordinary. Named Morgana by her parents in a burst of romanticism, she had always had an interest in the unusual. After all, Morgana le Fay was the half sister of King Arthur, and Morgana meant "dawn." Her namesake had been a witch in touch with all the forgotten magic of the dawn of time.

Patricia Stone hadn't wanted Morgana to be like all the other girls in Congreve, so she had sent Morgana to Barnard in New York for her undergraduate degree and encouraged her to get out in the world. Morgana had a high IQ, an easy way with words, an instinctive empathy with abnormal people, and her father's charisma.

Morgana had been settled into a teaching post at Columbia University when her mother had the stroke. Morgana vividly recalled the telephone ringing. It had been Ryan Stafford, the retired minister, who had called. At that moment, memories of her father's death had come flooding back. Her mother picking her up from school in the middle of the day. Breaking down and weeping on the way to the hospital. The nurse stopping them outside the room to tell them that Jack Stone was dead.

The doctors had predicted that Pat Stone would never walk again, but she had defied them all. Exerting her fierce will, she had recovered totally, but not before Morgana had moved back home to Congreve. Morgana's flabbergasted colleagues at Columbia had insisted on giving her leave of absence, which was now in an unprecedented third year. They asked why Patricia couldn't live up north with her daughter. But Patricia Stone wanted to stay in the town that she knew, the town where she had been so happy with her husband. And Morgana had been happy in Congreve. She and her mother got along in a way that most mothers and daughters didn't. Morgana had no interest in getting married unless the right man came along. Her mother had waited to get married until late, and she completely agreed with her daughter. Looking at the lives of several of her good friends who were in the middle of second and even third marriages, Morgana knew that she had made the right decision.

"You know, I'd just as soon you didn't get killed by one of your patients or your lab experiments or whatever they are," said her mother, following Morgana into the kitchen. "Whereas it is something of a source of pride to see my daughter a heroine on the evening news, I'd really like you to outlive me." Patricia poured herself a glass of grapefruit juice.

"I couldn't just let the girl jump," said Morgana. "You know that. Patricia Stone wouldn't if she were in my place."

"Patricia Stone doesn't hang around loonies. Those days you spent with all those cults and communes and things in California still make me shudder. I'm glad I don't know what really went on out there. Science is all very well, and so is human charity. But life's so short." Patricia shook her head. "We're here one day and gone the next. Why, just look at poor Drena."

Reading for the second time about Drena Wrenn's death in the morning paper, Morgana had been struck by the same emotion. Drena had been Morgana's summer neighbor at the beach house on Robinson's Island when they were children and one of her best friends many years ago at Hutton Hall, the exclusive girls' school in downtown Congreve. Like Morgana, Drena had had her eye on horizons beyond Congreve and had wanted nothing to do with marriage and kids. Now, as if life had become too much for her, Drena had killed herself in a fire in her elegant old house on Robinson's Island.

"I know," Morgana agreed. "Life is short. That's why I take chances. You've got to live out your own destiny."

"But sometimes, darling," Patricia said, "you take it too far." She paused. "I'm for helping humanity and all but . . . You know, this all reminds me of our minister, Chris Dixon. He used to go see Crawford in Reidsville. He's a humanitarian just like you."

"I guess Squirt mentioned that once," said Morgana. "Dixon was doing some kind of prison ministry."

"The wheel of fate," Pat said. "You know Chris has been—" She stopped short.

"Yes?" Morgana asked, mildly curious.

"Well, nothing really. It's just that he's been accused of something nasty by some sick soul at his former parish. Woman who killed herself. I've been asked to sit on a review board as a lay member. I'm not supposed to say anything about it because they are keeping it hush-hush. I'm sure he's going through hell. I really feel sorry for him."

Morgana shrugged as she went upstairs to get her things together for her night class. She didn't have much use for the country club atmosphere of the church and had only been there once since she'd been home. While Chris Dixon had struck her as good-looking, honest, and a good speaker, she didn't have much sympathy for someone who had committed his life to the hierarchy. His energies seemed misdirected at best.

● *10* ●

The night lay, a humid velvet cast, over the city. The stars shone like telescopic eyes. A smell of pluff mud crept in off the river, combining the aroma of wet marsh with that of rotting plants, stagnant water, dead fish, and mosquito larvae. Like the marine life that lived within it, the mud seemed to respirate on its own.

Exhaling the reek of the port city, the Reverend Christopher Dixon straightened his clerical collar, smoothed his hair, and admired himself in the church restroom mirror. He was pleased with his appearance: scrutinizing blue eyes, hard athletic body, cleft chin, Roman nose. He looked composed. He told himself to remember to answer every question only after careful deliberation.

A commode in one of the stalls flushed, and the lawyer, Brian Murchison, emerged, screwing the cap on his pigskin flask. Murchison gave Chris a crooked grin and shoved the flask into the inside pocket of his jacket. He was a lot bigger than Chris and his features were rougher. Though they were the same age, Murchison looked a good five years older. He wore a wrinkled blue seersucker jacket, khaki trousers, worn-out desert boots, and a frayed necktie.

"I was up all last night," Murchison explained sheepishly. "I needed an eye-opener."

The sight of the liquor filled Chris with a sense of foreboding. He couldn't have been wrong about this man. Murchison had a reputation as an impressive appellate lawyer. He had actually argued before the U.S. Supreme Court within the last year and won. Since Murchison was the only lawyer in town trained in ecclesiastical law, hiring him had seemed like a smart preemptive move on Chris's part. By retaining him as counsel the moment the trouble surfaced, Chris had deprived the Committee of the key man who might have helped them to a conviction.

"Don't worry," Murchison assured his client. "I've got it wired. I've talked personally to each of the Committee members except Pat Stone. They're impressed with you. Everyone loves you. This is just a formality. Ratteree's going to lead them through to a total exoneration. Just keep your cool."

"Of course I'll tell the truth," Chris insisted.

"Of course," Murchison said slowly. "But remember that they're just going through the motions. Don't get too nervous. That woman's husband is as big a nut as she was. We all recognize that."

"Why didn't you talk to Patricia Stone?"

"She's a hard old bat. Retired schoolteacher from Hutton

Hall. No-nonsense type. If I'd approached her, she might have gotten her back up. But she's a fair person, and women have traditionally had their reputation for hanging up juries. It's good she's on the Committee."

"Yes," said Chris, following Murchison down the hall and into the meeting room in the fellowship hall adjoining St. Helen's Church. "I just . . . can't believe this is happening to me."

Arrayed in a line were seven people, six clergymen and one laywoman. The laywoman was Patricia Stone. The clergymen wore ceremonial robes. Pat Stone wore a blue seersucker suit. They all sat at a metal folding table, Styrofoam cups of water in front of each of them. A formidable stack of papers was at the head of the table where Reverend Ratteree, the chair of the Committee, was sitting.

"Do come in," said Ratteree, rising to shake hands and introduce everyone. Chris knew all of them. Ratteree was a corpulent man with a round pink face. "Don't be alarmed by all these trappings." He waved his hand in the air.

"This is rather an awkward matter," he continued. "Frankly, none of us have any experience with an investigatory committee of this nature. I'm afraid we've had to rely on your esteemed counsel, Mr. Murchison, for advice as to procedure." He coughed.

"We . . . uh . . . we've been going over your church records," Ratteree continued, turning to Dixon and coughing behind his hand again. "You're to be commended, Reverend, for the phenomenal increase in attendance and membership at St. Helen's over the past year and a half. It even dwarfs your outstanding record in your parish in Tennessee."

The Committee members smiled at Dixon. "Well, are we ready to proceed, Mr. Murchison?" the Bishop said.

Murchison offered Dixon the seat to his right and sat down himself. "By all means, proceed, Your Worship."

"Well." Turning on a tape recorder, Reverend Ratteree coughed yet another time. "I will say from the start that our sympathies are totally with you, Reverend Dixon, and while we have no wish to disabuse you of the very solemn and serious nature of this proceeding, our hearts go out to you."

The others nodded their assent.

"Due to the quite lengthy nature of the evidence arrayed against you"—Ratteree indicated the stack of file folders and papers in front of him—"we cannot handle this in one sitting. Unfortunately, the Committee estimates it will take three meetings. Of course, this is all strictly confidential and we will meet at times of mutual convenience. However, each piece of evidence must be considered in its turn."

Murchison nodded.

"Needless to say, your accuser is not present, she being . . . um . . . deceased." Ratteree shuffled through some papers in front of him. "In preliminary motions, Counsel Murchison has called it to our attention that your accuser's husband has no actual firsthand knowledge of the alleged events that transpired. Mr. Danner's only knowledge of his wife's accusations comes from her diary." Ratteree held up a brown leather-bound tome gingerly, as if it were unclean. "Consequently, his testimony is what is called, I believe, hearsay. Therefore . . ." He cleared his throat. "Mr. Danner will not be asked to attend this proceeding to give witness, despite his repeated and somewhat strenuous demands."

A little wordy, thought Murchison. But he had understood the issues correctly, always an encouraging sign. All the committee members paid close attention.

"Now . . ." Ratteree paused, obviously choosing his words carefully. "The accusation consists of a claim that you held Carolyn Danner, this unfortunate parishioner, in a form of emotional and actual physical bondage. While she was in physical bondage, that you did flagellate her with whips and scourges and did have sexual intercourse both ordinary and in the nature of sodomy . . ." He paused. "With this . . . with this unfortunate. And all this was done while the unfortunate was under your spiritual care and guidance as a member of your parish in the County of Wessex, State of Tennessee. Now, Reverend Dixon, I presume you plead not guilty to these charges."

Chris raised his eyes above the heads of the Committee before he answered in a clear whisper, "Yes, Your Worships."

"Now, I believe it's appropriate for your counsel to give an opening statement. Mr. Murchison?"

Shoving his necktie inside his buttoned jacket, Brian Murchison got to his feet. "May it please Your Worships," he began in his deepest, most authoritative voice, "the evidence that has made the Reverend Dixon's life such a torment consists entirely of a series of hysterical and, frankly, demented letters to a variety of ecclesiastical and civil authorities and a diary Carolyn Danner claims to have kept during the course of her alleged degradation. Let me remind you all that at no time before her suicide did Mrs. Danner level any charges against the Reverend Dixon. The letters were all mailed just moments before her death by hanging."

He leaned forward and tapped the table authoritatively. "At no time did the plaintiff choose to even discuss the matter with her own husband. I submit for your consideration"—Murchison drew a folded piece of paper from his breast pocket—"a copy of a signed statement that her husband, Adolphus Danner, made to the police at the time of his wife's suicide. You will note that he says quite clearly that he never guessed at the possibility of any of these accusations although he was aware—and this I stress—he was aware of his wife's unstable mental condition and that she had been seeing a variety of psychiatrists for many years before Reverend Dixon even came to the parish.

"In fact," Murchison continued, his voice rising, "Adolphus Danner further states that many of the dates on which his wife alleges to have had intercourse with Reverend Dixon were days on which he himself recalls being with her all day." Murchison paused and looked at each Committee member in turn. "It was only later—much, much later, Your Worships—that in his grief and despair, Adolphus Danner decided to press these charges." He paused for effect again.

"You have the record of Reverend Dixon's performance

before you, Your Worships. He left Tennessee with all the evidence before you being known to the Church and the civil authorities, having been fully examined by both, yet he left with the blessings of the Church and with no charges being brought by any grand jury. It is frankly outrageous that he is being subjected to this now." Murchison's voice became lower, more intense. "We all know about jealousy and spite. I believe that that is what we see today in the charges of Carolyn Danner against the Reverend Christopher Lawrence Dixon III."

Chris started to relax. Murchison himself was thinking he sounded almost eloquent. How outrageous to think that someone with the status, presence, and education of Chris Dixon would do such a thing to anyone, especially one of his parishioners. It was good that a no-nonsense woman like Patricia Stone was here. She was a tough-minded schoolteacher. She'd recognize the charges for what they were: wild accusations totally without any foundation in fact.

● // ●

The blistering light of afternoon poured soundlessly over the burial ground of St. Helen's Church. The unseasonably early May heat sucked the moisture from the freshly turned earth and dried out the essence of centuries of compost, dead leaves, jasmine, honeysuckle, and ivy. The earth had been opened for the ritual of interment. The majestic towers of St. Helen's looked down upon mourners groping for remission of sins and life everlasting.

Lynn Stafford wasn't thinking about Drena Wrenn's funeral. Since her father had been a minister all of Lynn's life and Lynn had spent five years married to another minister, she had grown bored with death and spirituality. Instead, she was thinking about the hot weather. It was unbearable wearing black in the heat, and there were gnats and mosquitos everywhere. Waving them away with her black-gloved hand, glad that she had worn a veil, Lynn edged through the graveside crowd into the cool shade of a giant live oak.

Lynn felt possessive about St. Helen's. This was her church, filled with fragrant memories. She had grown up in the rectory and spent every Sunday of her life in the church until she had married Roger Frye. But she had nothing to do with the church officially now, and it had been a long time since she'd been to a funeral there. Though her father had been the rector at St. Helen's for twenty years, he had been retired for eight, and Roger had divorced Lynn nearly five years ago.

Thinking back on it, Lynn found it hard to believe that she had ever been married to Roger Frye—had ever used his name as her own. An idealistic, picture-perfect blonde set on living happily ever after, Lynn had married him right after she graduated from junior college. Roger had been a cadet at The Military and its regimental religious officer during his last two years. With his mind set on a ministerial career, he had seemed the ideal husband. The problem was that Lynn had pictured him getting a big church in Congreve just like her daddy right off. Instead, Roger had to work his way up through those dreadfully boring small-town parishes. When she couldn't seem to have any children, Lynn had become nervous and irritable. And she had been indiscreet with the local supermarket manager. When Lynn had found comfort in the arms of this incredibly understanding man, Roger had blown up, ordered her out of the house, and finally divorced her a year later. The experience had been humiliating.

Fanning herself with a limp Kleenex, Lynn thought about Drena Wrenn. Poor thing, burned to a crisp. The casket had been sealed at the funeral home since apparently there had been nothing left of her but ashes, almost as if she had arranged her own cremation. When they had all been students at Hutton Hall, Drena hadn't been a snob like so many of the others, even though she got accepted at Bennington College in Vermont while Lynn had to go to a technical school. Drena had even visited Lynn and Roger in Crossroads, Georgia, when she was promoting a bluegrass band to stardom. Drena had kidded Lynn about living in a hick town, and Lynn had enjoyed reminiscing about old times.

Drawn by curiosity to see who was in the crowd of mourners, Lynn moved out of the shade and into the knots of people around the grave site. The pallbearers were lowering the casket into the ground with ropes.

Drena was the first person to be buried in the newly cleared plot of ground right next to the church. Ryan Stafford had opposed the opening of that ground. When it was done, he, like everyone else, had assumed that only the big donors would be buried there. Lynn had disagreed with her father. She knew that Chris Dixon wasn't like that. He knew that Drena's suicide had been particularly tragic, and he wanted to accept her into the church with open arms.

Surveying the crowd from behind her black veil, Lynn thought that practically everyone from Congreve who had known Drena was at the funeral. There was that strange Irishwoman, Maeve or something, married to that crazy art professor at Hutton College. She had been Drena's big friend here lately.

Lynn's eyes lingered on Fran Maitland, one of hers and Drena's Hutton Hall classmates. Fran had been trained as a psychologist and had taught briefly at Hutton College before she married Dr. Ronald Maitland, a local internist. Now Fran lived south of Main and was in all the right social circles. In fact, when Lynn came back to Congreve to live after her divorce, Fran hadn't had time to socialize with her. Not that Lynn minded. She had never cared for Fran. With her mouse brown hair and flat chest, Fran Maitland was a snob, as far as Lynn was concerned.

Fran nodded to an attractive woman in a black dress, and Lynn recognized Morgana Stone, another old Hutton Hall classmate. She had changed her hairstyle and was just as attractive as Lynn remembered. Come to think of it, Lynn had read in the Congreve newspaper yesterday that Morgana was back in town teaching at Hutton College.

There had been a feature article on Morgana's rescue of a suicidal student on the Carteret River Bridge. Morgana had it all: brains and looks. She and Drena had been the smartest of their Hutton Hall class.

Lynn's memories were interrupted by the smooth, perfect voice of the Reverend Chris Dixon. In his white robes, he looked regal, almost immaculate. Reverend Dixon wasn't stuck-up like Roger. He was more like Ryan Stafford, Lynn's daddy. Chris Dixon was the way a minister should be, always in control, friendly, someone you felt you could confess anything to. Chris Dixon hadn't had to spend time in those boring small-town parishes. He'd gone straight to the top as minister of just the right church in Congreve. Chris Dixon was still on his way up. Everyone said he was headed for the top.

"I know this is not traditional," said the Reverend Dixon to the mourners, "but Drena left specific instructions for her funeral ceremony. Drena was always so vibrant and full of fun and love for her fellow human beings. She wanted music and joy around her when she died. She wanted her funeral to be a happy occasion during which her friends and family could rejoice at her journey to a greater land than ours. She didn't want tears. I entreat you all to respect her wishes and to be joyful at her release from the pain and tears of this world."

The Reverend Dixon's voice rose with sincerity and held the mourners spellbound. Some wiped their eyes. "Drena Wrenn's death was a terrible one, yet in pain she was released from the sinful husk of our mortal form. Let us listen to this, Drena's last communion with us."

The Reverend stepped back and let a young man wearing jeans and a T-shirt and holding a guitar stand at the edge of the grave. As the man tuned the instrument, people shifted restlessly in the heat. Lynn was more restless than the others. She shifted her weight first to one leg and then the other.

Finally the young man began to play. Though the music wasn't the right tempo, Lynn recognized it as something from the late sixties by Bob Dylan.

It was true. This ceremony was certainly not traditional. Some of the crowd began to squirm uncomfortably, but the majority listened patiently.

After several more minutes, the music ended. While the pallbearers shoveled dirt over the coffin, Faith Dixon stepped forward. In her black-gloved hand, she held a perfect red rose. Standing over the casket, she let it drop. "Goodbye, our beloved Drena," she said in a melodious voice. "We'll join you one day."

It was a touching expression of sentiment. Faith Dixon was just like Lynn's mother had been. The perfect ministerial companion, the perfect complement to the minister.

• 12 •

Fran Maitland got into her brand-new metallic blue Cadillac Seville and closed the door right in Lynn's face. She hated funerals and she certainly didn't want to stay around at the reception afterward listening to Lynn Stafford yack at her. Lynn talked just to fill the silence. She was filled with fears, the way Fran figured it. Fran was a psychologist by training and could always spot what was wrong with people. Immaturity. Suggestibility. An exaggerated need for approval.

The engine started smoothly, and Fran turned onto Quaker Street, heading uptown rather than down. After the heat and bugs, the air conditioning felt wonderful.

Turning onto Alexander Street, Fran drove past the campus of Hutton College. Despite two massive, modern, brick parking garages, it had the composure of two hundred years of history: Doric columns and arches, waxed magnolia leaves, meticulously restored old houses amid beds of lovely spring flowers. The main building was pink stucco. Amid a green yard of oaks, the cistern dated to 1890 and was flanked by a gate lodge and a small Classical Revival–style building. The walks were filled with blond coeds in cutoff jeans.

Fran didn't want to think too much about the college where she had had a brief career as an instructor in the psychology department after graduating cum laude from the University of Georgia. Her colleagues in the department hadn't liked her and were getting ready to deny her tenure when she waltzed out to marry Roland.

Poor Morgana Stone had been at the funeral. She was having the same trouble with the psychology department that Fran had had. Though she was almost forty, Morgana was still ravishing. The most beautiful girl in the senior class at Hutton Hall, Morgana was still the most beautiful woman no matter what room she stepped into. But her beauty got her nothing at Hutton College. Word was that she was soon to be denied tenure. Fran laughed to herself.

Well, Morgana had it coming to her. She was no smarter than Fran, and Fran had had problems. At least Fran had a husband who could provide for her. Morgana had never been much on men. For someone as beautiful as she was to remain unmarried, Morgana must be screwed up. Since Fran's clinical specialty at school had been sexual aberrations, she knew that more than sixty percent of American women were frigid. She figured Morgana Stone fell into that group. Most of the beautiful ones did.

Now that Fran was free of the college, Clarence Fuller, head of the department, was a good friend. He was a social climber, and Fran had social position now and moved in the best of downtown circles. She even played bridge every week with the wife of the president of the college.

Since Fran had slowed to a crawl, cars honked behind her, but she drove on at her leisurely pace, refusing to let them rattle her. Looking out at the life and spring around her, Fran found it unbelievable that Drena Wrenn was dead.

Fran knew about death. Her older sister, Cynthia, had died almost twenty years ago when she was barely twenty. It wasn't something Fran liked to remember. Like Cynthia, Drena couldn't feel or smell or touch or see anymore. Poor Drena. She had lived with such gusto. Drena had been into the occult: astrology and tarot cards and hypnotism. In fact, most of the time Drena had been flat-out weird with her visions of the cosmos and her fortune-telling with tea leaves and Ouija boards.

Fran didn't know why she had ever allowed Drena to do a star chart on her, back at Hutton Hall. Insisting there was destiny in the minute of birth, Drena had required the precise time. It had frankly scared Fran, especially when Drena had predicted that she would die before she was forty. But even if you believed that sort of thing, which Fran didn't, Drena had clearly mixed her up with her sister Cynthia.

Fran crossed Main Street where her house sat among a cluster of early nineteenth-century brick mansions. She remembered how she and Roland had talked about having children. Main Street represented all that was elegant and perfect about Congreve. The old city was as exquisite as some sculpture being slowly weathered in a square in Venice. In the evenings, she could watch the light slowly fade over the rooftops while she sat sipping sherry. It was a perfect neighborhood for children. But there would be no children. Roland had decided that on his own. He had had a vasectomy without even asking her.

"What do you care?" he had said to her. "You've got your big house and plenty of money. I don't want any more kids." He had two from his previous marriage.

Fran got out of the car to open the iron gate that barred her narrow driveway. Pushing the heavy decorative iron-work open on its hinges, she saw Rafe Artigues, her next-door neighbor, working in his garden. A Swiss-trained chef, Rafe owned a fancy restaurant downtown on the water and had moved in nearly a year ago. He was Australian by birth, and those who knew him better said he had left a wife and kids back in Melbourne.

Everyone knew Rafe. He had money, rode with the fox hounds, and played polo. His manners were rough but captivating, and Fran had been stunned when he made his first pass at her. She had never made love with any man other than Roland, let alone with some Errol Flynn–type dark adventurer in the hay of a horse loose-box. She had emerged sated, naked, and soaked with sweat, shivering in the chill autumn air, oddly at peace with herself.

Now it was May, and she had been sleeping with Rafe since October. He couldn't seem to get enough of her, but the word "love" had never passed his lips. Fran knew that men like him needed to dominate women to overcome their own feelings of inadequacy. With someone like Rafe, it led him to affect the lifestyle of a dangerous philanderer. No woman would do unless she was upper-class and already married.

Despite the certainty that she was being used in a sick game, Fran couldn't stop the liaison with Rafe. She had never had a man of such force and will need her. Roland was a do-it, roll-over-and-go-to-sleep lover, but Rafe drove her into frenzied orgasms.

As Fran opened her back door, Rafe was suddenly there beside her, his muscled bulk looming large. He pushed in with her, closing the door and locking it behind him.

"Please, Rafe," Fran begged, but he had her in his arms and was kissing her passionately.

"You need a man," he whispered. "Not some cripple."

Fran knew she shouldn't have told him about Roland's vasectomy. Rafe seemed to have an instinct for her vulnerable spot. He would talk about his potency all the while they made love. The desire for a child and the terror of Roland's reaction made her weak with longing.

Fran groaned with pleasure. When he put her on the floor, the chandelier above her seemed to move. Fran hoped she'd sweat. It made her feel like an animal.

• 13 •

Storming into his office, Chris Dixon tore off his clerical collar and slung it onto the massive George III desk. The reception after the Wrenn funeral had been interminable. He had barely been able to contain his panic through the slow performance of his ministerial duties.

Byron Moss was in Congreve! It was unbelievable! The bastard had driven up in a battered car that rattled and burned oil right as Chris was about to start Drena's funeral. He even had some teenage runaway in tow, dressed like one of those Hare Krishna nuts. Even though Moss had claimed that the girl was his daughter, Chris knew differently. Byron just couldn't keep his hands off the young girls. The filthy swine! How dare he barge in like this!

Chris paced the floor, wringing his hands. His head buzzed with fears. The Committee hearing on Carolyn Danner. Joan Scott trying to jump off a bridge. And now Byron Moss. Nobody would believe that teenage girl he had with him was his daughter. And it wouldn't take much digging to learn about Chris's past, especially since Byron knew it all! Why had Chris ever allowed himself to get hooked up with such low-life trash?

Faith had even seen Moss. She would remember him from the church in Tennessee. What would she say? What unpleasant questions would she ask? Chris struck the desktop with the flat of his hand and winced at the pain. He could hear Faith talking in his imagination:

"Anger is one of the deadliest sins. When it's turned loose, it gets control of you. It can destroy your whole body."

Chris flopped into a chair and put his head in his hands. The Committee inquiry was getting to him. He felt helpless and trapped, drowned by currents beyond his control. He tried to concentrate on the pictures on the wall—the prints of Dartmouth and Christ Church College, Oxford. He tried to think of old landscapes and elegant, historic structures, but it didn't work. He was hot and tired and the air-conditioning in his office was broken and it couldn't be repaired until the deacons approved the budget line-item by line-item.

Faith's voice seemed to glide through his mind: "You are strong. Go slowly and gather the power that lies within you. Anger is wasted power. In wrath you spend your strength aimlessly and at random."

"No!" Chris shrieked aloud, vaulting up out of his chair. He had to deal with Moss immediately. If Moss said something to the Committee, Chris was finished!

Chris bolted out of the room and strode rapidly down the hall to the cloistered courtyard that led to the carriage-house apartment behind the church. Still struggling to get a grip on his emotions, he sat down on a stone bench and listened to the coo of doves up in the eaves. He stared hard at an iron-bound door, but his eyes kept drifting to a stone crucifix set in a niche of the wall.

Powers lay dormant within him—powers he could build and use to put himself above other men. Powers it only took courage and concentration to exercise.

Chris clutched at the small brass cylinder he wore on a chain around his neck. The finger—the witch's finger—rested inside, withered and dry, with a long gray nail. He didn't ever seem to have the strength of will to throw it away. It hung there, a constant reminder of his bondage to evil forces. Always, the witch haunted him, whispering that he was bound to her, tempting him to follow the left-hand path toward Satan and evil.

Could it be that he really was fated to exercise great powers—to wield the might of the left-hand path? To brush aside the human scum like Byron Moss? To make women his slaves?

He had always felt he had powers lying sleeping within him. Frustrated housewives like Debra Mosley and Carolyn Danner, neurotic students like Joan Scott—it was so easy to manipulate them, to twist their minds and petty vanities into the patterns that he wanted. Perhaps it was equally easy to expand—to strengthen, build, unleash the true might of his will.

Feeling more hopeful, Chris mounted the outside stairs to the top apartment of the carriage house, where he had agreed to let Moss stay until he could figure out how to deal with the man. Without knocking, Chris burst in on Moss, who lay sprawled on a couch in sock feet, shirt open to the waist, showing his undershirt.

"What gives you the gall to show up here?" Chris demanded wrathfully. "That junk car of yours was spitting out smoke and oil and it was all right at the start of a funeral in front of everybody!"

Byron Moss chuckled. "How was I to know you were having a funeral? I let you hustle me in here, didn't I? I got right out of the way once you gave me a place to stay." He sat up on the couch and looked about the simple room. "Not a bad place, but could use a bit of sprucing up. I reckon it'll do fine. Did you bring me anything to eat from the reception?"

"You won't have time for a meal," said Chris. "You're getting out of here immediately. You're getting out of Congreve."

Byron chuckled again. "Now, Chris-boy, you know I don't take easily to orders. I really like this place. I think I'll stay for quite some time."

Chris simply couldn't credit the sheer worthless lethargy of the man. Kicked out of Oral Roberts University as a divinity professor for molesting sub-teen girls, Moss had wandered from one religious scam to the next. He actually reeked of liquor at four in the afternoon. It was disgusting. "Where's that girl of yours?" Chris demanded. "Where have you got her?"

Byron smiled broadly. "She's gone down to the market. After all those years in that there Hare Krishna commune, she just can't get enough of looking at the sights."

Chris stuck his jaw out. The back of his neck tensed. "She's your concubine, isn't she? Come on and admit it!"

Byron waved a calming hand. "Now, Chris-boy, just hold your potato while I eat mine. We all know about your little ways with the ladies. If I have a few motes in my eyes, it ain't nothing next to the beam in yours."

Chris turned red in the face, and his voice cracked. "Don't you accuse me of things—of things which you have imperfect evidence on!"

"You sound like a lawyer." Byron laughed. He reached over for an open pint of liquor. Raising it in a toast, he added, "It's funny you should talk like a lawyer when the very thought of lawyers ought to make you uncomfortable. If I was you and heard the word 'lawyer,' I'd think of Carolyn Danner and all those little spank-the-fanny sessions you used to have with her."

Byron's suitcase was open on the floor. Among the wads of dirty clothes was an open porn magazine. "Is it money you want?" Chris asked. "I'll loan you money. How much do you need to go on to wherever you're going?"

Byron pondered the thought and gave a hick grin. "You know, Chris-boy, you got to stop worrying so much and just roll with the flow. You got to get into your head that there's big money in this church racket, and this is just the place to make a score. Even up in Tennessee, I heard all about how well you were doing down here. New members flooding in. Why, with all them top-tax-bracket folks in your church, we can clean up. The older members will, of course, have their pledges tallied by the deacons, but I'll just bet all them new members are giving you free-will offerings and love offerings, half of 'em in cash, and nobody keeping track of nothing. Why, I bet you can skim off twenty-five hundred bucks a Sunday."

"You get caught diddling with the money," Chris threatened, "and I'll see that you go to prison!"

"Now, you wouldn't do that to old Byron," he drawled. "I'm your old buddy-row-pal. I taught you everything you know about this charisma business. Waving the hands over your head when you pray. The voice tricks. The big human need for heavy belief in a divinity. You weren't nothing but a little old frozen-up piss-ant rich boy when I met you. Now I've made you into a somebody."

"You were sent to me," Chris sneered. "You had no choice

in the matter. You were sent to me as an instrument, and when you cease to be useful, you'll be destroyed!"

Byron clucked his tongue. "Your destined path to power. You sound like Satan showed you the cities of the plain and you believed him. Well, you're nothing without me as a friend. You know why?" His voice became insinuating and sly. "If I'm not your friend, I just might talk about you and Carolyn. And until some thunderbolt carries me off, I'll be here with my catalogue of memories." He raised his hand to stop objections. "You couldn't have your parish know the truth and expect mercy. Me, I'm just loaded with mercy for your sins. I'll forgive anything. Ain't that what you preach? Forgiving anything? Anyhow, that's what you used to preach to sweet Carolyn."

Chris stormed out of the room and down the stairs, pursued by Byron's drunken laughter. How could anyone be so completely slothful and base and crooked? Sure, he had taught Chris about crowd control. No one would have believed the upper classes would have gone for it in such numbers until Moss had shown how it was done in Tennessee. But Chris didn't need the slimy bastard Moss anymore. He had just been a messenger, a tool, an instrument. And tools could be cast away.

● 14 ●

Early on the Sunday morning following Drena Wrenn's funeral, Morgana Stone decided to go grocery shopping in Lake Shores, a small shopping center just over the Elstree River Bridge. She tried to get her mother to come along, but Patricia would not stay in out of the heat. She preferred to garden. Driving over the Bridge, enjoying the brief glimpse of blue on the river with its border of marsh, Morgana told herself it was better for her mother to die happy than to live miserable.

Morgana smiled, remembering how her mother had skipped church this morning to read her newspapers. Patricia Stone took five of them and clipped articles for friends and neighbors. She had also written nearly twenty letters to editors. An ardent defender of the environment, Patricia campaigned loudly against nuclear power, development of the marshlands, pollution of the ground water supplies by trace metals, and a long list of pesticides. Morgana admired her mother's spunk.

After parking between the Piggly Wiggly and Belks, Morgana went inside the grocery store and got a cart. In front of her, a fat woman blocked the aisle, laboriously pinching and squeezing tomatoes. She looked frazzled. A kid squirmed in the seat of her shopping cart. "You're a doo-doo head!" yelled the child, a boy of about three.

"I'm not a doo-doo head!" the mother screamed, her face turning beet red. "You're the doo-doo head!"

Morgana edged around her, glad she didn't have the problem of children. As she approached forty, Morgana was unconcerned about her spinsterhood. She had just never met the man she wanted to spend the rest of her life with. At least her mother didn't nag her about it.

A face that looked oddly familiar broke into her train of thought. A man about her age reeled drunkenly toward the cash register, his cart filled with five cases of beer. He seemed to have drunk a case before he even came to the store.

"Uh . . . I'm sorry, sir," said the nervous checkout girl when she saw his cart. "It's Sunday and you can't buy beer."

"You're shittin' me," said the man.

"Sir, in Georgia you can't buy beer or wine in grocery stores on Sunday." Morgana silently took a bottle of wine out of her own cart. She had forgotten about the blue laws herself.

"You mean it's Sunday?" the man asked, puzzled. "What happened to Saturday?"

"It's . . . gone," said the cashier. Obviously apprehensive, she looked around for the manager.

Meanwhile, the customer stood helpless, trying to figure

out what to do next. Morgana peered at him. He was handsome despite his inebriation. He didn't look like he should have been a drunk. He wore old khakis and a blue work shirt. It was like a uniform out of the 1960s. At that instant, Morgana recognized him. "Brian?" she heard herself ask. "Brian Murchison?"

"Huh?" he said, looking around.

"It's . . . uh . . . it's Morgana Stone. Remember? We grew up together."

The man turned his head to one side and squinted. "Morgana . . .. Yeah, sure. Hutton Hall. I was at . . . the? I guess I don't really remember."

They paused awkwardly, neither knowing what to do or say. "My car's out front. Can I drive you home?" Morgana asked impulsively. She wasn't quite sure why she made the offer.

"Well . . ." he mumbled. She took him by the arm, told the clerk she'd come back for her groceries, and led him out of the store. When they passed an old 1967 Malibu convertible, he jerked away. "Let's drive my car," he insisted. He got in the passenger side and dangled his car keys for her.

Morgana slid into the front. The floor was loaded with wadded-up newspapers, fruit juice cans, and fast food wrappers. "Still beautiful," he murmured. "Perfect legs. Great figure. In fact, you always were the prettiest woman everywhere. The perfect southern belle."

Morgana said nothing. She didn't like to be reminded of those days. She had spent most of her life trying to shake that identity.

Murchison slid lower in his seat, as if he were going to take a nap. "Would you like to go to the movies? The theater over there is one of those dollar ones. That's why I was laying in supplies. Figured on a double feature."

Morgana shook her head. "What are you celebrating, anyway?"

Murchison shrugged. "Beats me," he said. "How about not having to go to church?"

"But why are you like this?" Morgana asked, her eyes

pleading. "You were the smartest guy in your class. You went to the University of Virginia."

"On a lousy football scholarship. Good old Brian Murchison, the jock."

"But you're a lawyer now, aren't you?"

Murchison laughed. "And a darn good one!" He punched his fist into the air. "Studied all kinds of places. Oxford University for divinity because it was a draft deferment. Then I faked the draft board out and switched to law. Then I faked myself out and got kicked out of school. But not before the glory. I played rugby before the Queen of England and won my blue." He shifted nervously, running his fingers through a full head of blond hair. "Never got the divinity degree, so the navy was a quick pick before the valley of the shadow of the draft. No combat until I got bored and selected fast boats and ended up on the Mekong, where I got enough combat for two lifetimes. Saw a lot of my friends die and I couldn't do a thing about it. Then I got out and went back to wa-hoo-wah UVA for the legal union card." He barely took a breath. "Sure, I'm a good lawyer. Put all my education to some use. Just helped get the famous Squirt Crawford out on parole. Aren't you impressed, little Ms. Psychologist?"

Morgana bristled. "Does it give you a thrill of power?" she asked sarcastically.

"I defended Squirt Crawford because he was there. He killed some people who were better off dead and our stinking judicial system didn't have the guts to do it," Murchison answered. "'Justice is justice,' they say. 'We can't bend the rules to suit ourselves.'"

Morgana rolled her eyes. "Where do you live? You're in no shape to drive home."

Murchison pointed to a tiny house within view of the shopping center. "Third down that street," he said. Then he quietly passed out. Morgana figured that was how he had missed Saturday.

Morgana bit her lip and started the engine. This man had been her first lover. There had been something about him—some unexplainable biological attraction—that still struck a spark in her. But Morgana didn't want to think about that. She had put it out of her mind.

She left him sleeping in his car in the driveway to his home and walked back down the short, tree-lined street to the big intersection and the shopping center. It was a curious place he had chosen to live, a little island of tiny postwar houses surrounded by major traffic arteries, as if he were living his life on an island of lost souls.

Morgana suddenly wished she hadn't seen Brian Murchison again. The memories were better than the reality.

• 15 •

Sunday morning sunlight streamed through the stained glass windows that depicted the great personages of Christianity in rich blues and reds. The interior of St. Helen's was a soaring, airy space with divided pews dating to the eighteenth century when families owned their own special seats and left them to their descendants in wills.

Lynn Stafford listened with awe as Chris Dixon delivered his sermon. She had heard many sermons, but none had been so eloquent: Chris Dixon had a voice that exuded both reason and emotion.

"Satan lives. He can enter into us. Satan is a force of universal evil. Our modern Western world is the only civilization to deny that an actual evil force is at large in the world. But our forefathers knew the truth. Even our parents knew the truth."

Some of the congregation shifted uncomfortably in their seats. Others sat enraptured. St. Helen's Church was packed. Even the balcony was filled, and TV cameras covered the service as a regular weekly feature of public television.

Lynn Stafford wasn't really listening. She was more hypnotized by the cadence of the words. They swept her away with feeling. Reverend Dixon was the ideal minister. Roger hadn't been at all like him, and neither had Ryan Stafford. Reverend Dixon was why the church wasn't completely dead. He talked about real life. He had feeling and love for his fellow man.

Lynn hadn't been around a man like Chris Dixon ever in her life. Ryburn, the high school principal she'd been dating, paled next to Chris Dixon. But the Reverend wasn't up for grabs. He was too devoted to his ministerial duties. He was on his way to the top of the church hierarchy, and he would get there.

Lynn's poor father had had this very church, but his stroke had canceled any chance of his becoming a bishop. In fact, he'd become an enemy to the church fathers in recent years, particularly when he had complained about opening the unhallowed plot of ground next to the graveyard of St. Helen's. Even though Lynn had spoken with her father and tried to persuade him to stop, he wouldn't see reason. He had some crazy notion about evil and witchcraft that made no sense.

Witchcraft? What in the world did that have to do with digging up a plot of ground for burial in twentieth-century Congreve, Georgia? It didn't make any sense to Lynn, even though she loved her father. It was so unlike Ryan Stafford, so out of character, and showed that he was getting old and senile.

Now her father was getting even worse. Lynn couldn't leave him alone because he left the gas burners lit on the stove and he was so deaf he couldn't hear any noises around him. More and more, Lynn feared for his safety. And he was a virtual recluse. The only company he would allow was Morgana and her mother. Patricia Stone could get him to smile when no one else could.

Lynn hated sickness. The sight of her father paralyzed down one side of his body from his second stroke, mouth turned down, drooling, was more than she could bear. She couldn't be expected to look after him in that condition. She was being forced to move him out of his apartment and into a nursing home fifty miles north of Congreve.

Lynn faded back into reality just as Chris Dixon was finishing his sermon. The Reverend bowed his head to deliver the benediction. Ever since childhood, Lynn had kept her eyes open and looked around during prayer. It was like being in a world all your own—as if everyone else was in a trance. She knew it didn't matter anyway.

Out of the corner of her eye, Lynn saw Patricia Stone. She had always been nice to Lynn and her father, particularly after Lynn's mother died. Morgana was another story. She never came to church and was very standoffish. That was just as well. Lynn had never been fond of Morgana Stone, but Patricia was someone you could talk to. Lynn decided to talk to Patricia about her poor father after church. Someone needed to help boost Ryan's spirits. Patricia was getting old, but she had a young outlook.

Glancing back at Chris Dixon, Lynn saw him looking straight at her. Their eyes met, and he smiled slightly at her irreverence without breaking the prayer. Lynn blushed and ducked her head.

• 16 •

Chris Dixon was thrilled when Squirt Crawford appeared at his office door the next morning. The man gave off such an aura of power. He was so small and insignificant until you looked into those flat, lifeless eyes—eyes that watched you like a reptile from under a rock.

Squirt had shaved his mustache and had his hair cut short, which gave him a startlingly altered appearance. He wore jeans and a denim work shirt and carried his few belongings in a paper grocery bag.

"How . . . how did you get here?" Chris asked, almost at

a loss for words. It had been more than a week since he had left Crawford at the junkyard in North Congreve.

"It ain't hard to hitch a ride, Reverend Dixon," Squirt said, affably enough.

"I've cleared everything with your parole officer," Chris continued. "He knows you'll be living here and working for the church. He's agreed not to tell anyone in the town here. That's smart of you to have altered your appearance. I explained to him that you were visiting some folks in North Congreve for a few days."

"Thanks, sir." Squirt smiled. "Being at a fine church like this is as good a camouflage as I know. I wouldn't want nobody mad at you for giving me a break."

Chris led Squirt to where he could live, in the lower apartment of the carriage house where Byron Moss was occupying the upper floor, and described the roofing work that needed to be done. Squirt set up a ladder, looked the job over, and quickly listed the quantity of shingles needed. Then he set to work in the heat. With his shirt off, he tore off old shingles and tapped and nailed in new ones without a break, never seeming to tire. Chris was awed. The man's adrenaline flow was incredible, and Chris found himself wondering if that gave him the power to kill.

This superhuman effort went on for hours. Squirt tanned but didn't burn in the sun and never flagged in his work. Though it was grueling and exhausting, he moved steadily.

Just at dusk, Chris watched from the narrow back window of his office as Cerise, the teenage runaway, went out to meet Squirt when he came down off the roof. She had talked to him off and on all day, and Chris noticed that she seemed drawn to the man. She was dressed in her saffron gown, barefooted, her long black hair hanging to her rear. She carried a six-pack of beer, held by the plastic rings. Hands clasped behind his back, Chris stood concealed in the dark room looking down as a drama began to unfold. A breeze rustled dead leaves in the green-patinaed copper gutters.

"Thank you, miss," Chris heard Squirt say, "but I don't drink. Not even beer. I could do with a Pepsi, though, if it won't trouble you none."

"All is one," Cerise said, her eyes half-lidded in a seductive way. Seemingly hesitant to leave Squirt, she stood for too long before disappearing upstairs into Moss's apartment. Squirt went in downstairs. Chris could hear the shower running, and he watched with amazement as the voluptuous girl returned with a soft-drink can. Her movements were smooth as a gazelle's. Without knocking, she entered Squirt's apartment and didn't come out.

About an hour later, Chris paused from reading a book and looked down from his office window to see Byron Moss prowling about in the dark, trying to peer in the windows of Squirt's apartment. When Squirt came out and spoke to him in a low voice, Moss went back up the stairs. Still, Cerise didn't emerge.

Chris took a walk at about midnight and paused ten yards from the carriage house. He could smell the climbing roses on the arches of the cloister. The overflow of the fountain irrigated the square of grass. A blossoming dogwood tree was blurred in the night like a Japanese print, lending an air of romantic melancholy to the scene. Chris could hear the girl's moans of pleasure clearly. It excited him unbearably, stirring up primal depths of human imagination. Squirt was obviously a man of monstrous power.

Several minutes later, Moss showed up at Chris's office. He was very drunk, his face pale, and began an angry tirade against Squirt, alleging the theft of his daughter. Chris lost his temper and slammed the door in his face and locked it. Moss pounded on the door angrily with both fists for a time, but finally went away.

Chris listened to the silence, his heart pounding. He had to get a grip on his emotions. He had to become as cold-blooded as Squirt Crawford. The man's actions were smooth and carefully thought out, not the result of erratic impulse. Only if Chris could become like that would he be able to unlock his powers.

Opening his office door a crack and finding no one there, Chris slipped out and got into the church station wagon. Driving over to the all-night Piggly Wiggly two blocks away, he bought cold 7-Up and two box breakfasts from the steam table before driving back to the church. It was near dawn. Several minutes later, Squirt emerged from his apartment to climb up on the roof to continue his work. His heart pounding, Chris stood beneath the ladder and asked Squirt to come down.

Squirt descended respectfully, apologizing for not having his shirt on. Chris told him he had brought breakfast and wanted to talk with him. They sat on a stone bench in the shade of the covered walkway of the cloisters.

Squirt was so polite, Chris found himself suddenly wondering if Crawford had really killed anyone. Yet no one could fail to notice that the man had been doing the work of ten men without rest. He had a maniac's strength. And he exuded a calm, almost awesome power.

"It's mighty fine of you to set me up and give me a chance like this, Reverend Dixon," Squirt began. "I owe you a favor. A big favor."

"Don't worry about it, Squirt," Chris said. He studied his own hands, uncertain how to proceed. "You know, as a minister . . . I'm obliged to respect confidences. That's to say, I'm not allowed under the law to reveal anything you might tell me . . . I mean, even if I wanted to—which I don't. . . ."

Squirt looked at him, his eyes watchful, but flat and incurious. To Chris, the silence was interminable. Finally, he took a deep breath.

"I—I'd like to know what it's like to kill someone," he stammered.

Squirt chewed thoughtfully on his scrambled eggs, grits, and sausage. "I wouldn't know about that. I've never done it."

"I . . . see . . ." said Chris.

Squirt spoke softly. "But being in prison and all, I've known plenty of folks what did. Even kill—you know—for hire, so to speak." He took a bite of biscuit. "They tell me it ain't hard to kill someone. You just got to know where to cut—or shoot."

"Did these . . . uh . . . folks ever feel remorse? You know . . . feel bad after killing?"

"I knows words like 'remorse,' Reverend Dixon," said Squirt earnestly. "No, they didn't feel bad. Not if the person needed killing."

Chris hesitated. "What—what about killing for hire?"

Squirt cocked his head to one side as he took another bite of biscuit. "Well, now, that's right different. That's like . . . killing someone you's hired to kill . . . It's kind of like fate, I figure." He studied Chris earnestly, obviously trying to put his thoughts into words. "That . . . that's like when the money goes down on the table, it's already been preordained. Somebody's going to pick it up. It makes no difference who does it."

An odd sensation overcame Chris. Suddenly he could feel the amorality of the man. Squirt was totally outside of society's laws.

"You know," Squirt continued, "she's a nice girl, that Cerise. She's just been raised by that crazy Krishna group. I've told her they were wrong to keep her penned up. She should get a education. Be somebody in life. Could find a good man and have kids by him. But she's all mixed up with that Preacher Moss nut. It's like she doesn't know what to do unless a man tells her. Lotsa women are like that. It's funny. It's like she wants to be free of him. She told me . . ." Squirt looked at Dixon intently. ". . . Moss was a sin-eater of the Reverend Dixon. She said I should eat his evil nature so the Reverend Dixon will be virtuous." Squirt rubbed his jaw thoughtfully. "Moss don't mean much to you, do he, Rector Dixon?"

Chris Dixon hesitated for only a moment. Squirt's message was a rhapsody. "No," Chris heard himself respond. "Byron Moss means nothing but trouble for me."

Squirt nodded. "I getcha," he said, and he got up to go back to work without another word.

The Reverend Dixon went home and went to bed fifteen minutes later. He had been up all night and he needed to rest. His heart was pounding.

● 17 ●

The hour was fast coming to a close, but Morgana's lecture had broken down twenty minutes before under student questioning about her talking Joan Scott down off the bridge ten days before. Morgana had been asked to appear on the local noon talk shows since the mayor of Congreve had announced he was giving her a citation for bravery. The announcement had reopened the publicity and the endless attention to Joan's case.

"She said she had no will of her own," said an intense, blond male student who sat in the front row. "That you had her completely under your control. Is that really possible? I mean, to control someone's brain like that? Is that what parapsychology is?"

Morgana grimaced. She had been talking about parapsychology, but she hadn't intended the discussion to take this direction. "The science of parapsychology," she answered patiently, "deals with the unharnessed power of the brain, the power to move objects or bend others to your will."

"Like telekinesis?" said someone from the back row. "You really believe in that?"

Morgana paused thoughtfully. "I've seen objects moved," she said finally. "And it wasn't a hoax."

"So you really think someone could control another person's brain?" a girl blurted out from the middle of the room.

"Most of us accept the idea of hypnosis willingly enough," Morgana answered. "In this case, we're just talking about a stronger form of it. Whether I actually had power over Joan's brain or not is open to debate. She was in a mood highly susceptible to suggestion."

"What about the light? The blue light Joan said she saw around you?"

66

"It's called an aura," Morgana explained. "It's like an envelope of light wrapping the human body. Long before Christian icon painters decorated the saints with haloes, the gods of Rome, the Nile, India, and Greece were depicted wrapped in brilliant mist."

"Does that make you seem like kind of a god?" one student asked with a laugh.

"No," Morgana said, smiling. "Everyone supposedly possesses the light. The Hindu scriptures call this essence 'prana.' The eighteenth-century inventor of hypnotism called it 'animal magnetism.' It's just that it supposedly can only be seen by people with special psychic powers."

"So Joan is really tuned in?" asked another student. "How do we know this whole business about auras isn't a fake?"

"It's been photographed by a Russian process called Kirlian photography," Morgana explained. "There's special photographic paper that catches luminous images. It seems that there's not only a general mass of light but little flares as well that leave the human skin. Apparently the flames actually correspond to the points where the Chinese have been applying acupuncture for centuries."

At that moment, the bell rang and Morgana looked up to see the head of her department, Clarence Fuller, standing in the doorway giving her a disapproving look. He had been in the habit of eavesdropping on her classes lately. "We'll continue this discussion next time," she said as she watched them all file out toward the hall.

With a shock of gray hair and a big body over six feet tall, Clarence was probably fifty years old. He might have been handsome except for the permanent sneer at the corners of his mouth.

Morgana looked Fuller directly in the eyes. "Is there something I can help you with?" she asked firmly.

He shifted uncomfortably from one foot to the other. "Yes, there is," he said, and drew himself straighter. "This . . . this incident with you and that poor girl—Joan—on the bridge. All the publicity is not a good thing for the department or for Hutton College. The whole incident strikes me as being remarkably unprofessional."

"I see," Morgana said softly, trying to hold on to her temper.

Clarence straightened his shoulders and shifted his weight some more. "I mean, all this talk about mind control doesn't support a view of the department as a place of correct scientific thinking."

"You mean dogmatic thinking," Morgana said. She could feel her bile rising.

Fuller's voice was a snarl when he answered. "Don't get cute with me, Stone. You won't get tenure without me in your corner."

Morgana stacked up her notes and walked toward the exit. If she didn't get tenure this year, she would not be allowed to stay at Hutton. "I'm sure we'll be talking about that soon," she said, feeling her teeth gritting. "Now, if you'll excuse me."

"Auras," she heard him snort. "Bullshit."

Morgana went out wondering why she lost her cool every time she talked with Clarence Fuller. He was so pompous she couldn't stand him. Surely the rest of the department could see through him. They wouldn't side with him against her for tenure. What had he expected her to do with Joan, anyway? Let her jump? Would that have been professional?

● *18* ●

Roland Maitland's office was in an old house on Rent Street with a yard full of palmettos and a narrow parking space for six cars. When she was first married, Fran had liked to go by at least once a week just to show the flag—let the nurses know the wife was around keeping an eye on things, watching over her territory. It had made Roland furious, however, and he had forbidden her to appear without calling first.

But today was different. Fran was so scared that a surprise appearance seemed like a small thing. For a week she had been nauseated in the morning and had been eating saltine crackers to keep from throwing up. She had missed her period and had had some spotting. Her breasts were incredibly tender. She was convinced she was pregnant.

As a second wife, Fran felt reasonably secure. One divorce was all Roland wanted to pay for, and his first wife had clipped him for plenty.

Fran tried to tell herself that vasectomies were sometimes ineffective. If Roland didn't have clear proof of her fooling around with Rafe Artigues, he'd have to assume the child was his. The money shouldn't be a problem. She just didn't know how Roland was going to take it. He clearly didn't want any more children, no matter how she felt.

Roland's kids by the first marriage were expensive because his ex-wife didn't want them underfoot and had them both in boarding school in Alexandria, Virginia. Tuition was enormous, and there were all the extras, plus the airfare three and four times a year. So she had to make sure he didn't squander money on his girlfriends or else there wouldn't be enough to go around.

Fran liked to tell herself that Roland only fooled around casually—a one-night stand here and there, typically at medical conventions. While not large, his sexual appetite was fairly regular, and he wasn't much on denying himself instant gratification. The truth was, he had had at least two serious affairs since marrying her.

The first she had found out about when a brand-new red MGB was delivered in their driveway and Roland got all upset and made a hushed phone call to the dealer. He claimed it was a mistake, but Fran had seen the personalized license plate that said "Kim," which just happened to be the name of his nurse.

The second one had only recently surfaced. The office accounts had been running short. Roland let his nurses keep the books and paid little attention to the cash flow, though he did notice when his income began to diminish while he was working at his normal pace. Two nights ago, Roland had been in a wild rage, storming around the house, bellowing that his nurse had been embezzling from him. Not just a hundred bucks here and there, but an incredible forty thousand dollars!

In a way, it was opportune. If the girl was stealing like that, she must have figured it was her due. Which meant Roland was on the defensive. He might accept Fran's pregnancy without complaint.

Fran parked her Cadillac on the street and sat there trying to gather her courage. Everyone had children. It was natural that she wanted a child. Roland already had boys. She'd have a girl. She'd name her Cynthia after her sister who'd died in New Hampshire.

Fran wrung her hands. She felt like she might throw up at any moment. It was so hot and Roland was going to be such a pig about the whole thing. Fran fought back her tears. All the women at the country club condescended to her because she didn't have children. It was so phony and smug, the way they told her she was lucky not to have kids.

Fran almost fainted in the rush of hot, sticky air as she got out of the car, She went in the front door of Roland's office building. Though the nurses eyed Fran suspiciously, Fran breezed on into Roland's office. Roland seemed to be in an examining room with a patient, so Fran took the opportunity to sit at his desk. Almost immediately, one of the nurses Fran had never met came in, and Fran stood up too quickly, despising herself for feeling insecure. It was her husband's desk and she could sit at it if she wanted.

Roland's nurses never stayed more than a year or two, so he was able to hire young graduates from the nursing school. The one who had stolen the money was named Jessica and had been dark and small. This new one was a knockout of the opposite type: tall, with long blond hair and a body that belonged on a Miss Universe. "Can I help you find something?" the nurse asked.

"Not at all," Fran said coldly. "I'll just wait."

The nurse cocked a hip as she gave Fran a look from

behind half-lidded eyes. "Dr. Maitland is with a patient right now. Can I give him a message?"

"You can tell him his wife is here," said Fran crisply.

The nurse switch-hipped out of the room like a cocktail waitress. Fran watched her go with disgust. The girl was at the age when she thought the world was her oyster.

Several minutes later, Roland came in red-faced, obviously irritated. "Frances, I've asked you not to barge in like this," he growled, closing the door behind him. "Don't you think I have enough problems? I just found out that bitch Jessica ran off with the money she embezzled. The police can't find her."

Fran walked over and laid a sympathetic hand on her husband's shoulder. "Roland, what are the chances your vasectomy was ineffective?" she said.

Roland's eyes suddenly narrowed. "I don't need this shit, Frances," he said with thinly veiled anger. "I've got enough problems!"

Fran's eyes filled with tears. "Roland, darling," she continued, unable to stop herself, "I'm . . . real sorry to have to bother you with this right now. I really am . . . but . . ." She took a deep breath. "I—I think I'm pregnant." Her lips trembled.

Roland paused only a second. "Who's the man?" he snarled.

Fran felt as if she had been slapped in the face. "Y—you, Roland. How could there be anyone else?"

Roland glowered at her. "I tested sterile. The chance of any sperm still being in my tubes or of the tubes becoming reconnected is next to zero. You're probably not pregnant."

"Roland . . . I . . ." Fran fumbled in her purse for a Kleenex.

"Well, there's no point in me getting my blood pressure up yet. Go see your OB. Get the tests run. We'll worry about it then." His voice became much more level. "Do you want me to call him and set it up?"

"N—no," Fran said, fighting back her tears. "I'd rather do it myself."

"Good. Go get yourself checked out. I'm sure you're

mistaken." He got up to leave. "I'll be home around nine tonight."

Fran walked out after Roland left, feeling her way with each step. The heat in her car was intense, and she sat there dripping with sweat until the air conditioner started to blow cool air.

"I will be calm," she told herself. "Roland behaves the way he does to compensate for his lack of social graces. He has to feel he's better than me."

Rafe Artigues was going out in his riding clothes as Fran drove up. When he saw her, he came across the yard to open the gate for her.

"Hello, beautiful," he said in his thick Australian accent. His shirt was open to show his chest hair.

"Hello, Rafe." Fran smiled. She was suddenly proud to be carrying his child.

"I'm going over the river for a bit of stick and ball. Why don't you come with me? All the ponies need to stretch their legs."

"No," Fran almost shrieked. "I'm sick! I've been sick for a week now!" She turned and ran into the house, slamming the door and locking it. When she peeked out the curtains, Rafe was driving away.

He hadn't understood she was pregnant. Or else he hadn't cared!

• *19* •

Around nine o'clock that evening, Chris Dixon stood in the open window of his office and looked across the cloistered yard to the carriage house. From his height, he saw Squirt Crawford open his door and stand framed by the light from inside. He was chewing the last of his dinner. He wiped his mouth with the back of his hand.

Cerise came up behind him. "That's strange food, all

them greens and beans," Crawford said to her. "Is that the stuff they eat in them Hare Krishna joints?"

Chris cut off the light in his office so he would be invisible. He couldn't hear Cerise's response, but Squirt's voice carried clearly on the still night air.

"You stay in tonight," Squirt told Cerise. "I'll be back directly."

Leaving the apartment, he went up the outside stairs to the apartment above. Byron Moss opened the door. He seemed to be eating cold chili from a can and drinking from a pint of vodka. He backed up when he saw Squirt.

"You get away from me," Bryon commanded in a voice that carried a note of panic. "I don't want nothing to do with you. Now, go on and git outta here."

"Hey, I come to bury the hatchet," said Squirt. "I took your girl. I've brought you one."

"What do you mean?" said Byron suspiciously.

"Bought you a night in a ho'house in North Congreve. Nice place. Suburban house with young girls. Some of 'em are under sixteen. They're picking you up in a car down at the end of Bayswater Street."

"That young?" said Byron.

"Well, it ain't a permanent replacement, but it's the best I could do under the circumstances. Well, whatta ya say?"

Byron hesitated for a moment. "Sure," he said, starting out the door, then remembered his pint and went back for it.

Realizing that something was about to happen, Chris started down the stairs. He was wearing casual clothes instead of the clerical collar that always made people stop and stare. By the time he reached the cloisters in front of the carriage house, Squirt and Byron had gone through the narrow passageway to the street and were walking under the streetlights up Bayswater Street.

Chris could hear snatches of the conversation as Squirt talked about the weather and the town like an amiable magpie. Byron ignored what Squirt was saying, unscrewed the cap from his vodka, and took a drink. By accident, he dropped the cap into the gutter where it promptly rolled down a drain. Hunkering down to look for it, he dropped the bottle, and the glass shattered on the pavement.

"Well, goddamn shit!" Byron yelled in disgust.

Chris slid into the nearby doorway of a closed bric-a-brac shop.

As Byron straightened up, he found Squirt's hard eyes on him. "Now, Byron," said Squirt. "You know there's women and children here in the market. They've just come down here to eat ice cream and have a good time. They don't need to be offended by your language."

Byron turned oddly weak under Squirt's gaze. If Chris had tried to chide him, he'd have been furious. But there was something about the stare from those penetrating eyes that seemed to take away his energy. "I dropped my drink . . ." he said weakly. His voice seemed to come from someone else. Chris's heart began to pound with excitement as he sensed the power Squirt Crawford was asserting over the weak, drunken Moss. Chris actually rubbed his hands together with relish.

"Well, don't worry about it none," said Squirt. "They'll have one for you in the car on the way up. Maybe one of them mixed drinks in a big chrome shaker with frost on the outside. In fact, I remember them saying they had one of them actual little bars right there in the backseat. Mix you up whatever the doctor orders."

"Yeh . . . okay," agreed Byron, allowing himself to be led along.

In the faint light, Squirt held up his cheap wristwatch close to his face, trying to read the dial. He looked up and down the parking lot at the end of Bayswater Street. "They're late," he said, scratching his head. "They said they'd be parked and flash their lights at us." He turned, looking across the parked cars. "Course, I don't know how they'd know it was us. It's supposed to be a big limo like from a funeral parlor. Hey, there they is." He pointed toward a few cars that were parked off the asphalt and in the brush that lined the river.

"That's not a limousine," protested Byron.

"Well, it's them just the same. They musta brought another car."

"But how can you know?" said Byron. He followed deeper into the shadows, as if he had no more will.

When they got to the fringe of the brush, Byron stood stock still, transfixed by the gaze that Squirt had turned on him. "There's no one in that car . . ." Byron said in a failing voice.

Chris was awed as he watched Squirt take his roofing hatchet from the back of his belt and cock it back.

Arms by his sides, Byron offered no resistance. The hatchet split his skull open squarely in the front. Byron gurgled and crumbled to his knees. The hatchet struck again, opening his head wider. Byron sprawled amid his own blood and brains.

Carefully wiping the hatchet on Byron's pants, Squirt put it back in his belt. Then he lifted Byron under the armpits and dragged him into the bushes and down a sandy track to the marshy edge of the Carteret River. Wading in to his knees, he pulled the body out into the inky black current and watched it drift out of sight. The water quickly enveloped its prey, sucking it down below the surface.

Squirt waded to shore. He started to throw the hatchet into the water but hesitated, finally sticking it back in his belt.

Chris watched from the shadows across the hood of a car as Squirt casually strolled back into the crowded market area and blended with the crowd. He had witnessed a cold-blooded, ruthless murder. A magnificent exercise of power and will. Chris was beside himself with joy. Byron was dead! Gone with a few easy motions. It seemed so simple to remove the impediments to his rise to power. If only he could teach himself to kill like Squirt Crawford.

Later that same night, Brian Murchison drove north on Quaker Street up the long gritty spine of the peninsula. Midway between Congreve and North Congreve there was a truck stop with an all-night diner surrounded by diesel pumps and a graveled parking area where the big rigs could pull in. Murchison usually went there when he wanted something to eat after midnight.

The night was liquid with humidity and the dull roar of traffic penetrated the glass front door of the diner as Murchison walked in. He ordered a BLT and a Dr. Pepper into which he poured a stiff hit of bourbon from a pint bottle when the waitress wasn't looking.

Drinking off a third of his concoction in one gulp, Murchison set his attention to the sandwich. The last client he'd gotten here had just had been pulled for DUI number three. The man owned a carpet cleaning business and had plenty of cash. He'd been the big talker/big drinker/big roll of bills, one-more-for-the-road kind of guy. Murchison had clipped him for two grand and gotten the man's wife to pick him up. It had been a fair night's work.

"You're one super guy, Brian Murchison," he muttered to himself as he shoved the sandwich into his mouth. "The night-stalker of Congreve. Playing in the fields of human garbage while good folks are at home in bed. Taking two thousand dollars off a man to try to save his driver's license which he deserves to lose. I'm surprised the Georgia bar doesn't give you some kind of special award."

His monologue was disturbed by a quiet voice at his elbow. "Mr. Murchison?"

Murchison gave a sideways look over his shoulder to see Squirt Crawford standing there in a work shirt that said

"Leroy" on one pocket and "Bing's Auto Elec." on the other.

"Mind if I join you?" Squirt asked in a voice so low it was more of a whisper.

"Pull up a swivel stool," said Murchison. He was amazed. In the two weeks since his release, Squirt Crawford had so altered his appearance that Murchison wouldn't have known him if Squirt hadn't spoken to him. Squirt's mustache was gone, and his hair was cut short and bristly. "So, what're you doin' here?"

"I'll have two chili dogs and a big Pepsi," said Squirt to the waitress. "I'm just hanging out," he answered Murchison. "The moon's full, so I been working into the night. Just knocked off. Hitched a ride up here to get something to eat."

Murchison downed more of his Dr. Pepper, listening to the loud voices of more truckers coming in behind them. Shoving and horsing around with each other, they migrated to the end of the counter and ordered Blue Ribbon beers and cheeseburgers.

"I been meaning to look you up and thank you proper for getting me paroled," said Squirt. "I knowed the justice system was fair and would finally get through to the right result. I just needed me the right lawyer, and that was you. I do thank you."

"Yeah," said Murchison. Yeah, he thought. A lawyer with a nasty little liquor habit and nothing much else to do.

"Did you say something to me?" said Squirt politely.

"Huh?" Murchison looked up. "No. I mumble to myself. Most times there's nobody else to talk to."

Squirt chuckled. "You know, that's funny. I do the same thing. It's almost like when I need to do something . . . you know . . . really important . . . I hear this voice telling me it's the right thing."

"Hey!" yelled one of the truckers down at the end of the counter. The waitress looked up and wiped a lock of dead blond hair out of her eyes with a tired motion.

"Hey, you! Yeh, I'm talking to you, lawyer!"

Murchison looked around slowly. The truckers were silent

except for one with a black beard and a green T-shirt that said, "Ask me if I give a shit." Leaning over the counter, he pointed at Murchison. "Ain't you the ass-wipe lawyer what represented my wife in our divorce?"

Murchison stared at him. He didn't want a fight, but his life had become such a blur that he had no particular motivation to avoid one. Pain and fear seemed to lack reality. "I can't say as I remember," he said solemnly.

"Yeh, well, I'll remind you," said the trucker, climbing off his stool and coming around the counter. The waitress moved her hand toward the phone. Murchison sat lethargically, observing the man as he approached. The trucker flexed his biceps, and, lacing his fingers, bent them outward to crack the knuckles. Though Murchison was football-player big, twenty years of almost no exercise and too much booze had slowed his reflexes.

But Murchison didn't have to worry. In an instant, Squirt Crawford was down off his stool, his thumbs hooked in his belt. Crawford was only five feet tall and weighed barely a hundred and ten pounds, but something about his manner demanded respect. "I think you might better leave," he said to the trucker in a low voice.

Over six feet tall with a thick chest and massive beer gut, the trucker appeared a human behemoth standing next to Crawford. He looked like he could snap Squirt's bones like twigs. "Who the shit are you?" the trucker demanded loudly, but a trace of uneasiness entered his voice.

"I only speak once, mister," said Squirt.

The trucker looked toward his friends for reassurance, then back at Squirt's hard, staring green eyes. "What the hell have you got to do with this? This lawyer cleaned me out, and I'm going to beat the shit out of him."

Squirt stared, his eyes narrowing almost imperceptibly.

"Hey, you got something you want to show off, little guy?" the trucker sneered. "What's your game?"

Squirt still said nothing. Instead, he took a roofing hatchet out of the back of his belt and put it down behind his thigh. "If you don't think I'll use it, just try me."

"You sorry little son-of-a-bitch!" cursed the trucker,

trying to mask the fear in his voice. "I ever catch you without that hatchet, I'll kill your ass!"

"You won't catch me without it," said Squirt.

The trucker paused, then stormed out, smacking the glass on the door with the flat of his hand. His friends trailed after him.

Murchison finished his drink. Squirt had no fear. He had let them all know that he would just as soon have split the man's head as finish his Pepsi. That was the mental edge he had over people.

Squirt let Murchison give him a ride back down the peninsula. Amid the narrow streets of the historic district and under the twin towers of St. Helen's, Murchison stopped the car at Squirt's direction and let him out.

"Why here?" Murchison asked.

"I live here. I work at the church. But don't tell nobody. It might spoil things. Lotsa folks believe all those lies about me killing people."

"Yeh . . . sure," Murchison agreed. "Look, thanks for saving my hide back there."

"It weren't nothing. If you ever have anybody . . . well, anybody you'd rather not see again . . . you let me know."

Murchison cut off his headlights as he watched Squirt vanish into the darkness of the church grounds. Bats flitted around the steeple. The man was an enigma. Somebody he'd rather not see again. Christ. Squirt seemed decent one minute and unhinged the next.

But then, so was Murchison. In the daylight, he told himself he'd never drink again, but as the day progressed, he couldn't do without it. Even the shame of having Morgana Stone see him like that yesterday in the grocery store hadn't seemed to bother him.

The beautiful Morgana Stone. He had had a chance with her once, and he had blown it.

• *21* •

The air of the spring evening was sultry, carrying a hint of the oppressive nights of summer. Tired after the Wednesday evening youth fellowship, Chris stripped off his jacket and clerical collar in the privacy of his office. In the darkened room, he sat, elbows on the windowsill, gazing out at the street and the graveyard beyond.

Though he didn't like handling the youth fellowship, Chris refused to hire an associate for the teenagers. Looking good with the young people was vital. Besides, their minds were fertile ground, perfect for the seeds he planted.

Chris wrung his hands nervously. The Committee was meeting again in five days, and Chris wanted it to be over. He did what most of his parishioners wanted, but there was always opposition to change. Chris was used to it. Some of the old guard were upset about his style of worship. They said he was deviating from the old ways too much. But the great majority loved it. After all, the charismatic movement wasn't new to St. Helen's. It had become a strong segment of the entire Church.

The Committee was different. They had power over him. They could exercise it in a moment and banish him to a hick town church. Chris remembered learning that Carolyn Danner had killed herself. Her husband had phoned. Numbed by grief, he had wanted answers to the tragedy. Carolyn had hung herself, he had told Chris.

When Carolyn had become inconvenient—talking about divorcing her husband and marrying Chris—Chris had often wished that she would kill herself by hanging. What a welcome surprise it had been when the visions had come to pass, like precognition!

Joan Scott was a similar nuisance now. Locked in the psychiatric ward, she was recovering nicely enough. But

Chris knew it was best if she would kill herself, too, and end her wretched misery, just like Carolyn Danner. Then Chris would have no more fears. He could handle the Committee on his own.

Raising the window, Chris looked out. In the distance, the old mausoleum sat shrouded by trees and darkness. Chris shuddered at the thought of the body inside. His shoulders trembled. The woman was so perfectly preserved. He still had nightmares about the night she had died. Her screams as the meat cleaver had opened her chest echoed in his brain. He had thought she'd never die. It was as if her soul had left her body and was hovering in the air, screaming.

Chris gripped the windowsill. He was frightened. That night he had entered a world of great power, a world that would help him rule others absolutely. The witch had put Satan inside him. It had been ordained by the powers. He had been chosen as one filled with promise. He had been put in bondage to a witch.

He was both exhilarated and afraid of his growing strength. It was so easy to manipulate people—to twist their simple brains. Just play upon their vanity, echo their self-delusions, and they were putty. Debra kept coming back for more and more. The last time he had put the lash to her. It had been a simple matter. Go into a feigned conscience crisis. Pretend remorse. Wail about chastisement and sin. She had willingly taken down her pants and let him whip her.

But where was it all leading? What dangers was he drifting into? The unknown was a black, gaping mouth waiting to devour him.

Chris shook with suppressed sobs as tears of pain and fear ran down his face. A nightjar flitted out of the dark and landed on the window ledge. Pulling himself together, Chris stared at it hard, trying to project calm, serenity. Strangely, the creature responded. The bird sat quite still, as if hypnotized, as Chris petted it with one finger.

Gently, Chris picked it up. As he closed his fingers around it, he could actually feel its tiny heartbeat. He had a sensation that he was entering the very essence of the bird with his will. He began to exult, to surge with pleasure. The bird became frightened, struggled, but Chris held it tightly. It stared at him with fear-wracked eyes. Chris laughed strangely. He squeezed the little bird tighter and tighter until it died in his hands, its guts forced out of its throat. Its head fell limp. Blood ran down over his fist.

Chris gloated over the gory little body. He had the power! He could do more than manipulate people! He could control their wills!

Setting the lifeless bird carefully on the ledge, Chris stripped off his clothes. Naked, he could feel the forces of the earth and the air. He built up a tiny fire of wood chips in the fireplace and placed the dead bird in front of it. Squatting, he slashed the bird open with a penknife, found its heart, and cut it free. He impaled the tiny heart with the point of the knife and seared it in the flames. Invoking the name of the Light Bringer, he began to recite the Lord's Prayer backwards.

"Ever and forever. Glory and power. Kingdom is thine. Evil from us deliver . . ."

His voice broke in a shrill laugh.

● **22** ●

Pat Stone had always loved to garden. Morgana's earliest childhood memories were of yardwork designed by her mother that always involved uprooting this and planting that. As a child, Morgana had hated the hot, sweaty work, but now she treasured the memories of quiet green shade.

"We live in a Darwinian world," Patricia said to her daughter as she walked back into the house to get the pruning shears. "You've studied human beings, Morgana. Do you think people can really hide their true emotions?"

Morgana was puzzled by the question. She couldn't follow her mother's train of thought. "What do you mean?"

Pat Stone paused briefly. "I don't know exactly. . . . I mean, people often seem outwardly normal, yet they're psychopaths or something?"

Morgana shrugged. "It's been shown to happen all the time," she agreed, studying her mother carefully. Pat had seemed under a lot of strain lately, like something was bothering her.

"What sort of a man might, say . . . beat a woman, yet seem perfectly composed otherwise and never give off the least sign of being a deviant?" Patricia asked.

"Some studies say that happens to men who hate their mothers," Morgana started slowly. "There's usually something from an early age that translates into a rage against women. It can be carefully concealed. Most of these people have that ability. Why are you asking all these questions?" Morgana tried the gentle approach, hoping it would work better.

"Oh, nothing," Pat demurred. "I was just wondering. I've got a daughter who's an authority on mind diseases. Why shouldn't I be able to ask her questions without a deeper motive?"

"Why not?" asked Morgana. "It's just that you've seemed kind of preoccupied lately. You haven't been yourself exactly."

Pat Stone shrugged. "It's just your imagination," she said. "With you coming up for tenure at Hutton, you've been acting different yourself. I was just reading in the paper about all this violence, and it started me thinking, that's all."

Morgana didn't say any more. When and if her mother wanted to talk, she would, but not before. And Pat was right, Morgana had been preoccupied herself with all the tenure business: writing letters, being interviewed, trying to figure out the political lay of the land. Morgana went upstairs to put the finishing touches on her Squirt Crawford paper. Of course, his name wasn't mentioned in it; only the psychological profile of the man was discussed.

Squirt Crawford, the alleged mass murderer, whom the police had been able to convict only of killing two baby-killers. Since he had been paroled, the press had forgotten about him. But Morgana still remembered vividly the answers he had given her on the Thematic Aperception Test, a series of cards with pictures of people in ambiguous situations. She had asked him to make up a story about each of the cards. By inventing stories, he'd revealed his own motivations.

Totally uninhibited, Squirt always saw the pictures as stories about himself—in fact, not so much stories as autobiography. Morgana had made tape recordings. The one picture that stuck in her mind was of a young boy imagining a surgical operation going on. Doctors in masks held scalpels over a patient on a table. Ignoring the boy in the picture, Squirt had launched into an account of killing a prison informer.

"Now, this is a man being patched up who was a squealer the first time I served a stretch in prison. He had squealed on a number of friends of mine to gain favors with the guards. As I'm sure you know, squealing like that is just not done. It's against the code and against all rules that guide prisoners. Now, he was treated fairly, and there was no summary justice about the whole thing.

"In fact, he was warned to stay out of the exercise yard, but he refused to heed the warnings, and he'd go out there anyway. Well, finally, after two warnings, he was attacked by prisoners and was cut in the stomach and the chest and the throat. The doctors are working hard to save his life, but he has lost too much blood, and they won't succeed. He'll die on the operating table."

"Were you one of the men who attacked him?" Morgana had asked.

"No, ma'am, I wasn't. I was one of the victims of his squealing, but some other people done the cutting on him."

The phone rang and Morgana answered reluctantly. It was a doctor she knew calling from the psychiatric ward of the hospital.

"I've got some bad news for you," he told Morgana. "You better sit down. Joan Scott killed herself last night."

"Oh, my God," Morgana breathed. "How did it . . .?"

"She hanged herself with a light cord. We thought she was sedated, but apparently she had been hiding her medication and . . . well . . . she was feigning calm."

Morgana was stunned. "How was that possible?"

"I—I don't know exactly. But we found her medication in the air-conditioning duct. She hadn't had it in the whole week she's been here. It was as if she was watching us the entire time, plotting her own suicide."

"I just can't believe it," Morgana said softly.

"Morgana, I know you're going to take this hard, but it happens to all of us who follow a patient. I know how you risked your neck to get her off the bridge. Now it all seems in vain. But you're going to have to shake it off."

"Did she leave any message? A note? Did she talk to anyone before she did it?"

"No one. She was by herself."

"So you're completely in the dark."

"Very much so. Although there was something very odd." He hesitated.

"What's that?"

"She had some scars on her buttocks and legs. As if she had been beaten with a whip. Did she ever talk to you about being brutalized by anyone?"

"No," Morgana answered. "Never. Could she have done it to herself? You know how she talked a lot about driving Satan out of her body."

"I don't know. We only noticed this during the autopsy. It's really grim."

"I'm sick. I'm just really sick." Morgana rubbed her eyes, trying to ward off the sudden feeling of enormous fatigue and nausea.

"Morgana," the doctor said quietly, "there's nothing more you could have done. People have their own private hells sometimes, and it's not always possible to reach them."

"But it is . . ." Morgana said softly. Then she hung up.

• 23 •

Brian Murchison sprawled in the chair behind his old scuffed desk, squinting against the sun and wondering why he had to put up with Maeve Sandor today. It was the last of May, a beautiful spring Monday. The windows were open and a breeze off the harbor funneled down Main Street. The view behind Maeve was of old rooftops that one hundred years before would have been lined with ships' masts. The cracked and peeling buildings all seemed to lean off their centers of gravity.

Murchison's office was a jumble of green file cabinets, papers impaled on spikes, accordion folders, racks of law books. On the walls were diplomas from the University of Virginia, an old map of plantations and parishes of the county, a print of the Charge of the Light Brigade, and a saber an ancestor had carried in the Civil War.

"You're quite a guy for a bastard," Maeve said, using her best roguish come-on.

God, I don't like her, Murchison thought. She had been hitting on him at a party last night, and he had agreed to talk business with her today. He had vaguely considered having sex with her last night, but in the sober light of day he was glad he hadn't. He couldn't clearly remember why he had been invited to the party or all that had happened there, just that it had been attended by a lot of the art professors from Hutton College.

The artists had gathered in a grubby, paint-littered house in one of the restored sections of Congreve, wearing grubby jeans, to get drunk, do dope, and screw. There had been a dragoon punch stirred with a hockey stick for those with that taste, and speed and acid for the others. The rest had been a blur. Except that Murchison had found them congenial enough, and far more to his liking than the upwardly mobile, hard-charging young attorneys on Main Street.

Especially Bojack Sandor, Maeve's husband, a small Hungarian who specialized in getting howling drunk and nailing rubbish to canvases. He taught art at Hutton, and he had been rolling on the floor amid the wood shavings with one of his female students for most of the evening. Murchison remembered now how Maeve had ignored her husband and talked to Murchison about Drena Wrenn when she'd found out that Murchison was the executor of Drena's estate.

"Now, about Drena," said Maeve. "Since you're her executor . . ."

Maeve crossed her heavy legs. She was six foot two, with a big-boned body. She wore a nondescript skirt and blouse and her hair was tinted a deep brown. Her face showed the crow's-feet of a woman of forty-five. "Do the authorities suspect foul play?"

"No. I don't think so. Drena wanted to check out. Might not be a bad idea for all of us."

"I have dark forebodings on the subject," said Maeve ominously. She fingered the carved green wooden balls of her necklace. "Drena and I were quite close, and she confided in me at length there at the last."

Murchison gritted his teeth.

"My mother had second sight," Maeve went on. "It's a common trait among the Celts. I have a touch of it myself. For example, the moment I saw you, I knew you were a man hiding from something. Perhaps hiding from yourself."

"Do you have a point you're trying to make?" asked Murchison impatiently.

Maeve stood up. "I suppose not," she said, crossing the room to look out the window. "Except that Drena was deathly afraid of witches. She seemed to feel that one had infected her with evil and that a spell had been cast over her and was directing her actions, making her do vile things."

"Such as?"

"The witch made her quite promiscuous."

Murchison shrugged and tried to subdue a smirk. "Drena

Wrenn was promiscuous from the cradle. It was part of her charm. I might even say her love of life. This witch must have infected her early."

Maeve winked at him. "You're not hinting that you did the dirty deed with her, are you?"

"No. And if I did, it's lost in the mists of time. The whole witch thing probably appealed to Drena's sense of drama. She loved an audience."

Somehow, Murchison got Maeve out the door a few minutes later. So Drena had acted weird before she died. Drena had claimed she could see into other worlds. Drena had been like that all her life. It was nothing new. But even in the doorway, Maeve resisted leaving. "Since you know where I live . . ." she began.

Murchison looked puzzled.

"You know, silly. You were there last night," Maeve continued. "Come by and see me . . . soon."

Murchison pulled an oak chair to the window. Filled with the numbed sadness of his life, he laid his head on the sill, letting the breeze bathe his face. On the street below, aggressive young lawyers in gray suits and power-yellow neckties strode toward the state and federal courts loaded with heavy briefcases and grim determination.

Shit. Drena Wrenn haunted by witches. She had once tried to raise the devil in a graveyard when she was in Hutton Hall. There was a big stink when she got caught. And all during college and after, she was into astrology, wanting to do star charts on people, hanging out with seers and spiritualists. Poor old Drena never had an axe to grind, never did anyone any harm. She had just wanted love and beauty and excitement. And she'd picked up every at-large lunatic available for romance. Even good old Murchison.

Drena used to write him letters asking him to marry her, and he'd thrown them away. One he had read aloud to a bar full of sailors in Saigon, and afterward felt like shit about it. Drena had been the only girl ever to write him the whole time he was in Vietnam. Not even Morgana Stone had written him. Morgana—the most beautiful woman he had ever seen. He had a special memory compartment for her—where he could picture her smile and the perfect green of her eyes.

There had been no reason for Drena to kill herself. They were all getting older. They had all lost some of their dreams. But maybe that was why. Maybe Drena had looked into the future and seen herself like Maeve Sandor and couldn't face it.

• 24 •

Chris Dixon put down the morning newspaper in his study, amazed at his sudden good fortune. Joan Scott had finally killed herself. And there had been no mention of the marks on her buttocks. He was in enough trouble with the Carolyn Danner business. He didn't need more.

Chris had been disappointed when Joan failed to jump from the bridge. Morgana Stone had saved her. Chris knew her vaguely. She was a professor at Hutton College, where Joan had been a student. Joan's statements to the press before being locked up had piqued Chris's interest in Morgana and had prompted him to do some research on her. She had written numerous scholarly journal articles. More astonishing, she was a member of his parish. Her mother was sitting in judgment of him on the Committee. Clearly, fate had brought them together in this bizarre fashion.

Joan had said that Morgana had controlled her will— made it impossible for her to jump. In trying to fight this, Joan had wanted to carry Morgana off the bridge with her, but Morgana's superior will had prevented this.

Chris sat back in his armchair and picked up the journal he had been reading. Joan was dead, he mused with pleasure. He had wished her to kill herself, just as he had wished the same for Carolyn Danner. Not that it was his idea in the beginning. Each of the women had conceived of

suicide on her own and pressed him with wild threats. As if
fear of their deaths would make him love her. How absurd.
But in each case, he had wished she would go on and die,
had even pictured her hanging by a cord from some high
place.

Had he dreamed up the method of death? Yes, certainly
with Joan. But that had been prompted by his memory of
Carolyn. Had he thought of that as a mode of death for her?
Chris couldn't remember. Though he tried hard, he just
couldn't remember. It nagged at him. He had to recall.
Something was at work. He had power over things—over
people—over their minds. He had seen it with the bird. The
thing had sat still and let Chris pick it up. It was a special
power that Chris had been given. And he had wished Joan to
hang herself.

Morgana's last article excited him even more when added
to the welcome news of Joan's death. It was about parapsychology, the study of inexplicable mind forces. "Physical
causality," it read, "is a transference of energy between two
bits of matter. A billiard ball striking another causes the
second one to move. The fact that we cannot always explain
causation in terms of modern physics does not mean that
one mental force may not be capable of moving objects or
controlling another mental force."

Chris had wished for two women to die. Had his wish
actually made them do it? Had he willed them to die? Had
he transferred his energy into them and controlled them?

"In historic times," the article went on, "magic was
believed capable of transferring energy between systems.
Witches, warlocks, and sorcerers could cast spells that
controlled weather, destroyed crops, or caused people to
sicken and die. While 'magical thinking' is largely discounted today, standard psychology recognizes such con-
cepts as the 'power of suggestion' and accepts that a witch
doctor could terrify a person into dying. The witch doctor
overpowers the victim's will and causes the victim to
destroy himself. An espousal of this fact must also accept
that humans can make a descent into their unconscious and
at that level take control of their minds and bodies. One

human can make the descent into the unconscious of another human."

Chris marveled at what he was reading. Morgana Stone knew and understood. Going to his desk, he got out the newspaper clippings from the day Morgana had talked Joan off the bridge. The photo was blurry, but it was clear that Morgana was physically beautiful. Morgana was the sort of woman he needed as his wife. She was approaching the same conclusion he was, but from the scientific end. He accepted his beliefs on faith—almost intuitively. Magic was real. It was a tool of Satan. It was all around us. Mind power. The ability to project one's will and control others. It was there to harness and use.

It was so easy to use imperfect people and then throw them away if they became a nuisance. Something had been transferred between Chris and Carolyn—between Chris and Joan. He had wished they would go ahead and kill themselves. He had pictured them hanging. Yes, he had imagined Carolyn hanging. It had come to him once when he was helping her with confession. He had pictured her choking with a rope around her neck, her tongue bulging out, gagging, gasping.

Morgana Stone would accept the truth even if it was a shock to her initially. Satan is a real evil force. He enters into us and offers us his powers. We can accept them if we have the courage. The witch had given him the courage and the power. And Morgana understood.

Somehow, the next hearing before the Committee no longer scared him.

• 25 •

"If I hadn't seen some familiar faces, I wouldn't have known I was in my own church," said old Mrs. Staley.

"I'm simply flabbergasted," agreed Mrs. Edwards with equal condemnation. "I thought I was in a dance hall instead of a church." They stepped out into the night of Bayswater Street. The emerging crowd swirled around them.

Trailing along behind the pair, Lynn Stafford heard the poisonous remarks. She couldn't say that she totally agreed with the Thursday night service. Guitars and tambourines, the hands held above the head when praying, all the amens from the crowd, the new hymns with that kind of rock-and-roll beat—they were shocking. And when that man in the back had starting talking in tongues, it had seemed more like an auction.

"You mark my words," asserted Mrs. Edwards. "It's a trick. He's going to keep the two services separate—charismatics on Thursday night, regular service on Sunday—separate until he's got the upper hand."

"What on earth do you mean?" asked Mrs. Staley.

"He's going to pretend he's serving the two different needs. *Pretend,* I tell you. What he's really doing is flooding the church with new members. Eventually they'll outnumber us, and you'll have this fundamentalist mess on Sunday morning."

"Why, that's ridiculous!" said Mrs. Staley indignantly. "I don't believe that."

"It's happening all over the country," countered Mrs. Edwards. "Once that charismatic crowd gets a grip, they don't let up. Did you notice how the church was half-filled with outsiders tonight? Those people don't belong here at all. They like Rector Dixon. That's what this charisma stuff

is all about. Following some preacher instead of belonging
to a church."

"That ghastly person in the back was talking in tongues,"
said Mrs. Staley.

"I couldn't believe it. I'm getting out. I'm moving my
membership to St. Bart's. It's not that far to drive."

"But—we can't. Tradition is . . ."

They moved off into the night to find their car. Stunned
and hesitant, Lynn stood still. On the one hand, she wanted
to chase after them and tell them they were all wrong. Chris
hadn't tried to pervert the church. He just believed in
ministering to people's needs. On the other hand, Lynn
wanted to warn Chris of how this group in the church felt. If
the church became divided into squabbling factions, the
Bishop might remove Chris and send him to some awful
hick church like Roger's in Crossroads. Chris had to be
careful.

But Lynn knew she couldn't just come out and tell Chris
Dixon he was wrong. It wasn't her place to do that. It would
give him the wrong impression and make him think she was
pushy and opinionated.

Several hundred people had been at the Thursday evening
service, and they took a long time to disperse. Clusters of
them stayed behind talking to Chris, telling him how moved
they had been, touching his arm. Lynn knew almost every
one of them. They weren't outsiders. They were members of
long standing who simply didn't come to church on Sunday
morning anymore. Now they were out in droves, all because
Chris Dixon was so inspirational. He was reaching people
who wanted to be reached. He was miraculous. God knew
who that old turkey gobbler had been in the back. He had
probably been there by mistake.

Faith Dixon was standing serenely off to the side, letting
Chris have the limelight. She was so youthful and classically
beautiful. She might have been Chris Dixon's sister instead
of his mother. Her manner was perfect. A nod here. A kind
word there. A smile. A hand pressed. Watching her, Lynn
made the decision to talk to Faith instead of Chris. Lynn
wouldn't just come out and tell Faith the Thursday service

was a mistake, because it wasn't, at least for some. But she'd mention that some of the old guard had their feathers ruffled. Faith would understand, and she might even use Lynn as an ambassador—a kind of go-between for the two groups. As the daughter of the former minister, Lynn would be perfect.

"Oh, Mrs. Dixon," Lynn gushed, clutching her white patent leather handbag to her breast. "It was such a perfect service! I do get tired of that stodgy Sunday ritual. Chris is a breath of fresh air. Not that I'm being critical of my father—you know my father, the former minister?—well, he *was* just a bit on the hidebound side."

"Of course I know Ryan Stafford," said Faith warmly. She took Lynn's arm in a confidential manner and walked down the steps with her and under the dark trees next to the iron spike fence of the graveyard. "Come to think of it, I bet you know absolutely everything about the church. The personal histories of all the members. Their likes and dislikes." She laughed. "Where all the bodies are buried."

Lynn laughed, too. "Every skeleton in every closet."

"You could be so helpful to my son. He's a bit impetuous, even if he is nearly forty. I'm such an overprotective mother—you must excuse me when I say such things. But then, I know I can rely on you to be discreet."

"Oh, yes, of course," said Lynn, her eyes bright.

"Why don't you come over to the manse now and have a cup of tea with me and a bit of a gossip?" Faith asked.

"Why, I'd love to," said Lynn, following Faith's lead as she headed toward the manse.

"Now, I want you to just tell me everything you can about this parish," Faith went on.

Lynn made herself at home in the manse while Faith made tea. She was very pleased with herself. The best way to a man like Chris Dixon was through his mother.

• 26 •

Fran Maitland couldn't believe she was talking to a minister. She had always been in control.

"And then he had a vasectomy," Fran heard herself saying to Chris Dixon. The man was so sympathetic and easy to talk to.

Outside, a woodpecker tapped at a tree. The sun was bright through the old leaded glass of the church administration wing. Inside, the objects in the room glittered in the sun. A big leather-topped desk was a George III. A *Times* crossword puzzle lay on one of the green leather club chairs. There was a rack of fine briar pipes, glass-fronted shelves with finely bound books, a small, heavily varnished English oil painting of cows grazing in front of Salisbury Cathedral.

Chris Dixon's blue eyes held both interest and intelligence. His smile was warm and understanding. As a minister, he understood social class, and he knew Fran's pain at not having children.

So Fran talked on, feeling at ease. "I wanted children," she said, fixing Chris with an intense gaze. "I still want children. Even if Roland is not the father." She knew Chris would notice the oblique reference to her affair.

"Have you committed adultery?" Chris asked with a gentle bluntness. He was so matter-of-fact.

Fran paused. "Yes," she said finally in a small voice. She knew this was why she had come to talk to Chris Dixon. She wanted to share both her joy and her shame.

Chris smiled warmly. "Sin is relative," he began carefully. "If consenting adults choose to find a moment of pleasure and can handle it emotionally without hurting someone else, then perhaps there's no real harm done."

"I . . . have often thought of it that way," Fran admitted.

She looked around the office. There was a photo of a rowing club behind Chris's head, indicating that he had pulled an oar in the Ivy League. That seemed so in character. Chris Dixon was manly and robust while filled with wisdom.

"Roland is so violent," Fran went on. "He collects guns. He nearly killed his first wife once, though he claimed he thought she was a prowler."

"Are you afraid to leave him?" Chris asked finally.

Fran paused. She balled up her Kleenex and then unballed it, flattening it out. "I'd like to leave him, Reverend Dixon, I really would. But it's not really possible. I feel I have a duty. Roland's first marriage ended so sordidly and he has to pay so much alimony. Even so, we have no financial worries, even with all of Roland's expensive hunting trips to Alaska and Africa."

"Would you bear a child by another man?" Chris asked. "Or have an abortion?"

"I want a child so badly," Fran sobbed suddenly. "A little girl, just like my sister, Cynthia."

"Are you fond of your sister?"

"I . . . was. She died when she was in college. I sometimes feel guilty about it. As if it was my fault."

"Why on earth should that be?" Chris Dixon asked.

"I don't know," Fran answered. "I guess it's because of deep-seated childhood jealousies. I used to imagine that she'd die and I'd have my father all to myself. Sometimes I wonder if you can make things happen just by thinking about them."

"I think you can make things happen by willing them," said Chris. "That's why we must be careful of our thoughts. Unclean thoughts have to be purged from our minds before they get control of us and make us do things we wish we hadn't. Have you wished for a child by this other man?"

Fran bit her lip. "I'm sure I have."

"Perhaps you made it happen, then. Well, where's the harm? You can have a child." Chris looked at her intently. "Provided your husband Roland doesn't find out it's not his."

"Y—yes," said Fran in a small voice. "But I had a test, and he'll find out . . . he'll find out eventually. He's a doctor."

"You must convince him otherwise," Chris insisted. "You just admitted that you've willed things that came true."

Fran had to leave several minutes later because the Reverend had another appointment. But she felt exhilarated. It was all so clear to her. Seeing the Reverend Dixon regularly would help her get through her pregnancy and have the beautiful little girl named Cynthia she had always wanted.

• 27 •

Morgana was surprised to see Chris Dixon in her office at Hutton College. It was ten o'clock on a Monday morning and Morgana was prepping for her next lecture.

Clearing a stack of papers and books off a chair, Morgana invited Dixon to sit down. He took his time, preferring to read through titles of books on some of the shelves. He behaved as though he knew her well. In fact, they had never met before. Morgana had seen him only once during a Sunday service, and then only from far away.

"I was next door at the campus ministry for a meeting," Dixon began, "and I had the urge to stop by since I haven't seen you in church lately." He smiled easily. "Please don't take that as some kind of a rebuke."

Morgana didn't answer.

"I was reading your recent article in the *Journal of Psychological Research* about mind control," Chris said, finally sitting down. "It was fascinating. Where did you get your interest in the subject?"

Morgana shrugged. "It's what I study. I'm a parapsychologist. I guess I've always been drawn to the occult."

"I have this theory," Chris continued, "that mind control is what evil is all about. I mean, witchcraft and satanism are just archaic tools people use in order to do evil. These forces help them focus their mind force."

Though the conversation struck Morgana as bizarre, she answered him. "I suppose we've all seen evidence of real mind-controlled evil. The charismatic monster like Charles Manson who manipulates people by force of will. The killer who can cold-bloodedly murder people, yet pose as warm and caring."

Dixon got an odd look on his face. "That's true, you know. I feel that Satan can enter into a human and gain total mastery."

Morgana listened quietly. She wasn't sure what to say. It was as if Dixon was delivering a sermon and only wanted her attention. "It's fashionable today to discount the frequent mention Christ made of Satan," Dixon continued. "Of course, Christ didn't mean some cartoon figure of a red man with tail and cloven hoofs, but an actual spirit of evil much like the Holy Ghost is a spirit of divine goodness. Christians are the only people on earth to doubt the existence of this evil spirit. I'm sure you know that in Hindu or Islamic lands or among animistic tribes, the satanic evil spirit is feared, appeased, and even worshipped." Dixon paused, but only briefly.

"You no doubt know about the classics," he went on. "The Babylonian name Beelzebub is often translated 'Lord of the Flies,' but it really means 'Dweller in the House.'"

Dixon's eyes took on a strange glow. "The Babylonian god was an evil one that came upon invitation and took over the bodies of willing men and women in special rituals of sexual rites and magic incantations. Witchcraft is a version of this. The witches' Sabbath is a ritual worship of Satan with all the magic and sex of Satan's priests. Beelzebub's flies . . . well, everyone believes that insects are sensitive to the spells cast by witches."

Morgana looked out the window at the students passing by outside. Witchcraft, Satan, and the evil that Chris Dixon was talking about seemed incongruous in her environment.

She didn't know exactly what he expected her to say or what she should say. As if reading her thoughts, Chris Dixon stood up.

"It's all only theory, of course. But it's so unusual for me to be able to talk to someone as educated in these things as you are. I guess I got carried away. I'm sorry. I'm sure you've got a lot to do, but maybe we can talk again—sometime soon, I hope, under less harried circumstances."

Morgana nodded and stood up uncomfortably.

Impulsively, Dixon reached out, grabbed her hand, and kissed it. Almost immediately, his face turned red. "I don't know why I did that," he apologized. "It was Beelzebub, I guess." He rushed out.

Walking toward her next class, Morgana tried to put her impressions of Chris Dixon into words. He seemed so intense one moment, and shy and boyish the next. He was certainly an odd person.

Morgana hadn't liked his touch at all. It had reminded her of something unpleasant that she couldn't quite place. And his infatuation with evil, Satan, and witchcraft was certainly macabre. It must explain why he had become a man of the cloth. To be closer to goodness and light.

● 28 ●

Murchison needed a drink badly. He fidgeted in his seat in the chapter house, wondering how bad it would be if he requested a recess to go to the bathroom. The second hearing on Chris Dixon before the Committee was taking forever. The first hearing had gotten bogged down in his life history and details of the parish in Tennessee. Now Dixon had diverted this one into a rambling Socratic dialogue on theology. It was a good strategy, exhausting the Committee with intellectual details. Who knew? They might be so bored they'd just fail to assemble one day, and the whole thing would be dropped. But, God, was it tedious!

"Satan can enter man," Chris continued to theorize, "but man must welcome him in. Hence the notion of the vampire being invited into the house before he can enter. This is a recognition of Beelzebub as the 'dweller in the house,' of cunning Satan, the 'ape of God,' beguiling man through the lusts of the flesh. It is the force of the evil will."

"Yes," Reverend Ratteree murmured vaguely. "The world, the flesh, and the devil."

Chris leaned forward in his chair. "In Acts, Peter told Ananias that Satan had filled his heart. We know for certain that Satan entered into Judas. We—"

Patricia Stone coughed behind her hand. "If I may interrupt, are you telling us that you believe in possession by Satan?"

"Once Satan enters into a man," replied Chris, "he may lurk dormant. He is waiting *achri kairou*—for the decisive moment."

"Yes," agreed Reverend Ratteree. "Of course, that's part of Church doctrine—the 'opportune moment.'" He chewed the end of his glasses thoughtfully.

"Gentlemen," said Pat Stone, "your little exchange of erudition is nice, but if what you say is true, how is it to be dealt with? By exorcism?"

"The ritual of exorcism," said Chris intensely, "was developed by the Church in response to a need that we currently ignore. The Scriptures are filled with evidence of cults devoted to worshipping a palpable evil substance. That strange part of the letter to the church at Pergamum which we find in Revelations—'I know where you dwell, where Satan's throne is'—has been shown by archaeologists to be a reference to temple worship of gods of malign powers. These gods were called by many names, but behind their masks was one universal evil. The Romans spread these cult beliefs throughout Europe. The worship survived in witchcraft and sorcery."

"You . . . you believe in witchcraft?" asked Pat.

"It is impossible not to believe in it," replied Chris Dixon. "The evidence of the existence of magic is too compelling. Pharaoh's sorcerers had mystical powers. Satan was called the Prince of the Air because his followers had the power of levitation. In our own time, telekinetic forces, poltergeists, and mind-reading have all been scientifically documented. Occult powers exist."

"What," said Pat Stone, "does this have to do with Carolyn Danner? Was she possessed by Satan?"

Dixon nodded almost imperceptibly as Murchison ran his hand through his hair and shifted in his seat for the hundredth time. God, he needed a drink. If this went on much longer, he'd have to down the whole flask just to get straight again.

On his yellow legal pad, in large letters, Murchison printed: "CHANGE THE SUBJECT," and emphasized it with three underlines and a brace of exclamation points. Dixon glared at him and talked on. Finally, Murchison leaped to his feet desperately. "May it please Your Worships, esteemed counsel is ill and needs to be excused."

It was as if Murchison had shattered a spell like crystal. Ratteree and the other members of the Committee rubbed their eyes. Murchison headed for the bathroom, getting the flask out as soon as the conference room door was closed behind him. He took a long, refreshing drink and coughed as it went down. He leaned over the sink as if he might throw up. Dixon slammed open the door and glowered at him in wrath.

"What the hell do you mean, doing that to me?" he demanded. "I had them in the palm of my hand!"

Murchison didn't turn away from the sink, but he could see Dixon in the mirror. He took another drink and gargled it before swallowing. His nostrils opened and he breathed in heaving gasps. "All they care about is church attendance and donations. They don't want a pentecostal firebrand. You had gone on long enough."

Putting his hands to his face, Chris smoothed out his forehead. "I had them spellbound," he insisted in a tight voice. "They understood evil. We all must understand evil. It is real. It is all-powerful!"

Letting out a fatigued breath, Murchison turned and leaned against the sink. His head sank to his chest, and he put his hand over his eyes. Dixon's gaze unsettled him. "Even assuming that's true," he said, "where were you heading? Were you establishing the sort of character who would never have tied up a woman and flogged the crap out of her? Were you painting a picture of yourself as the smiling, timid divine who wouldn't think of saying 'damn'? For shit's sake, get some perspective, Chris."

"I . . . I suppose you're correct," admitted Dixon. "I'm sorry."

"You weren't holding Pat Stone," Murchison went on. "You weren't convincing her of anything you wanted to convince her of. She was writing it all down."

Dixon looked abashed. "You're right. I didn't realize that." Suddenly he thrust his hand out and said, "You're right and I'm wrong. I apologize. I'll pay attention in the future."

Murchison looked down at the extended hand. Reluctantly, he gave it a limp shake. Suddenly he didn't like the feeling that passed from Dixon into him. It gave him the creeps.

● *29* ●

"You be careful of that!" Lynn ordered the moving men in a shrill voice. "That china cabinet has been in the Stafford family for nearly a hundred years!"

Mopping perspiration from her neck, Lynn sat down. It was so hot with the air conditioning turned off. Even with the men doing all the heavy work, she felt faint and exhausted.

Patricia Stone went on wrapping china in newspaper and ignoring Lynn's histrionics. She was helping out of friendship for Ryan Stafford, who was crippled from a stroke.

"Be sure and wrap those cups well," Lynn directed. "I couldn't bear the idea of any of Mother's china getting broken." Lynn took a swig from her Coke and dabbed at her neck and face again with a handkerchief.

Lynn had always been good at organizing people, and when she considered it, that was really the prime talent of a minister's wife. All men needed organizing, but ministers more than most. They had that tendency toward unworldliness.

"No!" Lynn shouted at the movers. "The refrigerator goes in the other truck! Father's not going to need that in a rest home! It's got to be put in storage!"

"I just don't know what I'll do if the landlord won't give me Father's damage deposit," Lynn said to Patricia, who was busily packing up the pots and pans from under the sink. "The apartment was a wreck when we moved in. It was such a shock after the manse. And now we're going to be blamed for defects that were always there." Her voice became hurried. "If I don't get the money back, I won't be able to pay for these trucks. Honestly, I don't understand why you thought I'd need two of them. And they're so expensive."

"Be calm, Lynn," said a fatigued Patricia Stone. "I'll lend you the money. You can pay me later."

"Oh," said Lynn. "That would be wonderful . . . if, of course . . . only if you *insist*."

It seemed simple enough to accept Patricia's money, since she was in a much better financial position and didn't need the loan paid back right away. Besides, Patricia was far too lavish with the movers, offering them Cokes and letting them rest every hour. She'd probably even tip them afterward.

Lynn was torn between showing her father her own new apartment on the Street Highway and hiding it from him. It was so shameful that she had to live there after the manse.

But in the end it wasn't a problem, because Ryan Stafford

became unruly when Lynn tried to get him into the car. He asked needless questions and was generally hard to deal with. Finally, it was Patricia who got him into the car. Because she had to drive him to the rest home, Lynn left Patricia to finish cleaning up. It was nearly an hour's drive up there, and it was late.

Ryan babbled all the way to the home. He fussed over his seat belt and asked Lynn a hundred times if the dining room table was properly wrapped with quilts.

The rest home was in a town north of Congreve that in historical times had been used as an escape from the mosquitos and heat of the coast in summer. It was approached along a road lined with gigantic live oaks, which were being cut one by one to make way for turn lanes and new apartment complexes and fast food outposts. The rest home had long verandas with wicker chairs and overhead fans, all banked around by shrubbery and overarched by big trees. Since it was run by the Church, her father got a special rate. Lynn talked about how nice the place was as they drove, gushing over the shrubbery, green grass, and spring flowers.

But Ryan Stafford wasn't listening. "They mustn't dig there anymore," he said urgently, his good eye imploring Lynn. "They mustn't tamper with it."

"Oh, really, Father," said Lynn in a disgusted tone. She knew that he was off on his kick about the "unhallowed ground," as he called it. It was so absurd, and she didn't want to listen.

"The body was unnatural. It was heavy. Easily three hundred pounds. With no reason for it. It took six men to lift it even in the plastic sack. We buried her at night so no one would know."

"Father, I just don't want to hear this," said Lynn, twisting the rearview mirror around to check her makeup.

Tears began to run from Ryan's bad eye, and the slack side of his mouth drooled. "They mustn't tamper with that body. They must leave it alone."

"I'm not hearing another word," said Lynn, putting her nose up in the air. She really couldn't stand it. Her own father had gone senile. It was like a dreadful warning of her own advancing age. Thank goodness he hadn't talked this way around Patricia Stone. What might she have thought? What might she have repeated? Lynn used to rely on her father for everything, but now she was clearly on her own. She had to be strong. She'd be strong enough to find a man to take her father's place.

● *30* ●

Fran Maitland's kitchen was perfect in every way. Gleaming copper pots hung from the walls in descending order of size. Her microwave was a Litton. She had a food processor and a toaster oven and two dishwashers for heavy entertaining. Cuisine was Fran's strength.

Magzie the cook had called in sick, but Fran figured it was a lie to get out of work. As one of her church duties, Fran had to participate in baking ten thousand cookies for the inmates of the Georgia prisons. Fran's share was five hundred, and it would take her all afternoon.

Chris Dixon was one of the most interesting men Fran had ever met, but his prison ministry was asinine. The idea of converting hardened criminals into normal human beings was absurd. The prisoners came to the Christian services merely to get out of their cells for a while. And when they returned, they were jeered at by the others as "Jesus freaks." To counteract this, some minister had conceived the idea of letting the Christian prisoners take cookies back to share with their fellow inmates.

It all seemed naive to Fran. Chris Dixon was so educated and human. He understood people. The idea that those beasts in a prison could be won over by cookies was absurd. Surely Chris could understand that. In fact, the ploy was guaranteed to make them howl with laughter. It was such a typical ministerial stunt. Cookies. Fran shook her head as she wiped the sweat off her nose with her apron.

She wondered why she had allowed herself to get roped into this sort of project. But she was keeping up appearances, doing the right things, like her mother.

Of course, she could have arranged to do the baking with someone else. But all the other women had children and talked about them nonstop, leaving Fran with nothing to say. They talked about Congreve Day School, soccer practice and ballet lessons, horseback riding and sailing lessons, car pools. It was as if they liked reminding Fran she didn't have children. Secretly, they probably talked about Fran being barren. They would never guess that Roland had had a vasectomy. After all, as far as they were concerned, he was a doctor and could afford all the children he wanted.

The bastard had left her without children. He had been totally insensitive to her needs, refusing to realize her humiliation. That was why Fran had let herself go with Rafe, and now she was going to have his child. Roland hadn't pressed her too much about the pregnancy. Fran figured it was because of the embezzlement and his affair with his nurse. She didn't care. She would deal with him just as Chris Dixon had suggested.

Fran sat down. At that moment, it struck Fran that Chris Dixon couldn't possibly believe in this stupid cookie business. He was like her. He was just doing what was expected. He had to blend with all those other insipid ministers and dotty women in the church. He had to survive the same way Fran did. That was why he had understood about Rafe and the baby.

Rafe Artigues was such a marvelous brute of a man. He could take her breath away just by running his hand down her spine. He was saddle leather and the smell of horses and hounds. He was all sinew and muscle. It almost made sense that she had let him give her a baby. It was as if she had willed it, just like Chris had said. Suddenly, tears rolled down her cheeks.

Fran was startled to hear the back doorbell ring. Quickly,

she wiped her eyes and looked at herself in the mirror over the sink. Her face was puffy and red. The bell rang again.

Faith Dixon stood at the door in her green shirtwaist dress, her deep black hair pulled back. Fran rubbed her hands down the front of the apron and confronted her unexpected guest.

"I'm so hot in here, I don't think I can stand it much longer," Fran said as an alibi for her red face.

"Why are we doing this?" Faith joked. "We must be out of our minds. I've been in the church kitchen all morning, and I thought I would die if I didn't get out. So I figured I'd drop in on my most valiant trooper."

Fran was flattered instantly. Out of all the women baking that day, Faith had chosen her to visit. Faith was such a figure in the church. Even though her role was a subservient one—always accepting, reconciling, submitting—she somehow made her presence felt. She had such perfect poise and elegance. It was easy to see how she had borne such a perfect son.

"Please come in," said Fran. "You're a lifesaver. I thought I was about to go out of my mind. Of course, the kitchen is a mess."

"I've always wanted to see your house," said Faith. "I saw the feature article on it in *Southern Living,* and I've been dying to get inside." She followed Fran's lead. It was clear she was impressed. "Why, your kitchen is just beautiful!" she said finally. "Why don't you put your house on the Congreve house tour?"

"I must confess," said Fran, "I always thought the tour was a bit common. People trying to show off their possessions. My mother always refused to be on the tour, and her house was just perfect. Come on, let me show you the living room. We had a new mantel put in from a house that was being torn down. Purists in restoration didn't approve, but I think you have to use some creativity in decoration. You can't be a total slave to the past."

"Oh, is this your family?" asked Faith, pausing and looking at a framed color photo.

"Yes," said Fran proudly. "My parents, the McAlisters,

and me when I was small. They were very prominent then. Father was building so many things."

"And is this a sister? I didn't know you had siblings," Faith went on.

Fran's face tightened. "Yes," she choked. "Cynthia was my older sister. She died . . . a long time ago."

"She seems almost familiar somehow," said Faith. "Like someone I might have known. Perhaps it's her resemblance to you."

Fran didn't seem to hear. She spoke as in a dream. "She was doing something she shouldn't have and was murdered. They wouldn't even let me see her body or tell me where she was buried." She began to weep.

Faith put a comforting arm around her and held her gently.

When Faith left several hours later, they had finished all the cookies. Faith had been so apologetic that she had even asked to hear more about Cynthia. She understood the grief Fran still felt. She was as understanding as her son.

● 31 ●

At the very back of The Military campus on a hill overlooking the marshes of the Elstree River was a thirty-foot wooden tower used for rappelling. Set among enormous live oaks draped in Spanish moss, it seemed an ideal place for a tryst. Debra and Beau had been meeting there ever since Wayne had moved back into the house.

Debra liked it because she could tell her husband she was going for a walk and simply disappear from sight. While he wasn't allowed off campus on weeknights, Beau could go anywhere he pleased on the grounds. Since the gym and the library were open, it was natural for the tactical officers to assume he was at one of those places.

The couple would lie in each other's arms and watch the

stars in a silence broken only by their breathing. When they made love, Debra liked the delicious sense of danger that came from imagining some outraged ROTC instructor at the bottom of the steps shouting at them to come down instantly. She imagined herself pulling her jeans back on slowly, bound by the knowledge of disgrace and doom. Perhaps in a final gesture of unconcern for her fate, she would let her panties drift down in the dark to drape the head of the blustering army jerk. She laughed aloud, thinking of it.

"Debra, baby, what's so funny?" whispered Beau. He was increasingly confused by her. She had been fired from her job at the bank and didn't seem to care. She had accepted Wayne's return to the house with total nonchalance. And she was totally unresponsive when he tried to talk to her about their future together. To him, his upcoming graduation next month and his commission in the army were the perfect provision for their security and love. He couldn't understand why she wouldn't want to leave her husband and follow him to Fort Bragg. They loved each other, after all.

Debra turned in his arms and nuzzled his throat. "Nothing," she murmured. "I just felt silly and thought I'd giggle."

"I don't understand you," said Beau suddenly in a sullen voice.

"What's to understand, babykins? I'm just a woman, and you're a boy. That's all."

"No, I'm not," he answered stubbornly. "I'm a man with a man's job in front of me. I've got my jump wings. I've got my commission. I can provide for you. I can protect you from that shithead you're married to. I can love you the way you should be loved."

Debra rubbed his smooth chest. His shirt was unbuttoned and the pants undone. The brass buckle on his belt glowed faintly in the moonlight. "Honey, you're just a boy who's made love to a woman for the first time in his life. That's all. It's just such a shock after groping with little teenage girls in the backseats of cars that you're just overwhelmed. You think you're in love, but you're not."

Beau sat up. "He's making you think that. He knows, and he's twisted your mind. Don't deny it. I know he's onto us. Every time he pulls an inspection, he reams me good. He's trying to give me so many demerits I'll get booted out of school. But he can't come between us that easy. I won't let him push me around no more than I'll let him hurt you!"

"You're wrong, babykins," said Debra, propping herself on an elbow. "He doesn't even have a suspicion."

"Don't lie to me," said Beau fiercely, smacking a fist into his open palm. "I've seen the welts on your backside even in the dark. And I can feel. I know your skin. He's been beating you. He's got you so scared you're trying to get rid of me. Well, he can't do that. I'll kill him first."

Debra tugged him back down beside her. "Lie down, baby. Someone'll see your silhouette. Wayne didn't do that to me."

"Well, who did, then?" He ran his hand inside her pants and stroked the flesh of his true love.

"The Reverend did, silly."

Beau couldn't believe what he had heard. "The Reverend? Are you crazy? What the hell's going on?"

"I'm a sinful woman," said Debra in a matter-of-fact voice. "That wipes away my sins. Just like when you were little and your daddy whipped you and it hurt and you cried, but afterward you forgot all about it. Your sins were gone. Daddy loved you, and he had whipped away your sins."

"You whip a child to teach him to do the right things," protested Beau. "What's he trying to teach you to do?"

"Nothing, silly. He's just getting rid of sin."

Beau didn't want to say it, but sometimes he wondered if Debra had a brain in her head. He wasn't the best of students, and was barely going to graduate with a 2.0 average if that vicious bastard in Business Law would give him a C. But still, when he tried to talk to Debra about even the most ordinary events in the news, she would stare at him blankly until he stopped. She didn't read a paper or any kind of book. She didn't seem to have any interest in anything except sex.

"Debra, that doesn't make sense. Grown men don't whip women unless they're some kinda sicko creep. What does he beat you with?"

"With a kind of leather whip he has. He soaks it in Vaseline so it doesn't hurt so much. It's not bad at all. He's really a smart man. I mean, he was the one who figured out how to handle Wayne."

"I'm lost, Debra," said Beau. He wanted to believe in his love for her. He wanted to believe in it so much. He had planned how he would break the news to his parents. He didn't care about his friends. But this was weird.

"It was really simple," said Debra, tracing an X on his chest with her finger. "He had this teenage girl they were giving shelter to at the church, and he suggested I hire her to baby-sit the boys. That way, Wayne would fall for the girl, and he wouldn't care about me anymore and I could have you."

"The minister planned that?" asked Beau incredulously.

"Well, just the baby-sitting part. The rest he just sort of hinted at. Or it seemed he was hinting. Anyhow, it sure worked out that way. I could tell right off from the way Wayne looked at her. She's a real piece of ass, that girl. Some kind of a nut-religion refugee. He's acting like a kid of twenty around her, all left feet."

"I'm a kid of twenty-one," said Beau. "And I love you and want you to marry me. If Wayne's got a girlfriend, then it's perfect. He'll be happy to divorce you."

"Beau, can't you just love without thinking about stuff that ruins love? Marriage is awful. You don't want any part of it."

"I do, Debra. I do."

"Shhh," she said, putting her fingers on his lips. "Be with me. Let's just enjoy the moment."

• 32 •

Bojack Sandor had thick black hair that he greased and combed straight back and a flat face with cheekbones so prominent they seemed to make his eyes squint. Barely five feet tall, he made up for his lack of size with a furious energy. An admirer of the late Jackson Pollock, he would fling paint frantically at a giant canvas while swilling red Hungarian wine. Paint splattered his coveralls until they resembled one of his creations.

His students adored him. His wife, Maeve, who was getting her master's in fine arts from his department at Hutton College, had considerably less respect for her husband. She had lived through eighteen years of his drunken rages and no longer found them charming.

"Knock off the creative impulse for a moment, will you, Bojack?" she said, pushing open the door to his studio in the fine arts building. Wet paint glistened on the walls, the windows, and a big octagonal canvas Bojack had built. He had just glued wads of newspaper to the wet canvas and was on the verge of scorching the entire thing with an acetylene torch while he drank wine from a jelly glass.

"I'm busy," he said in his thick accent.

"Don't be a shit," Maeve said. "I need five minutes, and I know I can't rely on seeing you at home anytime soon." Bojack kept no regular hours, often sleeping in his studio, under cars, or in the beds of whatever coeds were infatuated with him at the moment.

Maeve picked her way through the puddles of wet paint on the floor. The heavy smell of turpentine filled the air. "I've been talking to Clarence Fuller," she said. Clarence was the head of the psychology department.

"That scumbag? What was he doing, shrinking your brain?"

Maeve held on to her temper. She figured on getting her master's and becoming an art teacher herself. Not at Hutton College, but at an important place. She had an instinctive feel for faculty politics, which was why Clarence had asked her to talk to Bojack. "He's very concerned about you being on the campus-wide tenure committee."

"Concerned?" snorted Bojack as he fiddled with the acetylene torch.

Maeve jerked the torch away from him and put it on a shelf across the room. "You've got a heavy responsibility on that committee. You'll be the voice of the college in deciding on tenure. The departments will send their recommendations, and you'll shape the issues for the president."

"I know what we do on the committee," glowered Bojack. "I vote yes for everybody. I stand for total academic freedom. We give everybody a secure job."

"That's just the problem, Bojack. You need to curb your natural anarchy. Clarence is very concerned about someone from his department."

"Yeah? That Nazi Fuller wants to fire someone, as usual. That's all he wants. To terrorize people like the KGB. He should go and live in Hungary. He'd like it there. They could put him in the psychiatric terror police. He could shoot people up with drugs and burn out their brains. He'd like that."

Maeve rolled her eyes. "Don't you have any concern for the quality of the school? No wonder Clarence felt he had to talk to me."

"Quality?" said Bojack angrily. "Quality is shit. I believe in freedom. Freedom to do as you please. Let everyone do as they please. Then you get quality."

"Bojack, I'm trying very hard to be calm. This is important. Clarence is depending on me. There is a woman in his department who really just doesn't fit in. Her name is Morgana Stone. They want her out. There's no point in my going into the reasons. Just vote with them. Can you understand that? For once in your life, do the political thing and win some friends."

"Do I win Morgana as a friend? Hah? Do you think she

will like me for firing her? You make me puke." Bojack clamped a welder's helmet on and retrieved the torch. Turning on the gas, he ignited the flame with a roar. "Go fuck yourself!" he yelled from inside the mask.

A furious Maeve stalked out of the room and down the hall of the fine arts building.

The stupid shit, Maeve fumed. How did he manage to survive in his job? She had nothing personal against Morgana. In fact, she barely knew the woman when she saw her. But you had to be aware of what went on around you. Clarence Fuller carried a lot of weight on the campus.

By instinct, Maeve was a free spirit. But still, she wanted that master's degree, and she had to be realistic enough to see that someone like Clarence could be very dangerous if he decided to pick on her. When that guy got on your case, he didn't sleep until you had been run off. For some reason he was pissed at Morgana. Unfair? Perhaps. But that was life. Maeve had been born into poverty in a Liverpool slum. That had been unfair. And now she was going to get above all that. She was going to be an art teacher herself.

No more depending on Bojack for her living. No more having to scrimp and ferret away nickels and dimes for a new pair of shoes or even a decent meal while he drank like a fish and philandered with every coed he could lay his paws on.

The immediate problem was to mollify Clarence Fuller. He had come to her and put his trust in her. She'd have to tell him she had Bojack lined up. It was easy enough to lie. The tenure committee vote was secret, so there would be no reason for Clarence to know even if Bojack voted for Morgana.

Maybe she'd dope Bojack up on the day of the vote. He'd sleep through the day and miss the whole thing. That was an idea. She could use a little rauwolfia from her garden.

"Oh, wow, look at these books," said Cerise later that day in a voice that could only be described as laid-back. "I've seen stuff like this before. I've even read some of them."

Morgana was accustomed to young egoism and ignorance. She had received notice from her department head that Cerise was her new advisee and would be allowed to audit whatever courses she wished for the remaining month of the semester, preparatory to enrolling as a full-time student for the summer. There were neither SAT scores nor an admission application in her file. As far as Morgana could tell, the only reason Hutton College had let in this kind of student was to stem a declining enrollment.

"Well, what are you thinking of studying?" Morgana asked.

The girl ran her hand through her beautiful, long black hair and gave Morgana a dreamy look. "Oh, I don't know. History maybe. Or philosophy. Or maybe pre-med."

Morgana thought Cerise was improbably beautiful even for a student at Hutton. If there was one thing that could be said of Hutton College, it was that it attracted some of the most beautiful girls in Georgia. And either the human race was improving in appearance, or Georgia had an abnormal number of beautiful girls. But the voice was something else. It was like Cerise was talking to Morgana from out in space.

"Reverend Dixon said I should ask for you special as my whatchamacallit—my advisor. He said you were something —some word I've forgotten. Anyhow, he wanted me to get you, and that other man, your boss, arranged it." She smiled and continued to run her fingers through her hair, looking around Morgana's office, reading the titles of the books. "You can call me Cerise," she said, "if you're wondering which name to use. I've quit using the name I had at New Vrindaban. And I live at the church. St. Helen's. He lets me crash there. He's probably the nicest man I've ever met. I came with a not-nice man who picked me up in West Virginia. The commune where I was raised was in West Virginia."

Jesus, thought Morgana, this girl was spacy. There were two names in the file, Cerise Abrams and Sulocana Dageth. Cerise seemed to be one of the children of Hare Krishna.

"You just sort of went with this man and ended up in Congreve?" she asked.

Cerise crossed her shapely legs and swung her foot back and forth. She was wearing Adidas running shoes and ankle socks with little pom-poms on the backs. Her T-shirt, stretched tightly across her full breasts, said, "Krishna is Love." "Yeh, like I just sort of walked away from the commune one day. I got to wondering what life was on the other side of the mountain and I just kept walking. Like the bear in the poem. And like this man picked me up."

"Uh . . . what was your education like?"

"We read mystical books. And we had sessions at the feet of the guru where he instructed us in the Way of Enlightenment." She looked down at her shoes. "The not-nice man bought me these clothes. All I had was this T-shirt and a saffron gown. He had nasty habits. He drank a lot of liquor, which is bad for you. I guess he died of it."

"Died?"

Cerise smiled sleepily. "I don't know why I said that. It just came into my head."

"Who is this man? What became of him?"

"I dunno. His name was Byron something. I think he was a preacher. He's gone. I stay with another man now. A real nice man. Nobody's ever been as nice to me as him, ever. Not even Reverend Dixon. I like this guy I'm with now a lot. He's got some nickname. I don't know his real name."

"And the Reverend approves?"

"I dunno." Cerise shrugged. "The Reverend looks after me. He's found me a job. I baby-sit for this family at the

Military. That's a weird place. Like a commune almost, except all the men are in soldier suits. It's a nice family. The husband is real funny. I think he likes me."

Morgana did her best to explain what college was all about, but Cerise's attention drifted. Finally she got up and walked out with a simple "See ya around" as a good-bye. The best Morgana could do was to tell the girl her office hours and hope she'd come back.

Clarence Fuller came into Morgana's office shortly afterward. Fuller used his height to look down his nose at everyone. A specialist in early childhood development, he had started a private psychology practice on the side, specializing in the children of the downtown social set. Clarence was a pro at convincing all the parents that their little darlings were prodigies, and he milked this talent for big fees and invitations to blue-blood events.

For no reason that Morgana could understand, he had taken an instant dislike to her. She sometimes imagined it was her professional reputation, since Clarence had none outside well-to-do Congreve. Other times, Morgana thought it might have been the shock of running into her at parties where he assumed no one from Hutton College but he would be invited. Or perhaps it was a combination of both. A fear that she would know him for the hollow intellect and social climber that he was.

"Well," Fuller said, remaining standing. "I trust you've helped our new student get acclimated."

"You mean Cerise?"

"Yes. She was recommended to us by Reverend Dixon, and I can't tell you how much the goodwill of St. Helen's Church means to Hutton College."

Sure, thought Morgana, most especially to your social aspirations.

While Clarence stood with one hand on his hip as if posing for a heroic statue, Morgana explained that Cerise wasn't ready to register yet. Clarence didn't agree.

"You know, Stone," he said, "you had quite a reputation up in New York, but there's a noticeable failure on your part to fit into the program here. This . . . this specialty of yours . . ." He waved his hand as if brushing off lint. "It's such a narrow field of interest, it's really only appropriate at a large university where they have room for obscure elective courses. Much as I admire your research effort, I'm afraid I'm bending in the direction of the bulk of the department in feeling you'd be happier somewhere else."

The message that she was going to be denied tenure within the next few weeks was clear. "What have I ever done to you?" she asked finally.

Fuller gave her a funny look and put his hand back on his hip. "You know, you're a good-looking woman, Stone. Perhaps if you got to know me better."

Morgana folded her hands. "And just what does *that* mean?" she asked.

"My wife's out of town this week at a folk-dancing festival in Atlanta. Perhaps if you were to have dinner with me tonight and . . . well, make yourself agreeable afterwards . . . it might go a long way toward adjusting my attitude."

"What would you say," Morgana asked sweetly, "if I told you I had a tape recorder running in my desk drawer?"

Fuller's nostrils flared and his eyes opened so wide the white could be seen in a ring about the iris. Without another word, he stalked out. She heard him slam the door at the end of the corridor.

The son-of-a-bitch, Morgana fumed. She really ought to start recording her conversations with him and nail his ass good for sexual harassment.

● 34 ●

Chris blew on the small flame in the fireplace to get the wood chips ignited. They would make a nice blaze, just enough to heat the wax, and it wouldn't be too hot on a spring day.

With deft fingers, he molded a tiny man from a wad of black candle wax, talking under his breath all the time. Then he poked a tuft of hair into the abdominal region with a bone splinter and dunked the thing in the little mustard jar of menstrual blood. Chris laughed to himself.

That stupid ass Clarence Fuller had actually boasted about how he was going to can Morgana Stone. He had gotten drunk at a party Chris had attended last night and told anyone who would listen how incompetent Morgana was. Fuller had been proud of his little exercise of power over her. Well, Fuller would be a good one to start on just to see if this worked or not. Chris had only wished for the deaths of Carolyn Danner and Joan Scott. Now he would know if he could really kill someone.

It hadn't been easy to get the hair, but everyone had always laughed about how Fuller's wife cut his hair because he was too cheap to go to a barber. The Fullers with their big house, and Fuller sitting out on the back steps clutching a towel around his neck while his wife snipped away. Lucky that that same night at the party someone had recounted seeing the "Fullerbob," as it was called. Then it was just a matter of sifting garbage.

Why the Fullers were invited anywhere was a mystery to Chris. Fuller's wife did folk dancing or something. And all the downtown rich people thought of Clarence as just another servant. Sure, he did testing on their children, but that wasn't much different from someone who sold carpets, as far as they were concerned.

Well, this would all work out. Chris was confident. Fuller would die, which would be a good test, and Chris would draw Morgana closer. Two birds with one stone.

Chris had already brought Debra under his power. He could actually project ideas into her brain. And Fran Maitland, too.

This had all been promised to him! The power of the left-hand path. There was danger there—great danger. A curse could come back with redoubled force. But you were safe if you cursed those who deserved it. Clarence Fuller certainly fit in that category. He had gone out of his way to harm Morgana Stone. He had attacked her for the sheer malicious cruelty of the thing. The fires of hell would welcome his screams. His internal anger was such that it could be twisted and made to tear his own body to shreds.

Gripped by a sudden fear, Chris had trouble breathing. He'd had asthma as a child, and it often struck when he was under stress. He lurched to the window and gasped in the hot air. His mind raced with images of the girl in the mausoleum. She was doing this to him! She was striking at him! He almost screamed, but bit his hand to stifle it.

Gradually the crisis passed. His breathing returned with difficulty. The corpse was his to use. It was a gift of great power given him because he was worthy. He had done nothing wrong. He had been born to greatness, born to be higher than mankind.

Byron Moss had been out to destroy Chris, so his death had been essential. Chris hadn't struck him down, anyway. An instrument sent for the task had done the act. Chris had only followed the path of his destiny.

Yes, he was doing fine, he told himself confidently. The left-hand path was a hard one, but he had the strength. He had the will. An evil smile spread his lips. He pictured how Fuller would look as the pain began.

• 35 •

"You men just take a world of looking after," drawled Lynn Stafford later that same day in her best southern belle voice. "Look at that ash in the fireplace. It's almost June and nobody's emptied the grate." She wiped a finger across Chris's desk. "And look at this dust. You really could use a woman around here. I mean, other than your mother."

Chris smiled sheepishly. Lynn liked the effect she was having on him. The motherly approach was always the best. Show a man how useful you could be, edge in here and there with helpful hints, and before long you were indispensable.

"I suppose you're right," Chris allowed. "I am rather absentminded about those things."

Lynn busied herself with the fireplace shovel scooping around in the ash, although she had no idea what she really should be doing.

"Goodness! These ashes are still hot!" she exclaimed as a little trail of smoke rose. "What in heaven's name were you doing with a fire on a warm day like this?"

"Oh, I don't know," Chris said absently. "It gets cold here sometimes. I felt chilly."

"Well, why didn't you just open a window and let all that nice sunshine in?" Lynn babbled on. "Now, tell me all about these pictures. No, let me guess. This is where you went to college, isn't it?" She leaned close to read the titles since she was nearsighted but wouldn't wear her glasses. "Christ Church College, Oxford. My goodness, an Oxford man!" She clapped her hand over her mouth in surprise. "But of course I knew that, silly me. Christopher Dixon, you are about the most educated man I ever did meet. I'm just swept away."

"Well, thank you," said Chris shyly.

At the Women's Luncheon last week, Faith had mentioned to Lynn that her son was a trifle vain about his education, believing that the only real place in the world to be trained in religious doctrine was England.

It had been easy enough for Lynn to pump Faith for inside poop on Chris. If there was one thing Lynn knew, it was that no mother likes anything better than talking about her offspring. When it was an only son with father deceased, and an unmarried son at that, he was an object of worshipful reverence.

Among other tidbits, Lynn had learned that Chris's favorite meal was rare roast beef—bloody rare—with Yorkshire pudding. Lynn was known for her cooking. Most important, Lynn had learned that Faith fervently wanted grandchildren before she got too old. She was sixty-two, Faith revealed without even being asked. And Lynn particularly noted how Faith asked all the right questions about Lynn's background as though she was checking off a list of essential attributes.

Faith was so distinguished and aristocratic. She seemed more like someone who should have been married to Lynn's father than her real mother. Faith walked and sat and used her silverware as if trained at an old-time finishing school. She never said a critical word about anyone. Lynn would adore having her as a mother-in-law.

And Faith didn't blink when the unpleasant subject of Lynn's divorce came up. Such refinement came only with breeding. No doubt she accepted divorce as one of those things of a modern age. Not exactly to her taste, but something the young people did. There really was no way she could hold it against Lynn, particularly after Lynn told her about the unjust way Roger had treated her.

More to the point, Faith had practically given Lynn an invitation to go ahead and make a play for Chris. He was a man of forty, after all, and a little sex was a necessary thing. Of course, she hadn't put it in so many words, but Faith did say that her son was shy around women and let them take charge. That appealed to Lynn. She was good at taking charge. If Roger hadn't been so bullheaded and had let her take the lead, Lynn probably could have salvaged his career even after the scandal with the grocery store manager.

"It seems so lonely here in this office," said Lynn, sitting close to Chris and letting her dress ride up to reveal a good length of thigh. The dress was pure silk and had cost more than two hundred dollars at Talbots, busting Lynn's budget for the next six months. "Are you lonely? I mean, way high up in this cold tower with your little fire to keep away the chill while you think deep thoughts?"

Chris smiled and rested his hand on her arm. He wasn't quite so shy after all. "Of course it's lonely. Ministers are condemned to a life of celibacy, all the natural urges scrutinized by old women. I actually need my mother as a chaperone just to keep off scandal. She wouldn't be here if I weren't single. In fact, she's anxious to move out and get on with a life of her own."

"Well, then, why doesn't little old you just go ahead and tie the knot with some sweet young thing?" Lynn asked brightly. "All the little girls in their twenties just swoon over you like you're some rock star."

Chris laughed. "That's my secret lust. But a levelheaded person like you knows I need a mature woman. Young girls go off the deep end occasionally, and I can't afford any missteps."

"You really are ambitious, aren't you?" Lynn said carefully. "I like that in a man."

They talked well into the late afternoon. Gradually Chris began to unburden himself, saying that he feared his ambition to be a bishop was a mortal sin and he would be punished for it. Lynn hastened to assure him otherwise.

Then came his incredible confession of feeling smothered by his mother and his longing to find a wife and be rid of a chaperone. He admitted his biological urges in frank language and spoke of sex as the bedrock of love.

Lynn felt herself growing weak under Chris's gaze. Faith was wrong. He was not shy. That was just a mother's perception. Christopher Lawrence Dixon III was the most compelling, masterful man she had ever met. There was something special about his manner. Something that made her feel she was with her father, like she was a little girl all snug and warm and being tucked up in bed wearing footy pajamas.

Lynn got a sad, tender expression on her face and leaned into him. The kiss that followed seemed like the most perfect and deep kiss of her life. It was as if electricity passed between them in such a strong current as to bond them together. Like that painting in the art history course she had taken in junior college. Michelangelo or somebody had done it on a chapel ceiling: God reaching out his hand and giving life to Adam.

As the kiss went on and on and their hands groped and clutched and her body ached with longing, everything unspoken was understood. They had been brought together by some sublime fate. They were one another's destiny.

Finally, he tore away from her. "Could you love me?" he asked.

"Yes, yes," she whispered fervently.

"We'd have to go slow in public and give Mother time to get used to it."

"And all those old cats in the congregation with single daughters," Lynn said, giggling.

Chris laughed gently. "But in private, we could be all we're meant to be."

"Yes," she answered simply, and let him take her in another passionate kiss. This one was rougher, hungrier, a signal of his inner need. Lynn knew she could quench his flame of desire each time it blazed up. She was more than enough woman for any man. That stupid Roger just hadn't had the brains to recognize her life force for what it was. Airhead bitch, he had called her. She'd show him with her new husband and Roger still stuck in Crossroads, Georgia, population 2,753.

Chris's hands went between Lynn's legs as his tongue filled her mouth. She groaned with desire and spread her thighs to let him touch her center. His mouth began to bite at hers, to nip her lips, her chin, her neck.

"Chris, you horny man." She giggled. "If your mother

were to see hickeys on my neck—why, she'd think I was making out with some teenager . . ."

"I need your love!" Chris pursued in a heaving voice.

She put her mouth close to his and closed her eyes. "I have it to give," she breathed. "I'm not some spinster afraid of the word 'fuck.' I'll fuck you until you can't stand up."

"Will you be loyal to me?" he asked. "Will you undergo pain for me?"

He squeezed her upper arms so tightly she cried out, but she liked the rough treatment. She liked feeling his masterful strength. "Yes," she wailed, her eyes closed, her head lolling in surrender.

"Then prove it!" he snarled, slapping her a ringing blow across the face.

Lynn's head jerked back, and stars briefly spun before her eyes. Her hand went to her hot, stinging cheek. She stared at him in horror.

● *36* ●

Morgana wasn't quite sure why she had come to her Hutton Hall twentieth reunion. She found her old acquaintances a little alien with their talk of children, car pools, and what was going on in the downtown set. But it was a link to her younger days, when life had been more innocent and idyllic.

Long serving tables were set under the ancient live oaks on the lawn in front of the old mansion that was the school's main building. As late afternoon turned to early evening, Japanese paper lanterns were lit and hung from the trees. The delicious food was catered by an Australian named Rafe Artigues, who ran a popular downtown restaurant called Dalmazell's. Chris Dixon had been invited to do the benediction. Smooth and charming, he moved among the crowd, accepting the attention of Morgana's former classmates with good grace. He was handsome and he obviously knew it.

"This is certainly a touch of the old South," Chris said as he found Morgana in the crowd. "Tell me, what was Congreve like when you were a kid?"

Morgana took a glass of champagne from a passing silver tray. "Believe it or not," she said, taking a sip, "nothing like this. The market area was sailors' bars and brothels." She stopped, remembering how she and Drena had sneaked away from Hutton Hall one afternoon to visit one of the bars. They had ended up throwing up in the azalea bushes on the way home. But Drena was dead and, suddenly, Morgana missed her in a way that we can only miss those who aren't there anymore.

Chris shook his head sadly. "I'm sorry about Drena. Did you keep up with her after high school?"

Morgana was startled. She had forgotten Chris Dixon was there. And how had he known she was thinking about Drena?

"After all," Chris continued, "you both had an interest in the occult. She was mystical. I guess you're more scientific."

Dixon shifted his weight from one foot to the other, but he didn't leave Morgana even though he acknowledged several people in the crowd. "I know a little something about the occult," he said. "If people get involved in casting spells— or in laying curses around them—they can come back with redoubled force." His look was intense. "You're in parapsychology. You know about the power of the human mind. Most of the brain is never used. The mysteries that lie there can be unlocked only by occult forces of tremendous power. Telekinesis, poltergeists. Many of the objects that people move with their mind-force are dangerous. Knives hurtling through space. Heavy objects flying around. Metal bending. The power can be used to do evil. Someone who didn't know what he was doing . . . someone just fumbling around with it, learning by trial and error . . . might injure himself."

"Morgana, sweetheart," someone gushed. The voice

sounded like an imitation of a Hollywood celebrity. It was Fran Maitland; Morgana had never liked the woman. "I'm *so* sorry to hear about your little *fracas* over at Hutton College," Fran said confidentially. "I can tell you, it isn't worth fighting. Those people down there are so *entrenched* you can't budge them. I'm just glad I found the *right* man"—she beamed at the man at her side—"and got *out* of there. Now we dine with the president of the college often. Maybe I can put in a *word* for you. Oh, my goodness," she exclaimed, pausing to take a breath, "I *forgot.* You don't know my husband. Dr. Roland Maitland." She turned to him. "Darling, this is one of my little old juvenile delinquent pals from the Hall days. She's become quite the egghead, although honestly I don't know why she bothers. She could have married a millionaire by now. She was always so *popular.*"

"You a professor?" Roland asked, eyeing Morgana suspiciously. "What area you in?"

"Psychology. Like Fran was," Morgana answered.

Fran cleared her throat. "Uhm . . . well . . . not *exactly.* Morgana's in parapsychology, Roland." Fran's voice took on a disapproving tone.

"Parapsychology," said Roland, taking an autocratic breath of air, "is a pile of steaming horse dung." He turned and walked away.

The crowd shifted slightly, and Fran stood there uncomfortably. "Hello, Frances," Morgana heard Chris say. "You certainly seem to be feeling better tonight."

Some of the effervescence left Fran's face. "Yes . . . well . . . I really need to find Roland. So *nice* seeing both of you."

She nearly bumped into Rafe Artigues as she turned to leave. "Hope you're all enjoying yourselves," he said, winking at Fran.

Morgana nodded and took the opportunity to extricate herself from Chris Dixon. Spying her old eighth-grade English teacher, she crossed the lawn to greet her.

"You know," said Chris, coming up behind her several

minutes later while she was eating a smoked oyster, "you can't avoid me forever. I took a bathroom break, that's all. And I think I heard Fran in the ladies' room getting sick. She's pregnant, you know. By the way, what can you tell me about her?"

Morgana looked startled. "I'm sure not very much at all," she said guardedly.

"The child's not her husband's, you know," Chris continued. "She wants it to be a girl to take the place of her dead sister, Cynthia."

Morgana mumbled something about having to go to the bathroom herself and got away from Chris Dixon for the second time that night. He was really starting to get on her nerves. Where did he get off, acting as if he knew all about her and her old friends?

Fran wasn't in the bathroom. Morgana knew about Cynthia. The poor girl had been murdered in New Hampshire. Remembering the whole thing almost made Morgana feel sorry for Fran, except that the woman was so insufferable.

Morgana decided to leave several minutes later. Saying her good-byes to the headmistress, she slipped out. Driving her car toward home, she passed the stone and concrete breakwater on the harbor at the very tip of the peninsula. She parked her car there and sat in the dark, letting the salt breeze flow through the open windows.

Childhood. She could never recapture the feeling of youth again. Her father and mother. Their devotion to each other and to her. Her innocence. It was gone forever, just like Drena, just like the past. There had been graduate school at Berkeley, and her interest in communes. Even then she had understood that she should want something different from life besides middle-classdom. She had lived with flower children and Tim Leary's group and even ridden down to Tijuana with a lesbian bike gang from Pasadena, wearing a leather jacket and a spike bracelet, blowing dope and hooking down tequilas. It had all been so foolish and stupid, yet oddly understandable, even now. The danger had made her feel she was alive.

Half an hour later, Morgana started the car and drove toward Oglethorpe Street. She parked in front of her house and walked toward the wrought-iron gate. Patricia would be asleep, no doubt, since she usually retired at nine o'clock and it was nearly eleven.

Standing there amid the lush foliage of the yard, Morgana felt weird and unsettled. The old houses with their sagging piazzas and generations of secrets seemed sinister and strange.

"She was a witch, you know," a voice whispered from behind her back. She nearly jumped out of her skin.

"Chris Dixon!" Morgana heard herself say. "What are you doing here?"

"I came to see you," Chris said slowly. He drew her to him ever so slightly, but he did not press her when she pulled away. "I can't believe how attracted to you I am," he whispered roughly. His eyes held hers in an intense gaze. They were strangely bright in the dark.

Morgana turned and walked toward the front door. She felt on her key ring for the key and turned it in the lock.

"Look," Chris said, following behind her. "I'm—I'm sorry. I know there are many impediments to our love . . ." His voice became more shrill. "But I will remove them— you will see. You will get a sign . . . soon."

Morgana closed the front door and leaned against it as she turned the inside locks. An indefinable feeling of nausea had settled in her stomach. It was absurd that a minister had such an uncanny effect on her. He was strange, obviously repressed and a bit of a weirdo, but he was harmless enough.

• 37 •

At the early-morning meeting the next day to decide on Morgana Stone's tenure, Clarence Fuller outdid himself in his savagery. The normally outspoken Bojack Sandor couldn't get a word in edgewise. To Morgana's one supporter in the department, a shy homosexual named Garnet Quincy, Fuller seemed almost demonic in his red-faced anger.

"We will maintain standards at this college! We will keep quality high and not tolerate the least deviation from excellence! We will not close our eyes to error or be bound by rumored reputations at other schools! We are a college of the highest integrity, and this will be maintained!"

With the exception of Garnet, the department had already voted against Morgana for tenure. Her area, parapsychology, everyone agreed, was bogus. It was sensationalist. That was why her students liked her so much. She had to go.

To the assembled members of the department, that seemed sufficient. They were surprised by the passion with which Clarence Fuller proceeded to spread out Morgana's prior publications on the table and lambaste each one. The articles in German particularly aroused his ire because he couldn't read German, and he felt certain that they were filled with the largest number of errors.

"I have been through this—this *material*," he sneered. "I can tell you that in my professional opinion, it is wrongheaded, ill researched, and"—he leaned forward across the table and looked each person in the eye in turn—"I seriously suspect the data is fraudulent."

Fuller slammed the table with his fist. His face burned beet red. "This—this person is utterly incompetent as a researcher, a scholar, and as a professor!" As he hit the table again, a rancid odor of body sweat broke out on him.

Bojack Sandor noticed that the floor was skittering with roaches. It was a familiar Congreve plague, but there seemed to be an awful lot of them.

"This fucking bitch," yelled Fuller, "needs to be thrown out into the gutter and eaten by dogs!"

Everyone in the room drew back at this extreme outburst. They couldn't believe what they were hearing. The roaches were getting more numerous. Some people were stamping their feet.

"This—this *cunt!* This—this *dog shit* smeared on our shoes!" screamed Fuller. Then abruptly he stopped and stared at his hands. They were swelling, the skin becoming puffy, fat, and shiny-looking.

"Wh—what's happening to me?" he stuttered, then doubled over in pain. "Oh, God, I'm being burned! I'm burning!" Hunched over, his face suddenly streaming with tears, he began to wail. "I'm being burned! It's like hot needles are searing me! Gouging me! Please help me! Please help me!"

Fuller fell to the floor and writhed into the fetal position. "Please make it stop!" he screamed. "Please! Please make it stop!"

Everyone in the room sat paralyzed. No one reached out a helping hand. There was something about the shiny skin, puffy and reptilian, that repulsed them. Roaches were swarming everywhere.

A few moments later, when Fuller began to vomit a black, bilious substance, Bojack ran and phoned EMS. They came shortly afterward and took him away. Bojack noticed that the roaches disappeared the minute Fuller was gone.

• 38 •

"Clarence Fuller is self-destructing!" Bojack Sandor announced mockingly to his wife a couple of hours later. "It's like he's possessed by a demon!" Bojack took a deep draught of his lunchtime red wine.

Maeve stopped stirring the spaghetti in the pot and brandished the spoon at her husband. "You're actually reveling in it, aren't you?"

Bojack smiled maliciously. "I always knew there was a demon in him. But now it's ripped loose. It's clawing his guts, squeezing his brain tighter and tighter."

"Why don't you shut up!" yelled Maeve. She liked Clarence Fuller, and what Bojack was describing sounded unsettling—like black magic.

Bojack's voice went low and sinister. He tested the edge of a carving knife. "The demon was lurking there, waiting. Probing at him. Making him do filthy things." His voice rose dramatically. "But now it rips loose and rends his flesh, tearing and eating his guts!" Bojack made savage stabbing motions with the knife.

"I said shut up!" Maeve yelled, swinging around to strike at him with the big metal spoon.

Bojack jumped out of his chair, knocking it over, brandishing the knife between him and Maeve. "I saw demon possession back in the old country. It's only here that they dress it up in scientific garb. We know the monster for what it is. The monster that's squeezing Fuller's balls like grapes!" Bojack laughed cruelly. He liked watching the destruction of his wife's crony. "He deserves it, the bastard!" he shouted.

"Shut up! Shut up!" Maeve yelled. She picked up a porcelain dish and threw it in Bojack's direction. "You bloody little shit!" she screamed, heaving a frying pan at her husband's head as he fled out the front door.

Bojack Sandor stared at his wife from the porch. Then he threw the knife. It sank into the door as Maeve slammed it. "You freaking cunt! His anger did it! The bastard did it to himself!" Bojack yelled as he stepped over the broken boards on the front porch. In his paint-covered coveralls, he disappeared down the street.

Maeve glowered after him, both hands on her hips, fuming. Fighting with her husband always made her disoriented. There was a point during their shouting and screaming in various languages when she'd start to hyperventilate and lose contact with reality. Going back into the kitchen, she sifted the broken porcelain with her toe. Noon sunlight poured like molten fire through the dirty glass of the windows.

Fucking creep. What did those college girls see in him? She wasn't sure why she had ever been interested in the man, except that as a desperate Irish girl from Liverpool, anyone had seemed a welcome escape from the sooty, grim British midlands. When he had picked her up working in that tea shop and had spun his absurd yarn of traveling the world bearing culture like Johnny Appleseed, her head had filled with visions of Katmandu and riding elephants in howdahs. But life in a small American college was different.

He had thrown the knife right at her. He might have killed her. Bojack had had a brief career as a knife thrower in a Hungarian circus. That was what had brought him to England, where he'd defected, if that was the right word. Almost made him sound like some important Soviet going over the wall to the West, when in fact he was just a fraud with a blimp-sized ego, no talent, and a never-ending thirst for oxblood wine.

Well, let him clean up the mess. No matter what she did, he was dissatisfied. The Irish are pigs, he would say. Well, the Hunkies ain't much by way of cleanliness either, she thought. Descended from a pack of Magyar Hunnish yobbos. You could see it in his flat face and slant eyes. He'd look perfect in a ratskin cloak, drinking mare's blood.

About the right size, too. Easy to picture him sitting on some little squat pony admiring a pyramid of skulls.

Maeve brewed herself a cup of tea and rested on an unbroken kitchen chair. Steam from the kettle drifted like a thin white scarf. She liked the image of her husband as a Hun. She had an easy way with words and pictures. Imagery was a gift of the Celts. It was part of their mystic heritage.

Finishing her tea, she mounted the stairs to the second story. Bojack had smashed down all the walls in a mood of "creative" frenzy, determined to clear it like a New York loft. Maeve had shoveled all the boards and plaster out the upstairs windows, and it all still lay on the ground like some magic circle around the house.

Maeve looked out at her garden. Bright with sun, it meandered across the backyard inside a serpentine row of brick. The taller flowers were in the back—hollyhocks, delphiniums, foxglove, snapdragons, and nicotiana. In the middle, stocks, linaria, cynoglossum. And in front, pansies and dwarf lobelia.

Mixed in with all this were the medicinal plants she had learned about from her Aunt Fiona in Connemara, who was a white witch—one who had taken the right-hand path to do good. Figwort and turtlehead. Pokeweed and yellow dock. Eyebright, peppermint, and gypsyweed.

The dangerous ones she kept out of the garden and grew among the plaster and litter along the margins of the house. There she raised the darkly mysterious belladonna and henbane and the thorn apple with its ornamental trumpet-shaped flowers. Although she used dope when it was available, Maeve had never tried the hallucinogenic alkaloids from these plants or the datura that is made from thorn apple. She knew they were dangerous to play with, and she hadn't even told Bojack about them. He didn't know a real plant from a weed anyway. It was Maeve's secret from everybody. The dangerous plants were pretty, and it gave her a thrill, knowing they were staples in any witch's garden.

Maeve dabbed a brush in turpentine as she roamed among her canvases. She kept her work down at one end of the room, away from Bojack's shit.

Her paintings were much better, mostly a series of coniferous trees clinging to a hunk of granite that floated above a whitecapped sea. It was a period she was experiencing. She had seen it in a dream, and believed dreams were to be heeded.

Through the dirty window, she could see the woman next door making coffee with a special grinding machine and filter. It was all so yuppie. The woman was an intern at the hospital, and the husband was a lawyer with a bond firm. They had matching Mercedes SLs in candy-apple red. At least Bojack was like her. He was an artist, too.

So was Clarence Fuller. But he had screwed up spiritually in some way. Bojack was right. Maeve's Irish background had left her steeped enough in demon lore that she vaguely believed it all. Something was badly wrong with Fuller. Something that had nothing to do with mental illness as we know it. It was as if a demon or a curse or something had a grip on him. All the signs had been there. The roaches. The shiny skin. The swelling. The smell.

Under the dormer window, Maeve had a cedar chest where she kept all the material from the magazine that she and Drena had been working on. She and Drena were kindred spirits. That had been apparent from the start. Drena had been ecstatic when she found out how much Maeve knew about folk medicine.

Opening the lid, Maeve went through the paper-clipped copies of articles and recipes for herbal medicines. They had spent nearly six months gathering it all and doing up the grant application to the National Endowment for the Humanities.

So many of the potions had come straight from Aunt Fiona. Drena had compared them to mountain cures and correlated the different European and American plant properties to demonstrate how the medicinal effects were consistent and that the old wives had really been skilled chemists.

In leafing through the material, Maeve found a copy of Drena's black magic story. Maeve had Aunt Fiona, a real witch in her family background, after all, and she had figured it was essential to include material showing real-life experiences, along with some curses and love potions, to get everyone thinking about evil. Just the thing for a first issue of a magazine. But Drena had said no to including the story, and she had been guarded, and really scared, to talk about it to Maeve.

Maeve made the sign of the cross, thinking of Drena. Her only real friend had burned to a cinder. A taste of the fires to come. Well, Maeve would put all that out of her mind. Including Clarence Fuller. Otherwise, morbid thoughts could take hold of you and curses could spread from one victim to another.

• 39 •

Three days after Clarence Fuller came home from the emergency room, his testicles began to swell. Screaming and writhing in agony, he dressed for class on Monday morning in loose clothing and made his wife drive him to work.

"I'll show the bitch," he muttered in the car. "I'll show her she can't stop me. I'll get her yet." His eyes were yellow and wild.

"Who are you talking about?" his wife asked nervously.

"Morgana Stone, you idiot. Something's trying to stop me from firing her ass! Something's trying to prevent me from getting at her! I can feel it working. It's trying to control me. But I won't let it. I won't be stopped."

In the classroom, Fuller gave an incoherent lecture to his nine o'clock class, punctuated by angry outbursts at the students in the front row. "You ignorant brats. Are you in college or not? Do you know how to take notes? Well, then, write down what I'm saying! I'm not here talking for my health!"

All morning long, Fuller's bizarre swelling worsened, aggravated by the appearance of red pustules that turned to pus-filled cankers. These watered and ran with nauseating regularity. His clothes clung to his body from the sweat and discharge. His urine filled with blood, and his stool clogged in constipation one minute and exploded in diarrhea the next.

Fuller tried to ignore the stench and the pain. Instead, after lunch, he paced the brick walks of Hutton College, shouting.

"You swine! You pissants! You scum! You think I'm dying, but I'm not! I can take pain! I'll survive, you wait and see!"

No one showed up for the afternoon classes. Apparently the news of Fuller's erratic behavior had spread. His red eyes began to ooze a white discharge, gumming them with a sticky crust which he picked at with trembling fingers.

His anger became uncontrollable. Behind the locked door of his office, he rampaged and emitted pained screams. A smell of smoke pervaded the psychology department offices. Finally Professor Quincy called the fire department, and Fuller was found burning Morgana Stone's articles in his trash can. The room was swarming with roaches.

That evening, Fuller attacked his wife. Hearing her screams, neighbors called the cops, and EMS transported her to the hospital, where she was treated for multiple contusions and fractures.

The next day, Fuller, his legs swollen to elephantine proportions, tennis shoes cut open to let his flesh breathe, sweat pouring off his body, camped outside the president's office in Rand Hall demanding an audience, but the president refused to see him.

"She's doing this to me!" Fuller screamed uncontrollably. "She wants me to die! She's brought the pain!"

Overnight, hatred of Morgana Stone had become his consuming obsession. Finally, late that night, Fuller collapsed on the campus lawn, spitting up an awful green mucus filled with broken glass, straight pins, and tacks. He died of strangulation before emergency personnel could be summoned. No one could account for his ingestion of such sickening foreign objects or for the actual cause of his death.

Morgana had gone home when the whole thing started, but her phone rang constantly as colleagues updated her on

Fuller's behavior. After Garnet Quincy called to tell her that Fuller was dead, she put her answering machine on and turned on an oldies rock-and-roll radio station to take her mind off everything. She didn't want to think about what had happened.

• *40* •

Morgana met Ron Neville outside the psychology building on the first day she returned to class. She hadn't been back since Fuller had died. Now Fuller's death seemed unreal, as if she would go back and he'd be there still.

Ron was one of the stars of the chemistry department. He and his wife, Shirley, a doctor who was finishing her residency at the hospital, were among Morgana's best friends.

"It's an ill wind that blows nobody good," Ron said almost playfully.

"Please," Morgana urged quietly, "don't joke about it. It was all just too hideously weird."

"Hey," Ron continued matter-of-factly, "are you forgetting that Clarence Fuller was a vicious bastard who deserved everything he got? It was utterly berserk, the way he behaved. It was like some demon possession you'd read about in the Middle Ages. The world is well rid of him, and I don't care who hears me say so."

Morgana shook her head. "Ron, you're a great guy, but you have the emotional savvy of a four-year-old. Whisper when you say stuff like that."

Ron grinned at her. "Bigmouth Neville. Shirley's always telling me to shut up, too." He dropped his voice to a stage whisper. "I'm glad you're safe. The word's out. They voted you tenure. The department flip-flopped and unanimously recommended you. Your buddy Garnet asserted himself in a meeting and practically dared them to vote against you.

That crazy artist Sandor joined in loudly and demanded an open vote, so they all said 'yea.' The campus committee will rubber-stamp them, now that Fuller is no longer in the picture."

Morgana still felt uncomfortable with all this brash talk. She didn't like reveling in someone's death. And, in the case of Fuller, it had just been too convenient for her. Demon possession, Ron had said. Total anger had taken over Fuller and turned him into a demon with no normal emotions or reactions. But Clarence had gone beyond that. He had seemed actually to be torn apart by the demon. She looked around to see if anyone was listening. She had a strange prickly feeling at the base of her neck.

"Tell me," Morgana asked, "what did Shirley think of Fuller's death? I mean, what on earth could have killed him like that? What disease?"

"Her best guess is myxedema—it's caused by a thyroid deficiency," Ron said authoritatively. "Shirley talked with the pathologists over at the forensic lab about it. It's only a guess, of course. All medicine is guesswork, and you can't really believe doctors half the time, my wife included. But that's their current best diagnosis."

"But what about all that stuff he spit up?" Morgana insisted.

"I guess he just went around the bend with the pain," Ron answered. "You know, a lot of mentally ill people will swallow foreign objects."

Morgana felt oddly elated. It comforted her to know that Clarence Fuller had died of a real, identifiable disease, not something unknown and mysterious.

A few minutes later, she went to her office, where she sat trying to figure out how to help the students catch up on the work they had missed while she'd been gone. But for some reason, her brain kept playing back Chris Dixon's words to her the night of the Hutton Hall reunion nearly a week and a half ago: "You will get a sign." She stood up restlessly, telling herself that she was being ridiculous. Still, her hands trembled as she reached for a red-bound book on her shelf—a book about witchcraft called the *Malleus*

Maleficarum, or the *Hammer of Witches.* A sixteenth-century book by two German monks.

Searching the index, she found the remembered passage: "And lastly in the said diocese of the Black Forest said honest labourer was cursed by a witch and found a pustule to grow upon his face. It stayed constant for a day and then began to grow and spread to his neck and at length said labourer found his whole body to become puffed and swollen and horribly diseased. He suffered agony of hot needles being drawn through his flesh and cried out in distress describing the same feelings. On the fourth day he spit up black bile and pins and needles and other foreign objects and died in wretched agony."

Morgana shuddered. This is ridiculous, she told herself. Clarence Fuller's death had had nothing to do with her. It wasn't a witches' curse that had killed him. It had been a real disease.

● *41* ●

Morgana wrote "psychosomatic" on the chalkboard as she lectured her two o'clock class that day. "Standard psychological thought," she began, "holds that we should regard any phenomenon that does not answer to the known laws of chemistry and physics as being a fantasy of the human imagination. Any belief in the unusual or out of the ordinary should be treated as a sickness.

"A psycho*somatic* school of thinking, however, holds that in fact humans can make a descent into their unconscious and at that level take control of their bodies and minds—and actually control their own diseases. Most of you have been raised with such an acceptance of this way of thinking that I'm sure you believe that what we call the psychosomatic personality can bring on his own sickness. In other words, the mind can make the body sick."

The class nodded. Some took notes.

"At the same time, most of you would find it farfetched to suggest that some form of deep thinking could control cancer and prevent it from spreading. Or at least you would feel it would require a very powerful thinker. Like Rodin's man on the commode."

They laughed.

She walked over near the window, then back to the chalkboard, and wrote "parapsych."

"The school of parapsychology goes further than the somatics. This, of course, you know as the school that gives us studies of ESP and telekinesis. It tells us that there is a constant form of subconscious thinking that for some people makes them more aware of the mental and emotional states of others."

A hand went up. "Isn't that like what biological attraction is? A form of ESP between two people?" asked a girl in the third row.

"To some extent," said Morgana. "At least, according to some parapsychologists. And they take us even deeper in their speculation. They believe that those who are truly adept at this form of deep thinking can actually manipulate the mental postures of others and make them alter their behavior. This is mind control. This is faith healing. In its simplest form, it is something like hypnotism."

Another hand went up. "Professor Stone, can these people actually manipulate nature?" a male student in the back asked.

Morgana smiled. "You've been reading the book, I see. That's psychokinesis, the ability to move objects through mind-power."

"Wow," said a vague female voice. "Just like in the horror movies. Do you really believe in that kind of stuff?"

Morgana paused. "We don't have the slightest idea how the thinking process really works. In fact, we know almost nothing about the working of the brain. But we do have quite a bit of historical evidence. While what was dubbed witchcraft in other centuries was distorted by public hysteria and universal cruelty, there are known instances of levitation—of people rising above the ground. These were recorded in elaborate detail and witnessed by many people. Even if it was mass delusion, it was a form of telekinesis—of mind control exerted by one person over many. So, I think it's definitely worth studying. I wouldn't throw it out, like some of my colleagues."

"Jeez, so like this whole ESP thing might actually be for real?" asked the same girl sitting in the third row.

"There is some evidence—admittedly very slight," Morgana said slowly, "that what the Middle Ages called 'witchcraft'—what we call 'schizophrenia'—is actually a form of mind control exercised by powerful malign human beings over weaker ones."

"Yeh, like some of those cults where a dude had mind control over a whole gang. Right?"

"I have seen evidence of cults like that," said Morgana. "The control was powerfully complete. Many of the victims were emotionally distressed to begin with. Their states of submission were often aided by heavy doses of hallucinogenic drugs. But always there was a leader whose personality was near-hypnotic. When he—or she; often the shes are the most powerful—when he or she spoke, there was just . . . well, something about the manner in which they said things. The words were usually pure nonsense. But the tone quality, the force of the voice, the intense penetrating look of the eyes brought submission and obedience from the others."

Morgana listed the basic methods of the somatic school in teaching people to concentrate so deeply as to become aware of simple things of which they were ordinarily unconscious. She spoke about patterns of breathing, the actual sound of one's pulse and heartbeat. She went over textbook cases of spontaneous ESP experiences that had resulted from even the simpler forms of heightened awareness.

When the hour was nearly over, one of the girls asked, "Was there something odd about Dr. Fuller's death? I mean, something you would classify as psychosomatic or parapsychic?"

"I'm not sure I'm competent to answer that," Morgana said slowly. "I didn't really see much of him at the last. But he was diagnosed by doctors at the hospital as having myxedema. It's a thyroid deficiency of some type."

"It was really gross," the girl went on. "I mean, he threw up pins and needles before he died. He was surrounded by roaches. I mean, isn't that like controlling nature?"

The students shifted in their seats, packing up books and papers. Like a broken record, Morgana repeated the diagnosis, then dismissed the class. She had refrained from saying that spitting up pins was one of the classic hallmarks of witch possession. That wasn't relevant, after all, she told herself as she went back to her office.

Outside, youth throbbed with its pulsing libido. Abbreviated clothes, early tans, constant flirting. Morgana thought of the student's question about biological attraction. She was attracted to Brian Murchison for no logical reason. He was a helpless degenerate, a drunk with an absurd car and crummy clothes. But there was something about him, his eyes, his hands, his mouth, that had always drawn her to him. Her thoughts focused on an image of sex long ago, then suddenly veered off.

They were going to give her tenure. The academic vice-president had asked her to lunch today and told her. Amid much hemming and hawing, he had told her that the department had convened and unanimously voted her tenure. All criticisms were withdrawn. Nothing but praise had gone to the campus-wide committee. He'd cleared his throat several times before welcoming her as a permanent member of the faculty.

He had been especially nervous about Fuller's death and bothered by the man's deranged ravings against Morgana. He seemed concerned about the potential liability of the school should Morgana decide to press charges because of Fuller's treatment of her toward the end. Morgana felt vaguely ridiculous listening to him talk, almost as if she wasn't operating in the real world. She had no intention of hurting Hutton College. She only wanted to be able to stay and keep up her work and research.

• 42 •

Wayne listened to Cerise tell the story as avidly as his young sons. It was close to nine o'clock and, though it was dark out, the boys were still up.

"One day," said Cerise hugging her knees on the living room floor, "Nanga Baiga used a stick to scratch himself, and Bhagavan transformed it into a cobra. Nanga Baiga was bitten by the terrible snake, and he died. Which was how death came into the world. Death comes from the ill will of the gods toward man."

"And that was the end of Nanga Baiga?" said six-year-old Donny, sitting cross-legged up close so he could touch Cerise.

"Well, not quite. As he was dying, he told his sons to boil and eat his flesh. Well, Bhagavan couldn't have that, because it would make the sons immortal, so he came to them disguised as a holy man and told them it was a great sin to eat their father. So instead, they threw the flesh into the river, and the magic of Nanga Baiga was lost to man forever. But down the river lived three old women who ate the flesh, and they became witches."

"Tell us about the witches," said eight-year-old Wayne. He was amazed to hear such a dramatic story. His parents only told contrived stories with dumb meanings about going to bed on time.

"Next time, boys," said Cerise, picking up Donny and hugging him. "Now it's time for bed."

They followed her happily upstairs, competing for her attention.

Wayne got himself a beer from the refrigerator and marveled over how terrific Cerise was with the boys. Debra was always frazzled and worn out and short-tempered with

144

them. She had a hundred reasons why she couldn't play with them. Like now; she had used the excuse of going to the drugstore for hair spray when Wayne knew full well she was out seeing that cadet somewhere.

Well, he didn't care anymore. He was free of being jerked around by Debra. He had only moved back into the house so he wouldn't have to drive so far to work. He slept in the same bed with Debra, but they never touched each other. All he wanted was time to figure out how to get rid of her with the minimum of expense. A bitter divorce could wipe him out financially. Women always worked you over in a divorce.

When all was quiet upstairs, Cerise came down, running her hand through her long dark hair in that way she had. She was wearing shorts and a halter top that showed the edges of her full breasts. Her eyes were as peaceful and calm as deep pools of black water. Her red lips bowed in a light smile. She always seemed to be smiling at something.

"You're amazing," said Wayne. "Just amazing. Say, you want a beer? I mean, I know they've raised the drinking age in Georgia to twenty-one and all, but nobody's gonna know."

"I don't drink," said Cerise.

Wayne chugged the rest of his beer and crushed the can before throwing it in the trash. "You're smart," he said. "I've got to stop. Getting me a beer gut." He hit his stomach with his fist to show how hard it was.

"Your physique is perfect," said Cerise, still smiling.

Wayne turned bright red with embarrassment. She had said it so naturally, looking into his eyes, not really coming on to him or anything. It had seemed like a natural compliment. Everything Cerise did was natural. She made him aware of how many nervous gestures he had. Always shuffling around and looking off somewhere else when he was talking to someone. Cerise looked him in the eye when she talked, not really trying to stare him down like a salesman or his commanding officer or someone, just quietly giving him her attention like no one else in the world existed at that moment.

"Well, I better drive you home," said Wayne, looking at his feet, then catching himself at it and trying to look into her eyes.

Cerise wanted to know if the boys would be all right alone, but Wayne assured her that they were already asleep. It didn't matter anyway. They were tough. He had raised them tough. If they woke up, they could just lie there and wait for him to get back.

It was a relief not to have to open the car door for Cerise. Debra always stood there and waited for him to open the door like she was a queen getting into her carriage. It had seemed okay when they were dating as teenagers, but now it was ridiculous. She only did it to let him know that she was in control. Dream on, bitch, Wayne thought.

Cerise slipped into the passenger seat while Wayne revved the powerful engine of his Trans-Am. "Do you really believe those stories?" he asked.

Cerise stared thoughtfully into the headlights, where moths danced and flitted. "I think I like to believe them," she said at last. "I like the idea of them being true. It makes me more at peace to be able to shape the world through the stories of the gods."

Wayne thought that was really an amazing way to look at things. "You know, we're raised with all this science and stuff and after a while you lose your sense of magic," he said. "When I'm out in the woods hunting and fishing, I get in touch with magic, but then I come back here and just put it all behind me again. It's subconscious, I guess. I don't mean to." He put the car in gear and started off.

"It's not easy living in this world of yours," said Cerise with a touch almost of sadness. "At New Vrindaban, we were always close to nature. I felt we were one with it."

"I hate all this modern stuff," said Wayne, waving his hand in the general direction of the houses they were passing. "It gets you out of touch with your real feelings. I sometimes think that everybody in the world has got an evil streak in them. I mean, they must be evil to create this screwed-up modern world where we cut down the trees and everything."

"There is evil in all of us," said Cerise. "The gods put it there out of fear of man."

"I can feel a story coming on," joked Wayne.

"The gods wanted to destroy the demons, so they made man as a great warrior who could control thunderbolts. He killed armies of demons and drove them out of heaven. But the gods were afraid of man, who might become more powerful than them. So they put evil in him. Fatigue. The need for sleep. Hatred. Hunger. The urge to gamble. Lust for women. Man was left with only the smallest feeling that he had once been divine."

"Is sex an evil thing?"

"No," said Cerise, leaning her head against his arm. "Not if it is done gently and with love. Hatred and torment and pain are evil." She trembled and snuggled against him. "A man died. A professor at Hutton College," she said after several minutes.

"The one on the news? The one who puked up the pins and glass?"

"I saw his face. He died possessed by evil. It's all around us."

Wayne dropped her off ten minutes later. She was so serene and pure. Everything was evil next to her.

● 43 ●

"You cannot rid yourself of evil except through the suffering of the flesh," said Chris Dixon in a compelling whisper.

Fran Maitland shifted, trying to take the pressure off her knees. She had never knelt on a hard floor for so long, and it hurt painfully. She didn't want to be there, but she was afraid not to. Praying with Chris seemed endless. He would pray, and then he would whisper theology, and then he would pray in Latin that she couldn't understand.

Her mind kept going to sordid, awful things. Dirty bus

shelters in the rain. Trashy people whose cars boiled over on interstate highways. Children with snot running down their noses. Old men with cloudy toenails whose skin was so insensitive they would let flies crawl over them. Flush-faced winos who sat on the pavement with ulcerous legs and greasy hair.

"The saints are a testimonial to this great truth," said Chris. "The mortification of the flesh both gives knowledge of God and banishes all sin. Once you have suffered, you are pure."

Fran's body seemed to be stiffening in a rigid acceptance of permanent ache. The grinding agony went from her knees down to her toes and all the way up into her shoulders. Leaning her elbows on the desk relieved it only a little.

She wanted to believe what he was saying. She had suffered pain all her life. All the girls at Hutton Hall had snickered at her because she was so plain and prim. All those fraternity boys at Emory had mocked her when she was clearly above their social station. Roland was always such a complete swine. And Rafe. That was where degradation became pleasure. It must be what Chris claimed.

Roland always seemed to be staring at her in a secretive and peculiar way, like he suspected what was going on with Rafe. He knew she was pregnant by another man. Sometimes she was absolutely certain he knew, and other times she just told herself it was creeping paranoia on her part.

She hadn't wanted to go to the Hutton Hall reunion. It had seemed like a trap from the beginning, her with Roland and Rafe in the same room. She couldn't resist Rafe. When he had simply walked into the ladies' room that night, she had let him take her right there, standing up, not caring if anyone caught them. He had pulled her pants down, set her up on the sink, and forced her legs open. He had gotten her just to the point when she was clawing at his back and tearing at his hair, when she had sensed another presence in the room. She had looked over Rafe's shoulder to see Chris Dixon staring at her, the door wide open. His eyes had cut into her in some deep, vital way, seeming to strip her flesh from her bones. It was as if his mind was overpowering hers, filling her with terror at being discovered. But he hadn't done anything, and Roland hadn't found out either.

Chris Dixon had called her the next day and made an appointment. Fran had been thankful, because by then she had felt like her whole life was coming apart because of the guilt. Roland had screamed again that he didn't want children. Rafe was cooling now that he knew she was pregnant with Cynthia. It was so typical of men, Fran knew. Except for Chris Dixon. Handsome, blond, Adonis-like Chris Dixon. He talked about the privileges of the upper classes and the need to let out animalism and how it was all kissed away through pain. He smiled at her in that knowing way, like he could see into her soul. And Fran was suddenly hopeful. She was pregnant. The source of the baby didn't matter.

Her body had been set ablaze, and she was a woman. Not like that frigid snow queen Morgana Stone. Now she could forget about a barren womb and Roland divorcing her without a cent and Rafe ignoring her. She could believe that she was a lady, and as a lady of a certain class, she could take some Australian adventurer as a lover if it pleased her and discard him when she was bored, and there would be no punishment for it because that was the privilege of her class. Chris Dixon would banish all taint of sin.

"I saw you," Chris said. "It wasn't a dream. I saw you with your lover on a sink in a public restroom. I think we should talk about it."

Her euphoria vanished, to be replaced by fear like a cold blast of wind. "Please . . ." Fran sobbed, pressing her head against the hard edge of the desk. "Please don't tell . . ."

"You've been a bad girl, Fran. You've let the devil loose inside you. He has a grip on you."

"Please," Fran wept. "I'll do whatever it takes. I can't stand the pain any longer. Or the fear!" Tears streamed down her face. She reached out her hands, groping after his hands.

She felt something on her wrists and opened her wild eyes to find that Chris Dixon had handcuffed her to the funny iron ring in the desk. He was lifting her up, gently but firmly, moving her around so she could press her chest down on the leather surface.

"N—no," she stammered, her wrists twisting inside the pink-satin-padded cuffs. "I won't do this kind of thing! I know what you're doing, but I won't allow it!" She struggled against the manacles, rattled the chain.

"Naughty, Fran," he said in a firm voice. "A nice sting to your fundament is much easier to bear than kneeling on a hard floor."

Chris lifted her dress and draped it across her back. He slid down her white bikini underpants threaded with their tiny pink bows and laid her rump bare.

"You can't do this!" Fran insisted, suddenly frantic. "You're the Minister!"

"But that's precisely why I can do it, Fran dear," said Chris Dixon. "I'm wiping away your sins. When I'm finished, you will be clean. If I can't make you clean, then someone else will have to. Roland, perhaps? Hmmm?"

"Yes," Fran said weakly. "I want to be clean. Please make me clean, Chris. Please!"

It took nearly an hour. Afterward, Chris walked Fran down the stairs to the church as if nothing had occurred. Consulting his gold-banded wristwatch as though he was mildly pressed for other engagements, he reminded her of their appointment at the same time next week and held her hands in his. With a warm look on his face, he wished her the blessings of the Lord of Light before going back up the stairs to his office.

Outside, Fran sat stunned on the stone bench facing the sundial. Her rear hurt something awful. But his hands had felt so cool after the blows. It had opened a whole memory of being spanked by her father. Only twice had her father ever laid a hand on her, but she found she had total recall of each time.

It hadn't happened, Fran told herself, sitting there alone. Chris Dixon hadn't actually beaten her! And he hadn't really raped and violated her after that!

But the memory of the heat rising within her, of herself crying out with sexual need, was too powerful for her to repress. Though she had been debased, she wanted more. By doing it, she was being saved. Chris was exactly right, Fran knew it.

She fumbled in her purse, going over familiar objects, idly searching for her car keys. Tears streamed down her face and she began to sob uncontrollably. She scrubbed at her eyes. Her shoulders heaved as she made a helpless keening noise. A shadow fell across her, startling her out of her weeping. She looked up to see an unfamiliar man standing there with no shirt on and a tool belt with hammer and hatchet in it.

"Ma'am, are you okay?" he asked politely. He reached out a hand as if to pat her, then drew it back. His arms covered his bare chest in modesty. "Sorry to be standing here half undressed like this, ma'am. I been working on the roof."

Fran simply sat and stared at him. His eyes were incredibly direct, whatever the shy tone of his voice. The space between them was stitched with feeling. There was something hypnotic in his gaze.

● 44 ●

"I don't particularly like the guy," said Morgana, laying down her book. "Why are you so interested in my opinion of Chris Dixon all of a sudden, anyway?"

"I just want to know," Pat Stone answered. "Your opinion is important to me."

Morgana took a deep breath. "I don't like him," she said finally. "He just doesn't strike me right. It's almost something instinctive."

Morgana was worried about her mother. Patricia Stone had been acting differently for two days, as if she had gotten senile overnight. Yesterday she had even gotten into a ferocious argument with the paperboy and called the editor of the newspaper to demand his discharge. That was not the Patricia Stone that Morgana knew and loved.

The Stones had never had much money. Jack Stone had died of a heart attack when Morgana was seventeen, leaving only a small estate mostly burdened by debts he had assumed from a feckless grandfather's failed agro-enterprise. Without a word of complaint, Patricia Stone had dusted off her teaching certificate and taken a post at Hutton Hall, where she had lovingly put generations of giddy, foolish young girls through Byron, Keats, and Shelley.

When Morgana went off to college, it was with the understanding that she had to live by her wits, as her mother had little money to spare. Morgana never resented that, nor did she resent coming home to be near her mom. She merely wished her mother wouldn't go into crazy tirades against things beyond her control, that Patricia would be more like the wry, witty mom she had adored as much as the girls in the classroom had.

"Well," said Patricia, holding a needle up to the light to thread it, "the Reverend Dixon has certainly got one foot on either side of a split as big as the Rift valley."

"Really?" asked Morgana. "Is it all that serious?"

"The old guard is most displeased," pronounced Patricia. "Guitars in the church and hands held above the head while praying are not their idea of decorum. Plus they're finding that they look around on Sunday and see an ocean of strange faces. The church seems to be turning rather common."

An unnatural cold snap had interrupted spring. The wind blew hard outside, shaking the trees and rattling the shutters. The back screen door clapped against the house until Morgana got up and hooked it. White azalea blossoms blew past her as she looked out into the chill evening. It had been a gloomy late Friday afternoon. There had been a meeting of the elders Thursday night after the service. Pat Stone was an elder.

"Mother, what's bothering you about Chris Dixon, exactly? Come on," Morgana pleaded, "you can tell me."

"I'm wondering how to confide in my favorite daughter."

"You can tell me," Morgana repeated. "All we have is each other."

"He's on trial before a Committee of the church for

ministerial misconduct. We need to reach a decision to-night. At first I tried to believe it was absurd. But by the end of the first night, there was something so disturbing about it that I've been able to think of little else. It was as if he was growing in arrogance in front of our eyes. Lecturing us. That Brian Murchison—I feel sort of sorry for him. His drinking problem is so obvious. But he has the same spark as his father. The same insight."

"So what on earth has Chris Dixon been accused of?"

Patricia still seemed vague. "I began to think of Haw-thorne's *Scarlet Letter*. That he had taken a girl into the woods to meet the Dark Man. I began to feel Chris was growing out into the room, surrounding us. I felt he was listening to my brain."

Morgana was unsettled by what she was hearing. Her mother seemed all right. Everything in the house was familiar and normal: the carved birds on the mantel, the English watercolors of the Lake District, the old sofa where Penny the terrier used to sleep before she died. But the way her mother was talking sounded dangerously like schizo-phrenia.

"Mother," Morgana went on, "what do you mean he went to meet the Dark Man? I only vaguely remember that book. Are you talking about Satan?"

Patricia examined her hands. The knuckles were begin-ning to bulge with arthritis. "He's been accused of tying up a woman and beating her. She left letters describing it before committing suicide."

Morgana sat down carefully in a chair. "Do you think he did it?" She could feel her pulse quicken.

Patricia hesitated. "I . . . I don't know. It's just that he's so arrogant about the whole thing, so callous about the woman's death. And no one—and I mean *no one* on the panel except me—is interested in whether he really did it or not. When we consult alone, Ratteree only talks about fund-raising and church attendance. All the others just sit and go along with him." Patricia's brows knitted together and her voice rose in anger. "It's like all they care about is the money coming into the church! If he's bringing in money, they don't care that he might have brutalized this poor woman!"

"Mother, please calm down." Morgana rose to hug her mother. "You don't know that he really did it."

"But don't you see?" Pat screamed. "That's not the point! They don't care! They don't care if he's done something criminal!" Patricia's voice became hysterical. "I hate them! I hate them all! I wish they would die!"

Patricia put her head in her hands and wept angry tears. Her thin shoulders shook. Morgana continued to try to comfort her mother. When she returned with a glass of ice water from the kitchen, she told herself she was just imagining the blue light over her mother's head. It waved and shimmered with a fuzzy edge when Morgana reached out to touch it. Then it changed to pink, then back to blue. Morgana blinked. The light was pink again. Was it some effect of the lamp?

"Mom?" she said in a voice that held an edge of alarm. "Are you all right?"

Patricia continued to cry. "I hate them! I hate them all!" she screamed.

The floor was suddenly thick with roaches. It was as if they were swarming. They were coming out of the walls from every direction.

● 45 ●

Murchison was trying to get his drinking under control, and the effort of denial made him irritable and inclined to hallucinations. He knew he was in trouble, but previously there had never seemed any particular reason to give a shit. Now there was Morgana. And here he sat in front of her mother, hoping to appear an eligible bachelor.

He sat at the third hearing on Chris Dixon listening to Reverend Ratteree drone on about something or other that he couldn't quite focus on. Morgana's mother looked at him as if he were a curiosity. This is stupid, he thought. Why change his ways over someone he had loved when he was twenty? Why not just go to the restroom and have a good, serious, nerve-steadying belt of hooch?

Murchison tried to listen intently. Pat Stone had asked Chris about the character of Carolyn Danner. If Dixon had any sense, he'd say he didn't really know her. They had been over that repeatedly. But the stupid bastard was giving a detailed description.

"She was blond and over six feet in height," said Chris with a finger on his chin. "It gave her an air almost of a Valkyrie, except that she seemed mushy, emotionally flaccid, flabby, rather like housewives who dwell so much in the world of game show TV and personal soap opera daydreams that they become entrapped in apprehensions."

What the hell kind of a description was that? thought Murchison. Dixon was a real uneven guy. The kind who could go either the genius or the insanity route, depending upon how fate tipped the scales.

"I would say that she had what is called a 'Great Mother' complex," Dixon continued. "An obsession with the appearance of perfect motherhood where symbolic acts of mothering are all-important. Her household was immaculate. Her two children were in advanced placement and were stars in many after-school activities. Athletics *and* violin, Scouts *and* drama. Interpersonal skills were not her forte. Her relationship with her husband was merely one of respecting his father role rather than valuing him as a person."

Holy shit, thought Murchison. You're getting slow, Brian. Five years ago a client wouldn't have gotten the first sentence out of his mouth before you would have faked a coughing fit or epilepsy or something. "May Your Worships please—" Murchison interjected quickly as he stood up.

"I'm talking, Murchison," said Dixon through gritted teeth. "Please go back to your stupor."

Slapped in the face, Murchison settled back into his chair.

If the fucker wanted to crucify himself, what did Murchison care? It wasn't as if Murchison had a reputation to worry about. Why, only this morning someone had told him what trash he had turned into. Who was it? Of course. The circuit court judge. And then last week there had been the phone call from the committed, compassionate liberal on the Lawyers Caring about Lawyers Committee who had wanted to help Murchison on the road to sobriety. The jerk had thrown Murchison's old man up to him, reminiscing about how Murchison senior had been one of the great trial lawyers of Congreve. Jesus. Nothing like hitting below the belt.

"One facet of her character," Chris Dixon was continuing, "which I feel goes a long way to explaining her, was her tendency to always try to cadge something for free, whatever was out there in the way of free government services or complimentary tickets to cultural events."

"What on earth does this have to do with anything, Reverend Dixon?" asked Pat Stone.

"Her only relationship with other women was to catalogue what their kids were doing and force hers into the same activities, for free if possible. The overcrowded car pool where all the drives were already handled. The summer camp charity slots that no needy children had taken. I think this was to some extent an overcompensation for her not working or earning money."

"You seem to be . . . trained in psychology," said Reverend Ratteree tentatively.

"It's a hobby," said Chris. "Seeing inside the human soul and gauging the weak points, figuring where people will break under temptation."

The members of the Committee looked mystified. Pat Stone bore in hard. "You find this aids in your pastoral work?"

Jesus, thought Murchison. She ought to be the federal D.A.

"Satan," said Chris, "can enter into any person, given the right set of circumstances. In most of us, he simply lurks in residence, waiting for the circumstances to give him control. It is of more than academic interest to know this in advance."

"Satan is in you?" asked Pat.

Chris Dixon folded his hands in his lap. "I cannot deny that."

The panel members exchanged uneasy glances. "Um . . . if we could get back to the character of the unfortunate," said Reverend Ratteree. "Um . . . did her husband not earn an adequate income? Is that why she sought out the freebies of life, as it were?"

A sneer decorated Dixon's mouth. "Her *husband*"—he almost spat the word—"her husband was an egg-bald, stoop-shouldered man employed as a CPA. His income may be measured by the number of hours he is able to devote to totting up figures. Multiply that by an hourly rate, which in that community could not exceed fifteen dollars, and you may buy and sell such a man."

Murchison rubbed his mouth, his chin, the back of his neck. Was the man bent on self-destruction?

"I think," continued Dixon, "I can say that her husband never had the slightest notion of the turmoil that was going on inside his wife. In his inadequacy, he never wanted to glimpse the dark abyss of her mind."

Pat Stone spoke up again. "You seem more familiar with the woman than your counsel, Mr. Murchison, led us to believe," she said sarcastically. "Did you then know her so well?"

Dixon examined his perfectly trimmed fingernails. The manicured cuticles showed the white moons. "I knew Carolyn Danner quite well."

"Did you attempt to minister to her needs?"

Murchison caught his breath.

"I did," he heard his client say.

Holy Mother of God, thought Murchison.

"How did you counsel her?" Pat continued.

"The woman had an intense need to punish her flesh. She wanted to feel the wrath of God, to know the sharp blow of punishment and the peace of forgiveness that comes with the dissolution of pain. It was a need so sharp that she devolved into dementia," Chris concluded.

I've gone crazy and been put in the madhouse, thought Murchison as the members of the Committee sat in shocked silence. No one wrote a note; no one whispered. Finally, Pat Stone asked the deadly question. "Do you believe that flagellation might relieve the burden of the soul?"

"Ancient Christians held such beliefs. As for myself, I am not sure."

"Have you experimented with such methods?"

Dixon looked dreamily up at the ceiling, then at each member of the Committee in turn, his face wearing a broad smile. "No," he said simply.

Murchison turned sideways in his chair and twisted his fingers one at a time.

"If I may interrupt these proceedings," Reverend Ratteree began, clearing his throat, "it's gotten rather late and, though I had hoped to reach a decision on this matter tonight, it now seems impossible. I suggest we adjourn and set up still another meeting."

Murchison barely listened to the committee's brief discussion about adjourning. Pat Stone seemed to be the only one who wanted to continue.

Dixon seemed elated that it wouldn't be decided yet. It occurred to Murchison that the man had practically been doing a filibuster. Murchison didn't even talk to his client after they adjourned. He went straight home and drank himself to sleep.

• 46 •

"I won't have you telling the boys any more of these weird Hindu stories," Debra told Cerise firmly.

Wayne hovered near the door, ready to drive Cerise back to the church. Behind him, the night was hot and sticky. Cerise twirled her hair around a finger. "There's no need to be afraid of life," she said vaguely.

"What?" said a surprised Debra. "I'm not afraid of life! And I don't hide from it the way you do with your off-the-wall religion. I'm not unable to act because of some karma or something!"

"Now, that's enough, Debra," said Wayne. "There's no call for being rude."

Debra glared back at him. "We'll discuss this later, Wayne Mosley. See that you're back in half an hour."

Wayne fumed inwardly as he held the door while Cerise crawled into his red Trans-Am. Just looking at the backs of her taut thighs, her white socks and tennis shoes, filled him with a sexual longing he hadn't felt in a long time. He couldn't believe her. How had she learned such a serene, easy, no-hassle way of approaching life?

Ever since childhood, someone had been yelling at Wayne to hurry up, to get the lead out, to move his ass. Debra was no different when she demanded that he hustle right back. Where did people learn to move deliberately and perfectly and slowly like Cerise?

Wayne had never imagined such a girl, not in high school, not at The Military, not in the army at Fort Bragg, not even in Germany, where there were so many blond girls talking slow and natural in that foreign language.

It was no wonder Debra had seemed so attractive to him then. He had first met her at a party at The Military. Sure, she had just been a high school kid when he was in college, but she was a woman with a woman's needs, or rather that was the way she had presented it. And she hadn't been backward about opening her blouse the way his previous girlfriends had.

By the time Wayne graduated, they had been sleeping together and he was hooked. Looking back on it, he had just been a horny kid married in a fairy-tale military ceremony before he had even gone through airborne school. Afterward, when he was doing the ranger course and mixing with real men, he began to wonder about his wife back in that rented apartment with the jelly glasses and K Mart plates and the stupid balloons she hung up everywhere to create a festive air. She was just a child he had married with imperfect information about the future.

There were perfect moments in life; he knew that for sure. The first jump he had made from that old Dakota had been one. He had felt as if he were floating on air, like he was above everybody and everything, floating down armed with death to kick ass and take names. He had been in a realm that other people could only guess at. When Debra had tried to kiss him and make a fuss over him after he'd done it, he knew it was put on; she didn't really understand how he felt at all.

"Hey, I'm sorry about Debra," Wayne apologized to Cerise after his long silence. "She's just jealous of you. I think she suspects we've . . . you know . . . made love."

"It doesn't matter," said Cerise. "Life flows like a river. If you are with the current, if you are in tune with nature, then your emotions are true."

"You're right," said Wayne. "I mean, it's like you've taught me so much. There are people who are plugged into life and other people who just sit in beanbag chairs and bitch. Debra had the boys and that's nice and I love them and all, but right afterwards, she got fat. And if that wasn't bad enough, she wanted me to tell her she wasn't fat. Every morning when she struggled out of bed, resenting that she had to get up just because I went to work, she'd hold her arms straight over her head in front of the mirror to pull in her gut and ask me if she looked fat."

"Please," said Cerise. "Don't say such evil things."

Wayne's anger rose as he remembered. "Of course she looked fat. Her clothes were busting at the seams. But she wanted to hold her arms up so her gut pulled in as much as possible and suck the rest of it in and whine about how she needed to lose weight and did she really look so bad. I tried to not answer, but she'd nag at me, so I'd say, 'Well, what do you think,' or 'You're making progress, I guess,' but she'd keep after me. What she really wanted was for me to say, 'Go ahead and be a fat shit! I don't care! You can still use me as a meal ticket!' Instead, I got pissed and said she was a sweat hog, so she damn well knew the truth!"

Cerise stopped his lips with her fingertips. "Please," she whispered. "With anger you destroy all serenity."

Wayne gaped at her, exhausted from his outpouring of wrath, amazed at her simple logic. God, Cerise moved like some tawny wild animal crying out to be mastered. She understood life. Wayne had already told her about the army and about his life as a TAC officer.

Cerise loved hearing about Germany, too. Wayne had told her how he'd learned to ski in the Alps and how he'd hiked all through the Black Forest. She had asked him all kinds of questions about the plants and animals, and he didn't really know the answers, but he'd tell her how the water in the streams felt cool on his face and how the sun would come down through the tree branches.

Cerise knew so much odd stuff, too. She had told Wayne about the *I Ching* and how the zodiac doesn't really exist but is just a method invented by the Babylonians for keeping up with where the stars are at any given time. She knew about numerology and astrology and could recite whole passages out of *The Third Eye* by Lobsang Rampa. Though Wayne had once read a book about reincarnation, called *The Search for Bridey Murphy,* he still couldn't follow what Cerise had told him about harnessing lunar vibrations with your body.

At that moment, Wayne tried to kiss Cerise, but she stopped him. "Please let us go to a world of our own."

"Yeh . . . sure," he said, his mind racing. He started the engine and scratched out of the drive, throwing gravel.

She put a restraining hand on his arm. "No," she urged. "You are doing bad things to the car. You are not in harmony with it."

Wayne slowed down. His breathing came rasping and heavy.

It was weird the way the Hare Krishna people grew up knowing nothing of the modern world, but still Cerise was intelligent. Debra might read *Glamour* and watch sitcoms on TV, but Cerise knew the really heavy stuff about life and life after death. She could fascinate him by making the Hindu myths come alive. She even knew about akashic records, the records that are kept in light and sound waves somewhere out in space where they never die, the total of all sensory impressions that ever existed. She had read aloud to him from *The Secret of the Golden Flower*, and when she explained it, it all suddenly made sense.

Cerise was the philosophical, deep one, and he was the practical one. They went together perfectly. She was so appreciative when he told her about life in America. Clearly she was a woman who would love him and enjoy serving him. Plus her body was something else. She could have won awards in skin magazines. Just sitting next to her in the car gave him a hard-on.

At Hutton College, she told him to park the car and led him over to the big grassy yard with the old oaks and the buildings that dated to the eighteenth century. She was carrying a white handkerchief, which she opened to reveal fruit and flower blossoms. Placing it carefully on a large stone in the middle of the green, she sprinkled a little powder on it and set it ablaze with a match.

"It is a symbolic sacrifice to you," she whispered.

As the flames died, she wrapped her arms around his neck and kissed him deeply. "You are my karma," she whispered. "Karma is destiny."

"I'm crazy in love with you," he whispered, squeezing her tightly.

When he put his hands down her pants, she didn't resist. Instead, she tilted her throat back, groaned, and gave him the fullness of her lips. Her arms were supple and warm and held him tightly, not like Debra, who just flopped on the bed and expected him to deliver a magic orgasm. Her legs and the smell of her overpowered him. She gave it to him the natural way—no whining or griping or bitching. She set him on fire. He did it repeatedly. She was a responsive woman with whom he could hold a hard-on and bring her to an orgasm. Not at all like Debra.

● **47** ●

"I said, do you think it's possible to be serene and tragic at the same time?" repeated Maeve Sandor.

Murchison stared at her from within a vague stupor. He took a drink from the can of beer that he had laced with Old Crow. "I couldn't begin to say," he answered.

Chris Dixon edged out of the little group. He was disgusted with the party and couldn't believe he had come. Someone at Hutton College had invited him. He had learned that Morgana Stone would be there and thought it would be a chance to be with her, but she hadn't shown up.

Maeve had organized the whole thing. She was the wife of some artist at Hutton College who had refused to attend. She had the use of a beach cottage for the weekend and had convinced a bunch of professors and their wives to bring food and liquor for a party.

In theory, it should have been fun. Except the cottage was grubby and salt-stained and the people were eggheads. Faculty tenure and promotion backbiting seemed to be a major subject of conversation. Maeve was clinging to Murchison as if afraid he would get away. His presence irritated Chris. It reminded him of the Committee and what he had to do about Pat Stone.

"Well, I think he looks rather tragic," said Maeve, running her hand down Murchison's face as three other couples in the tiny living room gave it serious consideration.

As usual, Brian Murchison was drunk. "You people are like a bunch of derelicts in a tropical hotel in some Graham Greene novel," he said while the professors and their wives stared at him.

Maeve put her arm through his. "You're such a cynic, Brian," she said loudly. "But why don't we have fun instead of brooding." She paused to take a breath. "I know! Let's all go skinny-dipping!"

When no one else seemed to hear, she put her arms around Murchison, who teetered on his feet as if Maeve was propping him up as she led him toward the door.

Chris headed toward the kitchen, nursing a scotch and water. He added a little more liquor before he slipped out the front door and down into the sand. His tennis shoes squeaked on the beach. Far behind him, he could hear Maeve pressing everyone outside on the skinny-dipping idea. She was still holding on to Murchison. Most of the partyers were stammering their objections.

Chris gave the fire a wide berth and walked to the edge of the ocean. The moon glinted on the water in broken fragments. A lone figure was coming down the beach barefoot just at the edge of the water. It was a woman. She stopped a few feet from him, startled. It was Morgana Stone!

"Oh . . ." she said, seeing Chris Dixon. "It's you."

"I've been waiting for you to come," Chris said intensely.

Morgana seemed at a loss for words, but Chris convinced himself that she was excited to see him. He tried to capture her eyes with his in the dark.

"I just had a long walk and thought I'd come see what's to eat," she said with a forced cheerfulness. She started to walk toward the fire.

Impulsively, Chris reached out and grabbed her arm tightly, holding her back. "No, please don't leave," he insisted. "I have so much to say to you."

"What on earth?" Morgana said, pulling her arm away and continuing to walk.

"Your enemy is gone," said Chris as he followed her. "He died like a bug squirming on a pin. Didn't that make you feel good?"

Morgana ignored the question but speeded her pace.

"I knew he was going to die," Chris continued. "I had a flash of intuition—or more like a dream I had while I was awake. And I saw it all. I saw his burning flesh, I saw him cry out at the pain. Did you witness his misery? Did you see the bugs crawling around him?"

Before Morgana could say anything, someone approached them. The night made the shadowy forms recognizable only by their voices. Maeve Sandor was stumbling down the beach dragging Brian Murchison behind her. He was half out of his clothes and she was naked.

Murchison was holding a drink and talking to no one in particular, like a loud drunk who thought he was eloquent. "When I was a teenager, I used to swim off Robinson's Island at night with three other guys. We'd talk about sex and what we'd like to do to this girl or that one. Buster and Will and whatever the big one's name was. The one who was killed with the air cavalry in Vietnam."

"That sounds delicious," said Maeve, putting her hands down his pants. "Not that poor boy's death. I mean the talk about sex."

"I was shocked," Murchison continued, "to learn that we all had stories of carnal knowledge of your friend Drena Wrenn. I was further surprised to learn how deeply one Morgana Stone was held in awe. Buster announced he'd like to get in her box. A simple enough thought that we all shared. He didn't put forward some proposal for raping her or anything. It was taken for granted that it would only occur if she consented, and the likelihood of that was zilch."

Frozen in time, Morgana stood anonymous in the dark. Maeve was pulling Murchison out of his pants.

"Anyhow, the biggest guy in the gang—what was his name? Something Duesenberg or Duesenberry—proceeded to pummel Buster bloody for talking about Morgana like that. He said Morgana was not to be mentioned in the same breath as Drena. I didn't quite buy that argument, since I was fond of Drena, but still, I was awed by the beautiful Miss Stone."

"Shut up, you twit," said Maeve impatiently. "She's supposed to be here, you know, and she might hear you."

"The same ocean that rocked me in my best youthful lust," Murchison spouted as Maeve dragged him closer to the water.

"I've got lots of family still in Ireland," said Maeve. "My Aunt Fiona was a witch in Connemara. She sold love potions, and then ones for abortions to those for whom the first nostrum worked too well. Then there were my three old aunties who lived in a big house in Dublin. They pecked away at it with digging tools, carving out new rooms and hallways until their home resembled a rabbit warren. Not to mention cousin Sean, who took my virginity and was a drinking man and a fighter rather like you, Brian Murchison."

Maeve wrestled him into the water and Murchison nearly lost his drink.

"Come away with me down the beach," Chris said from behind Morgana. His breath was hot and wet. "I have to talk to you away from these idiots!"

"Leave me alone!" Morgana said fiercely.

"I believed in fairies as a child," Maeve was saying. "Did you believe in fairies? Not the fag kind, but the little chaps with wings on their backs?"

Murchison didn't answer. He seemed to be floating on his back with a beer can resting on his chest, staring up at the moon. "I wonder," he speculated sonorously from the darkness, "how far I could drift out to sea before the cold would seize me and drag me down into fathomless depths."

"How can you stay with these jackasses?" Chris Dixon demanded. "You and I have important business together."

Meanwhile, Maeve was dragging Murchison out of the water. She seemed to be telling him how a cousin in Dingle could see haloes of light, like auras, around people until he was twelve years old, when he repressed it so he could be like other children. The intelligent, nice ones had blue light. The color changed if they were going to be sick.

"Did you hear that?" Chris Dixon said as he grabbed Morgana's arm again, pulling her to him. "You know about things like those auras. You can help me in my work."

"I told you to leave me alone!" Morgana hissed, trying to pull away again, but Dixon's grip was too tight. Fiercely, Morgana kneed him in the groin. She ran the last thirty yards up to the fire. Several people were roasting hot dogs.

"And there he was in the rain knocking on the car window and telling the priest he wanted to be driven through the town," one of the women was saying. "Can you believe such cheek?" She noticed Chris Dixon walking up and engaged him in conversation almost instantly. "Reverend Dixon, where have you been hiding yourself all evening?"

Morgana caught her breath and decided to avoid Dixon the rest of the evening. It wasn't hard, since he had started talking theology with whoever would listen. But his eyes kept following her.

As the evening wore on, the party drifted back inside. Morgana wasn't quite sure why she stayed on. Continuing to drink, Murchison recited "The Charge of the Light Brigade" and "The Shooting of Dan McGrew." Everyone seemed to enjoy his boozy exposition, and at one point he and Maeve even sang some traditional Irish airs. Finally, someone started up the tape player again.

At that point, Murchison, who was spiking another beer with bourbon, noticed Morgana getting more wine. "Oh . . ." he said sheepishly. "It's me. The party boy."

Morgana stared at him. "You getting plenty to drink?" she asked sarcastically. She turned away.

With put-on affection, Murchison patted the approaching Dixon on the cheek. "Hello," he slurred.

"Don't you touch me!" Dixon snapped angrily. Morgana was saying her good-byes to everyone and he wanted to follow her outside.

"Right," Murchison leered. "We must keep the appearance of utter rectitude at all times. Rectitude for the Reverend. Hey, what a pun!"

Chris shoved him away. Pushing through the crowd, he finally caught up with Morgana outside getting into her car. "Wait!" he said, rushing toward her, out of breath. "I told you I'd give you a sign!"

Morgana got into the car and tried to pull the door shut, but Chris blocked it with his knee. "Let go of the door, dammit," she ordered. "I asked you to leave me alone!"

Chris smiled. "I knew it was going to happen. I knew this enormous anger—his internalized evil—would get out of control and become directed at his own body. That it would destroy him—tear him apart."

"Are you crazy?" Morgana said. "What are you talking about?"

"Has your mother told you about me? Is that why you're so afraid?" Chris asked, fixing Morgana with his gaze. His eyes were bright but cold as ice. "I've been accused of some filthy stuff by a crazy bitch who killed herself. You talk about crazy, now she was crazy. A dead woman is making my life miserable and your mother is one of my judges. She's a lay member of the panel. I'm sure she'll do right by me. She's not the sort to get eaten up by her own anger like Fuller. He was blind to the powers of the mind. He directed anger out at you, and it came back to destroy him."

Morgana pulled at the car door again, but Chris continued to block it with his knee. "I said, let go of the door, Chris. This conversation doesn't interest me."

"You shouldn't have hurt me like that down on the beach," Dixon said, ignoring her plea. "I don't like pain. No one likes it. Fuller died in pain. Just like the pain he gave out in his lifetime. Just like the pain he wanted for you. He died like a bug squirming on a pin."

Morgana started the engine of her car, jammed it into gear, and scratched off backward down the drive. Chris tried to hold onto the car door, but was thrown backward. He was furious, but invigorated. Morgana Stone was quite a woman!

He stalked between the beach houses and down onto the

sand again. He paced up and down, trying to calm his wrath. He had to concentrate and wield his powers in order to win her over. It was clear the woman only had eyes for the drunken Brian Murchison. It was also clear that her mother had told her to stay clear of Chris Dixon. But Chris could overcome both obstacles.

A plan formulated, Chris went to his car for a pair of scissors and returned. Patiently, he waited. Several hours later, he found the entwined couple—Maeve and Murchison—asleep after sexual union behind a sand dune, their bodies the color of putty in the dark. It was easy enough to cut a snip of Murchison's hair. It had been an insight, knowing that Murchison would end up blasted on the beach.

Chris knew people. By simply concentrating, he could get inside their minds. He knew that Morgana was uneasy because she sensed his powers. He had expressed his pleasure in Fuller's death because she was now safe from Fuller and would stay in Congreve. He wanted her to know that he loved her and that it was he who had helped her.

By describing Fuller's end, he had hinted at a knowledge he should not have had. It would leave her nicely mystified, but guessing the truth—that he had power over nature— that he was fueled by Satan, the Light Giver.

Chris tucked Murchison's hair into a little plastic bag. He didn't like the attitude Murchison was taking toward his defense or the fact that Morgana was attracted to the drunken fool.

Murchison would have to die. Along with Patricia Stone.

• 48 •

Chris waited for Squirt Crawford to come down from the roof in the gray-cloistered dark. For three weeks now, ever since he had first come to Congreve after getting out on parole, Squirt had worked steadily with no days off and no slacking. Even on Sundays—like today—Squirt worked.

"Evening, Reverend Dixon," said Squirt.

"I need to talk to you," said Chris as he motioned Squirt to sit down on the steps to the chapter house.

"I'm right here," Squirt said. He refused to sit.

"This is difficult to say," Chris began slowly, "but I know you'll understand. You see . . . I want you to quit seeing Cerise. I need her for something."

There was complicity in Squirt's smile. "I don't mind if you get some from the same gal."

"No. No, that's not it," Chris said. "She's going to be living in a dormitory at Hutton College. I'm sending her to school to get an education. It would be best if you didn't see her again."

"Well, I think that's just fine, her getting a college education," Squirt said approvingly. "If I had had me one of them, I might be somebody now."

"You play a vital role in the scheme of things as it is," Chris continued.

"Well, thank you, Reverend," Squirt smiled. "That's right nice. Now, if there's nothing else . . ." He turned to go.

"Sure. Uh . . . Squirt?"

Squirt turned around again. "Yes, Reverend?"

"What do you think of Fran Maitland? I saw you talking to her the other day."

"She's a fine lady. Not the sort of woman I'm accustomed to, mind you, but I knows a fine lady when I see one."

"Well, she's really a very warm person. I think you might

170

have some things . . . some things in common. Don't be shy around her."

"Well, thank you. That's good to know, Reverend, sir."

Chris took a deep breath. His heart was pounding. "Say, Squirt . . . I've been meaning to ask you—whatever became of Byron Moss?"

Squirt stopped and looked up at the bats flitting through the yard in hot pursuit of insects. He rubbed his chin, making a rasping noise on the beard stubble. "Well, me and him took a walk one evening. Went around the town together. He was drinking a lot, but we was right sociable. Went all the way down to the end of Bayswater Street where it leads off in that brush on the edge of the Carteret River."

Squirt looked down at the ground, rubbing the back of his neck. Then he looked up slowly, meeting Chris's gaze. "You know," he said, "it's funny. I never did see him again after that."

Chris felt the thrill all through his body as Squirt went across the grass toward the carriage house apartment where he lived. Chris's hands were trembling and his breath came in short gasps. It was marvelous, the total evil that had taken full possession of Crawford. Never had there been such a study in evil.

Squirt was perfect. Chris would rehearse him on a couple of other jobs, and then turn him loose on the big one. Squirt killed so efficiently, without fear or concern, that he couldn't fail. That must make it facile. If you had no fear and no sense of guilt, you could kill as easily as sitting down to breakfast.

Chris was thinking about getting Squirt to kill Fran Maitland first. The woman seemed to scream out to the world around her, "I'm better than you." Never had he seen social snobbery reach such an intense pitch. She had an almost feverish need to put everyone else down. It had been simple to twist her around to do his bidding. She had taken the whip willingly. She shrieked, but she had fought to hold the cries in as he lashed her. And she was too afraid of humiliation to expose him.

Chris would have liked to whip Morgana Stone, but he

would have to wait. She'd come around once he had killed her mother because then she'd be alone, and she'd need him. Her mother was an impertinent bitch and deserved to die. All those questions she kept asking him at the hearings. It would be as much fun to kill her as Fuller. Then he could find the love that had been denied him all his life. Faith wouldn't be able to stop that one.

Carolyn Danner had been such an ungainly thing. She'd only moved when he had her tied and whipped. Why had he ever felt he loved her? Just desperation. Fear of Faith. He laughed. Fear of Faith. He had no fear of faith in his destiny. He knew he was going to the top, and he could take Morgana with him. She could share his rise. With the proper submission, of course. Obeisance and humility were required, and Morgana would display these qualities when she grasped the magnitude of his powers.

He had Lynn to occupy him for the moment. She would come around within five minutes of his calling her. Faith would go out to call on the sick, and five minutes later Lynn would be there. And Lynn responded well to the whip, too. Submission was doing her a world of good. It was calming her. He'd have to dispose of her once he had Morgana, but that would be easy. He'd give her to Squirt.

Chris walked through the chapter house and out onto Bayswater Street. Behind the iron spike fence, the unhallowed ground was fully cleared. Chris stared at the old mausoleum with dread. Its dark bulk made the night hideous, and Cynthia's body hidden inside seemed like that of a rival, an antagonist.

It wasn't true, he thought angrily. He wasn't afraid of a corpse. He held the enigmatic knowledge. Carolyn and Joan had just been experiments. Since then, he had mastered the rituals and gained the power. First the bird. Then Fuller. The corpse was for his use. It would decay as he consumed its strength. All he had to do was reach out with his mind and pluck strength as he would a flower.

Standing in the insect-whining silence of night, Chris's eyes fixed on Venus as it hung low over the horizon of rooftops. He had the power! He had it!

• 49 •

"I'm just so amazed you never got married!" said a loud, abrasive woman Morgana vaguely remembered from Hutton Hall. "You and Drena, two of a kind. Two way-out eggheads. Of course, Drena met an untimely end." The woman clapped her hand to her lips. "That sounds just terrible, doesn't it! Like I might be predicting the same for you."

"Or at the very least, like you're being callous about Drena," said Morgana drily.

"Yes, that too," the woman agreed sheepishly.

Morgana wandered farther into the huge house. She hadn't particularly wanted to come to the cocktail party, but Patricia Stone had insisted. She didn't want to come herself, so she had urged Morgana to "put in an appearance."

Morgana vaguely remembered being in the huge mansion on Lee Street once before. A kindly old man had hosted a party for his niece's birthday there when Morgana was maybe seven. They had all worn frilly dresses and played party games on the lawn. Morgana had gone indoors in search of the bathroom, stared in awe at the big glass cases of Indian artifacts, and gotten lost and been unable to find the bathroom. She had finally sneaked out the back and relieved herself behind a tree.

The kindly old uncle was gone now, replaced by the niece, Mary Anne Whitehead. It was a touch of continuity to a part of town where so much had changed in Morgana's lifetime. Sure, the houses were the same, but there was a difference now. The tiny old community was lost in the frenzy of preservation. The unity of acquaintances was gone with an influx of new money, the sheer cost of upkeep, and the unavailability of servants at any price.

The house was huge and nicely furnished in an almost

173

exact duplication of every exclusive south-of-Main home in Congreve: reproduction furniture, interior-decorator color coordination of fabrics and carpet, big, colorful Audubon bird prints. But Morgana was longing for the remembered glass display cases of arrowheads and the musty worn smell of Mary Anne's old uncle as Mary Anne limped out of the kitchen carrying a bowl of curried dip. She wore a built-up shoe that caused her to walk funny. Had Mary Anne always had that infirmity? Morgana wondered. Had Morgana been so self-centered in her youth that she had never noticed?

In the kitchen, big chopping-block tables were covered with food under preparation. Brass pots hung in descending sizes on the wall. Tommy, Mary Anne's husband, was in an apron, loudly handling a cauldron of shrimp on the boil, bellowing for Mary Anne to come and help. Half a dozen other people were talking or getting ice for their drinks.

"Why, there you are!" said a loud, accusing voice. Morgana turned to find a wild-eyed Lynn Stafford coming straight for her, wagging a finger under her nose accusingly. "Where have you been hiding?"

Morgana smiled. Lynn was the same as always. She had been so nervous she couldn't sit still for the SAT test, and had always been high-strung and given to frenzies.

Lynn put her face right next to Morgana's. She seemed to have had too much to drink. "I know why you're avoiding me. You haven't fooled me one bit! You always were a put-on, like you thought you had everybody fooled! But everybody knew you wanted to take my Roger from me!"

Morgana was momentarily speechless at this attack from out of the blue. "Lynn, what on earth—?"

"Don't you deny it, Miss Bitch! You finagled Roger into asking you to The Military hop the year he proposed to me! I caught you! You think you're all intellect and real brainy and innocent. Looking up from a book like all you care about is going off to some big important university up north and becoming a big important world-class psychologist! Well, I've caught you again! I can't have anything that you don't want, you snaky bitch!"

"Lynn," said Morgana, suddenly angry, "that was twenty

years ago. Roger Frye proposed to me, but I turned him down. Then he got so pissed he claimed I'd asked him to marry me. Back off, will you?"

By now, everyone in the kitchen was staring. "I won't do any such thing, Miss Snaky Bitch! You and your lying friends! Drena would say anything to protect you! You all lied to me! You lied to me every chance you got! Make old Lynn the butt of your practical jokes! Stick toothpaste in her underwear and watch her squeal when she puts it on!"

Never one to let a bad situation remain un-taken-charge-of, Tommy Whitehead bulled across the room. "Lynn, calm down. You'll scare the horses." It was a stupid joke, but Lynn laughed hysterically.

"Ohhhh, Tommy, you're sooo clever and funny I just can't stand it!" she shrieked in a high falsetto. "Do tell us another terribly clever, witty witticism before I tear Miss Sugar Britches' eyeballs out!" She made clawing motions with her painted red nails.

Morgana backed around the table. She saw no reason to stay and be exposed to this sort of hysteria.

"She's up to her old sly tricks again"—Lynn raised her voice to be sure Morgana could hear—"and I call you each and every one as a witness! She knows I've got claims on Chris Dixon, and she just can't stand it unless she can steal him from me! She's shaking her little tight-packed buns in front of him, luring him down the primrose path to where she can get her tentacles all around him! Well, I won't stand for it this time! Do you hear me?"

Lynn looked around for an ally. Her heavily sprayed hair swung in a wide arch as she whipped her eyes to one face and then another, searching for sympathy.

Mary Anne appeared. She took Lynn by the shoulders and hugged her gently. "Lynn, I don't think—"

"I'll get her for this!" Lynn shrieked, throwing Mary Anne off. She snatched up a boning knife from the kitchen counter and brandished it in Morgana's direction. "You take my last chance for happiness, and I'll mutilate you! Do you hear?" She slashed out at Morgana, but it was more for show than an attempt to do any real damage.

With cool courage, Mary Anne went over to put her arm around Lynn one more time. Lynn leaned into her friend and began to cry violently. She dropped the knife point downward into the floor and allowed herself to be led weeping out of the room.

Several minutes later, Morgana left by way of the kitchen door and the back steps. The huge house loomed up behind, twenty windows all lit up brightly. The big oak trees sheltered the sky, blotting out the stars. Morgana paused. Around her, the night was filled with singing insects and tree peepers. It smelled of jasmine and honeysuckle.

Lynn Stafford needed help in a bad way. Her mother was dead and her father was senile in a rest home. Morgana knew Lynn had had an affair that had busted up her marriage. So now she had the hots for Chris Dixon. That fitted in with her need to be a minister's wife. Lynn always did have a father fixation. She had always worshipped Ryan Stafford. "My daddy thinks . . ." had always been the first words out of Lynn's mouth.

It was so sad sometimes, watching old friends change and even die. The loneliness of existence was overpowering. Suddenly, Morgana wanted to get home. She wanted to hug her mother and tell her how much she loved her.

● *50* ●

Maeve was pleasantly surprised when Faith Dixon came to see her the next day. Parking in front of the house in the distinctive old church station wagon on a Monday morning, Faith had half the yuppie housewives on the street wondering how Maeve rated a visit from the mother of the minister of St. Helen's Church, *the* church in downtown Congreve.

Bojack had been in one of his booze frenzies the night before, and the house was even more of a mess than usual. He had lit a bonfire in the backyard with some of his more frustration-inspiring canvases and then stumbled into it himself and caught his trousers on fire. The turpentine-impregnated cloth had blazed heartily, and Maeve had had a good laugh before she had finally doused him with a pot of boiling water from the stove. This morning, Bojack had consented to go to the hospital to get his burned ankles treated, but not before he had smashed their last table lamp all over the front hall as a way of showing his displeasure with his pain.

When Faith crunched over the broken porcelain, Maeve apologized about her husband's artistic temperament without explaining exactly what had happened.

Not being too certain of the state of the living room, Maeve decided to receive Faith in the studio, assuming that the mess there would be expected by anyone who knew that she and Bojack were artists. Faith didn't seem to be at all offended; in fact, she spoke highly of the tea that Maeve served.

"The unusual taste," said Maeve, "is due to the rose leaves. They kill the bitterness of Peruvian bark, which I drink to ward off sickness. Oh, yes, and just a bit of foxglove."

Faith's eyes brightened. "It contains digitalis . . . yes, of course. I had heard it was in foxglove."

"It strengthens the heart and acts as a diuretic," agreed Maeve proudly.

Faith seemed particularly drawn to Maeve's artwork. In fact, she dismissed Bojack's altogether once Maeve explained what was what. They talked at length about art and legend and the Celtic twilight. Faith seemed to have endless questions about Maeve's background, and Maeve rose to the occasion with one clever story after another.

Chris Dixon was mentioned, but only in the context of "Oh, my son adores Irish folktales."

"Do tell me about your son," Maeve insisted finally, when the conversation was otherwise waning.

"Oh, I couldn't," said Faith. "He's just a troublesome boy."

Maeve knew Chris had passed Murchison and her on the

beach. She didn't care if he had seen her in the buff. In fact, as the conversation went on, Maeve had the odd notion that maybe Chris had liked the sight of her and had spoken of it to his mother in such a way that she felt she had to reconnoiter the terrain. Was that why Faith was here? Because Chris had mentioned Maeve in a flattering way? Now, that was a nice thought.

But the longer Maeve talked to Faith about Ireland and artistic creativity, the more she became convinced that Chris had nothing to do with the call. Faith had heard of Maeve somewhere or other and was truly interested in her as a person.

An hour into the conversation, Drena Wrenn's name came up—"the muse by the sea," as Maeve was now referring to her dead friend. Nothing satisfied Faith but for Maeve to open the cedar chest and show her the entire magazine project, article by article. Faith sat for more than another hour, drinking tea and discussing each wad of papers. She seemed to recognize many of the folk cures, and Maeve was happy to find someone who could talk on the subject of herbalism. Naturally, they got around to discussing Maeve's Aunt Fiona, the white witch of Connemara.

Apparently Faith had always been drawn to the mystery of witchcraft with its air of womanly secrets. Maeve, too, loved to discuss her lifelong fascination with Medea, the witch of Colchis who'd used her spells to help Jason find the golden fleece but destroyed him when he was unfaithful to her. Maeve had long had a project in mind to depict heroic scenes from Medea's life on canvas.

Sifting through the piles, Faith found Drena's story "Dreams of Sabbat" and read it from start to finish while Maeve brewed more tea on the hot plate. Faith praised it and said she'd like to show it to Chris, who made a hobby of reading these things. Though Maeve had no objection, she insisted that Faith take a number of her own efforts as well, which Faith thought was a marvelous idea.

Of course Faith had to see the garden. Nervously, Maeve explained away the plaster and wood around the base of the house, but Faith wasn't listening. She was too intent on the plants. Faith was as enthusiastic as anyone had ever been, and this pleased Maeve enormously.

"Oh, my," said Faith, bending down and smiling knowingly. "That's not rauwolfia, is it?"

Maeve flushed with pride. "It relaxes you marvelously," she explained. "It was discovered in India thirty centuries ago. They call it *'chandra,'* which means 'moon.' It refers to the plant's tranquilizing effect on lunatics."

Faith seemed to know already all that Maeve was telling her, but the shared knowledge was still a pleasure to them both. "Do you boil the roots?" she asked.

"Yes. I drink it like an herbal tea, and I always have a cup when I'm particularly pissed at Bojack."

Faith laughed conspiratorially. Maeve confessed that she had once slipped her husband a dose of datura to try to scare him. Bojack hadn't noticed a thing. "He's always high on something or other," Maeve added. "You know artists."

Faith did know artists. She also recognized the thorn apple, belladonna, and henbane, and asked to take a cutting of each, which Maeve gladly gave her, wrapping them up in old newspaper.

Bojack called Maeve later from the hospital, demanding that she stop everything and come to take him home. He wasn't at all interested in Faith Dixon's visit.

● **51** ●

Chris Dixon stood in a brooding attitude on the vast stone porch of St. Helen's Church, looking out at the pale darkness of night. He was smoking a cigarette laced with hashish in an attempt to calm his nerves. His mind, though exhilarated by having knowingly killed Fuller, at the same time lapsed into depression with fears of humiliation and death.

Fuller had deserved every moment of the pain. It was a

pleasure to be the instrument of such torment when someone was so in need of it. Chris had actually watched from
near the fringes of the campus as Fuller died that last day
three weeks ago.

But despite the fierce surge in his powers, Chris was
afraid. The world he knew was so fragile. St. Helen's itself
could tumble the way it had once in history, and the money
could never be raised to restore it to its exquisite glory.
Indeed, fate could cause all of historic Congreve to perish.

The city sat on a major earthquake fault, and just as
hurricanes were inevitable, so was another devastating
earthquake. When the old houses tumbled, they could never
be rebuilt. There was enough squabbling with developers
under the best of conditions to prevent them from demol-
ishing all that remained of the old and graceful to make way
for federal urban-grant parking garages.

The world that Chris loved was like the warm glow of a
campfire with evil, angry eyes lurking outside the rim in the
dark. This well-lit world was one of great architecture
stamped with the patina of time, old books and paintings,
fine furnishings. It was the world of youth and university,
the world of the Church.

The world of darkness was urban housing projects and
trailer parks, plastic furniture in bus stations, sun-blistered
parking lots in shopping malls, faceless, unending suburbs.

Mitchum Avenue in North Congreve was to Chris a
gateway to hell. It went on for nearly fifteen miles, double
lanes of cars being sluiced through a gully of car washes,
Chinese restaurants, auto parts, porno shops, and bargain
warehouses. Chris sometimes joked that, if there was a hell
and he was condemned to it, he would have to drive for
eternity in intense heat along Mitchum Avenue with his air
conditioner broken, stopping repeatedly in backed-up lines
of cars for the never-ending traffic lights.

Chris was deathly afraid of what he had come to know to
be true: The good God had been displaced at the beginning
of time. A leering Prince of Darkness ruled the cruel,
cannibalistic world of men and animals and bugs. Safety lay

in embracing the Prince as a light bringer. Only there could Chris find cleanliness and solitude and escape from subhuman existence.

Pounding his fist against the stone pillar, Chris winced against the pain and mentally cried out for release from his plight. He sucked desperately at the last bit of the cigarette before he ground it to dust beneath his heel. Tears ran down his face.

He hadn't asked for this. All he had wanted was love. Simple physical love in which a woman gave herself to him without trickery and schemes and elaborate traps. Lust wasn't criminal. Otherwise there would be people unafflicted by it. But lust had trapped him. Entangled him with a witch who held him prisoner, unable to tell his plight to anyone. He could still remember the night of sex with that dark creature—hot, fiery sex like he had never known before or since. Only Morgana could understand. She knew about evil. She knew how men could be trapped. He would have to have her. He would have to go forward. Her mother was a threat to him on that committee. She wouldn't be swayed like the rest. He couldn't allow her to harm him. She had to die.

Rapidly, Chris crossed the street lined with parked cars that had spilled over from the bars and restaurants several blocks away. Pushing through the iron gate, he entered the silent graveyard, moving among the upright headstones that glowed not in moonlight but in the urban glow reflected off low-lying clouds. Fear prickled at his neck. Knowing that tramps slept among the graves, he paused and listened, but nothing was stirring.

Crossing to the unhallowed ground, Chris disappeared from sight among the somber yews. He'd had the door to the mausoleum carefully padlocked, and only he had a key. Once he was securely inside, he turned on his pencil flashlight, casting its thin beam around the tiny, cobweb-choked room. Roaches crunched underfoot.

Running tremulous hands along the cool stone of the sarcophagus, Chris hesitated in what he was about to do. Acrid sweat broke out under his armpits. Fear seized his stomach, making him dizzy and nauseated. He couldn't look at the body again. The face still came to him in nightmares. It was still so perfectly composed and real. Chris bit his own hand to keep from screaming.

He had to get a grip on himself. He knew the truth. Satan ruled. Satan was inside him, ruling his will and his body. Only Morgana could save him. Only she had the knowledge. Only she had the pure sexual love that would save him. He had to kill her mother to save his own immortal soul.

With a sudden surge of will, Chris wrenched the lid up and jerked it to one side. No odor of decay emerged from the crypt, only the smell of damp and mold. The flashlight beam shivered in his hand as he tried to focus it on the plastic-shrouded face. The lips seemed to hold a faint smile. The cheeks were full and perfect. Not rosy or healthy, but still undecayed.

The beam went down the bag to where the hands lay folded prayerfully beneath the breasts. Carefully he touched the slick plastic cocoon. Then, with both hands, he opened the seams to lay the body bare. When he touched the flesh, it was cold. The hands seemed incredibly heavy. It took all his strength to lift them and drop them by her sides.

It was there. The extra nipple beneath her right breast. The witch mark. The teat for giving suck to Satan. That was what had drawn him to the girl. He had convinced Drena to bring her to the Sabbath. They had been poor little fools with no idea of what was in store for them.

Chris felt a mild, triumphant elation. He had had the courage to do it. He could set the girl's strength free from her body. He could absorb her strength now and foster his own powers apart from hers. He would not be restrained by anyone now. Not by anyone.

• 52 •

Morgana was shocked when Brian Murchison showed up on the piazza at five-thirty carrying a manila folder. She was even more shocked when her mother invited him to stay for dinner.

"I just brought this by for Morgana," he protested. "I'm handling Drena's estate. There was a note leaving it to her." He wore a suit that looked like it had been pressed under a mattress. All his movements were slow but correct, and he had a dull expression of serenity on his face.

"We won't take no for an answer," said Pat, bustling him inside. "It's been ages since I've seen you. I mean, not counting the hearing at the church."

Murchison dropped the envelope on a chair and Morgana looked at it, but didn't open it.

When Patricia brought out the liquor cart, Murchison only stared at it fixedly. He wouldn't even have wine with the meal. Patricia kept pushing liquor at him with a sly grin, as if she was testing him. She broiled steaks and shucked shrimp and made vinaigrette dressing. Morgana just watched.

Patricia talked to Murchison as if he were the nice, well-mannered boy who used to stay down the beach from them summers on Robinson's Island.

"Now, tell me about your law practice," said Patricia once they were all seated at the dinner table. "I suppose everyone has a specialty these days."

"I sue people," said Murchison bluntly. "It's a sue practice. If that's a term. I also keep bums out of jail."

Murchison is such a boob, Morgana thought. He should have died at age twenty-one when he was still full of promise.

"Well, tell us all about Oxford," Patricia continued. She

183

seemed content to carry on the conversation without Morgana's help. "I visited there once on a tour of England. It was absolutely beautiful."

"I got kicked out," said Murchison. "That's why I became a lawyer."

"Don't run your profession down," Patricia chided. "Your father made an honorable career of it."

"Yeah," Murchison acknowledged. "But Dad had his own racket. He would fleece widows and orphans."

Patricia exchanged an odd glance with Morgana, who rolled her eyes. Undaunted, Patricia fixed Murchison with her best schoolteacher stare and smiled at him fiercely. If he was going to be Peck's bad boy, she could handle it. She was accustomed to unruly adolescents. "Well, then. Tell us about being kicked out of Oxford. I'm sure that was a broadening experience."

Murchison ate salad as if he were trying to polish off a year's supply of greens. "It was the Vietnam era. I got into a fight with another student. I defended America's intervention in Southeast Asia. Punched the little guy's lights out when he insulted me because of my opinion. Got asked before the dean. He was rabidly right wing and sympathetic to America."

"So, what was the problem?" asked Patricia.

"Oh, yes, do tell us," Morgana inserted sarcastically, stifling a yawn.

"Something just came over me. I don't know what. A mood. I started to sound like Jane Fonda. You know, Hanoi Jane, before the exercise book days. It thoroughly ticked off the dean, so I got the boot."

"What a colorful story," said Patricia.

Morgana stared at her mother hard, trying to figure out if she was putting them on. She decided to get Murchison talking about Squirt Crawford. That ought to thoroughly revolt her mother enough to send Murchison home. "Brian, why don't you tell us about how you managed to arrange Squirt Crawford's parole."

Murchison rose to the bait, gesturing with his fork. "Squirt Crawford," he said, "is a man of biblical proportions. He's a patriarchal father who kept together an adopted commune of drifters and prostitutes. People just join up with him because he's a natural leader. Working incidentally at the business of running stolen cars, he provided the income that bailed these people out of scrapes, put food on the table, and kept their kids in day-care. He took the women out of prostitution and made the men work in roofing. He would brook no dope, no alcohol, no foul language. The sheer mental force—almost like charisma— of the man is amazing," asserted Murchison. "Just being in the same room with him, you feel it. It's like a moral force." Murchison waved his hands expansively. "He's almost like some Abraham or Moses trying to bring the tribe through the desert to the next water hole. But break the fiduciary trust of the tribe—abuse the laws—endanger the safety of the others, and you invoke his wrath. And it is a terrible wrath indeed. That's what got him into trouble with the law. He killed those people who he knew had killed small, innocent children."

"You don't think that's a bit severe, taking the law into your own hands?" asked Morgana.

When Patricia got up to clear the table, Murchison turned his full attention on Morgana. "Squirt Crawford is . . . well, have you ever imagined what an avenging angel must be like? That's the way I picture him. He's not perfect, but then neither are any of us."

Morgana got up and took her plate and glass into the kitchen. A cluster of roaches scuttled away as she entered. At least they weren't as bad as when they'd swarmed the other night.

When she returned, Murchison still showed no sign of going home. He had total recall of all the girls in Morgana's Hutton Hall class and asked about each in turn. Morgana didn't know much about any of them, except the ones she'd seen at the recent reunion. Patricia, on the other hand, elaborated on the lives of close to twenty girls. Then she suddenly decided to bring up Chris Dixon, as if out of nowhere.

"Chris Dixon is guilty, isn't he?" she asked. Her voice was very intense.

Murchison sat silent for a long time. "You know we can't talk about that, Mrs. Stone," he said at last.

"He did it, didn't he?" Pat repeated, her voice suddenly angry and irrational.

"Let me help you clean up," Murchison said loudly, trying to ignore her comments. He stood up too quickly and jarred the table. "Whups. I'm not as clumsy as I seem. I'm great at washing dishes. I promise not to drop a one."

"You're winning, you know!" Pat Stone said, keeping her seat. "All they care about is church attendance. They're going to cover it all up! But I know the truth!"

Murchison sounded like an abashed little boy. "Mrs. Stone . . . I—"

"You're a fool to be representing him!" Patricia shrieked. "A fool and a villain!" She got up slowly and climbed the stairs, finally slamming the door to her bedroom. Staring helplessly after her, Murchison began to stack the dishes.

"I'm sorry," he said. "I didn't mean to set her off."

"It isn't you," said Morgana. "She's started to lose her temper lately. I don't understand it."

"Hey, I'm sorry I was naked on the beach," he whispered, changing the subject entirely. "That's not the real me. Honest. That woman with me—I barely know her. I mean . . . that didn't come out right. I mean, she's nothing to me."

"Very little seems to be of importance to you," said Morgana.

"Look, Morgana, I . . . well, we got off to a bad start that day in the grocery store. I mean . . . I don't know what I mean. I just came by to bring you the envelope."

Morgana crossed the room and picked up the manila envelope she had left on the chair. It contained a red-bound book, like a ledger. Inside, Morgana found quill pen writing and name and date entries going back to 1725. Beside each name was an entry like "witchcraft" or "idolatry" or "murder of slaves."

Morgana flipped through each page, then turned back to the first one. The book seemed to be a record of burials in the unhallowed ground beside St. Helen's. Turning forward, she found that the entries stopped in 1855 with an entry that read: "Jabez Guillam—perpetual blasphemy."

She showed the book to Murchison. "How on earth did Drena get this?" she asked, puzzled.

"She didn't have a will," Murchison explained. "There was just a note attached to this saying, 'Deliver to Morgana Stone.' It's not a proper testament really."

He flipped to the last page. There was a final entry in red ballpoint pen: "July 22, 1968. Cynthia McAlister. Witchcraft. May her soul rest in peace."

"Cynthia was murdered in New Hampshire. . . ." said Morgana. "I didn't know where—where she was buried. No one knew. Lynn's father, old Ryan Stafford, was minister at St. Helen's then. . . . I guess it's kind of logical. Fran's family was big in the church then, like now. They must have buried her secretly."

Murchison didn't reply. Instead, he went into the kitchen and leaned over the sink as if he was going to be sick. "Morgana, I've got this little booze problem. I'm sure it's no secret. What I'm trying to say is, often things look a little weird to me. But there's something . . . well, I don't know . . ."

"What on earth is the matter with you?" Morgana asked.

"It's your mother. When she was there at the table yelling at me, she . . . she seemed to be surrounded by a pink light. Is there a funny light in the dining room?"

Morgana didn't show Brian Murchison out. What he had said bothered her too much. For the past week, she had noticed a very faint light around her mother's head, but she had convinced herself it was all in her mind, that her eyes were merely tired and blurring from too much reading.

However, Brian's mentioning it now made it hard to ignore anymore.

• 53 •

The next morning, Patricia Stone got into a wild argument with Morgana. She sent her daughter out of the house, hurling abuse at her over a broken coffee cup. Morgana left for classes with the image of her mother in the doorway telling her what a clumsy, irresponsible child she had always been.

When Morgana returned that evening, she discovered that Patricia had gotten into a row at the meat counter in Murdock's and the security guards had put her off the premises. Then Pat had apparently driven to the Congreve newspaper offices to demand that an editorial be written on her outrageous treatment, and was thrown out of there. That night, Morgana went to bed early and lay awake hearing her mother nag at the portrait of her dad over the mantel. Patricia catalogued her ill treatment at his hands and dwelt at length on his deliberate unconcern for his family, culminating in his leaving them destitute.

At breakfast the next morning, Pat was still going strong. She went through the Stone family like a genealogical vacuum, sucking up all the dirt and spewing it out. Loans unrepaid. No gratitude for Christmas gifts and favors. For the hundredth time, Morgana tried to get her mother to take a tranquilizer, but Patricia ordered her out of the house.

"It's my house!" she screamed. "I paid off the mortgage! I worked for it! I won't have an ungrateful child in my house bossing me around!"

That afternoon, Patricia took on the light and water company as well as Southern Bell. In the evening, she called her sister long-distance in Pickens, South Carolina, and laid into her about borrowing and never returning her vicuña coat, which Jack Stone had brought her from Peru while in the navy. This event had allegedly taken place in 1957 on

188

New Year's Day. Patricia claimed to remember it clearly because that was the year her sister's husband had gotten Jack to cosign a promissory note for a bank loan.

Trying desperately to reason with her mother, Morgana got nowhere. She even called the family physician about having her mother hospitalized, but there was no way she could achieve that against Patricia's will without a court order.

Finally, Patricia paced the floor, railing about a bathtub that wouldn't drain properly and a leak in the roof that the contractor had gouged her on without repairing.

The next day when Morgana called in sick, her mother gave her a tongue-lashing about irresponsibility. "It's that Stone blood! No one on my side of the family has been shiftless or even dilatory!"

Morgana begged and pleaded with her to go to the hospital. As her mother got wilder and wilder, Morgana finally burst into tears. But Patricia didn't seem to notice. She was heaving things out of the downstairs hall closet and railing against the maid who didn't know how to clean decently.

"You can't get decent help anymore! No one wants to work! People wouldn't work if you held a gun on them!"

Morgana knew that half the guys she had grown up with were lawyers, but she couldn't think of any names but Brian Murchison. She phoned him. His answering service said he was out for the day. "More likely out for the duration," Morgana fumed as she slammed down the phone. "Down for the count. Out cold. Struck out."

By lunchtime, Patricia had calmed down some but was still muttering under her breath. "I'm just an old woman, and they want to get me," she was saying. "They're all out to take my money. They want every penny of it, and they won't rest until they have it."

"Mama, who are 'they'?" Morgana pleaded.

Patricia gave her an evil look, her hair hanging down in her face. She looked like an inmate of Bedlam. "You're one of them. You're part and parcel of the gang. I can't turn my back on you for a moment before you're stealing from me.

Go on. Deny it. First it was little things missing. I mention them casually, and you tell me I'm getting absentminded. But then it's more and more things and finally you find the money in the sewing basket. You've taken it, admit it!"

Morgana took her mother by the shoulders and shook her, yelling, "Please, Mother! Stop it! Stop it!"

Patricia broke away, ran up the stairs and locked herself in her bedroom. It was calm for nearly a half hour while Morgana cleaned up the lunch dishes and tried to figure out what she should do.

Shortly afterward, Patricia tore out of her room and down the stairs. From the window, she had seen the neighbor's cat in the back near the hummingbird feeder. She got the broom from the kitchen and went screaming out into the yard, chasing the cat and damning the neighbor for keeping a vicious animal. Patricia pursued the cat around the house and then collapsed on the front walk.

On her hands and knees, Patricia began vomiting up a black bile filled with pins and needles and broken glass. By the time EMS arrived, Morgana was covered with bile and had lacerated her hands on the glass. She was unable to get her mother to stop heaving, and the woman died in her arms, her nose running with blood and her eyes rolled back in her head.

"Please don't die, Mama," Morgana sobbed. "Please don't die! Not like this!"

Strauch's Funeral Home made all the funeral arrangements because Morgana was too distraught. The next night, there was a wake at the home; Morgana somehow managed to stand upright and greet old friends and school chums and the myriad of grown women who had been Patricia Stone's girls.

All the next day, Morgana wept almost nonstop; she was unable to sit through the whole funeral. Seeing Chris Dixon with his solemn-pious demeanor reminded her too vividly of all the things he had said to her.

She walked out of the church and down Bayswater Street and wandered the narrow, crooked lanes of the old city of Congreve, looking at the last of the blossoms drifting off the trees, remembering growing up. At the edge of the harbor, she climbed up on the Civil War cannon where she used to sit and read books when she was in her early teens.

Finally, she walked back to the house and poured herself a straight vodka, and turned on the radio.

She didn't answer the phone or the doorbell. She just wanted to be alone with her grief.

• 54 •

"You're certainly a strange little man," said Fran haughtily.

"Yeh," said Squirt. "Mosta my friends think I'm strange, too."

He was making chicken-fried steak in the tiny kitchen of his carriage house apartment, and Fran felt oddly hungry. She had asked for a drink, but Squirt had said he didn't drink and didn't care to have people around him doing it. Fran sat on the edge of the high kitchen stool watching him make dinner, wondering why she was there.

But the marks on her body were still there. She could feel them. Chris Dixon had absolved her of her guilt and it was all right. There was an animal inside her that had to be let out under controlled conditions. Chris was brutal and cruel, but just. He had lectured her on sin and pain. He had put on a weird leather mask that covered the top of his head, then he had manacled her. His whip had stung her again and again. When it was over, he'd told her to get dressed in a perfectly normal tone of voice. When she cried, he called her "my dear" and told her she was overwrought and needed to go home and lie down. His manner was so controlled and smooth. He had left her at the foot of the stairs of the chapter house, crying, while he went back up to his office to prepare tomorrow's sermon. Then this little man had come along, just as he had last time, and felt sorry for her. He'd invited her for dinner and showed her to the bathroom to wash her face.

Fran's whole world was falling apart. Roland was giving her ultimatums about an abortion. He said he'd kill her if she didn't have one. But she wanted her baby Cynthia so badly.

Was this what had really happened to her sister? Did she have only a short moment of terror before death, or had she lived the agony of the damned, as Fran was doing? When Roland cleaned his guns, Fran was afraid he was planning to kill her.

What if she didn't have the abortion? Roland had already said he was going to hire some swine lawyer to humiliate her in court and strip her of her pride and her dignity and every cent that was rightfully hers. What could she do? Crawl back to Hutton College to do temporary teaching? She couldn't go back to teaching. She'd have to leave town—but where would she go? The idea of having to clerk in department stores filled her with horror. Could she find something to do as a psychologist?

Fran's mind was enmeshed in constant brooding and fantasy so that she didn't know the difference between truth and reality. Now and then, she even heard voices. The first time she'd heard them, she was walking along shady Lee Street remembering a time in her childhood when the tides rose and the streets had flooded. She and Cynthia had floated around in the yard in wooden crates. They had been so happy then. Daddy still had the big construction company and was making all that money. In the middle of Lee Street, Fran had heard Cynthia's voice. With total recognition, she had heard her dead sister laughing and telling Fran to paddle over with her, as if they were still floating in the crates.

Since then, Fran had heard Cynthia's voice a lot. She had told Chris about it, and he had reassured her that she was all right. He had suggested that she talk to Squirt Crawford because he had gone through so much stress and still managed to survive. Fran agreed. The man was incredible, someone she could look up to. Not at all like Rafe Artigues, who'd disappeared as soon as Roland started getting nasty.

"So when the police came, I went out the back door and lit out," Squirt was saying. "Went to live with the Indians up in the mountains of North Carolina. I had to leave my wife, a girl of sixteen, with her aunts because they hated me and wouldn't let her go with me. One of them held a .22 rifle on me.

"But them Indians would treat a man straight up if he was honest with them. I treated them open, and we got on just fine. I got to living with an ole Indian who had a garage, and I'd repair the cars while he pumped gas. He had a young wife, couldn't have been more than nineteen or twenty. He was fat and had a bad case of whatchamacallit . . . asthma? He could barely breathe if he didn't stay right still. So you can imagine he couldn't . . . well, you know . . . do the right thing by his wife."

Squirt threw the frozen okra bag into boiling water and flipped fried potatoes with a spatula. "So me and her would get off together. He'd go outten the house down the road to the store where he'd sit and drink Pepsis and talk big jaw. Well, me and that gal would be in the bed together before he was out of the house good." Squirt paused and rubbed his hands on a towel. "Hope I ain't offending you none by talk like this, but you asked about my life outside of prison."

"No," said Fran weakly. "I am interested." She wanted him to keep talking. It soothed her. He had a sort of exaggerated gallantry and treated her like a lady, holding the door, calling her "ma'am."

"Well, anyhow, there was trouble up there in the mountains over some stolen cars, and I got blamed for something I didn't do, so I had to take off. There's tribal law up there on the reservation, but they had to do their duty and arrest me. They was my friends, so they warned me twenty-four hours in advance to give me a head start. Anyhow, I gassed up the car and took off with the Indian gal.

"We drove down off the mountains and swung by to get my wife in Florence. There was a fight with her aunts, and they threatened me again with the .22 rifle, so I had to take it away from them, and one of them aunts got struck by accident and knocked down. But we got away and made it through to Georgia before we hit the first roadblock."

Fran listened and watched his hands. There was something almost hypnotic about this man. His eyes looked right inside her. His voice seemed to wash around her like a bath.

"Anyhow," he went on, "about the third roadblock, I took off on foot and got down in the swamp. There was quicksand in there. You could tell because it was the spots where there weren't no weeds growing. So I'd get underwater right near the quicksand and the dogs would come up and go away, and nobody didn't never find me. And you know what the funny thing is?"

"No," said Fran. She was trying not to cry. Chris had hurt her badly. He had stripped her of all her dignity and left her like some smelly pile of feces.

"They all thought I was dead. Thought I had sunk in the quicksand. If I had just stayed out of sight longer and taken a new name—maybe gone to Tennessee or something—they wouldn't never have charged me with any of the stuff that Squirt Crawford was wanted for. Would've just wiped the books clean on Squirt Crawford."

Fran scrubbed her eyes with her fists as she started crying again. She didn't know why, but the story made her sad.

Squirt paused and looked at her gently. "Now, ma'am, the dinner can be put on the table," he said, "or you could get out of your step-ins and get up in the bed with me."

Fran's mouth fell open. His eyes . . . his eyes were looking right inside her.

The morning after the funeral, Morgana tried to pull herself together. Drained by exhaustion, she had slept until ten. The hot sunlight streamed into the house. Birds flitted around the feeder in the backyard. Everything around her was the same, except that her mother was dead now.

Morgana went through her drawers and dug out an old pair of jeans she had worn more than fifteen years ago when she was lining up acts for rock clubs down in Greenwich Village. On impulse, she put them on. There was a T-shirt that said "Grateful Dead" and had a picture of bearded Pigpen the organ grinder. She put on her leather wristband with the sharp spike studs on it for defense that she had bought in a kung fu shop on Forty-second Street. The clothes took her back to her youth, when she'd been more brash, more gutsy, and more alive. She had been the daredevil who used to walk the night streets of New York feeling invulnerable. The woman who had laughed at craziness and swore that all she wanted was to be surrounded by it forever.

The phone rang, but Morgana didn't answer it. She wasn't ready to deal with reality. On and on it rang, until she wanted to yank it off the wall. At last it fell silent.

Morgana ate dry toast, drank black coffee, and looked out the kitchen window at the garden. In just a matter of days, the weeds would start to take over. Her poor mother had put so many hours of loving care into that garden.

Morgana went out into the yard and got some gardening tools out of the shed. She worked for the next two hours in the heat, weeding among the flowers, sweating, wiping her wet hair back out of her eyes. So far, she had refused to think about wills or estates or all the legal mess of her mother's house. Morgana didn't know if there was a mortgage on it, didn't know if she wanted to keep the house or sell it and move back to New York.

Around two o'clock, Morgana went inside, put her head under the tap in the sink, and washed the grime off her hands. Then she went out in the tepid shade and lay in the hammock. The bugs were bad, but she fell asleep until around five, when she got up and redoused her head in the kitchen.

Knotting her hair up on top of her head, she dripped into the dining room and made herself a scotch and water. It tasted so good she had a second, and a third. She was feeling a bit tipsy when the phone rang. On impulse, she picked it up.

"Morgana," a familiar male voice said, "this is Chris. Chris Dixon."

Oh, shit, Morgana groaned to herself. Out loud, her voice was peeved. "Yes, Chris?"

He hesitated. "I've got something I want to show you."

Morgana repeated his words in a disgusted monotone: "You've got something you want to show me."

"It's important," Chris persisted.

Morgana considered hanging up. "Chris, my mother just died."

"I know," Dixon said impatiently. "I was there. This . . . this has to do with that." He rushed on. "Did you ever know a girl named Cynthia McAlister?"

Morgana felt a chill at the base of her neck. "Cynthia? Of course I knew her. We were in school together a long time ago."

"Well . . ." Chris paused briefly; then his voice became suddenly desperate. "She's buried here at St. Helen's. I want to show you her grave. Perhaps you can explain something to me." His voice became shrill and out of control. "It's important! You must come now. I'm at the church." His voice fell to a whisper. "Please." Then he hung up.

Morgana put down the phone. She didn't want to think about Chris Dixon. He reminded her of parts of her past she wanted to forget. She poured herself another scotch and took the phone off the hook, staring into space. Cynthia

McAlister. Fran Maitland's sister. The book Drena had left her mentioned that she was buried in the unhallowed ground of St. Helen's. Chris Dixon knew something. Chris Dixon seemed to be willing her to go to him.

Morgana crossed the distance to the sink and threw her drink down the drain. She wanted to know what Dixon knew. Had the man driven her mother crazy?

Walking down Oglethorpe Street, Morgana passed the familiar old houses that she had known since she was born. The evening traffic was thinning out, the maids had all gone home, the kids were being called in from play, the oleanders were starting to bloom despite the devastating heat.

Turning left onto Bayswater Street, she walked past the old Bowditch Hotel with its decorative iron balcony and then crossed over to Bayswater.

Chris wasn't on the steps of St. Helen's, so she sat down to wait. Time seemed to pass in a haze. The sun dipped lower in the sky. The sound of the traffic over on Quaker Street grew dim. Soft shadows lengthened in the graveyard and Venus appeared as a lone star in the sky just fading to mauve.

"I've been watching you from the window of my office," said a hushed voice behind Morgana.

Morgana jumped up.

"You've got a great sense of calm," Chris continued, looking right into her eyes. "You're like someone who's in touch with things larger than life."

"Sure," Morgana said. "Whatever you say." It was ridiculous, she told herself, how uneasy the man made her.

"It's Cynthia McAlister." Chris fixed Morgana's eyes with his own. "I've discovered her body," he whispered. "In the mausoleum."

"Isn't that where bodies usually go?" Morgana said.

"But, you see, she shouldn't be there," Chris said intensely. "She died in New Hampshire, after all, and her body disappeared there and was never found."

Chris's breath became more strained. He shook his head. "But there are no records. I've checked thoroughly. There was no record kept of the burial. And the church is very strict about that normally. We have to have a license from the county and account for the body for public health purposes."

Morgana suddenly became impatient. "I'm afraid I don't see the need for this urgency, Chris, or why you called me here."

Chris's hands were cold when he gripped Morgana's arm, and the sensation sent a wave of nausea to her stomach and the base of her throat.

"I want you to see something," he whispered, pulling Morgana across the street.

Up and down Bayswater Street, no one was around, but Morgana knew there were houses and people and restaurants nearby everywhere. All she had to do was scream. But why? Chris Dixon was an upstanding minister, supposedly. There was nothing to be afraid of. Yet fear lingered around her like a stagnant pool of algae.

As Morgana acquiesced, Chris led her through the iron gate and in among the headstones and obelisks of the main graveyard. He made a pathway into the new ground and led Morgana behind the yew trees that masked a tiny mausoleum. Opening the door to the small marble building, Chris paused in the doorway. It was dark inside. He flicked on a pen light.

Chris put a finger to his lips. "Shhh," he said. "She's sleeping."

He led Morgana inside to a stone sarcophagus. There was an open plastic bag there. Lying inside was the unmistakable form of Cynthia McAlister. Her flesh was starting to dry rather than rot, but bugs swarmed around her in sickening masses, unable to feed.

"It's her, isn't it?" Chris breathed heavily.

Morgana edged back toward the entrance, but Chris blocked her path. "Yes, it's her," she whispered. "So what?"

"She died twenty years ago, but the body is still intact. There's something going on that I know you can explain to me," Chris insisted. He ran a nervous hand through his thick hair.

"How can I explain it to you?" asked Morgana. She could hear fear starting to creep into her voice.

"You're an expert. An expert in the occult. Wouldn't you say that it would take witchcraft to keep a body like that?"

Morgana tried to get past Chris, but he grabbed her shoulders, putting his face close to hers. His breath smelled of mouthwash.

"I want you to touch Cynthia and tell me what you feel. Then I want you to show me your mark. Please."

"What?" asked Morgana, her voice rising. "What the shit are you talking about, Chris Dixon? You're stark raving mad!"

Chris put both arms around Morgana and gripped her tightly to him. "I've told you I want you, Morgana. I want you to love me. Open your blouse and show me your witch mark. You've got one. I know it."

Gently, Dixon threaded his hand in Morgana's hair and twisted her face around to where she had to look at Cynthia's body. "Look, hers is there, below her breast. The extra nipple. You've got one. Show it to me!"

Dixon's voice was eerie and excited. The smell of death was heavy in the air. The bugs swarmed with an audible noise. "I've arranged for us to be together, Morgana. It took some doing, but at last everything is ready. We're alone. Show me." As he spoke, he ran his free hand up under her T-shirt and squeezed her breasts each in turn.

Morgana screamed and slammed Chris in the jaw with her spike bracelet.

Under the impact of the blow, he fell back against the stone wall, stunned, the pain from shattered teeth and lacerated flesh rocking his brain. Morgana continued to scream as she swung at him again, but Chris cowered back, blood running out between his teeth.

"You get away from me!" he shrieked. "I can kill you! Do you know that? I can kill you! All I have to do is think it!"

In the split second of his rage, Morgana took another swing at Dixon. On the backswing, she caught him on the shoulder and felt the metal bite into his joint.

"You get away from me!" he screamed again as he

stumbled out toward the yew trees, tore through the rough branches, and finally lurched out of the graveyard. He was running, one arm hanging limp, as he rolled over the hood of a car parked on the street. With a surge of energy, he sprinted away into the main sanctuary of the church. Morgana could hear his running feet on the stone aisle of the nave. Panting from exhaustion, Morgana stared at the black, empty door of the church. She didn't go inside.

Glassy-eyed and mute, she wandered back down Bayswater Street. She didn't remember the walk home and became conscious only when she found herself on her own front porch. Very carefully, she sat down in an armchair in the living room, moving as though her bones might break. Her braceleted wrist was splattered with bright red blood. Her body trembled uncontrollably.

Morgana didn't know how much later it was that she heard rapping on one of the French doors that led to the screened-in front porch. She froze in fear, wondering if she could get to the telephone before Chris managed to get in. But the doors opened almost immediately. It was Brian Murchison. He smelled of liquor, and his shirt was missing buttons.

"Get out of here, you asshole!" Morgana yelled at him. Then she doubled up and clutched her knees.

Even in his drunken stupor, Murchison noticed the blood. "Looks like you could use a brilliant criminal lawyer," he remarked, grinning.

"Go away!" Morgana cried angrily. "Leave me alone!"

Murchison sat down heavily in a chair and crossed his legs. He didn't touch her. "Do you want to tell me about it?" he said finally.

Morgana didn't say anything. Instead, she took the glass of water Murchison offered her and let him wash off the blood with a cold washrag.

"I can still remember being down in the Village with the UVA football team when I was twenty," Murchison said softly. "Going into the Lounge Lizard and seeing the All Girl Rock 'n' Roll Revue. That was novel stuff in those days. You strutted out first in that blond wig and that hot pink knit dress without a stitch under it and mimed Martha and the Vandellas. At the break, you came back as Grace Slick with the Jefferson Airplane. You guided me back to your flat and took me to bed. Whatever became of that generous passion that burned in you? I thought you loved me then."

She didn't resist when Murchison laid her on the sofa and covered her with a blanket, or when he sat next to her while they talked, and finally she slept. She couldn't tell him about Chris Dixon and Cynthia McAlister. At least, not until she understood it all herself.

• 56 •

Wayne Mosley thought that the Reverend was the easiest person he had ever talked to in his life. It was like the Reverend knew his thoughts before Wayne even said them, like the Reverend was getting inside Wayne's head and saying the things that needed to be said. All of a sudden, Wayne wondered why he had never come to church before.

Chris's jaw was wired and he had to talk with his teeth locked together. When he related how he had been violently mugged by a group of black hoodlums, Wayne had an urge to hunt them down and kill them.

"I love Cerise very deeply," said Wayne. "Debra's a betrayer. She's making a mockery of me with the cadets." He fidgeted with his hands. "She'll destroy my career, and I'll never go anywhere in the army. I'll have to get out early and have one of those jobs that the retired army guys get. I won't be able to use my skills."

"You are a trained soldier," said Chris. "It's apparent in your eyes that you have the fighting man's instincts. That's why you're drawn to Cerise. She is your female opposite. She is the warrior's bride."

Wayne liked the way the Reverend talked. It was almost hypnotic to listen to him discuss manliness and war and a man's duty. Wayne would come out of the sessions they had with his head on straight and all the right thoughts. The Reverend knew Wayne could use his hands. He knew Wayne's strength. He knew Wayne knew about killing.

"Killing is the power of one man over another," Chris said.

As far as Wayne was concerned, the power to kill was absolute. Sometimes he'd sit in those awful meetings of the TAC officers and think of killing his commander. It made him calm to think that was what Reverend Dixon said Wayne should strive for—the calm that comes from power. Power over others that made you free from their individual constraints. Power over the terror that others could put in you, like the terror of humiliation. Though Wayne's commander was always trying to give him lousy merit evaluations and run Wayne out of the service early, Wayne figured knowing he could kill the man took away his own fear.

"Cerise wants only to be with you," said Chris. "She has confided this in me."

Wayne's heart beat with excitement. He knew Cerise told this man everything. Chris Dixon was like her father, and he didn't lie to anyone. If Cerise wanted him—Wayne—then everything was perfect. "I'll be with her forever," Wayne promised. "I'll never treat her wrong. I've never treated Debra wrong. She lies and makes up things that I've done or not done. She forgets whatever she wants to forget. If it suits her, she'll forget that she's been fucking cadets and making me a mockery. Well, I'm not ashamed anymore. Realizing I have the power of life and death over her has taken away my fear."

"Would it make things easier if she were dead?" Chris asked, his eyes boring into Wayne. "Then there wouldn't be a messy divorce to ruin your remarriage, or all those lawyers."

"I won't allow anything to hurt my marriage to Cerise," Wayne asserted fiercely. "Cerise is like cool water. Yeh. Just like cool water. When I'm with her, I'm in a cool bath and I just kind of float. I don't worry about my commanding officer and where my career is going. I know I'll get a good assignment and not be stuck in another lousy post or run out of the service early."

"While Debra's adultery will be easy to prove," Chris continued, "Cerise has come from an . . . an alien background."

Wayne stood up. "Alien? What do you mean?"

"I don't mean like Martians." Chris smiled. "I mean that it's alien to the middle-class values that guide our departments of social services and our divorce courts. Her education has only begun. Her life in the commune seems strange to most people who don't see her true goodness."

"I'll teach her everything she needs to know," Wayne said earnestly. "She's a natural mother. Anyhow, I don't really want the boys. Debra can have them. They're part of her, not me. My life is with Cerise from now on. I'm through giving myself to people who aren't grateful for it and don't know how to love."

"The cadet could still be a problem," Chris insisted. "You need to think about it carefully."

"Not if Debra's dead," Wayne heard himself say.

Chris lifted his eyebrows. "Oh? Is Debra in poor health?"

Wayne didn't answer. The Reverend knew what he meant, but it was like a game between them to pretend he didn't know. "Debra's in deep shit," he said finally. "There's some psycho calling her on the phone with death threats. He's been doing it for two or three weeks now. Telling her he's gonna kill her. I've told everybody at work it's going on and I'm real worried about her."

"Is it wise to go around telling everyone about this?" Chris asked.

Wayne laughed, very pleased with himself. "I'm way ahead of you, Reverend Dixon. I have to get the message out in case anything happens to her. If that psycho kills her, I want it known that it was him and that someone had been stalking her for some time. That way I won't get blamed for something I didn't do. Read me?"

"Loud and clear, soldier," said Chris.

When Wayne found himself outside on the sidewalk of Bayswater Street, he felt groggy, as if he had just waked up from a nap. Checking his watch, he was surprised to find it was three o'clock. He had been with the Rector for two solid hours. It didn't seem like their talk had lasted that long.

Wayne really liked the Reverend. They always talked about Cerise. Chris Dixon believed in telling a woman what you expected of her and punishing her if she didn't do it. The mistake he had made with Debra was trying to be too nice. Well, he was going to have to straighten out years of just letting things slide. He couldn't allow Debra to ruin his last real chance of happiness. The drastic measure couldn't be avoided. Debra sure didn't care about his happiness. If she was that unloving, then she didn't deserve to live.

Wayne thought of Cerise. She'd already be out of class! If he wasn't there right on the hour, she'd just wander off, and there were dozens of guys around her all the time. With their long hair and fraternity T-shirts, they looked at him like he was some kind of an old man who didn't belong, like maybe Wayne was Cerise's father or something. Little punks. They didn't understand love.

Wayne thought of how he'd like to teach them the meaning of his love for Cerise with a rifle butt. Maybe when they were all standing around trying to chat her up outside of class, Wayne would get out of his Trans-Am wearing his camos and spit-shined boots, carrying his M-16. One of them would make a snide remark and the rest would laugh. Wayne would move up real close, knowing they wouldn't dare touch him.

One sharp blow to the stomach with the rifle barrel, and when the little punk was doubled up, he'd shout at him above the roar of pain in his ears. Tell him this was what happened when you fucked with Wayne Mosley. Then up into the jaw with the butt so the punk fell backward. Smash his knees and legs. The rest would run away while Wayne worked on the guy's head. Let him live, but not before he was crippled.

● 57 ●

On the horizon, a hazy line of freighters sat waiting for the pilot boats to guide them across the bar. The silt-pregnant rivers sludged into the harbor, mixing their water, raw sewage, and chemical discharge with the salt of the ocean. Though the sea was high, the buildings on Main Street blocked the hot wind completely.

The steaming asphalt gave off a greasy reflection. Sulky-bodied secretaries ankled their way to the banks with the morning's deposits, their high-heeled shoes filmed with the brick dust of the renovation work on the old tobacco warehouse.

Brian Murchison was sifting through four boxes of rubbish that had just arrived from the National Endowment for the Humanities. They contained all of Drena's materials from her application for a grant, and had been returned to him since he was handling her estate. In the background, Murchison's window air conditioner banged loudly. Pigeons clustered on the window ledge drinking from the water drip.

It was simply incredible. Drena had sent stacks of notebook paper with herbs stuck to them with library paste. Poems and photographs. Jars of home remedies labeled as being effective for rheumatism, gout, arthritis, and impotence.

The impotence one especially interested Murchison. He could use that, since Morgana Stone filled him with fears of inadequacy.

Murchison laughed softly to himself. He had found the girl of his dreams. He was in love. Finally, he had something to live for. He would quit drinking, not tomorrow but today. In fact, he hadn't had a drink all day, and he had actually done a competent preliminary hearing in North Congreve on a drug bust. The smartass lawyer Murchison still had a few brain cells left.

He had even eaten a balanced lunch in a shopping mall cafeteria. Three vegetables, meat, bread and butter. Iced tea, no booze. He figured he'd exercise next, if he could remember how it was done. When he was in the navy, he could climb the rope all the way to the top of the gym. And guts? He had loved jumping into the flaming oil swimming pool when everyone else was cringing up on the tower.

The old Murchison would come back if Brian could just keep his grip and find something to occupy his time. Should he get busy and become one of the boy-lawyer millionaires, of which there were five— count 'em, five—in the city of Congreve? Would Morgana like that? Money? Mercedes SLs and Rolex watches? All that yuppie shit? Food processors, wine cellars, and trips to Tahiti? Would that impress her? Christ, he was sounding sophomoric.

Murchison went back to rummaging through poor Drena's boxes. There was a bottle of love potion, of all things. Maybe he'd take a swig. Or slip Morgana one. He was really in love. Just sitting next to her all night, watching her sleep, he had felt like a teenager again.

What else was in these boxes? Snake venom. That sounded useful. Laxative. Menstrual cramp alleviant. Alleviant? Was that a word, or had Drena made it up? Murchison had little knowledge of grantsmanship, but this sure didn't seem to be the right way to get money out of NEH.

He flipped through the formal application. Drena had stapled news clippings to it, reviews of some of her magazines, reviews of art shows. She seemed to be proposing that the NEH support her and the dreaded Maeve Sandor to the tune of sixty thousand dollars for a year while they pulled together this first of a series of new magazine issues on European/American folk medicine.

There were transcribed recordings of old mountain men telling how they prepared, prescribed, and used home remedies. A woman named Jedburg was heavily featured. Then there were stories and poems and music scores for songs. Drena had certainly covered all the bases.

"Dreams of Sabbat" was an unpublished manuscript by Drena herself. Murchison browsed down the first page. It seemed to be about a witches' Sabbath that Drena claimed she had viewed. Weird. The beginning described a New Hampshire farmhouse outside of Hanover, near Dartmouth. A girl who seemed to be from Congreve was there. There had been three people other than the writer: a woman who was a witch, a man, and the woman from Congreve. The man and the witch had laid the other woman out naked on an altar with black candles on her, and the author described a witches' ritual. The writing was amazingly competent, Murchison thought, but, good God, it was a gruesome story. The man and the witch sacrificed the victim to Satan at the end. They killed her with a meat cleaver, which the witch used again to cut off her left ring finger. She gave it to the man as an amulet, the sign of his bondage to her, their bondage to each other for the rest of their lives. The author vacillated between saying it was real and saying it was a dream. On the last page, Drena had written something in pencil: *"Cynthia McAlister. We buried her in a shallow grave near the roadside. It opened up at the first rain, and they took her home to Congreve."*

Murchison read and reread that passage. He was bothered by it. He had known a Cynthia McAlister.

Fran Maitland—neé McAlister—Fran's sister, Cynthia, had been in college at Wellesley. Cynthia had gotten the brains of the family, while Fran got the social snobbery. Come to think of it, Cynthia was dead. She had died in New Hampshire under mysterious circumstances, and her body had been discovered in a shallow grave.

An eerie feeling overcame Murchison. Surely Cynthia's death wasn't related to Drena's story. Then a light went on in Murchison's head. The bound book that Drena had left for Morgana. Drena had left a record of the burials in St. Helen's unhallowed ground to Morgana. And one of them was Cynthia McAlister. And Drena had killed herself. It all seemed so unreal, like something Drena would have pulled from her imagination laced with bits of truth. Drena had been like that, always making up stories that had some basis in fact.

God this was weird. It would be nice to have a drink. Perhaps just one. Nope, he told himself, not when he was doing so well. Murchison the man of iron will.

• 58 •

Later that same Tuesday, Lynn Stafford sat at the kitchen counter of her tiny apartment going over lists of guests. One contained the essential guests. The others were more peripheral. There were plenty of people in the parish who simply couldn't be ignored, even if it was Lynn's second marriage.

It was already the first week of June, and she would have to work hard to get out all the invitations before the end of the month. With Chris being married for the first time, it would have to be a big affair. There was the problem of the white dress, but Lynn had decided to wear one anyway. Let the tongues wag.

There would be crowds of people at the reception, but Lynn knew she could count on Faith to help plan that. Chris was her only son, after all. And since Lynn's mother was dead, Faith would have to be a mother to both bride and groom. That made it kind of nice, when Lynn thought of it. They were a unit. Sure, Chris didn't want to be too close to Faith after the marriage, and he had said Faith would have to go back to live in the family home in Tuxedo Park. Still, they could visit on holidays. With Chris's heavy responsibilities, he couldn't be expected to take off for New York, so Faith would have to fly down to Congreve—or take the train. Amtrak had a good schedule coming south.

Chris was being reticent about setting a date, but Lynn and Faith were so much better at arranging these things anyway. They'd set it up and then bring Chris around. He was really pliable if you knew how to manipulate him like Lynn did.

In her mind, Lynn enumerated some of the very fine things she was bringing into the marriage. Her mother's Wedgwood china was in immaculate condition. There were nearly fifty place settings, even though Roger had busted up twenty of them one night when he got to drinking. Not many members of the Crossroads parish had known he drank because Lynn had gone to such pains to keep it secret. Of course, it had all come out during the divorce when Roger was being so hateful to her.

Lynn also had her mother's crystal and flatware. The silver looked so nice when it was polished up. Finding a good maid for the manse would be tricky, but Lynn would manage. Being from out of town, Faith just didn't understand these things and how they were done in Congreve. They probably used Latin Americans in New York where she came from. Lynn knew that selecting and managing a maid and a cook was essential, and it was clear that the manse hadn't had the proper attention in this regard.

Lynn surveyed her apartment with disgust. She had tried to make it attractive, but there wasn't much you could do with these wretched modern apartments. The ceilings were low, the rooms tiny. Why, if Chris ever came home with her, he'd barely fit in the bedroom. But this was just temporary. She wouldn't have that problem at the manse, where the rooms were enormous. And Chris had such a perfect study for all his business, quiet and isolated. He and Lynn had even made love there, and no one had been the wiser.

Lynn ran her finger over the top of the picture frame that held her father's photo, rubbing the dust off. Dear Daddy. How proud he would be to see her living in her girlhood home again. Lynn knew that moving out of the manse was really what had killed her mother. The poor woman had had to live in some common little place next door to Patricia Stone. Her daddy had felt the strain, too, no matter how cheerful he tried to be. Then it hadn't been long before the stroke and the nursing home.

The dust made Lynn think of gloves. She would have to wear gloves to meet Faith. Her future mother-in-law was like that, perfectly styled, always wearing gloves. Lynn's mother had said that no woman was dressed to go out unless she had on a hat and gloves. Of course, that was back in the 1950s, and styles had changed, but it was refreshing to see someone who kept the old ways. If Faith did that, then Lynn would, too, no matter what Chris said about his mother choking the life out of him.

As far as Lynn was concerned, men were stupid. If they couldn't make a mess, or if they had to get dressed up on a week night, or if they weren't allowed to smoke cigars or watch football on TV, then you were choking the life out of them. And Chris didn't seem to have any of those habits, so Lynn wouldn't have any trouble with him.

Well, Chris Dixon did have one particular bad habit, but Lynn was going to deal with it head-on right this afternoon. Lynn wouldn't marry Chris until it was straightened out. She was firm on that.

The best thing would be for Faith to face the problem squarely and admit to what she must have known for years. Chris needed professional help—something discreet, however expensive. Chaseborn Hall was a nice place. All the better class of people went there for their problems. Lynn had wanted Roger to go there for his drinking. There, no one would know Chris was having treatment. In fact, any breath of scandal could destroy his future in the church hierarchy. That was why it was essential that this all be settled among them, and settled immediately and in absolute silence.

If there was one thing Lynn had been trained in early, it was keeping her mouth shut. In the manse, many parish secrets were aired at the dinner table, and as the child of a minister, Lynn had been taught discretion.

Lynn got her car keys and left the apartment. The crabgrass needed mowing, and the swimming pool was filled with leaves. The owner wouldn't clean and fill it until well into the summer, which was just as well, because it would probably attract kids from outside the complex. Lynn knew it would have crushed her mother to see her daughter living in such a place, but it was only temporary, after all.

The old Ford Pinto was hot inside and the air-conditioning was broken. Lynn worried she would start sweating during the drive. And if she let too much breeze in, she'd have to fix her hair all over again. She pulled into the traffic of the highway, just a short hop over the bridge, past the marina filled with boats, a twist and a turn, and she was on Bayswater, where her proper home was waiting. In her mind, Lynn went over what she would tell Faith Dixon. Faith might not care for the drastic measures at first, but she had to accept her share of the responsibility.

Wagging her finger at the windshield, Lynn pretended to lecture Faith. She'd use her best nonthreatening tone. "You've raised a very naughty boy, Mrs. Faith Dixon," she whispered, "and you're going to have to get him back on the straight and narrow. I am a modern woman, and while I am not proud of my first marriage, I am not ashamed of it either. I learned a great deal and have a great deal to offer. I am open-minded about sex. Indeed, in a playful or passionate mood, I am capable of vulgarity. But I will not tolerate being abused. Abused, Mrs. Faith Dixon. You ask for details? Very well, I'll give you details. Don't you call being tied up and beaten with a dog whip being abused?"

Lynn's voice rose in both anger and excitement. "I call it abuse to be raped . . . raped from the rear! I don't care how you feel about me as a daughter-in-law! Chris and I are adults and able to make adult decisions. He is going to stop this abuse of me, and he is going to marry me. He is going to marry me before the end of June! Do you hear me, Mrs. Faith Dixon?"

Lynn felt much better rehearsing it all. She'd be smoother then and less threatening to Faith. After all, she just wanted Chris to change a little. He was perfect otherwise, and Lynn knew he'd be the perfect husband.

The Split Beaver was the roughest cowboy bar on the Street Road, a long strip of neon that ran from the air base over into the morass of North Congreve. Speed freaks, bearded boozers, and teenagers with knives and guns hung out among the revolving beer lights while country and western bands played from noon to dawn.

Wayne couldn't figure exactly why Cerise liked the place so much. He wanted to be alone with her, while she wanted to go to the Beaver where she could drink beer and smoke grass. If Bubba and his team of bouncers came over, she'd just smile at them and offer them a drag, and they'd be charmed. Even the undercover cops knew her and let her get by with it.

Since Cerise had started living in the dorm at Hutton College, she'd changed a lot. She wasn't doing any real studying, as far as Wayne could tell. She never had any books, and she couldn't remember anything that was said by the professors in class. When he asked her about the lectures, she said she was just cruising around from one subject to another, trying to find what interested her.

When Wayne really pressed her, she'd say that geology interested her because rocks were the building blocks of the earth. Or she liked zoo lab because they were cutting up animals, which was really organic. Once she had looked through a microscope at a plant cell structure, and had said it was like looking into the eyes of God.

"I just love it in here," yelled Cerise over the din of the band. "I mean, everybody is just moving and being, like they're all reduced to basics. They're so primal."

Wayne didn't like the tone of her voice. She sounded like some sorority girl down at Hutton College. When he'd first met Cerise, she had been dreamy and ethereal. She had moved slowly like a plant growing or a tree shifting in the breeze. But those idiot college kids had changed her. They were twisting her around into something she wasn't. The way he saw it, Wayne was going to have to get Debra out of the way and marry Cerise so he could get her out of that dorm. All her friends made fun of The Military people.

When Cerise and Wayne were alone, she was okay. She was the old Cerise. She liked him to tell her about Germany and Texas and would show the depths of her wisdom by lying on her back in the grass in the night and pointing out the constellations. She could talk about the stars and how they were shaped and how they affected life and destiny. Her slow voice would lull him to a level where sex was as natural as crocuses coming out in spring.

"Hey, there's a wet T-shirt contest tonight!" she yelled. "I'm going to enter it!"

"You've got to be kidding me!" Wayne yelled back. "That's disgusting!"

Cerise threw back her shoulders and thrust her breasts out against her U2 T-shirt. "Don't you think I've got the equipment? All the guys say I have good knockers!"

Wayne leaned across the table and tried to capture her eyes. "Cerise, this is not you! You're not a crowd person! You're soft and quiet like spring rain. You're nice things. You're gentle things. You're a baby's laughter. You're a puffy cloud in a blue sky. This"—he waved his hand at the room of rowdies in straw cowboy hats, biceps bulging—"this is shit! This is like an old tire lot or a junkyard! This is some fucking river in Pittsburgh with oil scum floating on it!"

Cerise looked deflated. She leaned close, clutching his arm, putting her mouth to his ear. "I don't know what I am, Wayne. I'm confused. The world is such a weird and frightening place, and I can't figure out where I fit in. Those kids at Hutton are like all programmed to do that stuff, and I'm scared of it. I'm scared of the Street Road and all this shit along it. Please keep me. Protect me."

Wayne obliged, lifting Cerise out of the chair and leading her out through the packed crowd. One of the bouncers, unhappy at seeing her leave, muscled his way over. "This man bothering you, Cerise?" he demanded.

Wayne tensed. He had his combat knife strapped to his leg under his pants. He'd kill the son-of-a-bitch.

Cerise hugged Wayne warmly. "This here's my man!" she shouted. "Where he goes, I go!"

The bouncer looked at Wayne with contempt. "You oughta ditch that scumbag, baby, and find a real man."

Wayne glowered at him, the killing lust on him, but Cerise pulled him away and out to their car. The parking lot was littered with trash. Across the road, other bars mingled with Oriental restaurants and the lineup of American fast food. Derelicts wandered barefoot along the hot asphalt. The night sky was lit pink by the electricity of teeming civilization.

In the car, Cerise kissed Wayne passionately on the mouth, running her hands all over him. "Keep me safe, Wayne," she begged. "Please kiss away my fears and keep me safe."

Wayne was delirious with happiness. "Nothing bad will ever happen to you, Cerise," he said. "I love you."

I'll keep her safe, he told himself. We'll be together soon. I'm going to kill my wife.

● *60* ●

Beside the charred ruins of the Robinson's Island house, Drena's old herb garden stood untended and wild. To the untutored eye, it was just a patch of weeds. But Chris Dixon had no trouble spotting the henbane and nightshade. Carefully, he dug around the plants and put them, roots and all, into a cardboard box.

"Aha!" said Maeve Sandor, coming up behind him. "Caught you!"

Chris flinched, but relaxed the moment he saw who it was. It was just that crazy artist's wife who had gotten naked with Murchison at the beach party.

"The handsome young minister," said Maeve, "out digging up hallucinogens."

"How do you—know?" Chris stammered. He had difficulty talking; his jaw had been wired because of the damage Morgana Stone had done to it several days ago. Mercifully, Maeve didn't ask him what had happened.

Maeve put her hands on her hips and gave him her best come-on look. "I helped to plant them. It's really my garden."

"You're Maeve, aren't you?" Dixon said, putting on a difficult smile. "Mother has told me about you. How did you happen to find me here?"

"The witch in my blood," Maeve replied mysteriously. She liked the look of Chris Dixon. She wanted to intrigue him. In fact, she had been driving past the church when she saw him leave in the old station wagon. She had followed him on impulse. Whatever had injured him, she figured she'd learn in time.

"Tell me more," Chris said, interested.

"I was up there." Maeve pointed toward the grassy ramparts of the old Civil War fort in the distance. "I often go there to talk to the wind. You know, you can do yourself some real damage if you don't use those plants right. A lot worse than whatever hit you in the face."

Chris ignored the comment. He didn't like to remember what Morgana Stone had done to him a couple of days ago. He told himself it hadn't been her brain that had overpowered his. He'd just had his guard down because he loved her. And he was more convinced than ever that he wanted her for his wife. "Do you know how to use them?" he asked Maeve, meaning the plants.

"My Aunt Fiona did," Maeve replied.

"Say, I packed a lunch," said Chris, changing the subject. "Will you share it with me? We could sit on those old fort walls . . . and talk to the wind together."

With a giggle, Maeve agreed, and together they climbed

up to view the sea spread out at their feet. It was a hot day and the ocean was calm. The lunch was a bottle of burgundy, a container of barley soup, and three peaches, which Chris could suck through his wired jaws.

"So your Aunt Fiona was really a witch?" asked Chris Dixon. The stitches made it difficult for him to talk clearly.

"Only a white witch," said Maeve coyly. "Although it was rumored that Aunt Fiona could change the weather, she never did anything diabolical."

"What sort of things would she do exactly?" Chris prodded. He rotated his right shoulder gently, feeling the stiffness of the bandaged abrasions.

Maeve laughed, putting her hand over her mouth. "Sorry. I can't help but laugh. You look so funny when you talk, rather like my husband when he's been in a fight with someone bigger, which is most of the world."

A frown crossed Chris's face. He didn't like being made fun of. Drena had done that sometimes back when they were in college, and when he tried to correct her, she'd laugh even more. "I was asking about Aunt Fiona," he repeated.

"Oh, her." Maeve was disappointed that the conversation had moved away from herself. "Oh, she made some love potions. I have no idea if they worked or not. They tasted bloody awful. And she had cures for animal sicknesses. I suppose she was something of a veterinarian. Drena and I were working on assembling all her knowledge, but that worthless foundation wouldn't finance it. I'm convinced that Americans are anti-intellectual at heart. They'd rather bankroll a football team. You knew Drena, didn't you?"

"Uh . . . yes," said Chris. "Way back. When she was in college up north, we . . . knew each other casually."

Maeve cocked her head to one side. "Were you in a witch coven with her?" she asked.

"A witch coven?" Chris put down his glass of burgundy abruptly.

"I'm just kidding." Maeve laughed. "Drena had this real thing about witches. In fact, that was what drew us together initially."

Chris sank the bottle opener into the cork of the bottle of

wine while Maeve posed, her hair blowing in the wind, her gaze directed out to sea. "Oh, look, there's a phalarope. I like birds. Especially the ones who were messengers to the gods, like ravens and eagles. Wouldn't it be nice to have a raven come perch on your shoulder and tell you the gossip of the four winds?"

Chris pulled the cork out with a pop. The jerking movement hurt his shoulder terribly. "We were talking about Drena," he said firmly.

Maeve looked at Chris like a bird listening for a worm. He certainly had a temper, she decided, but she liked that in a man, especially one who was good-looking.

Maeve drank from the bottle before Chris could reach for her glass to fill it. "Drena had had a bad experience with a witch once," she began. "You see, Drena really believed that she had seen a girl killed at some sort of a witches' Sabbath a long time ago. You know the scene. Kids out horsing around for a thrill, biting off more than they could chew. They dropped acid, and she wasn't quite sure what happened after that. She even wrote a story about it." Maeve paused dreamily and took another slug of wine directly from the bottle. "The first time Bojack gave me acid, I was nineteen. It was during a party. I ran out of the house and refused to come back inside. Everyone said I looked like a hunted animal. Can you imagine?"

Chris took the bottle from Maeve, wiped the mouth carefully with his handkerchief, and poured some wine into her glass. "I think you'd be rather like a unicorn," he said.

"Cheers," said Maeve, downing the contents of her glass. She bit into a peach, deliberately letting the juice run down her chin and into her blouse. "Do you really think so? A unicorn?" She turned her head in profile so Chris could examine her from a different angle.

"You know," said Chris, "as close as Drena and I were, she never mentioned that story to me. Did she say anything more?"

"I thought you only knew her casually," Maeve parried. She wanted more wine, but she didn't want to ask.

"Well, I did. I mean . . . she just never said anything

about it . . . even though we did have some long talks about fate and destiny."

"Well," Maeve said to fill in the silence, "Drena seemed to have this mental thing about it. She was certain that the girl was dead, but she didn't want to believe it. I figured it was only a bad dream or fantasy, but still it was a real stain on her conscience. Drena was so tortured. She had this terrible self-imposed guilt."

As the afternoon wore on, Chris poured three more glasses of wine, and they talked about how they believed in living life, not worrying about material possessions.

Chris suggested that Maeve was wasted on her husband, and Maeve agreed with that through two more glasses of wine and a second peach. When he asked her what plans she had for the future, Maeve got up and did a pirouette and looked out to sea, in deep meditation. Then she launched into her project to paint the life of Medea once she was better at figure drawing, and her desire to go to New York to find a gallery that understood art instead of the local Congreve "galleries" that only sold bird prints to the tourists. Chris even seemed to know several gallery owners who he said would be happy to help her.

Maeve sat back down. "You know, I really rather fancy you," she said, leaning close. "I'm glad we talked."

Chris narrowed the gap between their lips. "You look like the kind of woman who would have no qualms about deciding on a man she fancied."

"You're not wrong," Maeve murmured as their lips met.

Chris drew back just a hair. "I'd really like to learn about those recipes your Aunt Fiona had for henbane."

"I can tell you all kinds of tricks," said Maeve as she pressed her lips gently to his, being careful to kiss around his stitches.

She knew too much, Chris figured. He'd have to kill her. She'd be easy. But first he'd toy with her.

• 61 •

By ten the next morning it was already burning hot, and Debra was miserable, sitting among the audience at The Military graduation. Dressed-up parents photographed ranks of cadets in white trousers and gold-braided gray jackets. A pompous bigwig delivered a canned speech about heading down "the long road of life." Local TV stations ran their cameras. The band played. Sweat trickled down Debra's back and added to her growing nausea. Wayne got to sit on the stage up under the awning.

Debra hated graduations and had always refused to come in the past. No one would know if she was there or not. Wayne's career was a joke, and who cared if his commanding officer noted her absence? Most of the graduates were too dumb to know whether their degree was a B.S. or a B.A.

Up on the stage, Wayne was standing, preparing to hand a rolled commission to each cadet who was now a second lieutenant as well as a college graduate. His exaggerated, stiff salute was designed to symbolize that the cadet was joining the grim-faced, serious world of Men, emphasis on the capital M.

Debra thought he looked ridiculous. And the cadets coming down the line holding their diplomas aloft like symbols of triumph looked just as ridiculous. To think that all over America, in similar ceremonies, kids were getting the same diploma made Debra laugh. The piece of paper meant nothing more than four years of parents' money spent for their children to hang around an advanced high school. All that a military school added to that experience was some organized hazing and a lot of guff about creating "real men."

Debra sat up in the front row, her back straight, her breasts thrust out, displaying her trim figure to the world

219

and fighting against heat prostration. Trying to ignore the heat, Debra mentally went over her new life, dwelling on each point.

First, she was a new person. She had sinned and repented. She had been lifted up into a greater awareness of her body and her mind. Her minister had guided her and absolved her of her sins. The sins had just been part of God's plan for her, anyway. Second, Debra was through with Beau. He was a kid she had taken in hand largely for his own benefit, and he had shown his childishness through a lack of gratitude and understanding of what she had done for him. That episode of her life was over.

Third, Debra was committed to getting out of Wayne what was due her. He was going to take care of the children while he paid for her to go to photography school. He owed her this because of her personal sacrifice in not going to college. Fourth, she was going to rise to her full potential. Losing weight had shown her that she could become whatever she wanted. She was going to make a successful career as a fashion photographer. She had both the ability and the insight needed to be a success.

Fifth, and finally, she wanted Chris Dixon. It was clear that to be worthy of Chris's love, she had to achieve something and find her own potential. That was why he wasn't seeing her as much, because he didn't want her to lean on him and be weak. He was doing it for her own good.

Wayne had used her. And Beau just wanted to put her through a rerun. He wanted kids. He wanted her to follow him around army posts. She had told him how she felt last night in the dark next to the chapel, and he had actually broken into tears and threatened suicide.

As far as Debra was concerned, men were like that. When you refused to let them use you, they fell apart. Chris Dixon had helped her see that. By taking her through pain, he had shown her that she could overcome any obstacle. He had shown her the mind of God, the third eye that lies within each of us. He had shown her that knowing herself meant giving in to angry impulses and asserting her own needs.

Debra had had enough of Wayne's fucking around with

that little Hare Krishna vamp. Right after ridding herself of Beau, she had gone home and gotten straight with Wayne. Hare Krishna was to go. His ridiculously low salary wouldn't stretch to send Debra to photography school and support his girlfriend, too.

Debra smiled to herself. She knew Wayne had been intimidated, just like Beau, except not quite as cringing because he was more callous than Beau. Wayne was a self-centered, ignorant, crude, selfish individual. He belched at the dinner table and pissed in the shower. He drank straight out of milk containers and blew his nose into the kitchen sink. He had stifled her at every turn. She was going to grow while she still had a few years of youth left in her. And Wayne was going to pay for it.

He had never lifted a hand to care for his kids. Well, he could just start getting used to that kind of work. She had been mother and father. He could play both roles for a while. The kids would probably end up raising him, and maybe they'd make him clean up some of his grosser habits—God knew Debra had tried and failed.

Meanwhile, Debra was moving off The Military campus. She had found an apartment at the beach for the summer and would enroll in a photography school in Atlanta for the fall. Reverend Dixon had actually found her the apartment, although Debra hadn't told Wayne that. She preferred that he think she had done it on her own.

Debra was tough. She looked tough with her new trim figure, the slight ripple of muscle in her biceps and pecs, her stomach that hadn't been so flat since high school. She also felt tough inside because of her mind-expanding sessions with Chris during which he took complete control of her psychic consciousness and carried her through the pain of this world into something so perfect that it relieved her of all her burdens of guilt. She was tough, and she had shown it by intimidating both Beau and Wayne.

She was proving how tough she was by sitting right here in the front row, looking good and letting the world know Wayne was hers. That bitch Cerise better not show up, either. Debra had made Wayne call her and tell her it was over while Debra listened in on the upstairs line. There had been a lot of noise and music in the dorm, and Cerise had sounded unconcerned. Of course, she always sounded that way, with all her Hindu pagan karma shit.

Wayne had seemed upset by Cerise's unconcern. He had shut himself in the bathroom and sat there in dead silence all night. He hadn't locked the door, though, which meant he wanted her to come in and hug him and say everything would be all right. But Debra had gone to bed instead. In the morning, she had opened the door and found him asleep curled around the toilet in his white T-shirt. Debra had even refused to make him breakfast and had told him he could take the boys out to Krispy Kreme while she ate yogurt.

The grisly ceremony was finally over fifteen minutes later. Several hundred cadets threw their hats in the air in a frenzy of mindless joy, while little children darted in among them trying to retrieve a hat as a souvenir.

Debra stood up and surveyed the crowd carefully. Cerise didn't seem to be there.

In the past, Wayne would have come home afterward expecting Debra to press his white uniform and hang it up just so until the same time next year. Well, this year he could damn well do it himself!

● *62* ●

"I've hired a P.I. out of Knoxville, Tennessee, to check Dixon's background," said Murchison over the wind roar as he drove south out of Congreve two days later. It was Saturday, and he had stopped by on impulse, he said, to ask Morgana to go with him to check on his beach house on Calloway Island. Apparently, he hadn't been out there in more than a month.

"A P.I.?" said Morgana, shifting her feet in the rubbish on the floorboard of the car. She couldn't quite credit that anyone would actually own, let alone drive, a 1967 Chevy Malibu with a jacked-up rear end.

"Private eye. Don't you watch television?" asked Murchison incredulously. He was driving with one hand, drinking cold tea out of a thermos. He hadn't had but one drink in a week, and he had felt so enormously guilty as that one went down that he had put his finger down his throat and thrown it up.

The consumer-age glut of the Street Highway finally petered out into small brick houses until the landscape was all pine forest accented here and there with tidal creeks.

"Why do that?" Morgana asked. "What do you expect to find?"

"Dirt. Filth. Slime. Everybody's got it somewhere in their background. I mean, look at us, or at least, look at me. I have plenty to hide about myself. And, besides, I've developed a real distaste for the guy. I don't trust him one bit. I figure an ounce of prevention . . ."

Morgana thought for a minute. She wanted to tell Murchison about Dixon and the night after her mom had died—had it just been eight days ago? It seemed like an eternity. But her instincts held her back. "All you've ever done is drink too much," she said instead.

"But with a vengeance. Don't forget that."

"How did you get started, anyway?"

"Oh, the really memorable demarcation was my first week back from Southeast Asia when I got blasted and passed twenty-four cars in a line on the two-lane road down to Petersville. Seven oncoming cars had to take to the ditch, but good old Bubba Wilcox, the oldest practicing member of the Georgia bar back then, defended me eloquently. I'll never forget his argument before the judge: 'Now, Judge, this boy's been defending his country. Why, I can remember when you and me came home from World War II. We used to drink a bit. Run around a bit.' That judge's eyes rolled back in his head in fond memory and he found me not guilty. From there on, I had my excuse. Look, you know I just use war as an excuse for behaving exactly like I've always wanted."

Morgana found herself liking Murchison again. When they were growing up, he had always stood out from the other guys. Not that he didn't have plenty of friends and play football and do all the usual guy things. But he had wanted to get out of the town to greener pastures and do something unusual. Just like Morgana.

Murchison stared out the windshield. "Got a package from NEH the other day," he said, switching the subject. "It was some more of Drena's rubbish. There was a weird story about a witches' Sabbath that she'd written. You know, Drena was the first to announce the coming of the Age of Aquarius way back on February 4, 1962, when we were all in junior high school, remember? The sun, moon, Mars, Venus, Jupiter, Mercury, and Saturn were all in Aquarius for the first time in centuries. As she explained it, slowly, over 2,170 years, the spring equinox was sliding over a zodiac sign. The Piscean Age was becoming Aquarian. Art, religion, and astral understanding would become one in the dawn of an Arcadian era. All of us shrugged it off as more of Drena's shit. It wasn't until 1967 and the musical *Hair* that we all heard the term again."

"To me," Murchison went on, "Drena was like an Eve figure, a big earth mother who longed to caress the whole mass of humanity. You know, one night she led me to the top of the ramparts at the fort and initiated me into manhood. It had a big impact on me."

"You're certainly open talking about sex," said Morgana frankly. "I guess it's because you're pushing forty. Or is this just some way to test my reaction?"

"I am available as a love slave." Murchison winked as he drove south toward Calloway Island.

Once over the bridge to the island, he turned onto a dirt road and drove past a shrimp fisherman's house and trawler on a deep-water creek, past tomato fields and the houses of black farm workers, into another pine wood with a house and a yard fronting on a tiny patch of rapidly eroding beach. The island had shifted slowly over the years, and radically during the last fierce storms. Murchison laughed to himself. Homo boobus couldn't accept that any seaside resort, however beautiful, was built on sand, no matter how deep the roots of the grass on the putting greens.

Morgana was captivated by the quiet loneliness of the tiny weathered house and the water that ran among the roots of dead trees almost to the front porch. In another year, the house would be undermined and would lie rotting like the trees. It was a picture of all that had been beautiful and swampy and natural about the Congreve of her youth before the population boom and the asphalt carpet.

Murchison flung open the front door of his beach house, revealing a bare single room with a fireplace in the far corner. "No furniture, electricity, or plumbing. This is Zen with a vengeance. You'll be right at home."

He seemed to have brought an amazing conglomeration of implements in the trunk of the car. Sleeping bags and foam pads. Skewers and pots. Boxes of food. Plates, forks, jelly glasses, and toilet paper. Towels and soap. "Tampax and gin for the ladies as needed!" he added expansively. Morgana laughed. She felt the warmest she had since her mother had died.

As they watched the sun go down from the perspective of the front porch swing, they ate steak. Overhead, ibis flew to their nesting grounds. The pines behind the house became a black wall against a deep blue sky of night, and the ocean in front turned to a hissing, breathing, amorphous mass. The fire in the hearth died to low coals.

Murchison fixed Morgana a gin and tonic, but drank straight tonic himself. As the night deepened and the stars came out, they delayed leaving, afraid to break the spell. It was as if they'd stepped back into a time warp where modern society didn't exist.

Murchison leaned back against a porch post and stood there, looking up at Morgana. "I still remember it in detail," he said finally. Even without it being said, Morgana knew that he was referring to their night together nearly twenty years ago. It was a bond that linked them, the ultimate communication.

"So do I," Morgana acknowledged softly.

"You were wearing the tiniest black underwear I had ever

seen. Your body was like some daydream of Cleopatra, or a sorceress like Circe or Calypso. I remember every move you made, every word you said."

"Please . . ." Morgana urged.

"We could go swimming naked in the surf," Murchison suggested. "Instead of remembering . . ." He put his arm around her tentatively. Morgana didn't resist. His touch excited her, as if her body was alive after years of frigid death.

"I still care for you, Morgana," he whispered.

"You're such a romantic," she said finally, following his lead down toward the water.

He bent to kiss her. The kiss was weak, then stronger as he spread her lips with his tongue. Morgana responded.

She went with him and helped when he got a sleeping bag out of his car and unrolled it on the sand. She stepped out of her clothes willingly and enjoyed feeling him hug her close against his chest.

The interlude went on for a long time, warm and pleasurable, before Morgana realized he couldn't get an erection. She wanted him then, and she was willing when he began to substitute his tongue.

She was taken to the heights of ecstasy, and did not feel apologetic or guilty afterward when she laid her panting heart on his chest.

The communication she had with this man was powerful. It had been reestablished and she was unafraid. She felt alive again.

• 63 •

Driving through the silent streets of Congreve the next night, Maeve knew that Bojack would be furious at her for taking his car, but he had passed out from all the rauwolfia she had given him, so she hadn't really been able to ask his permission. She laughed to herself. If he woke up before she got home, he'd probably think the car had been stolen. Plus, the thought of meeting Chris Dixon at the old abandoned county jail was just too delicious for her to worry about Bojack and how he felt.

Chris Dixon definitely had a kinky side, and Maeve loved it. She was just sorry they hadn't met much earlier. Chris had wanted Maeve's aunt's recipe for the witches' salve— henbane boiled and mixed with herbal ointments—which seeped into the pores and provoked wonderful hallucinations.

Maeve had toyed with Chris a bit, knowing she was in control. And gradually something deeper was creeping into the relationship. Chris concealed so much behind his gray suit and dog collar. Inside, he was like a low door into a secret garden.

Maeve had the ability to sense the paranormal in people. Her Aunt Fiona from Connemara had filled Maeve with a warm glow just by entering the same room. And, just like her aunt and even with his wired jaw, Chris Dixon fascinated Maeve with his talk about medieval magic, alchemy, Paracelsus, and man's early gropings for mind paths to the unknown. He was obviously educated in psychology, theology, and science, and the folklore he held in his brain was encyclopedic.

But clearly Chris was holding back in their relationship. Maeve knew that he was deliberately letting her coals smolder and glow. She had known that, just at some moment when they were primed to burst into flame, he was going to embrace her.

And, miraculously, that moment had come tonight. Chris had phoned and outlined his plan, saying he would have a side door open. They were actually going to break into the abandoned jail for their tryst. The idea exhilarated Maeve. She was tired of her Hungarian midget husband and the drunken Brian Murchison. She was ready to wrap herself around a man whose lightest touch was electrifying.

Chris was fascinated by her, Maeve knew for sure, because he had told her so himself. He was so honest and frank. He said it was the touch of the witch in her blood, just a little strain of what her aunt had gotten in a much larger dose. Aunt Fiona had been a seventh daughter of a seventh daughter, which had given her full powers. Still, Maeve's insight into character had always been remarked on by her aunt, who had urged her niece to go into fortune-telling. It was so natural to be with Chris; they were so different from other people.

The old Congreve County jail sat squarely in a patch of marsh on the edge of an unnamed finger of the Carteret River, just in the shadow of the enormous high span of a bridge. Both a public housing project and a truck lot were nearby, and the jail stood out on a gravel causeway in the marsh like a moated castle. Abandoned years ago, it sat silent as though it had been cursed by the human misery that had existed there at one time.

Maeve parked at the entrance to the causeway and flashed her headlights. From the distant, silent, brick building, a flashlight blinked twice in response. Overhead, there was the roar of passing traffic on the bridge. Amid the sound of croaking frogs, Maeve got out and walked along the gravel lane. Across the river, the lights of Congreve winked. A rat scampered out ahead of her and disappeared easily into the water. Like paper cutouts from Halloween, bats flitted past.

Maeve shivered slightly in the rather sinister surroundings. Chris had told her over the phone about men who had hanged themselves in the jail, and in return Maeve had told him about the Glory Hand, a legendary appendage cut from a hanged felon, which, with a candle burning on it, would force anyone to tell the truth. Suddenly, what had started as an enormous giggle terrified her.

Hurriedly, Maeve found an open door next to an oil drum filled with dirty water, a fallen drainpipe, and a burned pile of tin cans. River water filmed with oil lapped among the marsh grasses, which were already choked with floating rubbish: old tires, plastic bottles, and the silver bodies of dead fish lying belly up. A rank odor lay over everything. The door, with its little wire mesh peephole, opened farther, creaking.

Inside, it was dark. Maeve listened but heard nothing.

It was obvious Chris wanted her to walk into the black corridors. But Maeve was suddenly pissed at his little game, and at that moment vowed she wouldn't play it. She'd just stand here inside the door. This place was getting on her nerves.

To her surprise, Chris immediately came walking down the corridor, the blade of his flashlight cutting a path. "Isn't this perfectly, wonderfully ghastly?" he joked. He took Maeve in his arms and kissed her while the flashlight beam danced across the ceiling. When he dropped the flashlight and had to bend down to retrieve it, Maeve found that she was laughing despite the weird illumination on his face. He led her along the corridor to a bare room lined with barred cells. The familiar picnic basket was in the corner with the wine already uncorked. Crossing the room, Maeve drank from it deeply.

She noticed that Chris's eyes were bright with excitement. He rubbed his hands together as he spoke.

"I've brought you here to help me explore witchcraft. You're a marvelous woman of eldritch sensibilities."

Maeve laughed some more, slapping at mosquitos.

Chris moved close and unzipped Maeve's dress in the back as she drank from the wine bottle again. "A snake shedding its skin," she quipped as she shook out of her dress and let it fall in a puddle at her feet. Unscrewing a jar of dark salve, Chris was silent. Concentrating heavily, he began to smear it on her back. It smelled of rosemary.

"The witches' salve!" Maeve exclaimed with delight. "You made it? How naughty of you!"

Maeve enjoyed Chris's hands on her body. He smoothed it in, traced the crease of her backbone. She drank more wine as she watched him rub down her legs. "I'll stand here while you draw the pentagram and light the candles," she said with suddenly relaxed savvy. She could feel the cream seeping into her body. That, along with the wine, made her feel even more exhilarated.

"So you've done this before," Chris whispered.

"Every niece of an Irish witch knows this," Maeve said.

Maeve groaned aloud as Chris rubbed the cream into her breasts, squeezing them gently, his breath hot at the nape of her neck. She turned coyly against his body, her eyes closed, rubbing all over him like a cat.

The cream oozed into her system, giving her a feeling of intense heat all over her body as if she were about to burst into flame. The smell rose and drenched her nostrils, almost choking her with its rich, cloying odor. Her brain began to spin.

Dimly, she knew he was manacling her to the bars of one of the cells. But when the lash fell, it was only the barest of stings—almost like a lover's pinch. Maeve's mind was transported into a whirling ether where physical pleasure mounted to utter ecstasy.

She hoped it would never end.

● 64 ●

By the time Wayne had fed the boys breakfast and driven them to school, the day was already unbearably hot. It was Monday, and almost a week had passed since he had seen Cerise. Wayne hated the heat and heavy humidity of Congreve. He dreamed more and more of living high in the mountains the way Cerise had in West Virginia, with log fires in the winter and cool air in the summer.

His uniform clung to his sweaty body and irritated his skin. He had prickly heat all over his neck where he shaved. It was particularly bad now that Debra was refusing to do anything to help out. Wayne had to do everything, while she slept late and only woke up to go to the health spa. She wouldn't make family meals anymore.

Wayne was putting off giving Debra the money to rent the house she had found at the beach. He wanted to save his money, and he knew Debra didn't have any of her own. Even if she did, she couldn't make the first payment because he had changed their joint bank account to his name only. She had yelled at him about it, but Wayne had just ignored her. That was the only technique that worked with Debra. That, and just leaving the house and going fishing or drinking in a bar until she cooled off. Anyway, Wayne didn't want anyone saying he wasn't the perfect family man here at the last, so what else could he do?

Always in pursuit of that image here at the last, he worked around the yard every evening and touched up the paint trim on the house, even though it was The Military property and he didn't have to. He washed and waxed the cars and talked a lot to the neighbors about how Debra had always wanted a boat and he was buying her one as a surprise. Then he'd slip in the story about the crank telephone calls Debra had been getting and how concerned he was.

He was doing all this while that sorry bitch Debra was reading books on photography. It was clear she couldn't understand them, because she'd get confused and put them down. When they had first gotten married, Debra had taken a French cooking course that she had made a hash of. Now it was photography. Before that, it had been interior decoration, and before that, color analysis. She could lie around for hours doing nothing. Or she'd go to the spa and flirt with guys.

One of them had even followed her home the other day, but the jerk-off had turned his car around real fast when he saw Wayne come out of the house with his T-shirt rolled up over his shoulders, showing his biceps and his skull tattoo on the right arm. Not that Wayne really cared who Debra screwed. He just couldn't have anyone saying they were having marital difficulties. The Minister knew, but he wouldn't talk. He was Wayne's friend.

Wayne sat at his desk at work and drank a cup of coffee, still fuming about what a waste-wad Debra was. Why had it taken him so long to see the truth about her? He had thrown away his youth and the chance of so many women. Not that it mattered anymore, because he had found the one woman he needed, the only one who mattered.

Debra hadn't even had a driver's license when Wayne

married her. That was because she had lost it for reckless driving. For two lousy years, he'd had to chauffeur her around wherever she wanted to go. He had been stupid enough to think it was nice having her dependent on him. Cerise wasn't like that. She was slow and careful in all her movements, almost like a sleepwalker who can move without bumping into anything.

Debra had been fucking around on him for years. Wayne had suspected it when he went off to Germany six months before she came over there. Suspected, hell, he knew it; he just wouldn't admit it to himself. After all, he'd found all those love letters in the bottom of her dresser drawer that time. She had refused to even burn them, just hid them somewhere else. And this cadet Beau was just the final act of humiliation. Hell, she'd been balling that little twerp for close to a year.

Debra had lost weight only for that little asshole. For years she had been putting on the lard and getting huffy when he made hints about her losing a few pounds. Now it was the other extreme. Every meal was an agony of her saying she couldn't eat much and carrying on about the misery of dieting until finally she started eating a bite here and a bite there, counting calories in front of him, talking about how good she had been about not eating all day and how she deserved a break. Plus the kids always took her side.

Of course, the minute Wayne had started losing weight and looking good again himself, Debra got scared. Suddenly she didn't want to lose him. Nothing motivated her but fear. Well, he'd fucking well motivate her soon enough.

With the cadets gone for the summer, the staff had little to do, and even the commanding officer had lightened up. Most of the guys would go to the gym, jog, or run errands, as long as they checked back into the office periodically, like they were working.

Wayne slipped out without telling anyone; he could claim to have been in the building the whole time, and no one would be able to prove otherwise. It was a short walk across the track field to his quarters. The grass was already baked brown and crying out for rain. He noticed nature a lot more these days, since Cerise was practically a weatherwoman, always smelling rain or predicting things from the way the birds behaved.

Wayne liked that and knew he had always had a buried central part of him that was like that, too. After all, he liked the outdoors and was happiest out dove hunting or drifting in a boat with his fishing rod. It was a way to commune with the animals and find the primitive innocence that lay inside him before he got so worked over by Debra and the shit of the world.

Once he was with Cerise permanently, Wayne figured, they'd go on a trip down to the Everglades and camp out, just living off the land the way he had learned in the army. He could show Cerise a lot of stuff, no matter how smart she was at that kind of thing.

Cerise was okay. Even though she had asked him to stay with her and keep her safe, and he had left her to go home to Debra, he could make her understand once Debra was gone.

That cunt Debra had humiliated him by making him call up Cerise four days ago. Debra had laughed at him the whole time, telling Wayne that Cerise was probably blowing dope with some other man.

Debra wanted him to believe that just to make him cry. She wanted Wayne to cry. She had always wanted him to cry. She had gone through all that self-awareness shit in the women's magazines. She had bugged him about letting out his feelings and told him he was screwed up because he wouldn't show his emotions. Then, when he had been passed over for promotion and got drunk and broke down and cried, she had sneered at him and told him he wasn't a man. It had all been an elaborate trap. Everything the bitch did was a trap! Well, it was over! He was busting out!

The back door was unlocked, and Wayne walked in. He closed it softly behind him. Then he went upstairs. The shower was running. She had finally gotten her lazy ass out of bed. A cold rage overcame him at the thought of her sleeping while he worked.

Getting his Colt automatic out of the drawer next to the bed, he moved the slide back on it easily, jacking a shell into the chamber. The door to the bathroom was open, a slight steam drifting out. Through the shower curtain he could see the outline of Debra lathering herself under the water, stroking the new skinny body she was so proud of, the body that other men fucked.

She didn't hear him come in, she was so busy admiring herself. She didn't even turn toward him as he raised the weapon, pointed it at her, and opened fire. Glass and water splattered around him as he shot her. She didn't have time to scream before the first bullet hit her brain. Wayne reloaded twice and put all thirty-six bullets into her body. It lay twisted and torn on the floor of the shower. The running water carried the blood down the drain in a thick stream.

Everything became a blur after that. Wayne couldn't remember having any coherent thoughts or recall anything he did. Suddenly, he became conscious that he was staggering in the broiling heat along the Elstree River Bridge. He thought he might have thrown the automatic into the water. When a police car drove up beside him, he stood and stared at it in a stupor.

The two officers got out with their weapons drawn and told him he was under arrest.

● 65 ●

Morgana Stone walked along the beach on the cut between the two barrier islands to the north of Congreve Harbor— Robinson's and the Isle of Charity. A bridge joined the islands, usually clogged by fishermen with ice chests and their bored wives. Since it was a weekday Monday morning, the bridge was vacant and only an occasional car going past broke her concentration. Morgana was making the most of her two-day break between spring and summer sessions.

She stretched her limbs, exposing her flesh in its skimpy swimsuit to the sun. Soon the heat would be intolerable, but for the moment she felt it was baking poisons out of her body, aiding in the slow rebuilding of her psyche.

For more than fifteen years, Morgana had been emotionally flat, unable to experience wide ranges of love or hatred, pain or joy for any man. Her mind enjoyed comprehending sex and passion intellectually, but when men threatened her situation, she shut them off and retreated to her books.

The tide was coming in, and it brought with it a land breeze that carried gnats and flies. Her feet in the water, Morgana bent and splashed the wet over her body and ran her hands through her hair. The current in this particular spot held a vicious undertow that drowned two or three swimmers a year. Despite big warning signs, fishermen would get drunk and start horsing around, daring one another to take a dip, oblivious to the water's deadly potential.

As a child, Morgana had spent every summer on these islands. They had been largely covered with jungle growth then, not yet scraped clear for the streets lined with beach houses. Now only Robinson's Island still held thick foliage among old wooden houses that dated to the turn of the century.

Morgana's father had taught her how to crab and fish and oyster when she was barely six years old. He had learned diving in the navy, and he'd taken her out from age twelve with the tanks and a knife strapped to her hip. Once he had killed a shark right in front of her, and the story had attained legendary proportions among her circle of adolescent friends when her dad told them that Morgana had done it.

Yet as much pleasure as Morgana and her father took in each other's company, Jack Stone had always been filled with a deep sadness. Perhaps he had been too dreamy for such a practical wife as Patricia. Or perhaps he had simply lived with a premonition of his impending death. Such transcendental messages were possible, Morgana knew full well. In her research, she had seen many verified incidents of ESP and mind control. Despite frauds, some psychics were real and had very real powers. Morgana believed that in every one of us there was that latent power. Most people simply didn't know how to release it. Or were afraid to.

That stupid Brian Murchison. She hadn't seen him since that night more than a week ago when they had made love. He had been crushed by one stupid night of impotence, which Morgana feared she might have willed on him because of her own inadequacies. Afterward, they had slept in the sleeping bag on the porch of the little island house. Morgana had been awakened in the night by his screams, and like a child crying for his mother, he had related his nightmare to her. It had been some twisted story of a firefight on hot, murky waters, of a river lined by a steaming jungle. Death had brought its leering face close and singed Murchison with phosphorescent flame. He had fired .50 caliber machine guns at the front of an enemy boat and seen the tracers slice through men and dance out of their flesh like hot fireflies. It was not war that frightened him, he said, but some deeper terror. Morgana had pressed his head against her breasts, smoothed his hair, holding him in her arms, filled with her own fears.

Murchison had finally lifted her up and carried her naked to the water's edge. The tide had lapped against his little house. The trees had been barely visible against the blackness and he had lowered her slowly into the water. The cold had seemed like a baptismal font for washing away fear.

Deliriously happy, they had kissed with pleasure and slept again. But in the morning light, he'd hidden behind small talk, already drawn into a shell. He had still been kind and tender with her, but distant.

"The jerk," Morgana said under her breath. She had given him her virginity twice, and now he wanted her to chase him. It was as mindless as those women's rape novels where the first dark knight-errant who ravished the heroine turned out to be the man of her dreams, and all the violations that followed were washed away when he returned and offered her true love.

Morgana stood at the point of Robinson's Island where the land curved into the channel. The distance to the other island was easily three-quarters of a mile. Crossing waters ran over one another in a deceptively gentle line of foam. A group of brown pelicans cruised by, intent on the shadows of fish just below the surface.

So much had changed in Morgana's lifetime. Hers was the first generation to be bound together by television. However innocent Sergeant Preston of the Yukon and the Mickey Mouse Club had been, they formed a pointless, shallow bond that had set millions on the path of mass culture and mass consumption.

It had seemed refreshing when the counterculture revolted against suburbia and the discharge-at-will bestiality of the corporate world. Morgana's generation had been the first to know the pill, and so it had been nothing unusual for a nineteen-year-old virgin to be swaggering about the streets of New York posing as a leather queen in rock clubs. Morgana had just added her own poignant touch by choosing to cross the line to womanhood with the boy next door.

Morgana had done it first with Murchison on impulse, but it was a deep impulse founded on her need to recapture the warm starry nights by the summer sea and the beach bonfires and oysters of autumn. Murchison had always been in the sailing regattas, and he'd seemed to barely notice any woman, much less Morgana. Drena used to drool over him and talk in shocking detail about how she had given herself to him on the ramparts of the fort. Drena had done it during her period, she'd claimed, so she would mark him forever with her blood.

In the morning light of Calloway, Morgana had tried to make Murchison open up to her again. She'd told him how she had thought of him often after that first and only night in New York. She had wanted to somehow express her love for him and break through his carapace, but he had deflected the assault on his heart by joking about the leather jacket with the Vietcong flag on the back and the black lace underwear she'd worn all those years ago.

Morgana kicked at the sand in anger. Murchison was tied up in an emotional straitjacket, just as she was. She couldn't tell him of her certainty in forces beyond the knowledge of science. She couldn't tell him about Chris Dixon. What would he think if she told him Dixon might have influenced both her mother's and Clarence Fuller's deaths? Maybe she was crazy.

Filled with anguish, Morgana bent down to splash water on herself again. She ran her hands along her arms and down the trunk of her body. Then—without warning—her mind went into slow motion.

Every thought seemed at one-third speed.

Flies swarmed around her, and she tried unsuccessfully to wave them away. She looked back down the beach to where her car sat next to the piled rocks that formed a support for the Robinson's Island end of the bridge. She saw the hazy green marsh beyond that matted the inland waterway.

The water suddenly gripped her body like mercury rising in a thermometer. It was only a subtle, listless awareness that told her she was wading out into the water. She wanted to stop, but she couldn't! The current whipped her under!

Morgana's eyes perceived only swirling, muddy green, but her mind was now shocked wildly alert and her lungs and muscles screamed against the irresistible force of the water.

Another voice was in her head. "Breathe," it urged her in a velvet growl. "Breathe in. Breathe in."

Morgana fought the voice even as she continued to struggle in the water. "Breathe," it kept telling her.

On and on Morgana whirled in the water, head over heels, twisting like a torpedo fired from a submarine tube. The pain and terror of her plight hammered in her head with a furious noise. Her bursting lungs exhaled, and her mouth opened to take a fatal gulp of water just as her head broke the surface.

"I won't die!" she screamed, gasping in lungfuls of air. "I won't die!" as the voice splintered in an inchoate jumble before the battering ram of her will.

A mile from shore with no one in sight, Morgana lay on her back staring at wisps of clouds. The water was gentler now, but it drew her on. Fighting her nausea and exhaustion, she began a slow sidestroke, moving down the coast where she knew the current was carrying her, but still gradually angling toward land. Her father had put her out of a boat at age ten and taught her the technique, following her closely to give her encouragement. She had never had to use the knowledge since.

When at last Morgana lay on the shore, her hair tangled about her face, she felt as though her blood had been transfused away and replaced by fizz. Her muscles jumped without control in their knotted spasms. She stretched her limbs slowly as if testing for broken bones. She was suddenly conscious of a hand on her shoulder.

"Are you all right?" a voice asked.

Chris Dixon hovered over her. His jaw was still wired shut. His concern seemed genuine, but something about his eyes terrified Morgana.

She struggled to stand up, to stand as an equal to this man.

"I still love you," he whispered, "even after what you did to me, and I haven't told anyone."

Morgana said nothing. Her head was giddy. She gauged the distance to her car and ran, ran as hard and as fast as her newfound adrenaline would let her. But it wasn't necessary, because Chris Dixon didn't pursue her.

Morgana knew that something awful had come over her out there in the water. It wasn't sunstroke.

Something had taken control of her brain.

She had been conscious of what she was doing, but powerless to stop, because her own brain was doing it.

Her own brain had been influenced by some evil force, and it had something to do with Chris Dixon.

• 66 •

In the church station wagon, Chris Dixon took Maeve to a place south of Congreve in a very rural part of the county. He drove up a sandy road into a tangled wood threatened by a black-water creek. Crows called from the tops of the tall pines.

"I come here a lot," he confided to Maeve, "to gather herbs. It's a plantation owned by one of my parishioners."

Maeve found Chris's voice so compelling. She could see his smooth chest in his casual polo shirt, and imagined touching his body. An impending sexual encounter always filled her with exhilaration. She had wonderful memories of their very first encounter three days ago, when he had put the witches' salve on her. It had sent her spinning into another universe.

Maeve sat close to Chris on the front seat. "I want to fly again," she purred. "And this time, you come with me." She was thrilled that Chris had confided to her his deep interest in the occult. What with her Aunt Fiona, Maeve knew that Chris was both a bit awed by her and confident that she would understand his own interest.

Chris pulled the car off the road and shut off the engine. "Your Aunt Fiona warned that henbane is a very tricky drug to use," he remarked, laughing. "We'll have to be careful."

"Let's throw caution to the winds!" Maeve said.

"You know it's poisonous if taken in too large doses," Chris reminded her.

"There's more dark in your soul than meets the eye," Maeve said as she ran her hands inside his shirt. "What would your parishioners think if they knew we were out here alone like this?"

"Universal condemnation," said Chris, kissing her on the

mouth, sensuously running his tongue over her lips. "But the risk is always worth it."

Their heads stayed close as they mingled their breathing. Maeve's nipples were stiff against her blouse. "We're kindred souls," she said.

"If it feels good, do it," said Chris, running his hand along her jeans. "That's my theology." Maeve leaned toward him in response and groaned slightly. He held her away. "Let's get out of the car."

"Okay," Maeve agreed.

She watched while Chris took a blanket from the trunk. They walked along the bank of the creek where an animal trail went through brambles and blackberry thickets. Squirrels scampered around them. Chris talked about the Indians who had lived in the region before being exterminated by war and disease in the early eighteenth century. He seemed fascinated with their shamans and beliefs in evil spirits.

"I always used to like red Indians as a child," said Maeve. "Running around the woods dressed in breechcloths, their bodies all oiled with grease." She put her arm around Chris as they walked. "It's so sensuous to think of soft deerskin between the thighs and the rawhide thong around the waist." She broke Chris's grip to cross a field to examine some nightshade. "This was Drena's favorite," she said.

Chris had followed right behind. "I know."

"She claimed," said Maeve, "that she and some other people took some the night they had the witches' Sabbath. She said it allowed her to expand her senses. The ceremony was something she got out of a book that belonged to a minister, which they actually stole from a church. She talked about black candles and chanting. It gave me the creeps to hear her talk about it. You know, just talking about it, Drena became so paranoid she started to scream and fight me when I tried to calm her down."

They entered a clearing in which stood a mammoth live oak, its huge branches twisting down to the ground. "Do you think they really were worshipping Satan?" asked Chris.

The grass around them reminded Maeve of a meadow. She laughed nervously. "I believe in the other world. I believe that these things can be made to happen with the right ceremonies and thoughts," she said, suddenly breathless.

"Have you ever heard of the witches' cradle?" Chris asked.

"You mean, where the witches spin each other in a blanket until they hallucinate?" Maeve asked.

"Without contact with the earth," Chris said evenly, "the balance mechanism of the inner ear ceases to function. In the darkness of the blanket, perception totally changes." He took the blanket off his arm and opened it to reveal a length of stout rope.

"You certainly came prepared," said Maeve. "Let's try it."

Chris wrapped her in the blanket, tied the ends in a knot, and rigged the rope through the blanket ends and over a thick limb of the oak. Maeve weighed so much that Chris was barely able to get her off the ground. At last he succeeded. He wrapped the rope around the tree trunk and tied it.

I should kill her now, he thought. No one would hear her scream. He could just stab her through the blanket and watch the red blood drain down. It wouldn't even get on his clothes. And she couldn't stop him. There would be no scratch marks anywhere or little slivers of his skin under her fingernails.

Chris's heart pounded with excitement. He had never killed anyone with his hands, only through mind control. The knife was in his pocket, a six-inch stiletto he had ordered from a magazine. He took it out and pressed the button. There was the sudden snick of the razor-sharp blade. He nudged Maeve through the blanket. Her back was a curve at the bottom of the bundle. Just one good thrust right there to get going, and then as many as it took to shut her up.

But fear held Chris back. What if there was someone walking in the woods? Or on the dirt road? They might hear the screams. Chris didn't know how far sound might carry in the woods. What if Maeve had told her husband where she was going or left him a note? She seemed to despise

Bojack, so she might have told him she was out with another man just to taunt him.

Chris pressed the knife blade against the ground, forcing it back into the hilt. He was shaking with fear.

"Come on, now," urged Maeve from inside the blanket. "Let's get on with it. It's hot in here!"

Chris acquiesced. He twisted Maeve's body in the blanket repeatedly so that it spun wildly when it unwound. His brain twisted with it. Why had he been so afraid to kill with his hands? He could do it with his brain. Squirt could kill with his hands. Why not Chris?

Chris spun the blanket more violently. Maeve moaned and talked senselessly inside. Why couldn't he strike the death blow? Did she have some control over him? Like Morgana Stone, did she have a will that resisted his?

Lowering the blanket to the ground half an hour later, Chris opened it to see Maeve lying in a semicomatose state. Her eyes were turned back in their sockets.

He could still kill her! One quick slash to the throat. Do it! Do it, his mind urged him. Do it! Get the knife out and cut her throat!

But still Chris Dixon resisted the angry voice inside him. He was afraid. Aroused by Maeve's helplessness, he wanted her. After all, she might be useful later. She had some of the characteristics of a witch in her blood. She would help him worship Satan on the summer solstice, June 23. Now that he had the power of Cynthia's body, he would celebrate the witches' Sabbath and worship Satan at the Black Mass. He could kill Maeve later.

He pulled off her jeans, but she didn't even notice his attentions. Afterward, while they were sleeping, she woke up long enough to vomit violently.

Suddenly, Chris was thoroughly disgusted. Clearly he should have killed her.

The air-conditioning in Murchison's office was busted, and even at nine on a Wednesday morning the heat was burning. With the windows and doors wide open, the yellow miasma from the chemical mills to the south filled his office.

Two weeks ago, Murchison would have been drunk and mostly oblivious to discomfort. Now he was sober. He was also trapped in his chair, trying to concentrate on what Lynn Stafford was telling him. Going off booze had produced a near-miraculous defogging of his brain, but the unaccustomed sensory reception was so startling that he had trouble sorting and filing all the information he was receiving from the world. Food had flavor again, but the noise pollution was intolerable. It was as if he were Rip van Winkle, awakening to find the landscape had changed. And it was all because of Morgana Stone. He loved her still. He didn't want to be impotent; he wanted to be strong.

"My daddy always used your daddy for all his legal matters," Lynn was saying. "So I thought it was natural to come to you."

Murchison was more cynical. The way he had it figured, no other lawyer in town wanted her case. She was all dressed up, wearing stockings despite the heat, a hat, and—of all things—white gloves. He mused as to whether she too had been asleep, only to wake up to find she was dressed for church.

"I swear," Lynn pattered on, "the world has just become such a strange place that I hardly know what to do. Why, when we were growing up with my daddy as minister of St. Helen's and your daddy practicing law here on Main Street and everybody going to Robinson's or Flat Rock in the summer—everything seemed so ordered. But now it's different, with all this change. You know, building and land development going on, all the new people from out of town, and all the traffic. Well . . . I just can't seem to think straight."

Murchison nodded vaguely. As far as he was concerned, Lynn Stafford had never been able to think straight. He could still remember being dragged to church each Sunday to daydream through the service and, at the end, hearing Lynn and her mother outshrieking each other as the Minister and his family greeted everybody going out.

"You know, my ex-husband, Roger Frye, used to say Congreve was going to change to where we couldn't recognize it one day, and all the old guard would be punished for their pride. And when you kind of think about it, he was right. Not that Roger was right about many things. But you just look at how south of Main has been turned into a tourist attraction. Why, motor homes are parked outside all night and tourists constantly dump litter down here. But the good old City Council just keeps raising property taxes. I mean, you'd think they'd give the people down here a break on taxes since they're supporting the whole town through the tourist trade."

"Look, Lynn," Murchison said slowly. "Can we get down to why you're here, please?"

The corner of Lynn's mouth twitched and her eyes blinked unnaturally fast. Her face was suddenly pale. "I mean, I still remember Hutton Hall and what it used to be like here growing up," she said, taking a handkerchief out of her white macramé handbag and dabbing the corners of her eyes. "Life was worth living then."

Murchison shifted uncomfortably in his seat. "Well, uhmmm . . . Lynn—" he began lamely.

But she cut him off. Tears streamed down her face. "It's—it's just that . . . people seem so nice one minute, then . . . suddenly they turn ugly." She took a deep breath. "Brian . . . it's Chris Dixon. He . . . he b—beat me horribly."

Murchison would have put her out of his office immediately, had he not, over the past month, been sitting through a hearing where very similar allegations had been brought against Chris Dixon by a woman who seemed to have been unstable after the fashion of Lynn Stafford. Instead, he tried to comfort Lynn enough to find out what had happened. There was a fairly clear pattern to Dixon's victims, he realized as she sobbed out her story. Murchison felt his stomach tense with the vile knowledge of what this man was doing. It was just too much of a coincidence, and the whole Carolyn Danner thing had been kept too quiet for Lynn to have known about it.

"Have you considered going to the district attorney?" Murchison asked finally. "If this was done without your consent, it's punishable as a crime."

Lynn wiped her eyes with a Kleenex. Her pain seemed genuine. "I . . . I couldn't face it," she whined. "My father was once the rector of St. Helen's and all, and the questioning . . . they—they'd turn it around to where I was the criminal . . . And I don't know that I didn't consent. I mean . . . I let him do it, didn't I? . . . I'd be . . . hum—humiliated." She sobbed violently into her hands.

Murchison sat calmly. He had learned long ago never to pat crying female clients on the shoulder. Some of them took it as an advance. A divorce client was perfectly capable of going back to her husband and making the lawyer into the villain who'd split up the marriage in the first place.

When Lynn had calmed down, Murchison explained the concept of civil actions for injuries such as assault and battery and the intentional infliction of emotional distress. Lynn didn't interrupt and seemed to comprehend. But after listening to everything Murchison said, she stunned him by saying: "I want you to sue him for breach of promise." Her fear had been replaced by a sudden hardness.

"I . . . don't understand," Murchison said cautiously.

"You know," Lynn repeated. "Breach of promise. After all, he promised to marry me and now he won't."

"You . . . want him to marry you?" Murchison asked incredulously. "After all that he's done to you?"

"Well, I mean, we are in love and all," Lynn said

plaintively. "He's just got this little problem, and while I can forgive and forget, I think it's just too good an opportunity to miss."

"Opportunity?" Murchison repeated.

"Yes. To get our understanding straightened out once and for all. I mean, the rest of the world isn't as broad-minded as I am about these things and would be shocked. Let's face it, Chris can't stand exposure. I want you to sit him down and have a talk with him about what might transpire if he doesn't become more cooperative in living up to his promises and in getting professional help so that he can overcome this mental thing he's got. I mean, confidentially, between you and me, I think it's some kind of mother hatred. I must confess I share it, because I tried to work it out with Faith and she just . . . she just . . . she treated me like dirt under her fingernails. I mean, she totally ignored my plight and said I was crazy." Lynn began weeping again.

With great difficulty, Murchison got Lynn to make a statement into a tape recorder about her experiences with Chris Dixon. With far less shame, she produced color photos of her striped buttocks and legs after one of the sin-absolution sessions. She claimed to have held the camera behind her and snapped the pictures. They were amazingly clear.

Lynn absolutely refused to go to a psychiatrist. She said it was Chris who needed a shrink. Finally, she exhausted her emotions and left without any real resolution of what Murchison was to do for her.

Afterward, Murchison sat with his hands behind his head, suddenly reveling in the possibilities the stench-pregnant day had brought him. He hated Chris Dixon. Obviously, the man was sick, but the private eye in Tennessee had been unable to find anything on him. There was no way Murchison could sue for breach of promise. The idea of suing on marriage contracts because of shame in the community was as out of date as buggy whips. Besides, Lynn had admitted that no one else knew of the alleged engagement, so her shame was purely in her mind.

Assault—that was the only way to get Dixon. But first

he'd have to break the lawyer-client relationship he had with the man. Of course, Dixon disliked Murchison now anyway, but Murchison was scheduled to do the last Committee hearing tonight. He'd have to do something right away.

● *68* ●

In the heat of the late Wednesday afternoon, Chris Dixon went into the unhallowed ground and sought the shade of the small mausoleum. Concealed against his body from the curious eyes of casual tourists on Bayswater Street was a plastic freezer bag with a living toad inside. The zip-lock top was slightly open so the luckless creature could breathe. It pressed its squat, wart-covered head against the opening, its mouth sucking rhythmically. Occasionally, its tongue would lick out, testing the edges of its prison.

Chris had caught the toad the night before in the grass of the cloisters. He chuckled to himself, thinking of the fools who discounted the old witches' brews with skin of toad. Science had recently determined that toad skin contained a powerful narcotic, lethal in heavy doses. However, Chris had other uses for the toad.

Ten yards away was the simple marker that showed where Drena Wrenn's ashes were buried. Chris felt no emotion. She had been just a tool sent for his use. If she hadn't killed herself, he would have had to do it.

Pausing at the entrance to the marble tomb, Chris took a long look back at the iron fence and the porch of the church. Tourists idled in front, taking pictures. In the graveyard proper, some roamed among the headstones, marveling at the dates. Chris smiled, thinking how simple their brains were. They were children who would never grow up, while each day his powers mounted.

Fran Maitland was his latest conquest. She was helplessly under his control now. She was suffering intense, free-floating anxiety punctuated by fear of her husband finding out about her affair with Rafe Artigues. She wanted the child she carried so badly that she would not have an abortion; yet she was terrified that Roland would throw her out of the house. She was so completely contorted mentally that only Chris's orders made any sense to her.

Just to torment her and prove his power to himself, Chris had driven her to a grocery store in a black district of the city this morning and made her wait in the hot car while he went inside. Fran hadn't even questioned why they had gone; she had simply followed his directions. And Fran had sat there, twisting her Lalounis necklace, scuffing the toe of one Gucci leather shoe with the other.

Chris had deliberately stayed inside the grocery store for forty-five minutes, knowing Fran would be repulsed by the poverty and terrified by the dudes hanging out in the parking lot. Sure enough, he watched from inside the air-conditioned store while she rolled up the windows and locked all the doors. All around her were beat-up cars and hustlers selling stuff out of their car trunks. Ragged kids juked to boom boxes. Drunks and dopeheads reeled by. Chris stood next to the gumball and pistachio machines, sipped a cold drink, and browsed among the tabloid newspapers near the checkout lanes. The security guards ignored him because of his clerical collar.

When Chris finally returned to the car, Fran was almost delirious. The smell of her sweat had even overpowered her Paloma Picasso perfume. Chris had driven away, listening to her talk of her need to be a woman and how Roland had stripped her of it. But now, she said, she was going to have her baby Cynthia and she was sure she would be happy.

Fran had begged Chris to make it all right: her sins, her needs, her degradations. Finally, he had stopped the car and allowed her to be sick in a gutter filled with litter and broken bottles across from a ramshackle ice cream shop where blacks in stocking caps sat swigging beer from brown paper bags. Chris offered Fran his handkerchief while she wept uncontrollably, her forehead pressed against the dashboard.

Despite Fran's pleading, Chris had refused to drive on

and just remained parked there under the impassive gaze of the blacks. Periodically, the woman who ran the ice cream store would come to the door to see if they were still there. She would stand there wiping her hands on her apron, and disappear again.

After two hours of this, Fran was completely weak and subdued. She sat there as though hypnotized while Chris concentrated on the inside of her brain, focusing all his thoughts on an image of it, wrinkled, gray, and shiny, sitting on the brain stem inside the white skull covering. He concentrated so fully that he could see the skull, clenched teeth, and empty eye sockets inside her head.

Without moving his lips, he planted there the need for Fran to poison Morgana Stone's mind against Brian Murchison. He told her to go to Morgana and tell her some vile gossip about Murchison. Then he took her home.

It was a subtle plan that Chris was particularly pleased with. Morgana was strong. Her powers could resist him. What he needed to do was totally isolate her; make her feel that she was all alone and could depend on no one else in the world. Under such circumstances, even the strongest of mortals began to weaken and became prey to their fears. Once fear was gnawing at her, Chris could strike. When she was alone in the dark with her fears, his mind would come to her.

Chris fingered the stitching in his jaw, the evidence of his last encounter with Morgana Stone. The skin pulled against the stitches still, especially when he smiled. But he'd make her submit. He'd show her the source of light and make her worship the Prince.

Glancing around to make sure no one was watching, Chris unlocked the padlock and slid inside the mausoleum. It was cool inside and he was no longer afraid. Snails had left their slimy trails across the walls, but Chris was not repulsed. The truth had been revealed to him. He knew that the dark Prince reigned. As a servant of darkness, Chris held power over the very air itself. Even the witch couldn't stop him now!

The stone lid to the sarcophagus grated as Chris lifted it.

Inside, insects swarmed ferociously: beetles, roaches, worms. A sliver of light from the barely cracked door rested on Cynthia McAlister's folded hands, which were dry and scaly now, lacking their former life. Without hesitation, Chris lifted them and let them drop. The insects shifted in a gray mass. The hands seemed light, almost weightless. There was no rot even in this wet, tropical air. The body was drying out as though it were in a desert.

Taking the toad from the plastic bag, Chris squeezed tight against its frantic kicking. He squeezed until the guts began to spew from its mouth. Then he carefully dribbled them the length of the body up to the throat.

Cynthia's face was going, too, the cheeks sinking in cavernously, the eyes shriveling. The hair had turned an iron gray and was dry to the touch. She was slowly decomposing, not from carrion bugs and muggy heat, but from Chris drawing out her essence. She had been sacrificed to give him power, and Chris was making full use of her. His strength grew with his delight in the horribly evil things that had once depressed him.

Now Chris found that he loved to drive through the filthiest places in North Congreve. Mitchum Avenue, where the whole carnival of human monstrosity was on display, was particularly delicious. Beneath revolving billboards and gigantic American flags, slack-jawed teenagers with straw-colored hair hanging in their eyes shambled barefoot along the hot pavement. Low-life women lived on welfare and fed small children on junk food. Unwashed fat men in under-shirts guzzled from gallon wine jugs on the front porches of tiny cracker-box frame houses. Bruised waitresses trudged to work in crummy cafés.

These people made Chris feel joyous now instead of repulsed. Rather than a fragile refuge, his satin-lined existence had become a reward that he knew would always be his. It was the one solid thing in a rotting, decomposing world. It was his reward for knowing the truth and having the power of the truth. Soon he would have his bride. When the summer solstice came—the longest day of the year, with

Venus sitting bright on the horizon—the time of the witches' Sabbath, then he would make another sacrifice, and he would have her.

Kneeling, Chris clasped his hands in prayer. His voice was furry and thick-tongued. "Light Bringer! Please bless me!"

• 69 •

At the last minute, Morgana decided not to teach summer school. The students were impossible in the heat. She had made up her mind to sell her mother's house and go back to Columbia University. It would take her the summer to clear everything up. So after turning in her spring semester grades, she went to her office to collect some of her research notes and papers. There was nothing to stay here for anyway. Except Brian Murchison.

"Knock, knock," Morgana heard as a head peeked into her office. "Spring cleaning?" It was Fran Maitland. Fran was wearing a new summer outfit of white linen, matching Bally of Switzerland handbag and shoes, and a diamond Piaget watch. She had a brittle look about her face and her movements were quick and birdlike. She seemed nervous and under stress.

"I guess I'd forgotten how cramped these offices are," Fran said, shifting some papers from the visitor's chair onto the floor so she could sit down. "I'm so glad to be out of this hole! I don't know how you stand it. Particularly after New York. This must be such a comedown. Are you going back there? I mean, there is nothing to hold you here in Congreve now. Unless it's"—she assumed a knowing expression—" oh, my . . . your *friend*. Is that what I should call him? I don't know what language to use these days, particularly since I'm out of touch with the students and I don't seem to have any unmarried friends our age."

Morgana thought that Fran had certainly done well for an opening gambit. In one short soliloquy, she had managed to sneer at Morgana's job, be callous about the death of her mother, and announce that she knew all about Brian Murchison.

Morgana suddenly had no patience for it. She looked pointedly at her watch. "Fran, I'm real busy," she said curtly. "I've come here to get a few things done. Could we talk some other time." It was a statement, not a question.

It wasn't at all clear that Fran was listening. She did stand up to examine some books on the shelves and look at the pictures and diplomas. "Oh, I'm so sorry," she said finally. "I didn't mean to hurt your feelings. I assumed you wanted the world to know about you and Brian. I mean, neighbors are going to talk, and he has always been rather known for his promiscuity with the women. You should remember what a close little community we are here in Congreve. He does have the family house, but it sits vacant—why, I don't know. He's letting it run down something awful, and there's talk of a neighborhood committee going to the zoning board to make him do something about it."

Morgana looked out the window pointedly. But Fran was not about to be put off by anything short of an eviction. She had often been rude, but today she was being worse than ever before. She almost seemed to be talking to herself, rather than to Morgana. Morgana wondered briefly if Fran was on amphetamines.

"You go ahead and work," Fran said cheerfully. "I don't need your full attention." She perched on the edge of Morgana's desk and ran her fingertips through the dust. "It's a good thing he's got you as his therapist now," Fran rattled on, going back to the subject of Brian Murchison. "He's such a mess. You know he was engaged to Bitsy Wycombe about ten years ago. But one night, when he was drunk at her parents' house and was left alone for only a moment, he took one of her father's shotguns, loaded it, and fired it through the wall. The worst thing was, it went into a closet and shredded her father's suits. Well, you can imagine the wedding was off." Fran studied her fingernails pensively. "Was it really ten years ago? It seems odd to imagine that Murchison's been a problem drinker for so long.

"Before that, he was a doper. Speed. Cocaine. You name it. He was thrown out of the yacht club for that—had his membership revoked, and those are like gold, with all that out-of-town money pushing in and fighting over the available slots. Look, Morgana, sweetheart, I just came to warn you about what you're getting into. I mean, Brian has a big inheritance from his father, who left him a ton of real estate. But it's in some kind of trust for Brian's children so he can't get to it. Poor thing. His father didn't think much of him and didn't want him to squander the money." Fran sighed and took a breath.

"To make the story really interesting, Brian had a serious bout with cancer, which he claimed was caused by Agent Orange in Vietnam. Of course, Roland says it's a lot of bunk, like all those environmental things. He says it's just more of those Vietnam vets bellyaching and wanting money out of the government. You couldn't tell to look at Brian that he had enough chemotherapy to kill an elephant, but he did. He's even kept all his hair. When the cancer went into remission, he was left with a dope habit that was followed by a liquor habit, and that gives us the man today. Of course, you know he's sterile. So I guess he'll have a hard time getting at the money his father left. No kids, see? Money but no money. It's called a spendthrift trust. That's it. I'm sure that's why Brian's drug- and alcohol-dependent. He's trying to bolster his lagging potency."

Fran rattled on and on.

"Then there was his period with sluts and his endless drunken project to write a book on outlaw women," Fran went on. "He lived for a time with a female bouncer at Ward's Beach who wore a fake cast on her arm for smacking unruly men. She typed his manuscript and then burned it in a jealous frenzy."

Morgana finally reached her limit. "You know," she began slowly, "I don't really like you, Fran. You've always been mean and vindictive. You cloak yourself in social snobbery and think that redeems you. Well, it doesn't."

Morgana was beginning to warm to her subject. Her adrenaline was flowing. But she stopped short when she realized that Fran wasn't listening. The woman had gotten down off the desk and was standing in the middle of the floor, her arms slack at her sides, staring at a spot midway up the bookcase. Her head was cocked to one side, and she seemed to be listening to something.

With her right hand, Fran made a feeble plucking motion in the air as if she were trying to grasp a dust mote. "Yes, Cynthia," she said. "Of course I can hear you. Oh, you've heard about my baby. Isn't it wonderful news? I'm going to name her after you." She knitted her brows in concentration. "You're growing faint. Don't go away. Please don't go away and leave me."

She delivered the last sentence in a small, helpless voice; then she looked back at Morgana, her eyes unfocused. With tentative hands, she touched her hair, patting it into place. "I'll be going," she said vaguely.

Morgana watched Fran disappear out the door as abruptly as she'd come half an hour earlier. All the woman's stress had finally short-circuited her brain neurons in some way.

Morgana looked out the window as Fran walked toward the president's house, where everyone knew she double-parked on the basis of her M.D. license plates and the big donor sticker on the windshield. She walked briskly and as if full of purpose.

She is not my problem, Morgana told herself fiercely. I'm not bound by some Hippocratic oath like a doctor. Her husband is a doctor; let him worry about her.

But the incident was still preying on Morgana several minutes later. On impulse, she picked up her telephone and called campus security. They promised to check it out and make sure that Fran had gotten home all right.

Super, thought Morgana. Now she was left to think over what Fran had said about Brian Murchison. It was all pretty sordid. But Morgana had heard most of the stories already, plus Brian had told her about the cancer that night at Calloway. The only major thing she didn't know about was the inheritance, but that wouldn't have mattered to him anyway. Murchison didn't care about money, as far as Morgana could tell.

● *70* ●

As far as Murchison was concerned, sitting next to Chris Dixon at this final Committee hearing was like being in bed with a snake. For Murchison, the man had come to exude a poisonous air. Tonight Dixon had insisted on summing up on his own in front of the Committee. Murchison sat slouched in his chair. Reverend Ratteree had insisted that Brian finish this out. In fact, when Murchison had called Ratteree to resign early this morning after Lynn's visit, Ratteree had nearly become violent.

Despite his wired jaw, Chris talked fluently in a weird, tight voice. He lectured the committee on theology and Church doctrine. He spoke about Carolyn Danner and how he had tried to save her. As far as Murchison could see, the man did everything but admit he had bound and flogged the woman. Without Pat Stone, the Committee members just sat there, absorbing what grew into a tirade without interruption. Near the end, they tried to regain some semblance of authority when Ratteree interrupted Dixon's monologue and asked him point-blank whether he had beaten Mrs. Danner.

Exhausted, Chris Dixon sat down heavily in his chair. "No," he said with a dismissive wave of his hand. "We've been over that, and you know the answer. The woman should have been in confinement somewhere."

The committee members all stared at Dixon. "Do . . . do you wish to continue?" Ratteree asked finally.

"No, no. I have finished." Chris looked like he'd had his train of thought interrupted and wasn't going to resume.

"Are you sure?" Ratteree asked. He seemed worried that he had inconvenienced Chris Dixon in some way.

"No. I am *quite finished,*" Chris repeated, emphasizing each word. Then he smiled, as if to soften the impact of his words. "I guess I have to lay down the torch sometimes."

While the Committee retired to another room to confer, Murchison turned in his seat so he wouldn't have to look at Chris. Their exchange of eye contact made him feel queasy. It was unbelievable how the man seemed to move in and out of sanity.

Chris sat with folded hands, breathing heavily as if he had just run five miles. As his air intake calmed to a more normal level, he began to clean his fingernails with a paper clip. After less than ten minutes, the Committee members filed back in. There were only six, since Patricia Stone had not been replaced. After her sudden death in the middle of the hearings, no one had wanted to back up and start all over again, which would have been required with a new person.

The Committee stood to deliver the verdict. Murchison felt the tension at the back of his neck. Ratteree closed his eyes. A broad smile spread across his face. He pronounced: "We would like to compliment the Reverend Dixon on his great patience with the procedures necessary to safeguard the best interests of our parishioners. Despite the heavy emotional burden that we feel this has laid upon him, he has conducted himself with dignity, honesty, and even compassion for the soul of a false witness."

Murchison ran his hand through his hair. Holy shit. It was going to be a complete whitewash, just like they had promised from the beginning.

"We, the assembled Committee, find the charges against the Reverend Dixon to be totally false and without foundation," Ratteree went on. "We find the Reverend Dixon innocent of all charges, and we commend him both for his forbearance in this matter and for the excellent work he has been doing at St. Helen's Church in the area of recruitment of new members and in the collection of tithes and offerings." Ratteree opened his eyes and smiled. "Congratulations, Chris. You've done well."

A murmur of agreement broke out from the others.

"A job well done for you, too, Brian," said Ratteree. "Even though you flagged there at the last and made Chris do all the talking, but then maybe you'll adjust his bill for that." He winked, then asked Murchison and Dixon to join them all for sherry. Murchison declined.

After everyone else had filed out of the room, Dixon turned to Murchison. "Don't worry," he sneered. "You don't have to adjust my bill. Just keep away from me. You're lucky you're alive at all. You exist at the sufferance of forces you don't even understand." His voice was suddenly sinister.

"You're fired, by the way," he hissed. "I never want to see you again."

Though Chris was clearly angry, he seemed in control. Rather than turning red, his skin became a pale ivory, almost gray. "You will also stay away from Morgana Stone, if you know what's good for you," he whispered through gritted teeth. "She is facing a world that she cannot comprehend, and that you cannot guard her against."

Dixon's eyes seemed to bore into Murchison's guts, making Murchison hot and feverish. Sweat broke out all over his body, and his knees began to give way. Try as he might, he couldn't seem to break eye contact with the man. He had the strange feeling that he *wasn't allowed to.* Then Chris looked away, and the paralysis ended.

"I think I'll take sherry with the others," said Chris, suddenly calm.

Murchison was left alone, still sweating and feeling drained as if he'd had the flu for a week. Odd pictures of bilious-colored shapes with fuzzy textures filled his mind. What the hell was happening to him? Was he sick? Or was this what happened when someone gave up drinking?

Murchison tried to concentrate on the fact that Dixon had

fired him. The attorney/client relationship was broken. Plus Murchison planned to see Morgana Stone as much as he wanted. Morgana could take care of herself. They certainly didn't need Chris Dixon's permission to do anything.

● 71 ●

The humid night air was oppressive yet typical for Congreve in mid-June. Though Morgana was soaked with perspiration, she still felt great. It was as if all evil were gone from the world. After almost two weeks of silence since Calloway, Brian had called her again and asked her to have supper. It was wonderful just to be with him and talk about absurd things.

Brian was in high spirits, too, and his attitude was infectious. He had taken her to dinner in a Greek restaurant, and they had eaten lemon soup and meat on a skewer and swapped yarns with a pair of cops who were in there. Afterward, walking in the dark down Oglethorpe Street, he held her close.

"So, tell me about outlaw women," she said, laying her head on his shoulder as they walked. "I hear it's a horrible life."

"What?" asked Murchison. "Why do you bring that up?"

"Fran Maitland. She came by yesterday to tell me how bad you are for some spiteful purpose all her own."

"That must have been a two-day visit," Murchison remarked, smiling.

Morgana wrapped her arm around him tighter as she wiped a line of sweat off her forehead and flung the little splatters of moisture into space.

"Women beyond the law." Murchison laughed. "It was one of my projects when I was younger. Women who like to live on the edge. Motorcycle girls. Dope-runner women. Most of them middle class and in rebellion. Women like you who genuinely like danger. I even wrote a book on it, but my girlfriend at the time burned it up. Death of a great manuscript."

"So, I didn't know you were engaged to be married once. Why didn't that come off?"

"Her parents took a sudden dislike to me," Murchison said as he ran his hand up and down her side.

"I hear Bitsy's dad was real attached to his suits," Morgana supplied.

Murchison pulled Morgana's hair playfully. "Am I naked before the world? Are my most intimate secrets bantered around on the street?"

Morgana pulled his shirttail out and rubbed his moist, perspiring skin. "I think I'm jealous," she pouted. "Bitsy was *the* Congreve debutante in our time."

"I don't think you need to worry about debs," Murchison said. "But women who like danger . . . I go weak at the knees around them." He turned to kiss Morgana full on the mouth; then they walked all the way down past Main Street necking like teenagers. All the shops were closed for the night. Bats flitted around the steeple of a downtown church. A car passed, bathing them in the lemon yellow of its headlights. Then, as suddenly, darkness flushed back. A shadowy cat slinked into an alley. Night lights swarmed with bugs.

"It's funny," he said, "how this town doesn't seem to hold much for us."

"Yeah," said Morgana. "I've decided to go back to Columbia. There's nothing to hold me here now."

Murchison paused. "You didn't tell me you were thinking about that."

"Well, you haven't been around," Morgana said. "You screwed me, then disappeared for two weeks. I had to work my problems out alone."

Murchison got serious. "Well, I can see why you don't want to stay here. Not with Columbia University and all of New York City panting to have you back."

In silence, he walked her down Lamb Street toward his old family house. "The old man stole this property from somebody when he was young. He stole a pile of real estate one way or another, and then put it in a trust because he thought I was a crook. Now I guess it'll stop with me. It's been a long time since I came here. Couldn't face it. Look, Morgana, I'm sorry I snubbed you, but I have my own problems. I'm trying to pull myself together." He put both arms around her. "I . . . care for you . . . very much," he whispered.

Morgana watched as he opened the door with his key. She let him lead her into the darkness. The house had the air of an abandoned palace waiting for the return of an exiled king. They walked from room to room among dustcovered furniture and lusterless black mirrors.

As they reminisced about the past, Murchison took her upstairs and opened a window in his old bedroom to let in the night air. The yard was weed-grown, and bats and nighthawks dipped by the windows in swift pursuit of insects. An abandoned rabbit hutch stood next to an empty doghouse and a shed with the door hanging limp on its hinges. A sickle moon the color of old ivory rode high in the cloudless sky.

They talked about their childhood summers on Robinson's Island. "I never killed the shark," Morgana confessed. "It was just a story my father made up. He killed it."

"I'm still impressed," Murchison answered. "I couldn't even imagine witnessing the combat."

"You know, I used to watch you from a distance in the summers. You were always out on your sailboat. As a teenager, I wanted to have an affair with you. I've always been irresistibly attracted to you." She leaned into him and nuzzled the base of his throat.

"You'll think this is low," Murchison said as he held her to him, "but when I was a teenager, I used to lie in bed in this very room and dream of your body while I masturbated."

"I think it's deliciously low," Morgana said, wrapping her arms around his neck.

The bed was stripped to the mattress. Murchison drew her to it, undressing her with much pausing for long kisses from his wet, anxious mouth. Then he got on top of her and got a big erection inside her. She gripped him between her thighs while he thrust into her repeatedly. "I'd like for you to have my kid," he said softly. "You're the only woman I've ever said that to."

Afterward, they lay in a great sadness, both silent; Morgana was wrapped in regrets that she could never carry his child. Unable to express to him her sorrow, she traced a finger from the tip of his nose down to the middle of his chest, down to his navel with its line of hair beneath. She touched his genitals, gently clasping them.

In a moment of longing, she willed that they heal and bear life once more—that they splash inside her a fertile seed. She willed that they could be complete as a couple and know love and peace and have a child.

After a time, she got up and crossed the room. As she reached the door, he called, "The water's turned off. You can't use the bathroom."

She paused, her nude body leaning against the doorframe. "So what do you suggest?" She giggled. "Should I go in the backyard?"

"That would be exciting," Murchison said as he got up to join her.

Distracted, Morgana rummaged around in Murchison's old desk. There was a quartz paperweight, old letters, a funny hair bracelet. She picked up the hair and examined it in the soft, blue darkness. "What is this thing?" she asked, suddenly frantic.

"I don't know." Murchison squinted. "I've never seen it before."

Morgana held it up to the moonlight coming through the window. It was like a little pigtail, tied at each end with . . . thread? Or horsehair? An odd chill went through her. Carefully, she began to go through all the objects on the desk.

"Brian," she whispered fiercely, "tell me what this is."

"Hey, I told you I don't know," Murchison said, trying to turn Morgana around. "What's wrong with you?"

Then she found it. A scrap of paper with "Brian

Murchison" written backwards on it. Her heart started to pound. She held the woven hair up against Murchison's head to compare hair color. It was identical.

"He's been here," she said, her voice rising with terror. "He's been here to try to get near your mind."

Murchison grabbed her by the shoulders and held her firmly. "What is wrong with you? Who's been here?"

"Chris Dixon. He's out to get you! I've seen these things before!" She flung the hair from her in revulsion.

"You're crazy! There's no such thing as sorcery! Don't believe that crap!"

"No! No!" Morgana screamed. "Please don't let it be true!"

As Murchison shook her violently, Morgana felt herself retreat into a posture of near-frozen withdrawal.

She crossed the room to pick up the amulet. She put it in her pocket.

That bastard Dixon was going to get them one by one. Just like Clarence Fuller and her mother. He was going to get them. The only way to stop him was to kill him.

• 72 •

"Lynn tells me she's going to marry the new minister," mumbled Ryan Stafford. He was paralyzed down one entire side of his body and spoke only with difficulty. The right side of his mouth curled down, and his right eye watered constantly. His right hand twisted inward like a claw. A book of crossword puzzles lay open on his lap. His socks drooped down over his ankles.

It was Sunday evening and Morgana had driven out to see him. It was an old town north of Congreve, a summer residence for planters' families in earlier centuries where women and children would come to higher ground in order to escape the heat and mosquitos of the coast while the men stayed with the slaves in the stagnant, fetid rice fields. Graceful homes had been built surrounded by oaks and hollies, magnolias and boxwoods, and a town had grown up with churches and small stores and winding lanes.

Now the town was being assailed by population crush and "good growth." The fifteen miles of live-oak-shrouded road on the way to Congreve had been savaged to make room for turn lanes to the new apartment complexes.

From where Morgana and Ryan Stafford sat on the veranda of the old wooden house, they could see headlights of cars in almost continuous circulation along the narrow road. The trees were a futile screen against the flashing lights, which flared across the old man's face in repeated spurts. The old people in the nursing home seemed like passengers on a frail ship of refugees stranded on an alien and unfriendly planet.

"I—I'm glad to hear that, Mr. Stafford," said Morgana weakly. "I know she'll be very happy." The car lights kept flashing by with the regularity of neon signs. A broken muffler tore up the night. Morgana was looking for anything, any information she could find about Chris Dixon. Stafford had written letters to the newspaper about the unhallowed ground. Drena was buried there. Chris Dixon had shown her Cynthia McAlister in the crypt there. Morgana knew it all was linked. She was seeking that link; but confronted with this poor crippled man, she wondered why she had thought he might be able to help.

"The young man came to see me," said Ryan. "We talked about the church. I think it was him. Lynn wasn't with him."

"Chris came alone? Why not with Lynn?" Morgana countered. The idea that Lynn was engaged to Chris was absurd. Lynn was falling into some deadly trap.

"Lynn doesn't come to see me much," Stafford struggled to say. "But she's a big girl now, and she has concerns of her own. Her marriage to Roger Frye ended badly. I guess you know that. Lynn was always high-strung, just like her mother. I had to be very patient with both of them." He fell back in his chair from the effort of talking.

Morgana rubbed her fingers over the arms of her wicker chair. A uniformed nurse moved among the old folks, handing out decaf coffee or warm milk on lap trays with little dishes of brightly colored pills.

A slight breeze brought in the smell of honeysuckle. For a brief moment, the car lights ceased and the unlighted porch was dark. Morgana could recall Ryan Stafford so well when he was a minister. He had always had infinite patience, and everyone had respected him and loved him despite the wife's erratic and often nasty behavior. That was no doubt where Lynn had gotten it.

The old man looked so fragile now, almost like dried papier mâché. A puff of wind might blow him away. Drool came out of his mouth and tears flowed continuously from his eyes. He dabbed at the wet with a Kleenex that was wadded in his good hand. He was so different from the strong man who had spent a lifetime shielding his wife and daughter.

Morgana took a deep breath. "Mr. Stafford, you wrote a letter to the newspaper," she began tentatively, "a letter of protest against the digging in the unhallowed ground next to St. Helen's. Could you tell me about it?"

Stafford leaned forward, his good eye suddenly bright. His claw hand clutched spasmodically at the chair arm, trying to get a grip. "The unhallowed ground," he croaked. "They . . . they shouldn't dig there. It has been used . . ."

Morgana's heart beat faster. "Yes?" she asked, prodding.

"The young . . . the young McAlister girl. The one who . . . who died in New Hampshire."

"Fran Maitland's sister? I mean, Fran McAlister's sister?"

Stafford breathed a sigh like air going out of a tire. "There's nothing wrong . . . with my memory. I married Fran and Roland. I know the Maitlands. Yes. It is her sister. A great tragedy for that family, the death of Cynthia McAlister. Everything seemed to fall apart for them after that. Her father lost his construction company purely through bad decisions. The mother came to me often. It seemed he simply couldn't keep his mind on business. But instead of selling out and retiring with his wealth, he kept bidding on projects that would go wrong on him. The mother died of a broken heart." He made a small gesture with his good hand. "That sounds like a minister's talk, doesn't it? But people do die of grief, you know."

"How did she die?" asked Morgana slowly. "Cynthia, I mean. What happened exactly?"

Stafford cradled his bad elbow in his good hand, rocking it as one would a baby. "They found the body in a shallow grave up there and brought it home to Congreve. It was . . . it was perfectly . . ." He struggled to pronounce the word. ". . . preserved. In a way no one could understand. The pathologists at the hospital were mystified. Particularly since it weighed so much. Nearly three hundred pounds."

"But she was a small girl . . ." mumbled Morgana.

"Yes. She was," Stafford agreed. "But it took four men to move the body in the plastic laboratory bag. We buried it at night so no one would know."

Morgana took Stafford's crippled claw in both her hands and held the dry, cold appendage. "Why? Why did you want it to be a secret? We all liked Cynthia. It was Fran—" She held back from saying how despised Fran was. Lynn and Fran had been the two outcasts of Hutton Hall, and they had hated even each other.

"We had to bury her . . . apart from the others," gasped Stafford. "She was different. Something had happened. Something terrible."

"But what had happened? What was wrong with her?"

Stafford's bony knees clicked together twice. "It was unhallowed ground, you see. We couldn't put her in the Christian earth. She was damned. There was a ritual . . . to put her soul to rest . . . so it would leave Christian folk in peace."

Morgana stared at old Reverend Stafford. He was so gentle and kind and forgiving. He was the only minister she had ever felt could understand human weakness and sin. The only minister in her life she felt held the true gift of understanding, of pardon, of forgiveness.

"Cynthia had become involved with something . . . quite terrible," the old man went on. "Something that even the church has little power over. We had to resort to ancient ritual to put her soul to rest. There was no other way."

"What was wrong with her?" repeated Morgana desperately. Even though she had known the answer ever since her mother died, Morgana had still subconsciously wanted to block it all out.

"She was . . . she was a witch."

The old man's eyes began to bulge out of his head, and his limbs shook all over with a terrible vibration.

"Mr. Stafford . . .?" said Morgana, reaching out to steady him.

"I feel like my skull is shrinking," he mumbled, grimacing horribly.

Out of the corner of his mouth poured a pinkish liquid like calamine lotion. It ran down his stringy neck and into the open white shirt. The vibrations grew so powerful that he lurched forward out of the chair and fell face down on the wooden porch.

One of the old people cried out, and while two attendants rushed to help Stafford, others moved through the crowd trying to calm everyone down. "It's all right. It's all right now. Everyone stay calm. There's nothing to be afraid of."

But Morgana knew differently. She couldn't ignore it anymore. Cynthia McAlister had been a witch when she died. Drena had experimented with witchcraft and had known where Cynthia was buried. She had left Morgana word. Drena had unleashed something terrible and she had wanted Morgana to know.

Morgana fingered the dreadful hair bracelet in her pocket. She had kept it so Chris couldn't use it again, to protect Brian Murchison. She had kept it almost like a talisman.

"I don't believe in witchcraft," said Brian Murchison. "I'm sure I should, but I don't. So there you have it. It's just one of my many shortcomings."

Exasperated by his smugness and driven by her own fears, Morgana beat her fists on the windowsill of Murchison's office. The sun was blistering, and the rusted window-unit air conditioner was obviously broken. She had told him everything she knew about Chris Dixon, but Murchison was unmoved. He wanted to go after Dixon through legal channels.

"Please, Brian," she pleaded, "don't be stupid. I watched Ryan Stafford die in front of my eyes last night! I watched my mother die! Clarence Fuller died! They all died the same way—spitting up pins and needles! You fuck with him, and he'll kill you, too! We have to get him his own way!"

Murchison slung a leg up on his desk and rocked back in his swivel chair. His manner was bland and self-satisfied. "Morgana, baby, you have your little body of knowledge, and I have mine. I'm very open about admitting that most of the law is bullshit designed to confuse the common man and help lawyers profit at his expense. So why can't you just be honest and recognize that all this mind-control shit is just that? Shit. Chris Dixon can't make someone die with his mind. That's flat-out ridiculous! Unleashing evil through witchcraft?! It's just plain mumbo jumbo!"

Morgana tried to remain calm. She lowered her voice several decibels so as not to appear hysterical. Taking the bracelet out of her pocket, she brandished it as a reminder to him.

"What I'm telling you is not the accepted academic line. What I am telling you is laughed at by the mainstream. But it's something I've seen with my own eyes. This is something

I am convinced of. Not something I read in a book. Goddammit, you were the one who saw the aura over my mother! So, wise up to the fact that you are playing with fire!"

Murchison grinned at Morgana in a way that she found infuriating. "I agree," he began, "that Chris Dixon is a first rate wacko. In another age, I might have been obliged to kill him for attacking you. But I find myself somewhat shackled by contemporary mores. If I kill him, I'll end up behind bars. So I have chosen the civilized path, which happens to be one I know pretty well. I have been practicing law many years and I do know something about it. That's the only way I know to get him."

Morgana shook her head. She had needed to share her thoughts with someone, so she had come to Murchison. But he didn't seem to understand. He was off on another track, raging about what Dixon had done to Lynn Stafford and how he was going to report it to the Reverend Ratteree. He was convinced that was the only way to get Dixon out of their lives. But Morgana knew differently. Chris Dixon would never go away. He could only die.

"You go to Ratteree about him, and Chris Dixon will sue you for slander! He'll hire the biggest firm in town to beat you! You're the one who tells me people get as much justice as they can afford. Chris can afford plenty. He'll smother you!" Morgana screamed.

"Thanks for the vote of confidence," Murchison said. "All I need to do is bite off a piece of him. He can't take that kind of pressure. Not after what he narrowly skittered out of in Tennessee. The least breath of more scandal, and Ratteree will run him out of town."

"He will kill you!" Morgana continued to scream. "Can't you see that, you stupid shithead!"

"The Vietnamese tried to kill me, and they were a hell of a lot meaner than he is," Murchison said quietly.

Morgana's voice trembled with pleading emotion. "Please, please don't go to Ratteree about Lynn Stafford! Chris is not going to come at you with a gun! Didn't you see the news about that guy at The Military who killed his wife?

Chris was into him somehow. I know it. Chris had a drifter girl named Cerise over there baby-sitting for them. He's tied up with that murder somehow! He toys with people's brains! He kills them for pleasure!"

"Morgana, I'm not sure I could accept life if I swallowed notions like that," Murchison answered slowly. "Mind control from long distances and modern-day witchcraft just don't check out with my view of reality." He held up a restraining hand. "Yes, I know what you told me about Stafford and Cynthia McAlister and all that. All it means, as far as I'm concerned, is that we're dealing with first-rate crazies. I've been around crazies all my adult career, and I've yet to meet one who had magical powers."

Eyes widening so far that the white could be seen all around them, Morgana railed at Murchison, furious. "You ignorant asshole! Don't come whining to me once you're dead!" She stormed out of his office, slamming the door so the pebble glass rattled.

Running down the narrow stairs and into the sun-blinding street, she was even angrier at herself for making such an asinine remark. "The stupid, stupid asshole!" she muttered to herself. "Why am I in love with such a fucked-up, no-mind jerk?"

Well, fuck him anyway, she told herself. She didn't need him! She didn't need any man! She'd lived without them for more than fifteen years. She could take care of herself.

• 74 •

Later that same Monday Chris Dixon went to see Wayne Mosley up at the county jail in the patch of buggy woods off the Street Road in North Congreve.

Everyone knew Wayne was crazy. Chris was aware that Wayne had told his jailers that the minister had made him do it. But everyone knew that Wayne hadn't been inside a church since he had been married ten years ago. Only the psychiatrists didn't think Wayne was crazy. They had been specially selected by the solicitor so they wouldn't pronounce Wayne crazy. That way, Wayne could die in the electric chair.

Still, Chris had to be careful. That cadet who had been in love with Debra had phoned the church, half out of his head over her death. Faith had talked with him, and when the boy made his wild accusations about Debra and Chris, she had hung up on him indignantly. Then he had phoned both the Congreve newspaper and Debra's parents on the Isle of Charity with the same story, but no one had been able to make sense of what he was saying. It was all so unpleasant. But the cadet had finally left today, at least. He was off in the army now. The Military had verified that.

Chris went through the entry book procedure at the front desk, clipped the plastic ID to his jacket lapel, and strolled down the corridor. A steel door was opened by a guard in an armored booth that sat like the hub of a wheel at the intersection of all the corridors. Prisoners milled around the cell corridors wearing the army fatigues and shower shoes that were jail attire. A heavy stench of cabbage came from the kitchen. Guards were dripping with perspiration in the heat.

The interview room was a tiny one with no windows, painted cinder-block walls, a wobbly table, and two plastic chairs. Cigarette burns marked the edges of the table like milling on a coin. "Fuck you butt hole" had been written with magic marker on the wall. Chris felt the heat for the first time in the airless room. He wondered why the county wouldn't at least air-condition the part of the jail where visitors came.

Two guards brought Wayne in handcuffed. Apparently the jail was so crowded these days that Wayne was sleeping in a corridor. Normally he wasn't even handcuffed, because, since Debra's murder, he had been gentle as a lamb. Only his wild talk about Reverend Dixon had dictated the current precautions. Still, Chris and Wayne were allowed to talk in private without a guard standing by. Chris had especially requested that.

Chris had come willingly to see this poor soul who associated him somehow with his misfortune. Yes, it was terrible about Debra. No, he hadn't really known her, although apparently she had been attending his church just before her death. That was why he felt somehow close to the tragedy. That was why he felt he had to try to find answers, to discover for himself whether he might have been able to do something to prevent it.

When Wayne was brought in, Chris introduced himself as if they had never met. With a thump of the heavy door, the guards went out. Activity in the corridor hub could be seen through reinforced glass. Clanks and bangs from the kitchen penetrated the room. They were alone.

Wayne sat on the edge of his chair looking at Chris warily. "Why'd you act like you don't know me?" he asked. "Are you ashamed to know me?"

"Is there anything I can do for you?" asked Chris, ignoring the question. "Is there anything I can do to lighten your burden?"

Tears began streaming down Wayne's face. "I didn't mean to kill her. I just lost control of myself there for a long time. You let me do it. You just sat and watched me plan it. You helped me plan it." His voice was plaintive and unaccusing, a simple statement of fact.

"I could take a message to someone, if you wish," Chris proposed. "Your family perhaps? Your boys?"

Wayne grimaced, fighting back the tears. "I'm dead to them," he pouted. "I'm already dead, and I want to remain dead."

"Is there no one else?" Chris asked again.

Wayne gulped down the lump in his throat. "Cerise," he said in a choked voice.

"Yes? I see Cerise quite often," Chris said. "It would be simple enough for me to take her a message."

"Tell her I love her. Tell her I did it for her, not because I'm evil or anything, but because I just lost my mind. I can barely remember what was going on for whole weeks at a time."

"Cerise has confided in me," Chris went on. "She wants a memento. A lock of your hair."

Wayne gave him an up-from-under look, his eyes filled with faint and futile hope. "Are you serious?" he asked.

From his pocket, Chris produced a pair of tiny sewing scissors. "We must be quick. The guards might look in." When Wayne bent his head, Chris snipped off a piece of hair, tucking the scissors and hair into a plastic bag.

Wayne straightened up. "Tell me about her," he said longingly. "Tell me how she looks, what she says."

"She's as beautiful as ever," purred Chris. "The long dark hair is still like a waterfall; the mysterious look is in her large, dark eyes."

"What does she say? Tell me the things she says." Wayne's voice was urgent with need, pleading for comfort.

"Oh, she doesn't say much of anything," said Chris. "Mostly she's with Squirt Crawford."

"Wh—what do you mean?"

"Well, she gave up on college. I think the shock of your being a killer was too much for her. She couldn't concentrate on the future very well. She moved back to the church, and since there really isn't any room in the manse, Squirt took her into his apartment again. You know she was there before you came along."

"No . . . no I didn't." Wayne hesitated.

"Oh, really?" Chris continued. "I thought you knew. She's not very strong, that girl. She just latches onto whoever will give her shelter. All of her . . . um . . . physical skills are just her method of paying room and board. And since you're not around to provide it, she's paying someone else. He's really kind of a scrawny little wretch, this Crawford fellow, but I suppose he's good enough for her. I mean, what does it matter who she's with?"

Wayne stared at him with uncomprehending eyes. "But she asked for some of my hair . . . ? Doesn't she remember me at all? Won't she come and see me just so I can say good-bye and kiss her cheek one last time?"

Chris shot him an odd, puzzled look. "Hair? What on earth are you talking about?"

"My hair!" Wayne shouted with rising emotion. "You just took some of my hair! I'm not crazy! I know what you did!"

"My, my, we're getting riled," said Chris calmly. "I'd better call the guards. They'll know how to deal with you. I've never understood you myself."

"You son-of-a-bitch!" Wayne bellowed, lurching up out of the chair. "You made me do it! You got control of my mind somehow and made me do it!"

Chris jerked open the door and gave out a feeble cry for help. Three guards piled into the room and smacked Wayne up against the wall like a football blocking dummy. One held a hairy forearm across Wayne's throat while the other two each took a shoulder. They ground his handcuffed wrists against the cinder blocks.

"The bastard took some of my hair!" Wayne screamed. "He's got scissors and he cut some of my hair!"

It sounded so absurd that the guards burst out laughing. "Wal, shit, maybe he'll trim your toenails next, buddy-row," said one. The others laughed even louder at the joke.

"You don't believe me?" yelled Wayne. "You think I'm crazy? Search the son-of-a-bitch! It's right there in his pocket in a plastic bag! You'll see I'm not crazy!"

Chris shook his head sadly. He went out toward the hub, waited for the door to buzz open, and headed to the reception desk.

"You bastard!" Wayne screamed after him, his voice filled with a terrible pain.

At the front door to the jail, Chris paused and chatted with the sheriff, who had come out to meet such an important visitor. Chris seemed distracted, almost totally disinterested in the sheriff's earnest efforts to be polite. Taking a tattered copy of *Field and Stream* off a reception area table, he thumbed through the pages.

"He sure is a first-class mental case, ain't he?" said the sheriff.

"I'm afraid it's all too true," Chris agreed. He dropped the magazine back onto the table, gave a brief smile, and went out to his car. The air-conditioning inside felt good. It had been disgusting in the jail.

Wayne alternately wept and screamed with rage all afternoon. He said he was going to tear down the walls and kill Chris Dixon with his bare hands. The other prisoners yelled at him to shut up, and when he wouldn't, they punched him around. Wayne crouched on the floor, covering his face against the kicks and blows, still screaming that Chris Dixon had made him kill Debra and that he was going to kill Chris Dixon himself. Finally, the guards came and closed him up in solitary, a dark closet of a room with a narrow slit of light marking the guard's watch-hole.

Wayne crashed against the confining walls as if he were trying to break his bones, all the time raging and wailing. He kept this up for hours, yet no one decided to call a doctor and sedate him. The whole jail was tense and edgy with the unending display of animal madness.

Around nine o'clock, Wayne finally fell silent. Hours later, no one heard the choking noise.

When they opened the door at six the next morning, Wayne was found curled in a tight fetal knot, and the floor was drenched in blood and vomit. Roaches swarmed everywhere. A huge hairball such as you might find in the stomach of a Saint Bernard was lodged in his throat. The doctors said it had smothered him in a hideous asphyxiation. Even worse, Wayne's eyes had popped out like grapes.

The coroner said it had been some kind of brain hemmorhage. He didn't order an autopsy. The District Attorney was glad the county had been saved the expense of a trial.

Murchison knew he was being stupid from the beginning in going to Reverend Ratteree against Chris Dixon. One side of his brain kept telling him he was stupid. His secretary told him he was stupid. Morgana Stone had already told him he was stupid and had gotten into an argument with him. Still, some crazy instinct drove him on and kept him on track every time he wavered.

Lynn had given him the recording. She had signed the written transcription as well. She had talked with Murchison countless times, usually at night when he wanted to be doing something else—anything but talking with her. She dithered and backpedaled, but always she returned to the same story with all the details exact. And always she insisted she wanted the world to know about Chris Dixon.

So Murchison had called the Reverend, bluntly told him the story, and proposed a meeting. Ratteree was in no hurry, and Murchison had had to press him to set a date for the meeting on June 11. Ratteree was reluctant and expressed concern about Murchison breaching attorney-client privilege because of his recent representation of Dixon before the Committee.

"I wonder," Ratteree had said over the phone, "what you will do in the event Chris Dixon is obliged to question your ethics."

Murchison gave a barking laugh. "I wonder what you'll do," he parried, "if Dixon beats up some more women." He was pleased with himself, feeling the old bravado he hadn't felt practicing law in five years or more. He wanted to get on with it. He was going to prove he could run Chris Dixon out of town.

The stinking hot days of June had crawled by in a record

drought that parched the trees and grass and left the city gasping under a pall of dust and pollen left over from spring.

Morgana refused to see Murchison no matter how hard he tried, citing a list of grievances that included his personal habits and not really believing he had given up drinking. She didn't like Congreve, she said, and she wanted to move out without being tied emotionally to anyone. He represented forgotten things she wanted to remain forgotten. She was scared of Chris Dixon and she didn't trust Lynn Stafford and knew anything involving her would surely turn into a disaster.

Murchison had seen her on the street that morning and she had stood still for a moment, trying to find words, and then suddenly burst into tears. She'd talked about Lynn's father and how he had died vomiting at the nursing home. How Wayne Mosley, who had murdered his wife, had died vomiting. How Clarence Fuller at Hutton College and Patricia Stone had both died vomiting. She just kept repeating this. Not just normal puke, but revolting foreign objects that no one sane would have swallowed. While some of them had been insane or very nearly so at the time of death, Stafford hadn't. Morgana had been sitting there holding his hand, having a perfectly normal conversation. Morgana didn't want to think too carefully about her mother's death, but other than the final days, Patricia Stone had been perfectly normal.

Murchison had made a desperate attempt to comfort Morgana and reason with her, but she had torn away and run down lower Oglethorpe Street, leaving Murchison to twirl his straw hat on his index finger while the tourists stared at him blankly.

Murchison was still uneasy about Morgana's witchcraft theory. The power of the mind over the body. People only use ten percent of their brains. Murchison could buy that part. If they could ever learn to open up the other ninety percent, there might be latent powers there of incredible magnitude. Viz, witches were nothing more than people who had learned some form of psychokinesis through extreme concentration.

Though Murchison didn't want to believe it, still, it was unsettling. Morgana had told him in detail of some of the things she had seen in her studies. There was a woman in the mountains of North Carolina who could take the pain of childbirth out of the woman actually giving birth. Morgana had seen a woman bring forth a child from the womb without the slightest expression of pain; all the while, the witch had writhed and screamed in agony on the floor nearby.

Chris Dixon was demented, Murchison was sure of that. But there was no way he could have such evil powers as Morgana attributed to him. Sure, he had the power of the lunatic. Squirt Crawford was brimming over with it. But Squirt couldn't control people's brains; at least, not from miles away. And Dixon couldn't even control his own brain. It was absurd to think otherwise.

With all the care of the experienced lawyer, Murchison had coached Lynn before the meeting with Ratteree. He had devoted the entire morning to asking her such questions as might be asked. She answered them all smoothly and perfectly. She was exact in every detail. He had seen clients fall apart without such coaching and he wanted to take every precaution, especially since Lynn's father had just died and he knew she was even more distraught than usual.

Murchison and Lynn had lunch in a sandwich shop on Main Street and watched the clock tick toward 2 PM. Lynn was wearing a pale blue suit and white gloves, which she removed to eat a chicken salad sandwich and drink iced tea. As the time passed, Lynn began to get agitated. With hand motions and exaggerated facial expressions, she began to talk about Hutton Hall and how she had never had a chance to do well there because the other girls had all hated her and that had meant she couldn't get into a decent college. If she had gone to a decent college, she wouldn't have had to marry that clod Roger Frye and wouldn't be divorced and in this mess. She'd often thought she'd make a terrific lawyer. That was really her calling. Didn't Murchison think so? He agreed as he watched the clock strike one forty-five.

In blinding sunlight, Murchison led Lynn across Main

Street to his car. Together, they drove up to the Church of St. Martins-in-the-Field, where Ratteree had his office. The yard was shaded by old oaks. The building held an air of peace and repose. Inside the administration building, a brass plaque signaled Ratteree's office. Lynn stood staring at her own dull reflection in the plate.

"Lynn," Murchison said. "We've got to go in now. You know what's got to be done. You'll be terrific. Now, let's give 'em hell." He tried to sound enthusiastic, but his voice trailed off when the expression on her face didn't change.

Lynn allowed Murchison to lead her in like a zombie. He had just about decided to announce she was sick and call it all off when Lynn recognized the receptionist and began talking in animated fashion about how embarrassing it was to be in "such a mess"; how her mother and father had led lives untouched by the least scandal and had never had any dealings with lawyers except once when they sold an inherited farm. The receptionist looked at her curiously but said nothing.

Murchison knew he was sunk from that point. He asked Lynn if she was sick and she said yes and found the ladies' room. She stayed in there so long that Ratteree came out of his office to ask if she would like to reschedule the appointment. He was obviously sure that Lynn was scared to death of the charges she was about to level.

Lynn came out finally, and shook hands with the Bishop and called him by name. Of course he knew her father, the former minister of St. Helen's. Ratteree said that Stafford's death was a great tragedy and a loss to the community, but thank goodness he had gone quickly. Lynn accepted a Coke to settle her stomach, but she insisted on going on with the meeting.

She walked the short distance to the interior office with her jaws set tight and little knots of muscle appearing at the corners. Her eyes were wide and staring, and her nostrils kept spreading with deep breaths.

In the inner office filled with leather furniture, Chris Dixon was waiting, all smiles and condescension. Murchison was stunned by Ratteree's treachery. Lynn jerked Murchison out into the hall and, her face red with anger, hissed at him: "You get that Chris Dixon out of that room, and I mean this instant!"

Ratteree came out, a sickly grin on his face. "I think it's best in such matters if we air the issues fully with all concerned parties being present. Don't you agree?"

"What are you trying to pull?" demanded Murchison.

"I think that's a question more properly directed at you," retorted Ratteree coolly. "You've made some very serious accusations. If you lack the courage to confront the accused, then perhaps you should rethink your position."

Murchison looked at Lynn. Her eyes seemed glassy and blank. "No," she said. "I do believe you're correct. Anything I have to say had best be said in Chris's presence."

They went back into the room and seated themselves around the desk. Murchison noted that the walls of the room were filled with black and white photos of Ratteree greeting political bigwigs. Chris Dixon made a tent of his fingers and pressed them gently against his lips. His manicure was perfect; his face was composed.

"Now," said Ratteree, "let's talk about our little difficulties."

"Where would you propose we begin?" growled Murchison.

"Perhaps Lynn should tell us a bit about herself," he replied. "While I knew her father well, I haven't seen much of her."

Lynn needed no prompting to talk about herself. She leaned toward Reverend Ratteree and began to talk in a confidential way as though she were gossiping over tea at the manse. For half an hour she talked, providing ornate detail on each stage of her schooling. She expressed her familiar refrain of how she had gone to junior college because Hutton Hall had let the other girls pick on her, and that was why she had bad grades.

Next, she discussed her marriage, going into detail about her extramarital affair. As Lynn told it, she was innocent of all wrongdoing, and, while she had committed adultery, she said it was perfectly justified under the circumstances. After all, the fact that Roger Frye was a homosexual was well known and documented.

Chris and Reverend Ratteree exchanged knowing looks. Lynn lidded her eyes to shut out the terrible impression she knew she was making. Murchison slid lower in his chair. He knew he was lost.

Slowly, Ratteree edged Lynn onto the substance of the complaint. "Now, Lynn, your attorney—I presume that is his present capacity—informs me that you sought counseling from Reverend Dixon. Could you describe the circumstances, please?"

"Counseling?" said Lynn, obviously flustered. "No, I never said that. No, that's not right. I . . . well, I went to see Chris—I mean, Mr. Dixon—because he asked me to. He wanted to marry me, you see, and he made up some excuse to get me into his office. Of course, I could see it was just an excuse, because as a minister's daughter I know about human passion, and besides, he made his intentions plain quite early."

"He wanted you to marry him?" Ratteree probed.

"Oh, my, yes," Lynn answered. "We had an understanding. I was to have sex—well, I guess that's the only way you could put it—have sex with him because we were engaged to be married, and he didn't want the community to know since so many women in the parish would be jealous. I mean, all those homely unmarried creatures couldn't help but be jealous with me on my second husband and some of them without the prospect of even a first."

"I see," Ratteree continued. "And your . . . your *attorney* . . . tells me that you were bound and beaten in the church office."

Lynn's hand flew to her mouth. "Oh, my, no! That never happened! Chris would never do that to me!"

Ratteree bore in for the kill. "Well, excuse me for being stupid, Ms. Stafford, but if it never happened, then why did your lawyer claim it had?"

Lynn didn't hesitate. "I—I don't know, sir, but coming to you was Brian Murchison's idea. I mean, I'm just utterly naive about the law, and the whole thing was . . . well . . . he was supposed to sue Chris for breach of promise. Chris promised to marry me and broke a promise. Brian—I mean—Mr. Murchison, told me coming to see you would throw a good scare into Chris and make him see the light."

Ratteree took out a briar pipe with a bowl so tiny his little finger would barely fit in it. He clamped it into his jaw without lighting it. "So . . . let me understand you, Mrs. Stafford . . ." He paused. "You accused Chris without any regard for the pain it might cause him, purely because you wanted him to . . . marry you?"

"Well, like I said, I don't know anything about the law. Mr. Murchison told me to, and I had to depend on his advice, especially since Daddy's dead and there's really no one else to turn to. That's what lawyers are for, isn't it?" She reached across the table and laid her white-gloved hand on Chris's arm. He didn't draw away, just gazed at her with an expression of pity and kindness.

"Chris, honestly," Lynn pleaded, "I didn't mean to hurt you. I knew this was wrong, but he just kept pushing me to do it. He kept making me say things into tape recorders and sign statements I knew were lies. I'm sorry. I'm sorry!" Tears streamed down her face. Finally, she jumped up and fled from the room.

Ratteree took a long time to look down his nose at Murchison. "I imagine you'll be hearing from Chris's attorney directly," he said. "Also no doubt from the state grievance committee."

"Fuck you, Ratteree," Murchison spat out. He got up so suddenly he knocked his chair over backward.

He walked out into the church yard. Halfway across the graveyard, Lynn turned to face him. She pressed one gloved hand against her chest delicately. He called after her, but she ran away, looking back to see if he was following.

"Mother-fucking bastard!" yelled Murchison to no one in particular. He kicked a tombstone.

Everything had certainly gone up in smoke, and Murchison had made a total fool of himself. No doubt the grievances would be filed, and Lynn would tell her berserk story again, adding even more lurid details about his coercion. Murchison figured Ratteree would be extra helpful in assisting Lynn on filling in all the details. Disbarment would come next. The bar was merciless with solo practitioners when it came to grievance issues.

But why, he asked himself, should he give a shit? He had never really liked practicing law. Dixon could sue Murchison and get zilch, since all his assets were tied up in that crazy spendthrift trust for children who would never appear. Murchison figured he'd be able to get a job at the marina scraping boats. At least that was honest work.

After nearly a month without booze, Murchison decided he needed a drink. Not only did he need one, he deserved one. Not only did he deserve one, it was almost like a territorial imperative that he put a drink inside himself.

What else did he have to do? He had no one to turn to. And nothing special to do.

• 76 •

For the next week, the heat wave continued unbroken. It was the nineteenth of June and summer was well settled in. All over the city, trees and shrubs lost yellowed leaves, shedding their foliage in nature's effort to carry less baggage. The air-conditioning compressor in the big central unit for St. Helen's blew, necessitating a special Tuesday-night meeting of the vestrymen to discuss expenses. The budget, like all church budgets, was strained. The fiscal conservatives had no trouble remembering the days before air conditioning and urging the congregation to swelter through the summer with the windows open.

Chris ended the logjam by introducing a new church member who had generously offered to bear the entire expense of repair. The officers of the church were stunned. Despite the wealth of the parish, most members were tight with their wallets. This was unheard of.

The new member was in the used-tire business and was frequently seen in local TV ads touting his sales and service from a variety of North Congreve locations. He was not quite what St. Helen's was accustomed to by way of membership. He wore white shoes and a matching white belt. He drove a fire-engine-red Cadillac with the name of his company emblazoned on it. Still, he wrote out the check right in front of them with a fountain pen and then waved it in the air to dry the ink. He embraced Chris and thanked him for doing the Lord's work. There being no other business, the meeting broke up early.

Charles "Chuck" Ransom Prettyman was the head vestryman. Short and corpulent with a shock of full snow-white hair, he had the air of a man whose opinions were always treated with careful respect. As a prominent Congreve banker, he kept his fingers in most financial pies and had surrounded himself with a chorus of yes-men. He had maintained an unaccustomed silence during the meeting, as though there were more weighty matters on his mind. Chris Dixon was not surprised when Chuck pulled him aside after the meeting and said, "Let's talk."

Chris took him to the church office and poured his favorite Napoleon brandy. Chuck said he hoped the drink didn't come from the church budget, and Chris joked that he had bought it by cutting corners on air-conditioning repairs. Chuck laughed hugely at that. He knew the size of Chris's personal bank account, and appreciated inherited wealth. He had himself inherited controlling shares in the bank from his father.

"Chris, lemme talk to you like a son. Okay?" said Chuck, swirling his tulip glass of brandy and giving it a careful sniff.

"Go right ahead . . . Dad," Chris answered, smiling.

"I won't talk about your preaching. Everybody else does that for me. And of course they think it's first-rate. You've done a great job of balancing the . . . uh . . . the newer element with the old. Keeping them on Thursday nights is just fine by me and everybody else.

"What I'm really impressed by is how you've beefed up the church finances. You had a reputation for that in Tennessee, and that was how come I voted to bring you down here. No, don't thank me. I'm sure you knew I had a major role in that. Anyhow, all that aside, we got problems, Chris."

Chris evaded Chuck's gaze only for a second. He seemed to be glancing out the window at the darkened graveyard below. Then he looked sincerely and intently into Chuck's eyes. "Please, let's be open about this. What's the trouble?"

"It's that fella you got working on the roof. I mean, I'm just amazed he's doing the job for room and board, and there's no complaint about his work. You know me and finances. Nobody rushes ahead of me in wanting to save a buck. And here we're talking thousands of bucks. Why, the man's a human roofing machine."

Chris gave a slight, knowing smile. "Yes, but I know that it's gotten out that he's done time in prison, and some people don't like that."

Chuck seemed almost relieved. "Somehow I knew you were already aware of it. I told all the vestrymen you couldn't be blank ignorant of what the congregation was thinking. Now, understand where I'm coming from, Chris. I know your style. You wanted to save money, and that's just great. I know we see eye to eye on the limits of Christian goodness." He chuckled lightly. "I mean, I'm prominent in this church, but I can't turn into a communist at the bank just because of Christian strictures about giving to the poor."

"Not with my money, anyway," Chris said, joining in the humor.

Chuck made a slight gesture toward the healing wound on Chris's face. "I mean, look at you. Try to do something for the poor, and what do you get? Belted in the chops. Like I always say, look after your own poverty first. And you are doing just a super job with fund-raising. I was talking to

Reverend Ratteree at the country club just the other day, and I put in a good word for you." Chuck leaned forward and patted Chris on the knee affectionately. "Yes, I know about that crazy dame up in Tennessee. I know all about it. Nothing goes on in this town I don't know about. And I know about the other thing, too."

Chris's mouth twitched just the least bit at the edge.

"Hell, Ratteree and I go way back. We grew up together. There's no way he's going to hold back on me." He slapped Chris's knee again. "Hey, relax. I understand. The Stafford women never were too tightly wrapped. Everybody knows that Lynn is half out of her mind. I mean, these things happen. A good-looking young guy like you is bound to be a lightning rod for that kind of crazy accusation. Anyhow, Ratteree tells me he doesn't believe a word of what she says."

Chris rubbed the back of one hand and cast his eyes down modestly. "I appreciate your confidence. It's just that lawyer—Brian Murchison. He seems so devious. His . . . drinking habit. He's like a loose cannon. You don't know what he'll do from one moment to the next."

"Hey, not to worry. Like I say, the local grievance committee'll be on him like a duck on a June bug. It's a pity Murchison doesn't owe anybody any money. Most lawyers exist off of thirty-day notes. Bank can stop their line of credit and have them on their knees in twenty-four hours. But he lives like some kind of bum."

"What can I do about him?" Chris asked earnestly.

"Leave it to me. This just requires a more circuitous route. He can't operate without malpractice insurance. I got some buddies here and there in insurance. I mean, what banker hasn't? Do you catch my drift?"

"Yes, I believe I do." Chris smiled.

"And I think you ought to go see some lawyer friends of mine and explore the idea of filing a lawsuit against that little pissant." He winked. "I mean, providing you aren't such a Christian you feel like you have to turn the other cheek or something."

Chris looked at his lap, then gave Chuck a sly up-from-under look. "These irresponsible lawyers have to be curbed. They're becoming a national menace. Insurance rates are going up for everyone."

Chuck laughed loudly. "I knew we'd get in harness together. Now, this Crawford fella, you've got to let him go, Chris. I mean, he's done time and all. Some folks are real upset about that, particularly since he actually lives next to the church. It's just a matter of time before this whole thing explodes."

Chris tensed. "Look, Chuck, he's almost through with the roof. It would be a real mess if we had to go out and hire a contractor now. More meetings like tonight." He rubbed his hands together. "I imagine I could push him along and have it wrapped up by the end of June. Do you think you can hold them off until then?"

Chuck chewed his lower lip thoughtfully. "I do hate to spend money unnecessarily. Maybe I can keep them quiet that long. Yeh, I bet I can. I'll accept full responsibility. Yeh, I'll do that."

On the way out, Chuck paused and scanned the titles of some of the books lining the walls. "Is this that Marquis de Sade fella?" he asked. "I mean, the sadomasochist guy?"

"The very man," said Chris openly. "I have to keep abreast of evil as well as good."

"Yeh." Chuck laughed. "There's a touch of the demon in all of us. Especially bankers."

Chris stayed up most of the night reading. He didn't have much time.

When it first opened, Fran Maitland had adored the new downtown renewal project with its galleries of expensive stores like Lord & Taylor, Talbots, and Banana Republic. It had once given her enormous satisfaction to be able to breeze in and command attention from multiple salesclerks as she ran up huge bills on her charge cards. In her opinion, the renewal was just what Congreve needed to revitalize the decaying downtown area and bring in high-quality stores. It was just perfect, just like New York, Atlanta, and Charleston.

Usually Fran went with a friend from her charge account stratum to have lunch in one of the intimate French restaurants before they went shopping all afternoon.

Lately, however, Fran had shunned her friends, and even shopping didn't hold its old allure. She was losing her figure since she was carrying Cynthia, but she didn't mind. Instead, she found herself going almost daily to the carriage house behind St. Helen's to meet Squirt Crawford. He would come down from the ladder at lunchtime or at twilight, depending on his mood. He was so different from anyone she had ever known, so powerful and self-sufficient. When he first touched her, Fran had felt like a schoolgirl. He was so down-to-earth, manly, and imposing. And Fran loved sex with him because he loved her growing belly. Anyway, if he didn't want to do it at lunch, he'd tell her without making her wait too long. Always, she felt the rejection keenly and worried if he would want her in the evening.

Fran had never had such sex. Squirt Crawford made her soar to heights she'd never dreamed possible. Rafe Artigues had been a child by comparison. She avoided Rafe now like the plague. And Roland wasn't even worth considering. He scarcely touched her anyway, and when he did, she was totally unresponsive. He didn't seem to notice.

Squirt talked to her in his nasal hick accent, and his breath often smelled of peanuts or packaged sweets. His body looked emaciated and undernourished, like a tenant farmer who lived off fatback and cornbread. But his strength was incredible. He dominated her with a kind of mystical power that made her body totally submissive to his. She sweated from every pore and lost all control, screaming and crying out violently, tearing at his flesh.

Fran found it to be like a drug she couldn't get enough of. Thoughts of it consumed her all day and into the night while she lay next to a snoring Roland. She neglected all her club-going and bridge playing. She practically forgot she had a horse stabled out at the hunt club. She didn't want to risk running into Rafe anyway.

More unsettling, Fran was becoming forgetful even about things she knew threw Roland into a frenzy if she forgot them, like what he wanted for dinner, getting his shirts from the laundry, or picking up the parts for the sailboat that had arrived at the marine supplier.

Fran found herself in a constant daze in which fears of the loss of all she prized hung perpetually over her head. She couldn't stay away from Squirt, but she knew her absence from normal haunts was becoming obvious. Friends were making remarks to Roland about not seeing her out or at lunch at the club. And Roland was constantly pissed about some chore she had neglected to do. Fran figured it was because she had refused to get an abortion, and Roland had figured out that he couldn't afford another divorce. Still, sometimes Fran wondered if she was simply going to break down and start screaming with fear. But she could always use the excuse that she was pregnant and felt horrible, even though she felt the best she ever had in her life.

That excuse had gotten Fran through many bad situations lately. She had run over a neighbor child's bicycle and crushed it flat with the car. She had walked out of a shop wearing clothes she was trying on and leaving hers behind.

There had been a stink over that until Fran reminded them how much money she spent there.

Even Roland was acting different. He had given up criticizing her shortcomings and now seemed to be plotting something. Sometimes she caught him giving secret signals to people around her. When she demanded to know what he was doing, he would only stare at her in his familiar sly manner. Fran didn't really know how to combat it. So she ignored him, which was easy most of the time because Roland was almost never home.

As a consequence, Fran spent a lot of time naked and sweating in Squirt Crawford's bed. There, she could forget the problems in her life and, most of all, she didn't hear her sister's voice there. She forgot Cynthia's laughter, which would come floating out of corners of rooms at odd moments and so absorb Fran that she would call out to her sister without thinking about who was with her at the time.

It seemed like all Fran did now was live for the moments when Squirt was humping away on her, like she was some *Tobacco Road* slut. She needed that release as surely as a heroin addict needed a fix. Then and only then did she feel she was alive and pregnant with the real Cynthia, the Cynthia who would be her child, not the Cynthia who had been her sister.

This Wednesday evening, Fran drove her Cadillac back home at close to eight o'clock. After seeing Squirt, she had stopped at the club briefly and had heard that something weird was going on that involved Lynn Stafford and Brian Murchison, but no one seemed to know the details. Fran didn't really even care. She had just gone so that she could tell Roland she had been there. He was supposed to be doing rounds at the hospital anyway and wouldn't be home until after ten. She knew she had time to fix him dinner and have everything normal when he came in.

"The trashy little man," Fran said aloud, following it with a high, nervous giggle. She was thinking of Squirt and their few hours together earlier. Suddenly, she became aware of her own voice and stopped, listening. She didn't want to hear Cynthia speak to her. Cynthia hadn't spoken all day. Maybe she would leave Fran alone today.

Fran opened the iron gate to her driveway and drove into the narrow space next to the house. The garbage cans had been left in the drive by the sanitation workers, but Fran didn't notice. Her clothes were a bit wrinkled and her makeup was smeared, but she didn't care. She looked all right. She couldn't bathe anyway because Cynthia always talked to her when she was in the bath. They had taken baths together when they were little, Fran and Cynthia, and Fran could still remember Cynthia splashing and talking in the baby talk she thought was cute when she was four.

Edging in the side door, Fran stopped, aghast. Roland was sitting in an armchair with his standard rye and water beside him. Roland never drank scotch because he didn't believe in consuming foreign products, so the scotch was kept for others at Fran's insistence. The bottle was out now—Glenfiddich, because Fran always insisted on the best. The triangular green bottle stood next to Rafe Artigues, who seemed a little unsteady as he tried to rise and instead settled back in the chair.

"Hello, dear," said Roland. His voice sounded mean. The room was deep in shadow and Fran could barely discern his face. The carved gilt mirrors reflected vacancy.

"Roland . . . Rafe . . . ? What's going on?" Fran heard herself say weakly.

"Nothing," Roland said as he got up to kiss Fran. "I just invited Rafe to dinner." Roland was wearing grass green trousers and a pink Lacoste shirt. His eyes were lidded. His voice purred like a torturer extracting a confession. "You seem so fond of him, I thought we needed to get to know one another better."

"Damn good scotch you keep in the old manor house," said Rafe in his put-on squire accent. He was balancing a glass on one knee and an ashtray on the other. His voice was slurred. Behind his head were sea-green-and-white-striped wallpaper and prints of white egrets, one of which held a frog in its scissor bill.

Fran sat down on the edge of her beige Chippendale sofa,

but stood up again almost immediately. Nervously, she straightened a picture on the wall, an English eighteenth-century oil of a scarlet-coated hunter and hounds, in the fashion of Stubbs. Her mind twisted and turned desperately, seeking a bolt hole. The room was dark. They couldn't see her exactly. Rafe was drunk and he had obviously been there some time. "I've been out riding a bit," she lied. "I've neglected my horse lately. I knew he needed some exercise and I guess I just lost track of the time. Anyway, I—I thought you were doing rounds tonight," she said to Roland.

Roland lifted his drink to his lips and paused, looking over the rim. His eyes were the only feature on his face that showed. "Plans change," he said. He sipped and held the liquor in his mouth as he set the glass down before he swallowed. "My, my, you must really be feeling better, darling," Roland said with what to Fran sounded like sarcasm. "Is riding the best thing for our little Cynthia, do you think?"

Fran's eyes roamed the walls. Rafe is here, she kept thinking. If Roland suspects I'm doing something, it can't be with Rafe because he's been here. Who would he think of? What was he up to?

Roland dabbled an index finger in his drink and sucked the liquor from it. "Listen, Rafe, m'man," he said. "Why don't you stand over there with Fran."

"What for?" asked Rafe, sitting forward in his chair.

"You make such a cute couple," Roland said, smiling, his voice soft and poisonous.

Rafe grinned stupidly. "We do, rather. Say, now, why don't you lend me the use of your wife one evening when she's unoccupied? I'd rather like that, you know."

"Just stand over there," said Roland in a firmer voice. He produced a revolver from under the chair cushion.

Fran's heart started pounding. She knew the gun. It was the Colt Python with the long barrel, one of those magnums like the cops in the movies love. Roland was always cleaning it and making it shine. He could shoot the hearts and spades out of playing cards with it.

Rafe did a "surely you're joking" routine until Roland put

the barrel up against the side of Rafe's head. Then Rafe began to sweat, and his eyes showed white in the dark. He did what he was told, being careful not to touch Fran.

Fran was too frightened even to cry as Roland shepherded them up the stairs toward the bedroom. She knew his cruelty and his violence. She had seen him stop his car to shoot a stray dog, just crippling it so he could walk over and blow the brains out while the poor thing kicked and struggled. She was suddenly terrified.

Roland backed them up against the big canopied bed with the carved posts that Fran had gotten at Congreve Reproductions. Everything she loved about the room seemed evanescent: the Colefax and Fowler chintz pattern on the armchairs, the framed architectural views, the chinchilla throw on the bed. It was all like cheap theatrical props on a stage set. Items barely noticed as the action unrolled.

"Both of you take your clothes off," Roland ordered.

Fran obeyed. It was all a nightmare, the culmination of her fears over the last few months.

"Now, see here—" Rafe started to argue in a tone he used only for servants. Roland said nothing. In silence, he lashed the man across the face with the barrel of the gun. Bleeding, Rafe obeyed and stripped naked.

"Now get on the bed," Roland ordered.

"You can't get away with this," Fran said hysterically. "You can't pretend to have caught us. Someone will know you were home from the beginning. You'll be caught."

There was a cruel edge to Roland's laugh. "Okay, big boy," he said to Rafe. "You like her so much, now fuck her."

"What will you do?" Rafe blubbered.

"I'm not going to shoot you, stupid." Roland gave a smutty grin. "I just want to see why you're so good."

Fran moved like an automaton through what followed. Rafe actually got an erection. This apparently appealed to his love of danger in some perverted way. His face held a rapt, excited expression. Blood ran down from where he had been hit with the gun and dripped on her neck, into her hair.

As his thrill mounted, Rafe's hands wrung her flesh, but Fran felt no pain. Her dazed eyes read the names of the perfumes and cosmetics lined up on the dresser: Estée Lauder. Revlon. Clinique. She had never felt so trashy, so utterly slovenly and unclean.

Roland took repeated snapshots of them screwing. The white stabs of light froze them in peculiar forms. Dark shapes danced on the walls like shadow puppets.

When Rafe was finished, Roland dragged Fran by the arm downstairs and threw her out of the house naked. She lay there crumpled on the small patch of lawn. He chucked her car keys after her.

"Go charge some new clothes somewhere," he told her. His laugh echoed flatly on the night air.

• 78 •

Chris Dixon could feel his strength growing with each day. He was draining the energy from Cynthia McAlister. Soon he would have exhausted it, but his rebirth was only four days away, and there would be another body then. He had almost total control. By heavy concentration, he could project his powers over staggering distances. Ryan Stafford and Wayne Mosley had been easy to verify. They were the farthest yet. Morgana Stone was harder because he hadn't killed her. It wasn't certain how he had affected her on the beach, but it was bound to have been strongly. Anyway, he hadn't wanted to actually kill her, just scare her so that she would come to him.

It was only Faith he feared. The rest of the human race were just jabbering animals who could be destroyed as easily as paper dolls. But Faith terrified him. Her smooth skin that never had a blemish or a wrinkle. Her calm gaze that cut through his flesh like icicles probing his heart. She, and only she, filled him with palpable terrors that were hot and cold at the same time and made his breathing difficult like when he had asthma as a child and had to lie in a dark room with the humidifier running day and night and be carried to the hospital for shots.

Chris had hated asthma. It had filled him with a perpetual fear that his throat and nose would clog and he wouldn't be able to breathe. His mother would go off shopping, promising to leave him only for a moment. She would call from the doorway into the dark room where he lay fidgeting and restless with only his imagination for comfort, promising to be back soon. The door would close. He could hear the car engine start and go down the drive. The time would tick away endlessly. Then his breathing would get difficult. He'd lay his head back, gasping, afraid to make sudden movements, afraid that exerting himself would shut down his breathing altogether. He would want to scream for his mother, but he was too afraid to scream; he was afraid to be afraid.

Prep school had ended all of that. Amid the merciless bullying from all the guys, he had learned to lash out with violence and watch them cower back. He had gotten up the nerve to go out for crew and found that he actually had a body that could be used. It was lightweight crew and it took him years to develop his muscles after his childhood inaction, but still, he developed, and with his body grew the certainty of his will.

Chris had never actually fought with people physically. Rather, he had learned the pleasure of secret revenge. He would use a razor to slash a closetful of clothes belonging to someone who had bullied him. The jerk would come back to discover the destruction and afterward live a prey to nameless fears, never knowing who had victimized him. There had been one particular lout on the football team who had a soft spot for stray animals. He'd rampage through the dorm at night terrorizing the little guys, but he adopted a stray mutt and kept it in a shed. Chris had fed it rat poison one night late, then hung around outside the lout's room listening to him cry once he had discovered the dead dog. That had felt really good.

Shortly after that, Chris had set his French teacher's car on fire because she had laughed at his pronunciation in class. She had let her insurance lapse because her measly salary wasn't enough to make ends meet, and the headmaster had actually taken up a collection to try to buy her a new car. Chris had put in a dollar.

Whenever someone picked on him, Chris had learned to take a secret, violent revenge that was all his own. He had learned that people were so high-strung with fears that any anonymous vandalism sent them into withdrawal as severe as that of a heroin addict deprived of a fix. They crept around suspicious of everyone, kept to themselves, and lost their spirit as thoroughly as a whipped dog.

In college, Chris began doing it to women who displeased him. He was sure of his physique and his brainpower by then and usually had his way with the women he wanted. After the death of his father, he had had a bottomless bank account and had delighted in buying women expensive gifts. The low-class townies had been particularly susceptible to a college boy treating them like "ladies", but the hard-bitten amazons of the northern universities had their vulnerability as well. Chris found that once he had them hooked on their greed, he could strike out and hit them the way he had never dared to hit his mother when she left him alone to gasp to death.

When the respectful knock came at his office door, Chris graciously invited entry. Squirt entered and stood there with his hands shoved in his pockets, an eager look on his face. Chris came around the desk and offered Squirt a chair, thanking him for coming. He inquired as to the progress on the roof. Squirt assured him that he would be through within the week and seemed anxious for praise. Chris praised him generously, and Squirt beamed.

"Now, tell me how you're doing otherwise," said Chris, sitting down. "I believe you've got Cerise living with you again?"

"Yessir," said Squirt carefully. "She's got nowheres to go. I make her clean up and do the laundry. You pay me enough to feed two."

"And does she go out when you . . . um . . . entertain Mrs. Maitland?"

Squirt turned his head slightly to one side as if he were looking at Chris with only one eye. "Yeh, uhm, if that's your question."

"Tell me, Squirt, are you happy here?" Chris leaned forward gently to inspire confidentiality.

"Yessir, I am." Squirt's head bobbed up and down.

"Do you feel you have a full life? That we're doing as much for you as possible under the circumstances?"

Squirt looked slightly puzzled. "I'm right grateful for what you've done for me, if that's the question. All I ever asked for in life was honest work. I don't want no handouts. I'll work for my keep. You seen that."

Chris ran his thumbs along the edge of the desk. "Yes," he agreed slowly. "You do earn your keep. But tell me. You will do a job for hire, won't you? I mean, a job like with Byron Moss?"

Squirt ran a finger over his teeth as if he were cleaning them. Finally, he settled on picking a back molar. He didn't speak for a long time. "Byron's gone," he said finally.

"Precisely," Chris agreed. "And suppose I wanted someone else gone like that? Would you be interested?"

Squirt stared out the window into the hot sunlight. The air conditioner hummed quietly, spewing visible water vapor into the room from the heavy humidity outside. "We talking money?" he asked.

Chris reached inside the long desk drawer and brought out two stacks of bills in a bank wrapper. "Five thousand dollars in hundreds," he nearly whispered.

"Who seems to be causing you trouble?" said Squirt.

Filled with a premonitory dread, Chris pronounced each word separately, but in a whisper: "Faith Dixon."

Squirt sat as still as a lizard on a branch. His skin was tanned a deep leather color from constant work in the brutal sun. "That's your mother," he observed.

Chris tensed, his hands on top of the desk with all ten fingernails showing the white moons at the cuticles. "Correct."

With just the tiny, pink tip of his tongue, Squirt wet his

thin lips. "It ain't right, killing your mother," he pronounced emphatically.

Finding himself getting angry, Chris had to struggle to remain calm. Why was Squirt being so difficult? He had killed plenty of women, no doubt. They were all somebody's mother. Or at least somebody's daughter. And what was the difference? "The money's on the table," Chris said tersely.

Squirt shook his head slowly from side to side. "You better put it away. It ain't right for me to kill her. What's she ever done bad to you?"

"That's not your concern," Chris said through clenched teeth. "The money's on the table. That's the way it works, isn't it? Once the money's on the table, fate is set in motion. If you don't pick it up, somebody else will."

Squirt rubbed his jaw, then scrubbed both palms on his thighs. He reached out for the money, hesitated, then reached farther, picking up one stack in either hand. Setting them on his lap, he riffled the bills. He stood up and dropped the bound stacks inside his shirt, where they lay in baggy lumps against the belt. Without another word, he went out of the room, shutting the door silently behind him.

Chris went down to the kitchen and made himself a snack of rye crackers and cold smoked salmon. Back in the office, he put on his pale purple silk dressing gown, lit black candles in the wall sconces, and uncorked a bottle of Chateau Margaux.

Breathing in the heady scent of the wine, he felt elated. The deed was done! The job was hired out. It was just a matter of time. Squirt was a genius at picking the moment. He had killed for years without anyone catching him! Faith would simply disappear. At last it would be at an end. He'd be rid of her!

• 79 •

Two days later, Chris sat in his office armchair watching Venus above the rooftops in the long summer twilight. The sky had been red this morning, reminding him of the old rhyme, "Sailors take warning." The breeze from the open window pleased him and made him feel close to the forces of nature as well as those of the air.

Around an index finger he had tightly wound a little love knot of Lynn Stafford's hair. This he would occasionally rub against his face. He still needed ritual to be able to exert the fierce concentration he required. One day he hoped to be able to do without the deaths of toads, menstrual blood, and low fires. But for the present, he still needed all the trappings. By closing his eyes, he could picture Lynn in every detail. By blocking out his other thoughts, he could send his message.

Wayne Mosley had been an experiment. Chris had taken a lock of Wayne's hair just to be sure. On impulse, he had abandoned the ritual briefly and simply sat in his chair with his body open to the air and sent a message of doom. The next morning's paper had carried the article about Wayne's gruesome death.

It had all been so simple. Chris now understood such ancient legends as the evil eye—by simply staring at someone, you could will them to sicken and die. It had been done since the dawn of time by men chosen for their innate power, by men who had dared to know the truth about evil and worshipped it as the divine force that it was.

There was no God, Chris knew, only the evil force that men called Satan. An evil force that dwelt in the air and was all around. A force that could enter in and take control of us all, bringing power and pleasure to some, destruction to others. Chris was in tune with that force. He could will it to do his bidding.

Chris chuckled to himself as he whispered Lynn's name. "Come to me, Lynn. Come to me and be my slave. Come to me and do my bidding."

He could see her face so clearly, could hear her voice rambling on and on. She had looked so ridiculous in front of Reverend Ratteree. And that drunken boob Murchison who had thought to do Chris injury. Well, Murchison would be next. Tomorrow—on the summer solstice, the time for the witches' Sabbath and the Black Mass—Chris was going to thoroughly dedicate himself to Satan and make himself Satan's highest servant. And Lynn would be the altarpiece. She would take Cynthia McAlister's place.

"Come to me, Lynn. Come and be my servant. Come and serve Satan through me."

Chris was not surprised when there was a timid tap at the door half an hour later. Outside, the wind was picking up, blowing the leaves on the trees. The sky was dark.

"You may enter," said Chris.

The door opened. Lynn stood there looking disheveled and glassy-eyed. She spoke in a monotone. "I love you, Chris. I didn't want to harm you. I didn't mean to harm you."

Chris viewed her with contempt. "Of course you meant to harm me, Lynn darling. You wanted power over me. You thought you could force me to marry you."

Lynn didn't react. She behaved as though she was hypnotized. "I won't harm you," she said plaintively. "I only wanted love."

"Come closer, Lynn," he commanded. "You may touch me. Touch the servant of the Light Bringer. Know the joy that comes from worshipping the True Lord."

Lynn took a stumbling step toward him, hesitated, then came forward.

"Down on your knees. Get down on your knees where you belong. I am your master. I am filled with the forces of the air. I have let the Light Bringer into my soul and he has

300

given me power over all men and women. Kneel in my presence."

Lynn kneeled before him. Her head lolled drunkenly on her shoulders. "Please don't punish me," she begged. "Please don't punish me any more."

Chris wrapped her hair around his hand and twisted her head back. "Tomorrow is the twenty-third of June," he hissed. "The time of great festival. A time to worship the Light Bringer. He has sent a storm as his message. A message of his power. Of the power of his servants."

"Please love me," Lynn mumbled. "Please let me be your bride." She had begun to cry.

"Yes, you will be my bride," said Chris. "But you must share me with your sisters. They will join us soon. Together we will worship the Light. You will have a special role in that worship. You will be the altar. On you will be placed the sacred candles and the holy eucharist. You will be joined with the Light Bringer through me. You will unite your flesh with the true God of all things. You will feel the surge of his power. You will take his power into you and give it to me in turn. You will give me even greater strength."

Lynn's eyes rolled back in her head. "Yes," she wept. "Yes."

● *80* ●

On Saturday, June 23, gigantic thunderheads began piling up over the ocean and kept building into the afternoon. With their mountainous white, they dwarfed the city of Congreve like a testimonial to the puny efforts of man. There was an appearance of whipped cream about them, a look of piled, thick froth; yet instincts deep inside everyone whispered of the violence of nature and the powers of the air and belied the innocence of that white foam. The drought was about to break with torrents of rain and wind lashing the land.

Morgana had taken most of her files home from the college to her mother's house on Oglethorpe Street, where she pored over dead memories. The fortune-teller who had lived in a trailer park in Tempe, Arizona, came to mind. She had worn harlequin spectacles, teased hair, and a miniskirt over fat thighs. A gypsy who claimed to be clairvoyant, she had shown her power by listing each plant in the back garden of Morgana's family home in Congreve, even naming them in the order in which they were lined up.

The Gurdjieff study group in southern California was the subject of the next file. Gurdjieff had been a Greek from Russian Turkestan who said he had the ability to teach telepathic contact with others. Though he had died in 1949, some groups still practiced his techniques. The mental strain was intense as the mind was trained to concentrate on individual thoughts and fight against the multitude of distractions in the world. Gurdjieff proposed ritual as a method of aiding concentration. Once the art was mastered, the ritual was no longer needed.

Then Morgana found what she had been looking for. The file on the Esalen Institute at Big Sur, California, where an experiment called "Symbo" had created a unified group-intelligence among six people. By a slow development of the ability to focus on group activities, they had created a common emotion and intelligence that arose and grew from no one individual. They had created an actual mental organism composed of the unit.

Pacing her upstairs bedroom, Morgana wrung her hands. Her nerves were on edge. The afternoon sky was growing darker as the clouds moved in from the sea. Soon the temperature change of the vapor over land would bring the rain. A brass barometer on the wall registered a steady fall. Morgana knew the effect of air pressure on the human nervous system and accepted it as natural that she might feel skittish.

But something deeper was pulling at her. It was June 23.

The summer solstice. It was a major festival night in the tradition of witchcraft. Witches' Sabbath, the night of the Black Mass.

Looking out her window over the trees, Morgana could see flickering bolts of lightning coming out of the distant reaches of the clouds. Like a quilt being drawn over a bird cage, a blacker cloud shadow moved across the yard. The wind picked up suddenly, whipping the trees as big splashes of water struck the windows.

Morgana bit down hard on her lips to try to keep her nerves from jumping. Rushing into the hall, she tried to call Murchison at his office. No one was in. The answering machine voice sounded drunk. She called his house, got no answer there, then slammed the phone down in frustration. She didn't know why she was calling him anyway.

She had treated him like crap, yelling at him about Lynn and refusing to talk to him afterward. How could she have done such a thing? All he had wanted to do was help her. A lot of men hankered after that, and they were certainly preferable to the callous, ego-bound types who always had snappy lines like: "Excuse me, but I believe you're mixing me up with someone who gives a shit." Morgana had had plenty of experience with men like that in college.

Her freshman year, she'd had a blind date with a guy from Columbia who'd presented her with an English theme paper titled "Copulation Before Conversation." The jerk had just stood there in the foyer of her residence hall holding out the paper and saying nothing. When she had told him to quit being an asshole, the guy had finally started to talk. Later she got drunk on vodka and grape juice at a fraternity party and threw up all over him.

Her sophomore year, Morgana had had a date with a fledgling Wall Street stockbroker who wanted her to meet him at his Upper West Side apartment. When she got there, the door was open and he was lying on a daybed, naked. "Well, let's get down to it," he'd greeted her. She had broken a lamp over his head, and the next day he had the nerve to have a lawyer call her and threaten litigation.

There had been others. The history grad student who

turned out to be a religious nut who wanted to listen to Oral Roberts records and talk in tongues. A Hindu who wanted her to live in purdah back in his hometown. A chemistry professor who wanted to make it with her among the mice cages in his lab while the white creatures rustled over their bodies. A medical student who expected her to come over on Tuesday nights when his wife was out playing bridge.

Murchison had always been different. In teenage days, he had been like a big, clumsy bear. Once he had gotten drunk and stepped out of a moving car thinking it was standing still. Even though he broke his leg and ended up in a cast, he had still sailed in the summer Regatta with tarot symbols Drena had drawn decorating the cast.

That night at age nineteen in New York when she had recognized him in the crowd at the Lounge Lizard Club, Morgana had felt as if she was falling in love for the first time. After the hassle of the big city and adapting to the pushy Yankee ways and the mad-dog competition of Barnard College, he had been like a gentle breath of air from the southlands. She had gone to bed with him and given him her virginity with a skill that surprised both of them. She still had a perfect memory of his hands running up and down her back. It had been as perfect a loss of girlhood as anyone could wish for.

Morgana dialed both numbers for Murchison again, with the same result. Why didn't he understand what she knew and feared? But then, how could anyone without her experiences and knowledge fathom the terror that she knew lurked in the world?

Morgana had seen it all. Not just the psycho-butchers so popular on TV, but the true dark forces that lurked in nooks and crannies, mastered by oddballs who gave up all normal life to learn occult powers. Morgana knew such powers were real. They were emanations of the minds of those who had learned to open up the unused recesses of the brain. They were mind forces that could control other minds, physically move objects, make people sicken and die.

A tremendous sizzle of lightning hit the transformer on the pole outside the house, flushing the bedroom in darkness and ramming a deafening crack of thunder through the house like a cannon shot in a cave. Morgana was untouched by the bolt of lightning, but the noise seemed to echo through her mind like a wave of blackness. She stood paralyzed for an interminable time; she felt herself transported outside by something beyond her control. It was as if she were floating above her body, watching herself, powerless to change her course of action.

When Morgana became aware of herself again, she was standing outside the huge wooden doors of St. Helen's. The bells were pealing eleven o'clock. Rain was coming down in buckets, obscuring objects no more than a few yards away. Water was ankle-deep in the street.

Morgana was aware of the cold from the rain that was creeping into her system. Still, her limbs moved involuntarily. Mind currents ran past her, dragging her on.

The front doors of the church were barred, but the small side door was rimmed with light. Without wanting to, Morgana pushed on the door and saw it open. The source of the light was far down the huge aisle at the nave. A hurricane lantern burned on the altar beside an upside-down cross and a goat's head.

Morgana told herself not to go inside as the cold worked its way through her. Her shuffling feet seemed to be burdened by leaden weights. She moved drowsily, saw everything as though it were underwater. She could count her heartbeats and hear her own respiration in the slow-motion world.

She knew who was waiting!

Naked beneath a black satin cloak, Chris Dixon proffered a jeweled dagger and goblet. At his left hand stood the solemn nude forms of Maeve Sandor, Lynn Stafford, and Fran Maitland. Morgana would be the fourth. Chris reached out his arms to her, and she walked toward him, step by dragging step.

"Come to me," Chris whispered inside her head. "Come and be my bride. Come celebrate our divinity."

Morgana knew the ritual. In whatever variation, there was

a recitation of the Lord's Prayer backwards, the drinking of a satanic wine of blood and semen, then group sex with Satan's priest. Chris would enter them each front and rear. Frenzied with henbane and the power of his mind, the women would cry out with both longing and joy.

It was coming, and she was powerless to prevent it. He wanted her as his bride. He had said so. He had killed Clarence Fuller and Patricia Stone to prove his power to her. He had thrust her into a riptide. Now he would spill his seed in her and own her.

Morgana's brain registered intense terror.

Almost on cue, Faith Dixon entered the church from one of the side doors behind the choir. She was dressed in a raincoat and boots and held a dripping umbrella. When she saw the spectacle, Faith's mouth fell open in horror. The umbrella dropped with a clunk.

Chris's mother obviously didn't know about her son, and now she had found him in the middle of a satanic ritual. His own mother who lived in his house! She had found her son in this blasphemy!

Hysterically, Morgana laughed aloud. A corner of her brain fought the spell with vehement laughter that wouldn't stop. The darkness shattered at the edges and lifted. The wild, spiraling laughter echoed through the upper reaches of the church. As Morgana laughed, a faint heat like a flame path ran through her, and she could feel her fingers and toes once more.

Lynn, Fran, and Maeve stood still, staring blankly at her. Faith seemed paralyzed. Grimacing in anger, Chris dashed his goblet to the stone floor and twisted the hilt of the dagger in both hands.

Suddenly, Morgana's laughter was replaced by fear. It wracked her with cold that hit her body with a sudden impact like crashing through a door.

Spurred by terror, Morgana turned and fled. Chris started to run after her; then, sputtering with anger, threw the dagger down with a clash.

Hunching his shoulders, he tried to concentrate on stopping her with his mind. He put both hands to his ears to stop the noise of her laughter, to block his mad rage, and concentrated on stopping her.

Morgana ran out into the downpour, splashed into the standing water, and sprinted down Bayswater Street. The houses were dark and looming shapes veiled by a waterfall of rain. Streetlights showed an eerie glimmer against the blackness of the gloom. She fell once, picked herself up, and ran on.

I've broken it! I've broken it, she told herself through labored breathing. I've broken his hold! I can fight him now!

At the corner of Main and Oglethorpe, she fell back against the side of a building, heaving, her lungs drinking in the air. Rain flowed in a torrent. No movement was visible anywhere around her. She could see; she could feel; she knew cold and fear!

It wasn't like before. She was her own master!

● 81 ●

Fran felt like shit the next day. Images of feces and human defecation kept running through her brain. She was wearing clothes that Squirt had bought for her at K Mart. She made meals for him and scrubbed the floors on her hands and knees with a scrub brush. When he corrected her, she apologized. She shared his bed with Cerise, feeling each time she performed the sex act that she was competing with this younger, more attractive woman for his favor.

She'd had nowhere to go when Roland threw her out. She couldn't face her friends, naked and abandoned by her doctor husband. She couldn't tell anyone of her humiliation at the hands of her sick husband and Rafe Artigues. Roland used guns to extend his penis, and Rafe had to have danger to feel like a man.

Fran's world had disintegrated. She had lost the baby

when Roland threw her out five days ago. It had been so early in her pregnancy that a D&C had not been necessary. But Cynthia was dead. Only Squirt had cared. Roland had simply laughed when she'd called to tell him. So now Fran was clinging to Squirt for protection because she had nowhere else to go. She didn't even own the Cadillac. Squirt had suggested selling it to a used-car dealer on Mitchum Avenue, but the title was in Roland's name.

Fran was hearing Cynthia's voice even more now. Her sister talked to her almost continuously, except when Squirt told Fran to shut up because she sounded like a crazy woman.

Fran blacked out a lot, and then she'd become conscious suddenly like she had waked up from a dream. Last night, for example, she'd come to, standing in a pouring rain on Bayswater Street in the middle of the night, and she had no clothes on. There were lash marks all down her back like Chris used to put on her. She felt sick and weak and unclean. When she returned to the carriage house, Cerise was asleep in bed with Squirt.

Violence was all around her. Squirt had told her at breakfast this morning that Lynn Stafford had been found in a patch of marsh near the Coast Guard station "slit open with a knife straight down from throat to pussy." She had been "gutted like a deer," he said, and the buzzards were all around her. That was how she was spotted. Blood and death. It was everywhere. It was going to devour Fran, just like it had devoured both Cynthias.

Three nights ago, Fran had driven over to her old home late and rung the doorbell. When Roland came down, she'd cried and begged him to take her back. She had begged him to keep her from a death like Cynthia's. She promised she'd do anything he wanted.

As Roland was standing naked in the doorway, a woman's voice had called down from upstairs, asking him who was there. Fran had recognized the voice. It was one of Roland's nurses. Unaffected, Roland had told her he'd been hoping she'd drop by because he had something to show her.

Inside, Fran had wiped away her tears. Laughing, Roland

produced his will, which named her as sole beneficiary. He tore it to shreds in front of her and threw her out in the street again. From an upstairs window, he called down to her that he had hired that awful bastard Bugle Gaston to handle the divorce for him.

From that moment on, Fran knew she had him. A plan formed in her mind. She had often pondered the problem of Roland's will before and what she would do if he cut her out, and had talked for hours with lawyers about a widow's right to dissent against a will, about will contests, about proof of insanity at the time of making a will.

Most interesting, she had learned that if Roland died without a will, the law of intestate succession dictated that the wife got half and the children collectively got half. Roland had children by his first marriage. His first wife was eliminated by the divorce. Fran was the wife who got half. Roland had more than three million dollars in life insurance alone. If he died while Fran was still married to him, she was very nicely taken care of.

It wasn't hard to explain the plan to Squirt Crawford. He listened impassively, only once drumming a horny fingernail against the tabletop with its red-checked cheesecloth. At the end of her explanation, he thought quietly for a long time while Fran sat with her hands in her lap and waited. She had been taught at Hutton Hall to sit with her hands in her lap and not to lean on tables. After a time, Squirt said, "I'll go get me a gun."

Two nights later, on the evening of June 26, Squirt and Fran went out and got into a Chevrolet Nova. It was raining again. When Fran asked Squirt where he'd gotten the strange car, he told her he had found it. Fran figured he had stolen it, but that was okay. It wouldn't do to have the Cadillac recognized.

Fran had phoned Roland and told him she was coming by with her new boyfriend to talk about the divorce. She was willing to give up all claims if he would give them a check for five thousand dollars immediately, she said. Roland hadn't been able to control his mirth over the phone. He couldn't wait to meet the new boyfriend. If he was common enough, Roland might be prepared to give up the pleasure of humiliating her in court. Fran knew the car would be a good touch.

Squirt sat outside in the rain with the windshield wipers going while Fran ran to the front door. It had been raining for four days straight, and the city was flooded continuously, especially at high tide. The decrepit sewer system couldn't handle the tidal backup from the rivers, particularly on full-moon nights. With the waxing moon plus the rainfall, Congreve was virtually drowned. Water was over the tires of the cars and sloshed inside on the floorboards. Fran had to wade to get to her house.

Roland didn't want to come out to the car, but Fran convinced him that her boyfriend was the sullen type who would feel inadequate in the house. Roland looked at the Chevy Nova and smiled. Wearing his docksiders, duckhead pants, and a red polo shirt, Roland waded out and got into the backseat. Squirt had slid over in the front, leaving the driver's seat to Fran. As soon as she got in, she put the car in gear and began slowly moving through the deep water. The car made a wake like a boat.

"Hey, where we going?" demanded Roland.

Squirt turned and fixed him with his eyes. "Just a ways 'cross the bridge," he said.

Roland felt for the door handle, but Squirt reached over the seat and held his wrist. "Don't do that," he instructed. Oddly, Roland obeyed. For the first time in his life, he seemed lethargic, slow, unsure of himself.

The streets rose slowly in elevation as they approached the Elstree River Bridge. The rain still fell, but on the far side of the bridge, they were out of the flooding. They drove past Lake Shores Shopping Center and down the road that led to Crosland Island.

The island was one of the Atlantic barriers, but it had no view of the ocean. Girded with marshes, bunkered by golf resorts, it was a place of trailers in patches of woods, small tomato farms, decaying country stores. Fran knew there was a dirt road on the edge of an expanse of marsh. She had been out there with Squirt earlier so they could rehearse everything.

Roland sat silently the whole way out. It was as if he had an awareness of death and felt helpless to prevent it. When Fran stopped the car, she heard him in the backseat. He was crying. The poor, mean bastard was afraid. He had sat there through the ride knowing that Squirt had a gun on him.

"Please," Roland said weakly. "Please don't."

Squirt said nothing. His yellow eyes shone in the dark, never wavering in their hold on Roland.

Fran laughed. "Do you like the feeling, Roland dear?" she chanted in a singsong voice. "Do you like the taste of fear? Do you like the smell of mud and death?"

Fran got out of the car and was almost obliterated by the rain. Faint lights shone distantly across the wide sea of marsh grass. The sky was black. "I should make you masturbate in front of us, you bastard!" Fran shrieked. With her hair streaming slack with water and her cheap clothes soaked, she looked like a hag out of a nightmare.

"You best get out of the car," said Squirt quietly. He revealed the magnum revolver for the first time.

Roland knew what the gun could do; he even knew its range. He jerked open the door, jumped out, and started to run up the road. He was visible in the headlights as he made a beeline for beckoning safety. He seemed to be racing the light, straining to get out of its beams.

Calmly, Squirt slipped out of the front, laid the magnum down on the hood with a two-handed grip, and squeezed off a shot. Roland jerked and fell forward.

Squirt walked through the rain to stand over the struggling body. Roland had been shot squarely in the back. He could still move his limbs, so the bullet had obviously missed the spinal cord. His hands clawed the soft mud. Squirt cocked the hammer and shot him through the back of the head. The report was muffled by the downpour.

Squirt looked at the gun with momentary regret, then chucked it into the marsh as far as he could. When he returned to the car, Fran was howling with wild laughter.

"You funny little man!" she shrieked. "You're such a funny, trashy little man!"

Standing there drenched by the rain, Squirt pondered his situation. "You don't intend to split the money with me, do you?" he asked.

"Of course I will!" Fran screeched in a voice that said she was out of control. "There's so much more to do yet! There's so much more I need you for!"

"I don't rightly feel I can trust you, Miss Fran," said Squirt.

Fran fell silent. She allowed him to lead her back to the car and stood in the rain while he cut off the headlights and killed the engine.

"We've had some lovin' times," he said gently, putting his hands on her hips.

"Please," she said. "I love you. You know that." Cynthia's voice was calling to her. She gave a high-pitched, involuntary laugh.

Squirt made her get out of her underpants. She took off her shoes to do it and stood with cold mud between her toes. Her panties lay beside the rear tire. Squirt put her in the backseat and they made love in their filthy, mud-stained clothes.

She climaxed twice before he took out his hawksbill knife and cut her throat.

● *82* ●

Maeve Sandor felt that her husband had been looking at her in a sly way ever since last night. She had appeared soaking wet with her dress in tatters and soaked with blood. It fueled her fears and made her certain that he and any number of other people were intent on killing her.

To wake up on a side street in Congreve and find yourself standing barefoot in the rain was one thing. She had had that happen plenty of times when she was drunk, particularly if she had been doing dope along with alcohol. She had slept with any number of men with little or no memory of the event, and had even found herself on strange streets with half her clothes missing.

What was so frightening this time was the feeling of utter exhaustion, as if she had been jumping up and down for hours. There was a feeling of sexual exhaustion as well, the kind that came from multiple partners. And then there was the memory of seeing a woman killed. It was like what used to haunt Drena.

Maeve wasn't clear on all that had happened. She did remember that Faith Dixon had tried to break up the party, but Chris had called her off. And also that Chris had tried unsuccessfully to get Morgana Stone to come back.

Maeve had a perfect memory of dancing naked, of watching herself—as if she were outside her body. Her mouth had been open, her tongue hanging out like a dog's. Drool had run down her bare body; foam had flecked her lips like a horse on a hot day. Then Chris Dixon had lifted a dagger over the body of the naked woman Lynn, whom Maeve had never seen before. Limp and perspiring, the woman had lain on the altar as if she were faint from exhaustion.

Chris had rubbed the flat of the dagger over his genitals and held it high. It seemed to glisten with sweat. Light glanced off the blade. Maeve had wanted to stop the blade from falling, but she wasn't inside her body.

Down it had come, hacking and tearing and slashing like someone cutting into a difficult packing case. Blood had flowed. The body of Maeve Sandor had rushed forward and lapped at the blood like a thirsty dog. The blood had run down the corners of her mouth in runnels.

When Maeve had found herself in the street without shoes, her dress was dark with stains like cheap red wine. It was only this morning when she had inspected the sodden mess at the front door where she had shucked it that she began to wonder if it was blood. Driven by the haunting memories, she had built a fire of the boards and lathe she had tossed out of the upstairs window on a patch of high ground in the backyard. The rain lifted only periodically, and the dress wouldn't catch fire, even when doused with gasoline. The yuppie bitch next door had come and railed at her about the stench. There was something about her eyes and the hard edge of her mouth that made Maeve afraid of her for the first time ever.

Taking the garment inside, Maeve had dried it in the oven and then tried to burn it in a metal pail in the middle of the kitchen floor. That was when Bojack had come downstairs yelling about the smoke and wanting to know if she was trying to set the fucking house on fire. Using a barbecue fork, she had heaved the flaming dress at him, and he had tried to hit her with a chair. Meanwhile, the dress scorched the linoleum and nearly set the dry-rotted boards underneath ablaze.

Finally, Maeve had taken the charred fragments out and chucked them into a garbage dumpster down in the public housing project. She carefully cut out the label beforehand, even though it was from Sears and the dress was secondhand via a thrift shop.

She had never known such fear. Not even when her crazy cousin blew up the postbox and spray-painted IRA slogans all around the council flats had she been so scared. He had hidden gelignite in the family flat in Birmingham, and Maeve had lived with fear of a sudden explosion or else police intrusion and a life spent behind bars in the women's division of Wormwood Scrubs. That was nothing like the terror of living with a memory of a savage murder dedicated to Satan and the image of yourself drinking blood.

That shit Chris Dixon! He was behind this. He was a demon. He had suckered her, using that lash on her to make her cavort around under the sting. It was revolting. That had been like a dream, too. Except that Maeve knew it was real. The red weals on her butt were very tangible.

You're a bleeding idiot, Maeve, she told herself. What could be more tangible than a bloodstained dress? You were present at a murder. That woman who was found in the marsh all chopped up today. Buzzards had pulled out her entrails like wiring from a tumbledown building, buzzards playing tug-of-war with her guts. She had been the altar, the altar to Satan.

Maeve had been drinking heavily all day long. She didn't want to remember it. She wanted to forget. First, she had finished off the half-gallon of gin, and then she'd taken to the brandy. It was some kind of nasty Greek stuff called Metaxa. It made her crazy; her mind turned cartwheels, spinning through the hideous memories over and over again. Aunt Fiona had been a good witch, one who took the right-hand path to do good. Chris Dixon had taken the left-hand path, and he reveled in evil.

Bojack was building a four-foot-high McDonald's Big Mac out of polymer in his studio. He was trying to give it a slick, wet look like those wet brands of women's lipstick. He seemed to feel it would be the ultimate statement on American cuisine. Lately, he'd talked of nothing else. He wasn't interested in Maeve and what troubled her.

Bojack was up to something. Maeve could see the wheels of his brain turning. He was plotting something. He had found a new conquest, some new student, and he was very pleased with himself lately. He had been suggesting that Maeve look for a job and leave home.

It didn't take much for Maeve to see what he was up to. Bojack wanted Maeve out of the way so he could do what he wanted at home with other women. That was clear. He was trying to scare her away. Night before last, he had beaten her with a belt buckle and then thrown a kitchen knife into the wall while she was frying hamburger patties for dinner. She had felt the blade slice past her face and turned around to see him sitting at the rickety table hugging a bottle of red Gallo, laughing like a hyena.

It was clear he wanted her dead. This out-of-body experience with the murder and Chris Dixon last night at the witches' Sabbath had convinced her. Actually, she had done nothing wrong. It had been only an example of nature in the extreme, only a premonition to warn her of future injury. What she had thought she was doing was only a warning of what Bojack would do to her. That stuff on her dress was just black tar from the high waters that covered Congreve. The whole city was underwater.

Maeve carried the ironing board and iron to a surplus store down the street and sold them for seventeen dollars. Then she bought a quart of scotch and carried it home in the continuing downpour. By that time, Bojack had gotten frustrated with his Big Mac and heaved it out the window into the backyard. It lay there like a decoration in the middle of the fish pond, nacreous green lettuce sticking out under a plastic burger and tan bun. He himself had disappeared.

Mixing some booze with Gatorade, Maeve sat down at the open front window with the rain splashing on her, trying to think. Something was badly wrong. She was being warned. Her mind wasn't working right. She kept having blank periods like LSD or marijuana flash-blacks. She would seem fine, and suddenly there would be a gap in time. She'd wake up on the commode or holding a paintbrush, and her body would be terribly tired, as if she had been holding the same position for hours. Looking at her watch, she discovered it was later than she'd thought.

Something was working on her brain, trying to get to her in a subtle, insidious way. She had always had an urge to jump to her death from the Elstree River Bridge, and it was even stronger now. She'd often talked to Bojack of her desire to do that. One morning very early she had even gone out there and left the car on that little pull-over for broken-down vehicles. She had put the keys under the floor mat where he could find them. Then she had climbed over the fence and hung out there, leaning out over space, her arms behind her gripping the metal. Down below was the island of fill dirt with the scrubby trees where the ibis nested, green dotted with myriad white birds. It was the one place the developers couldn't stick condos on, so they called it a bird sanctuary.

You've always liked birds, she told herself. You should die among them. Just go and swan-dive hundreds of feet down. King Kong was eighty feet high. Remember how tiny Fay Wray looked in his hands. Now you can picture eighty feet.

Imagine how many eighty feets you'd fall before you'd be shredded by the tree limbs. She figured she'd wear a white dress. With the blood, it would look like a Red Cross flag waving from up high.

Maeve sat quietly drinking scotch and Gatorade and watching the rain pelt down into the growing, muddy lake that covered the city. Rubbish from the Piggly Wiggly was floating down the street: sodden cardboard boxes, vegetable leaves, paper, milk cartons, bottles with their necks up like something you'd send a message in from your marooned island in the South Seas, a dead dog.

Jesus, was that really a dead dog? Yes, it was some kind of ocher-colored creature with its stiff legs sticking up above the water. It had lodged against a spindly tree across the street. The whole city smacked of stagnation. It was built on mud and garbage landfill, which was fine to layer over with soil, plant tropical trees, and build jigsaw wood houses. Except that you were building on dead, inanimate filth that would one day swallow you up like quicksand.

Bojack came wading down the street up to his short little waist in water. He was pushing his bicycle, but fifty yards from the house he became fatigued with the chore and dumped it into the water so the bike disappeared from view. By the time he made it to the front door, dripping, Maeve was furious.

Just two weeks ago she had gone over to the police station and bid for that bicycle at the auction they had every year for unclaimed stolen goods. It had cost her ten dollars. That bastard Bojack thought nothing of money. He was always nagging her to get a job and bring money in, instead of making it himself. He brought home whole shopping carts filled with liquor and wine and tore up the new clothes she got if they displeased him, rather than letting her return them for a refund. It was a protest against capitalistic excess, he claimed. Just like that party where he had provided stacks of one-dollar bills and encouraged the guests to burn them in a fire.

"Worthless bastard!" Maeve yelled at him as he came dripping into the living room.

Bojack had been drinking and his face showed it. He growled at Maeve and began to heave some loose pieces of plaster that had fallen in the hall in her direction. A glass lamp filled with seashells exploded against the wall near her head, shells scattering in a shrapnel burst.

Unable to control his wrath, Bojack continued to storm at Maeve. He flung open a drawer of kitchen utensils and began trying his old circus skills, doing his best to skewer her with a set of Japanese steak knives. One narrowly missed her throat. Letting out a wail, Maeve hurled the coffee maker in Bojack's direction; it caught him on the head and closed one eye with blood and immediate swelling.

At that, Bojack retreated toward the outside front steps and into the rain, and began wading down the street. He was wiping at the blood running into his eyes, trying to clear his vision of blood and pelting rain.

Filled with rage, Maeve snatched up her car keys. Telling herself to be calm, she tried to start the engine of her car. At first it seemed hopelessly wet; the battery moaned and the engine made pathetic noises. Then, almost as if by Maeve's force of will, it jumped to life. Maeve carefully fed it gas so it didn't flood out and edged it down the drive into the deep water of the street.

In the distance, she could see Bojack struggling through the thigh-deep water. Even at a reduced speed, she narrowed the gap between them rapidly and nearly came even with him before he turned into a side street lined with a fence of iron spears. The windshield wipers were swishing back and forth valiantly. Maeve saw Bojack look nervously back over his shoulder. It was as if she were looking through a gun sight.

Bojack hugged the fence. He kept looking back even as he flailed his arms in a swivel motion to help move him through the thick brown water. Maeve began to build up speed. As she got up to forty-five miles per hour, all her building resentment and hate exploded. She was right on him with the car. He was in front of her. She would run over him if she didn't stop. She laughed and closed her eyes briefly. Something inside her drove her on.

Without regret or hesitation, she drove him through the metal fence, wedging his body between the car hood and the iron spears that splayed out on impact like buck teeth.

Maeve laughed grotesquely as she backed the car out from the fence with a grinding and scraping of metal. Bojack's dead face seemed to scream silently at her. The mouth was pressed against the windshield in a cruel smile and had given a last breath that fogged the glass. All the gold fillings in the molars showed clearly. His hands clutched the windshield wipers and held them as if he were stopping a clock. From the shoulder blades down, he was pulped red flesh. A short stream of blood came out of his mouth and ran down a wiper blade as if it were a gutter.

Within seconds, the rain diluted it to pale pink.

• 83 •

During the two weeks since Lynn Stafford's disastrous visit to Reverend Ratteree, Murchison had begun to drink again. Though he kept it confined to after five o'clock, he was clearly off the wagon. He had already received the notice that his malpractice premiums were being trebled, and there was some question as to whether he would continue to be insured at all. When he called the insurance company, he had gotten the runaround and vague references to the computer. The heat had broken with the torrential rains. Murchison was still out of touch with Morgana and had even quit trying to call her, at least for the time being.

Murchison sat with his second drink, watching the Monday night TV news. He sat up when it started reporting a weird story about finding the body of Lynn Stafford in the marsh near the Coast Guard station. Despite the intense downpour, buzzards had collected over the nude and mutilated body of the daughter of the former rector of St. Helen's. Appalled, Murchison switched channels desperately, listening to the accounts over all three television stations. Then he stared into space. Lynn Stafford was definitely dead, by all accounts. And he couldn't help feeling he was somehow responsible because he had taken her to the Bishop. He was convinced that confronting Dixon had somehow led directly to her death.

Consequently Murchison made a resolution to go on a serious binge. It began amid water on the floor and the smell of stale beer at Captain Bill's Red Snapper bar. It continued through a series of bars in town and out on the island. Murchison decided to spend the night in the backseat of his car whenever he felt like sleeping. The torrential rain wouldn't stop. It washed the grime from the streets and sent garbage swirling into the drains. The air smelled clean and free of sweaty humidity.

Murchison drank slowly but steadily, pacing himself, and making a catalogue of his life year by year. He mentally listed triumphs and failures, joy and pain, lust and love. He took time out to talk with anyone who would listen, encouraging old cranks to spout their theories about creeping communism and the spread of AIDS. He admired tricks performed by bar dogs, made clumsy passes at ugly waitresses, sat in on card games, once winning five dollars, once losing twenty-five. He helped a man push a car out of a rain-drowned ditch in exchange for a six-pack of beer. He argued with a woman police officer outside a 7-Eleven, but charmed her out of arresting him and convinced her to go out with him after she got off duty.

In the course of his mental compilation of history, Murchison especially dwelt on Drena Wrenn. She was the one girl he had actually been able to talk to as a teenager. The rest had seemed to be watching him warily, as if he were expected to perform a role and had flubbed his lines.

He remembered Drena trying to use a divining rod to locate fresh water out on Robinson's Island and citing as her authority a Soviet army study reported in *True* magazine. Drena never hesitated to tell him exactly what was on her mind, and she told it like a delicious secret that he alone was privy to. She would actually pass him notes in church, expecting people to hand the folded paper down the entire row of the pew.

When she went on her tarot kick, she forecast all her friends first and saved him for last, asserting that she wanted to master the art perfectly before tackling his awesome future. She had laid the cards out in the ten-card Celtic pattern, explaining their origin in 1200 AD Egypt and how they were an occult teaching device for showing the flow of time and the fusion of thesis and antithesis into synthesis.

The Hanged Man turned up in his future, which Murchison thought was funny as hell, but Drena took it very seriously. She had gazed at him with sad, solicitous eyes for days afterward, and finally took him onto the grassy ramparts of the fort and made love to him on a star-filled night. She said he didn't dare wait any longer to enjoy the sweetness of life, and she owed him a gift of love in exchange for her clumsy message of doom.

Later, Murchison remembered her turning up on the University of Virginia campus in hippie jewelry, Mexican peasant blouse, and those flat sandals that made her feet slap the pavement. She had ceased shaving her legs, so they were covered with fine blond hair. Drena said she was upset by the configuration of the planets and felt that something terrible was about to happen to her. At the time, Murchison had been trying to get into the pants of a little sugar britches from Hollins College who would tell you right up front that her daddy owned three Ford dealerships and she had been a state debutante. He had told Drena to get lost.

Afterwards, though, he'd often wondered what had been bothering her and if he could have helped her in some way. She had wanted warmth and love, and he had rejected her because he had the hots for the heiress to three Ford dealerships. Drena had never ceased to love him, writing him in Vietnam, later asking him to marry her when he was doing so much cocaine and his life was at an ebb. Now she haunted him, as if she were more alive because she was no longer there.

Murchison read the newspaper account of Lynn Stafford's death while he was having a breakfast beer and a hot dog at the Hog Locker on Artillery Road in Mount Meade the next morning. Rain beat on the bottle-cap-paved space near the gas tanks. An old man in a yellow slicker pumped gas. Lines of commuter cars, windshield wipers working overtime, streamed toward the big Carteret River Bridge and Congreve.

The newspaper headline and pictures of police hauling the body bag out of the marsh reminded Murchison of his most grisly memories of Vietnam. In one of the pictures, tiny against the background sky, could be seen circling buzzards. Murchison had even seen pigs eating bodies in Vietnam.

The obituary listed Lynn's parents, both deceased, her education at Hutton Hall and St. Mary's Junior College, and her marriage to the minister Roger Frye. The news article described Lynn as having been slashed in a ritual pattern. Murchison found himself wondering if Dixon would twist the events at the Bishop's in such a way as to make Murchison a murder suspect.

Disbarment was nothing, since Murchison had never particularly liked being a lawyer. The only pleasure it had ever brought him was its excuse for being rude to people he didn't like already. Otherwise, it made him feel like a blind horse driving a millstone round and round. But doing life for murder was not Murchison's idea of a pleasant alternative to practicing law, either. Absentmindedly, he started to make a list of his alibis at particular times of the past days on a napkin, but found there were too many gaps.

At a series of rural gas stations, Murchison indulged himself in beer all morning. Near noon, he drove into the city and went by his office. There was a note from Sue, his secretary, saying she had left early. For an hour or so, Murchison sifted through the mail.

Finally, he left his office and had the first of many bourbons at lunch at a pool hall in North Congreve, then ended up at Captain Bill's for the evening traffic. His bourbon-laced beer glass bubbled at the brim. Bugs swarmed about the bare light bulbs. The TV above the bar showed police officers searching among the skein of tangled brush and trees on the island under the Carteret River Bridge. White ibis squawked and flapped away as the fatigue-clad cops struggled through the mud and guano in a steady rain. Cars were jammed on the towering bridge like a clotted artery.

The bartender explained how some crazy artist broad had rammed her husband through a fence in town and then crashed her car through the railings of the bridge. Both husband and wife were dead. Their name was foreign and funny. Bojack something. Or something Bojack.

Then Murchison heard the names. Maeve and Bojack Sandor!

Vividly, he pictured Maeve Sandor's car spiraling down through the air like a dropping football never to be received. Down, down, to land in mud, not with a fiery explosion but with a splash! It was about then that he began to feel sick and heaved his guts up all over the floor. He found himself unable to walk, and his eyesight was growing blurred. Some of the regulars who knew him drove him home and saw him through the front door.

He waved good-bye at the headlights of their car, took off his shoes and socks, and got the Old Crow out of the liquor cabinet. He began to have fierce chills and decided against ice, drinking straight out of the bottle. He thought about putting his shoes and socks back on, but the effort required was too much.

Morgana Stone came in when he was a third of the way down the bottle. She lit into him about being a drunken slob, but stopped in horror, her hands clapped to her mouth, when she saw how his feet were swelling. Cockroaches were swarming out of the walls by the hundreds.

"What's happening to you?" she yelled. "What are all these bugs?"

"Thank God you're here for moral support." Murchison laughed. "For a moment there, I thought I had the DTs."

His feet continued to swell until the skin was shiny tight. The pain was intense, but everything seemed funny to him. When a roach crawled onto his shoulder, he said, "Look! It thinks it's a parrot and I'm Long John Silver. Hey, pieces of eight, pieces of eight! Right? Isn't that the line?"

Morgana hugged him and kissed his beard-stubbled face, then ordered him to try to walk to her car so she could get him to the hospital; he was too big a hulk for her to carry. Murchison swigged from the bottle and argued that medical science could do nothing. He knew what was happening as well as she did. That bastard Dixon was coming for him. Morgana had been right all along.

"I can take it," he said. "You wouldn't believe the roentgen rays or whatever the fuck it's called they poured into me when I had cancer. I'm tough. You have to be tough to put your body through the abuse mine has weathered over the years. Hell, I could go on the sumo wrestling circuit in Japan. Bounce off those big soybean porkers and feel no pain." He drank again. By then his face and hands were swelling, too.

His eyes were nearly swollen shut when his genitals started to enlarge. Morgana had to help him tear open his pants to release testicles the size of baseballs. His hands were useless blobs, tiny fingernails set into putty.

"Doesn't it hurt?" she demanded, pleading for a response.

"Of course it hurts! It hurts like shit! But I love it! This is the first action I've had in days of despair. This is something tangible I can fight! This is the dark night with a promise of a new dawn at the end!"

Outside the rain fell steadily. The roaches swarmed in mad patterns over the furniture, the walls, the floor. Some took flight, buzzing through the air, striking one another, falling into the squirming mess on the floor. Murchison dribbled liquor into the tiny mouth of his dough-wad face and continued to make bad jokes. Then he started to vomit.

For over an hour he heaved out bile and shit bloody diarrhea all over the floor where he writhed and tossed. A hairball got lodged in his throat, and Morgana had to pry open his jaws and drag it out with her fingers. He spit up paper clips and bottle caps and pop tops from cans all mixed with bile and mucus.

Morgana prayed and begged God for mercy. She talked and reasoned and lectured in a meaningless monologue. She began to scream and yell, cursing Chris Dixon, damning his eyes, damning his soul, cursing him with every ounce of her fiber. She used biblical language like an exorcism.

Finally, she took the lock of hair she had found in Murchison's desk and concentrated all her will on the object. She was sweating and her eyes were filled with tears, but her knuckles were taut with determination.

Five hours later, in the gray, rainy dawn, light barely leaked through the windows. Murchison lay on the floor, his head back. He had lost consciousness. The swelling was going down. He was still alive!

Morgana went into the bathroom still clutching the amulet. She was exhausted. She fell asleep standing up over the sink.

● *84* ●

Morgana woke up on the bathroom floor several hours later. Murchison was stirring in the living room. Morgana cleaned him up, stripped him, and shoved him in the shower, where he sat on the floor of the stall while the water pounded him. Though he kept asking for a drink, she poured out all the bottles from the liquor cabinet into the kitchen sink.

She coaxed him through dressing, drove him to the hospital, and checked him in, signing as the responsible party for payment of the bill. They diagnosed him as suffering from exhaustion and sun exposure, which made Morgana laugh, given the fact that it had been raining steadily for a week. When Morgana left him in the hospital bed, he weakly gripped her fingers and told her she was a brick.

Outside, the central city was a shallow lake that rose and fell with the tides. Stalled cars were parked at odd angles.

Police patroled in four-wheel-drive vehicles. A heavy surf was crashing so high over the harbor wall that it sprayed the houses. Most normal work had stalled with the commuter cars. The mayor was asking the governor for emergency relief.

Morgana decided to walk the rest of the way home when she saw the immense, two-block puddle on Oglethorpe Street. It was still raining, but she parked and got out and waded, soaked quickly by the rain. The only people outside were police in yellow rain slickers. The coffee-colored floodwater had joined with that of the man-made lake in the middle of downtown near the hospital. Seagulls floated everywhere looking for rubbish. The vegetation seemed all the more green and luxurious for being drowned.

Morgana didn't focus her mind on anything but the things around her. The historic downtown was certainly different from where Murchison chose to live, west of the Elstree River. There, most of the houses had been built after World War II and were like dollhouses with tiny rooms and only one bathroom you could barely turn around in. Cut off from the rest of Congreve by a maze of roads and interstates, Murchison's neighborhood was like a beleaguered island in the midst of an angry sea of traffic horns, headlights, and exhaust fumes. The yards were thick with oaks and azaleas and clumps of Spanish bayonet. In a funny way, it was like a tiny tropical Eden. Walking south of Main where the vacant Murchison family house stood, Morgana could almost understand why he had elected to live there among old retired people who puttered in their yards oblivious to the surrounding traffic jams.

The alternative was a suburb jammed onto filled land smack against a marsh with expensive homes and hard-charging neighbors. In the family house on Lamb Street, he would have been surrounded by rich doctors or pretentious lawyers.

Morgana continued to wade down Oglethorpe Street. The water was up to the top step of her house, but it hadn't leaked inside. She closed the door, breathed a sigh of relief, and stripped off her dirty clothes, then dried herself with a towel and sat in a living room chair naked except for the towel wrapped turbanlike around her wet hair.

She had saved Brian Murchison by the sheer force of her will. She knew this to be true. Her parents had at times called her dogmatic and stubborn, yet Drena had sworn that Morgana had the gift. It was not by accident, Drena had claimed, that her parents had named her Morgana. Morgana was gifted with the ability to open up that other ninety percent of the brain that most people couldn't use.

Only a very small percentage were born understanding. Those had the second sight, though they often sublimated it.

Others acquired the understanding through desire and careful study. These were often erratic and incomplete in their powers, sometimes able to produce results, sometimes not.

Still others acquired the gift by accident. Car wrecks, blows to the head, explosions, brain injuries that brought strange insight and spiritual peace. Typically, this was the group with the greatest power but the most hesitancy, since they also had the greatest understanding.

It was not crazy to believe that under the emotional jolt of the death of her mother and the attack by Chris Dixon, her power had been brought into focus. She had resisted, the night Chris brought her to the church. She had fought him and matched him last night when he had tried to kill Brian Murchison.

Morgana ran her hands up and down her body, stroking it in a sensual way and thinking of her desire for Murchison even after seeing him a bloated mass of putrefaction. She desired him in a way that gave her the will to do what must be done.

It was useless to even think of revealing what she knew to anyone other than Brian. It was too out of line with ordinary thinking. She would be tranquilized and locked away. Chris Dixon would beat her accusations the same way he'd beaten those of Carolyn Danner and Lynn Stafford. No, Morgana would have to destroy Dixon diabolically.

The flesh must breathe the air. She pulled off the towel turban and scraped her scalp with her fingernails. In her upstairs bedroom, she got dressed and went through her files to locate the one on spells compiled from Appalachian Mountain settlers. Leafing through it, she found what she wanted. It sounded absolutely stupid.

Bind a cat to a bedpost, it instructed, and lash it with tufts of grass. Then the witch who hates you will come to the door on some trivial errand. The witch will make a request to borrow something, which, if refused, will put the witch under your power. The person will become agitated and angry, but will be unable to leave.

It was like something out of a fairy tale, but the old woman in Maggie Valley, North Carolina, who had told it to Morgana had been revered by her neighbors. Besides, Morgana knew the truth behind the ritual. Quite simply, she would be willing Chris Dixon to come by using the power of her mind over his. The ritual would focus her power.

Without Patricia Stone shooing them away, the neighbors' cats roamed the yard at will. By luck, one of them had been trapped on the back stoop by the risen waters and was meowing in complaint. Though it could have swum back home, the poor cat obviously found the thought so distasteful that she preferred to sit there, crying, unable to leave.

Morgana brought her in, tied a noose around her middle, and tied that to the upstairs bedpost. The cat struggled wildly until Morgana fed her a bowl of milk and sardines. Contented, she ate and settled down to lick her fur. Morgana squatted on her haunches and tried to put herself in the right frame of mind.

Trying to block out other images, she recalled an evening as a young girl when a dense fog had blown in off the sea, smothering the town in its wet blur. Sitting in her room, she had been unable to see more than inches into the pea soup. It had seemed to her then that the world was gone and she was all that existed. By focusing hard on this, she put out of her vision the trees and the falling rain outside.

Taking some grass she'd plucked from beside the house, Morgana scrubbed it up and down the cat's fur, all the time concentrating on Chris Dixon, willing him to come.

Come to me, she thought. Please come to me. Come to me now.

She struggled to impose her will far out into the night, even performing other rituals with the cat's hair on an amulet. Eventually, her thighs were screaming from her position on the floor, and she straightened up. The cat slept, exhausted. Doubts crept into Morgana's brain. What she was doing was absurd.

She went downstairs and put tomato soup on the stove to heat. It reminded her of being sick as a little girl and her mother bringing soup on a tray to her in bed and reading her poems from *A Child's Garden of Verses*. Morgana became so lost in her reverie that the sound of splashing coming around the side of the house was a shock.

Standing on tiptoe at the kitchen window, she saw Chris Dixon out in the backyard. He was wearing rubber boots and a raincoat, carrying an umbrella. There was an anxious look in his eyes.

Morgana's heart quickened. She knew what she had to do next, and it terrified her. The man was a demon!

Slipping a drawer open, she took out the old wooden-handled carving knife. The knife dated to the first years of her parents' marriage. Its broad, fat blade had been honed down over forty years of sharpening, but it was always razor sharp.

The screen creaked open and a light tap sounded on the glass of the door. "Hello?" said a gentle voice. "Anybody there?"

The handle turned, but the door was locked.

"Morgana? Are you there, Morgana?"

The voice sounded insane, insane yet cunning. This man had killed, and he knew that Morgana knew. He had called her to the witches' Sabbath, the Black Mass in St. Helen's Church only a few days ago, but now he was outside the house talking in a perfectly normal tone of voice as if nothing at all had happened.

"Please! I need help," he called, knocking again. Shading the glass with both hands, he peered inside. "You can help me! I know you can!" He was silent for a moment, then he called again. "Are you there, Morgana? Just tell me if you're there. I won't come in! I'll talk to you through the door."

Morgana showed herself at the glass. She held the knife behind her and hooked the other hand in her jeans.

Dixon's mouth was still scarred at the corner where she had hit him with the spike bracelet. It crooked into a grin when he saw her. Morgana suddenly wished she had that spiked bracelet on now. That, or a loaded gun.

"Please, Morgana, open the door so we can talk," Dixon said persuasively. "We've had a misunderstanding that I can clear up. It's all been a mistake."

The rain was pelting on Dixon's umbrella and streaming down in rivulets. Morgana could sense his trying to put a mental net over her. It was weak and feeble, a slight tug like a child's grasp, an impulse to let him in that just barely tugged at her will.

Feeling the surge of her power, she heard herself say, "I can't help you, Chris. Go away."

He looked startled, and then his face became incredibly sad. Dropping his umbrella into the standing water, he wept and pleaded with her. "Please. I need help! I'm in the grip of Satan! I can't control it! He makes me do his will. I've been in bondage to a witch since college. She makes me serve Satan. Don't you understand? I have no free will. I have no soul. That's why I came to you—I know you can help. Satan is making me do evil things! Please help me!" He pressed his face and hands flat against the windowpane and rubbed his foggy hot breath on the glass. Rain ran down, distorting the image even more, giving him a ghoulish hall-of-mirrors look.

"I've done terrible things!" he confessed. "I'll put it on tape, I'll sign confessions! I'll tell about the murders! I don't care how I'm punished. They can jail me, electrocute me. I don't care anymore! I'm too tired of hiding, too tired of fighting against it. I just want rest for my soul! I want my soul back!"

Moved by his piteous cries, Morgana reached for the doorknob, but drew back when she saw the quick flicker of a grin. The look of a monster came over his face, twisting his features into contortions, rolling back his lips, baring his teeth.

As she backed away from the door, Chris smashed the glass with his fist and rammed his bleeding hand past the shards to reach for the knob. Morgana raised the knife to strike, but his will got a grip on hers and paralyzed her uplifted hand.

With a growl, he turned the knob and shoved inside. "You bitch!" he snarled. "I wanted to make you my bride. You could have sat beside me in power. You could have helped me. My bondage will be broken soon. I'll be free and unmastered in my own power. You might have tasted my flesh and known my joys."

The knife fell from Morgana's loosened grasp. The point struck the floor but didn't stick. Chris kicked it under the table and laughed deep and low. "I'll have your flesh. I'll make you lick my sweat and beg for me to stop hurting you. I'll suck the marrow from your bones with my hunger."

Chris grabbed her by the shoulders, his fingers biting deep. Morgana's head was swimming. She had been so sure she could overcome his will. She had done everything she was supposed to do. Had she failed? Was she going to die when she wanted more than ever before to live? She continued to struggle, and his teeth sank into her shoulder.

The pain was excruciating. But it was also delicious. It was as if it took the paralysis out of her!

She kicked violently at his groin in instinctive defense while her hands grabbed the pan of soup. Oblivious to the searing pain in her palms, she heaved it in his face.

His head was coated with the burning red liquid. He was silent for one startled moment. Then his piercing shrieks burst forth as he clutched at his eyes, scrubbing and wiping at the agony.

Scrambling under the table, Morgana grabbed for the knife, but Chris was on her, shrieking like a soul damned in hell. He tore at her clothes, belted her across the face, stunning her, spinning her head with stars. He jammed his knees into her stomach repeatedly to knock the air from her, and then gripped her throat with both hands. She tried to claw him and tangled a hand in a chain at his throat, which snapped, sending something rolling across the floor.

He told himself he had Morgana now. Such a little pressure on the windpipe, on the arteries, and the blood stopped to the brain, and the victim passed out. He wailed with evil laughter, dripping red soup, gnashing his teeth like a rabid dog.

Morgana's hand closed on the knife at last, and she jammed it into his left side with all her force. She felt his hands release her a split second before his screams crescendoed to new heights. He lurched up, Morgana after him, and stumbled out the back door as she continued to jab at him with the knife, plunging it down with both hands, trying to find a vital spot. Blood was flung around them in a maelstrom of screams and howls.

Chris blundered out into the pounding rain as Morgana fell back against the wall and slowly slid to a sitting position. She told herself she couldn't let him live. Whatever her fears of the left-hand path, whatever the cost, she had to use it now. Whatever it might send back at her, she had to destroy him.

Her eyes caught sight of a brass cylinder on the floor, and she remembered the chain around Chris's neck and recognized it as a talisman. Unscrewing the top, she dumped out the withered finger. It lay on the floor, the curled yellow nail pointing at nothing in particular. Hatred overcame her revulsion. She cut repeatedly at the finger with the knife, chopping it into small bits. She cursed and muttered and wished every vile death she could imagine on him. She pictured him eaten by ants and gnawed by maggots. She saw him dead in a ditch, mangled by dogs. She saw his head smashed open with hammers. She planned a scene in elaborate detail of his walking in front of a bus and being squished like a bug.

She willed stomach cancer and brain tumors and polio on him. All the while she jabbed the floor with the knife and muttered.

"Die!" she screamed at him. "Die!"

She concentrated for hours, thinking only of Dixon's death and watching the clock on the wall advance like a symbol of doom.

At last, exhausted, she fell into trancelike quiet.

● *85* ●

Chris Dixon waded back to the church, leaving a bloody wake through the deepening waters. His mind was a frenzy of pain. He couldn't concentrate on anything but his hatred, and then only in fragments. Images of his own hideous death kept screaming against his eyeballs. Pictures of his flesh tortured by medieval instruments, torn by hot pincers, his bones splintered on racks, branding irons searing deep into his muscles.

She was beating him! The bitch was beating him! He couldn't let her win! He had come so far! Faith would be dead soon! Then he would be free again. His soul would be his!

His breath was labored and desperate. His nostrils seemed to be closing up like in an asthma attack of his youth. With long, deep, straining pulls, he fought to get air into his lungs.

Oh, shit, the pain! He couldn't stand the pain! He hated pain! He was an instrument for the delivery of pain; he wasn't destined to be its victim! It wasn't right! It wasn't fair!

The rain beat down furiously. The palmettos on Main Street seemed to be growing in a river. Their leaves rattled under the assault in a sound as loud as the hammering of the heavy surf of the Elstree River. No one witnessed the lone figure staggering along, or if they did, they assumed he was a booze-blinded derelict.

Chris pounded on the big doors of St. Helen's. They had

been kept locked since he'd had his jaw broken by Morgana and told the lie about being mugged. The church was dark. Behind him, water descended from the stone porch in a wall like Niagara. The gutters gushed their own roaring cataracts.

Leaving a weaving trail of blood, Chris made his way across Bayswater Street and into the standing water of the graveyard. Splashing through water up to his knees, banging clumsily against tombstones, he passed into the unhallowed ground, staggering past Drena Wrenn's grave. The mausoleum stood before him among the dripping yew trees. Chris staggered inside to find the floor deep with water and the body bag that held Cynthia McAlister floating. He fell to his knees in the water and pushed the water-sodden corpse away from him in disgust. Insects clung to the body in heaps, trying to stay above the rising water. He clasped his hands in prayer for mercy.

"Light Bringer!" he gasped. "Please help me!"

He clutched at the brass cylinder at his throat and, for the first time, found it missing. Panic infused his pain. His throat seemed to close. He could barely breathe with a thin, whining noise. Still, he continued to beg:

"Light Bringer! Power Giver! Hear me!"

A splashing noise signaled the approach of someone. Grimacing against his agony, Chris twisted and looked up to see Squirt Crawford standing there with arms folded. Squirt's hair was plastered flat; his face ran with rivulets. Chris whimpered. There was something about that grim face, those stony eyes, something that made him look like a messenger of death.

Chris crawled toward him like a bleeding animal. "Please help me," he begged. "I'm hurt. I can't go to a doctor. I can't let anyone know about this! You've got to help me! You've got to hide me where she can't get me!"

"It ain't right to kill your own mother," said Squirt, his mouth the barest slit.

"Please!" begged Chris. "I'll give you money! Any amount you want!"

Squirt put his foot on Chris's neck, grasped his hair, and jerked the head back violently; the spine snapped. Dropping the limp head into the water, he stepped back to inspect his work. The mouth hung slack. The eyes were rolled back so only the whites showed. It looked like the face of someone damned to the immolating fires of hell for all eternity.

"No one should want to kill his own mother," Squirt muttered.

• 86 •

Morgana sat paralyzed with her back against the kitchen wall. The blood on her hands had dried to a brown crust. As the big hand on the clock came up to the twelve and the little hand to the eight, a great wave of peace came over her. She felt tired and weak but satisfied. She knew she had been successful. She knew Chris Dixon was dead.

Ointment and gauze anchored with adhesive tape made the burns on her palms cool. Getting out sponges and scrub brushes and every kind of cleanser in the house, she went to work on the tomato soup and bloodstains, rubbing and scrubbing until they were gone. The chopped-up bits of finger she gathered and packed into the cylinder. She poured Lysol into it, screwed on the cap, and then went out to the street to drop it down a rushing storm sewer. Back in the house, she let the floor dry and then went over it again. The still pelting rain had washed the porch steps clean. Every trace of the violence was removed. The rain sounded softer now, like some great burden had been lifted from nature.

Morgana poured herself a scotch and sat in her father's old armchair in the living room to listen to the ormolu clock. It had a peaceful tick that soothed her even more. The savage scene with Chris Dixon might never have happened. The certainty of his death made the horror seem like a movie she had once watched late at night, just a memory of someone's morbid imagination. Only the red marks on Morgana's throat anchored it all in reality.

The scotch tasted wonderful, and she began to wonder if Murchison didn't have the right idea when he stayed permanently soused. Life seemed like a battle to the death for the mere permission of survival. No one with any sensitivity of soul could avoid becoming either a mystic or an alcoholic.

By nine-thirty the rain had stopped and the clouds cleared. A full moon shone on the flat, brown mat of water that covered Congreve. Morgana put on rubber flip-flops, rolled up her jeans, and walked up to the hospital. Murchison was sitting up in bed reading the newspaper and eating canned applesauce. He looked weak but at ease. He held her bandaged hands and looked at them quizzically.

"You know," he said, "eating pop tops was never one of my party stunts at UVA. I can't figure what forgotten debauch I was in when I swallowed all that metallic junk, or why it wasn't picked up on X-rays before."

"Because it wasn't there," Morgana whispered. "He did it to you, but he's dead now and he can't do it again."

Murchison reached up to finger the marks on Morgana's neck.

"I'm certain he's dead," Morgana continued. She sat next to him on the bed and told him the whole story in a whisper. After a while, she fell asleep from exhaustion. When the nurse came around to clear out visitors, Murchison put a finger to his lips and said, "Shhh. Patient's asleep." Accustomed to Murchison's nonsense, the nurse decided to let Morgana sleep there instead of arguing with him.

In the morning, Morgana went down to the cafeteria for breakfast. There she read in the newspaper about the death of Rector Dixon. His body had been found in the graveyard, stabbed repeatedly, and the neck had been broken. The police suspected robbery as the motive; there had been other problems with looters in the midst of the flooding. The lead editorial sounded off about the sleeping beast in mankind and the need to cleanse society of its basest elements by use of the death penalty or any other means at hand.

Morgana put her face in her hands and tried to sink into deep, peaceful meditation. Her trance was broken by a doctor in a green scrub suit who sat down at her table and made a big effort to hit on her. She interrupted a description of his Porsche to tell him she had syphilis. He gave her a funny look and slid away.

The flood took a week to go down, and during that time Murchison was kept under observation at the hospital. The run of deaths from vomiting glass and pins had become a pattern, and the doctors were fascinated. Murchison merely irritated them with his contradictory stories, utter lack of cooperation, and personal quack medical theories.

All week, Morgana carried him food and magazines, watched him fidget, and listened to him blow off about his boredom. They took to playing Parcheesi every night, and once barred the door and made love. She was particularly pleased that he never asked her to smuggle him a drink.

The time for her period had come and gone, so Morgana went for a pregnancy test. The doctor confirmed sadly that she was pregnant. But Morgana was ecstatic.

"What are you thinking of doing with the rest of your life?" she asked Murchison.

"I'm through practicing law," he said decidedly. "I'll leave that to the guys in the yellow neckties. Maybe I'll open a saloon or run a towing service or become a tennis pro in Katmandu. If I had kids, I could live off their trust fund and sit around and be a full-time daddy. I'd call myself an investment counselor, though. Hang out at the yacht club reading the financial press and drinking tonic water."

Morgana ran her hand through his hair. "Whoever told you you were sterile?" she asked.

"Lots of people," Murchison answered. "I'm sterile, uncultured, boring, and backward." Then he saw her smile. He closed one eye. "Don't tell me . . ." He stopped in midsentence. "It can't be mine?"

Morgana held his hand. "I haven't been touched by anyone but one Brian Murchison, esquire."

"Jeez, I'm rich," Murchison said suddenly. "Plus I'm on the wagon. Let's get married."

"Maybe," Morgana said. "What do you think about a

wedding on a boat in the harbor? Like overage hippies with flowers thrown in the water and poetry by T. S. Eliot."

Murchison nodded and kissed her. He felt like a kid again.

● *87* ●

Morgana's doorbell rang at about nine o'clock three nights later. She answered it to find Faith Dixon standing on the porch, immaculately dressed in a lightweight summer suit, hat, and gloves. Morgana eyed her cautiously. Why should the woman come to see her? Faith's presence reinforced a vague foreboding Morgana had been feeling.

The funeral for Chris Dixon had been held that afternoon with eulogies delivered by the mayor and one of the many Church dignitaries who had attended. Both had spoken of the tragic loss of human life and the declining morality of society. The turnout had been heavy, the divided parish uniting once more to pay its respects to the dead.

"I'm on my way out of town," said Faith. She was very composed. Not at all distraught over the loss of her son. "I don't want any of our possessions. The church may do with them as it wills." She stood there briefly. Morgana said nothing.

"May I come in?" Though her voice was courteous, she clearly intended to have her way. Morgana stepped back.

Faith looked around the living room, touching one of the better pieces of furniture with her white-gloved hand. "You're a strange woman, Morgana," she said. "I'm not sure you realize how highly Chris spoke of you when he was alive. I must say, I had my hopes . . . . But tell me, how did you come to have such a name as Morgana?"

The comment struck a chill note. Morgana turned on another lamp to brighten the room. It lent her courage. "My parents were romantics," she said simply. She did not ask Faith to sit down.

Faith put her head back, closed her eyes, and took a deep breath. "I like to think of myself as a romantic." She rolled her head as if her neck was stiff and hugged her elbows. "I've been in love with love many a time. It's made me waste myself on some very choice specimens of foolishness. No doubt you've had similar experiences. I see you're pregnant. It's a boy you're carrying, isn't it?"

Morgana backed up against the mantel and laid her arm on it, seeking strength from its solid shape. Faith seemed suddenly ageless; her face—that of a woman beyond forty —was flawless, unmarred by any wrinkle. Her hair was a perfect, natural black. "How can you know any such thing?" Morgana asked, panic rising in her voice.

"My dear," said Faith warmly, "I know many things." She began tugging off her gloves. "You could, too, you know. You've got the gift. Drena spoke of it. She only had it in the slightest way, poor thing. She wanted so badly to embrace the light, but she just couldn't manage. She was a bit too squeamish, I suppose."

The gloves were off now. Faith flexed her fingers. She wore a bright topaz ring on her middle finger. She was missing the ring finger on her left hand.

A terrible awareness came over Morgana. She didn't know how much of it was logical reasoning and how much intuition, but she knew all the same. "Why did you come here?" she demanded. "Why did you come to this town?"

Faith let her attention drift back to the room, admiring the furniture again. For that instant, Morgana felt a weight lifted from her. Something had been pressing down on her without her even realizing, but she knew once it was lifted. Faith wandered into the dining room, switched on the lights, inspected the mahogany table, the big sideboard, the china cupboard. Morgana followed her.

"Poor Chris," she sighed. "He was so weak. I really shouldn't fall for rich boys, but they have such sleek, self-indulged bodies. I just shiver all over when I see them. The sloth. The petty greed. The rank cowardice. It makes them positively voluptuous." She turned her green cat's eyes back on Morgana. The weight returned. It seemed to be pressing about her throat and nasal passages, making it hard to breathe. It was like a severe attack of asthma.

"I suppose," said Faith, "you have similar emotions. Your Brian Murchison. What a perfect wastrel he is. It gives a woman such a sense of power. But of course, weak men have their drawbacks. Once they're given power, they decide they're important. Then they have to be chastised. You certainly did a number on my Chris." A faint smile played about her lips.

Morgana had a terrible urge to pick up a heavy candlestick and smash it over the woman's head. But she couldn't lift her arms to do it. They were leaden. They hung slack by her sides and couldn't be used.

Faith moved to the far side of the table. Her reflection shone deeply in its polished surface. "But you asked a question. Why did we come here? We came because poor Chris was weak. I had to convince him that power came from the sacrificed. It is the most powerful mind-bender I know—to make someone believe that power comes from the deaths of others.

"But you see, Chris was afraid to kill. At least at first." She raised her eyebrows in an ironic expression. "Later he came to like it all too much. But in the beginning, I had to make do with that pathetic creature who . . . expired . . . in New Hampshire so many years ago. Chris just wouldn't concentrate decently until I got him close to the body. It was a problem locating the girl again, particularly after the efforts her parents and that minister devoted to concealing her."

Faith took hold of a candlestick but didn't lift it. Her simple act of touching the metal seemed to increase the pressure on Morgana. As she talked aloud, a telepathic message seemed to carry mocking laughter: *You'd like to lift this, wouldn't you? But you can't, you see. Not without my permission. I could give that permission. I could teach you all.*

"Poor Chris," were the words she actually spoke. "The years I spent feeding that boy's vanities. College in Europe.

Cultural affectations. Expensive trips. Power-seeking in the Church. He was such a coward. He wouldn't even have entered the ministry if it hadn't been for the war and the draft. Time passes by, and we fritter away our efforts on failures. It's most discouraging. But then, what's time to me, I suppose?"

Morgana's words were thick and almost unintelligible. She had trouble even speaking. "How . . . old . . . are . . . you?" she asked with a gasp between each word. She felt like an automaton.

"One never asks a lady's age," said Faith with a smile. "It doesn't really matter. I'm quite ageless."

She's mad, Morgana thought. She's stark, staring mad. She's only a crazy old woman. Maybe she's flipped out because of the death of her son.

Faith's lips were perfectly still. But Morgana could hear her hushed voice: *I'm not, you know. I am what I say. Can't you feel my force? I can bend you to my will.*

Faith lifted her hand to inspect it under the light. Her nails were perfect red talons. The topaz shone. The missing finger was a jarring note. "Do you know what this means?" she asked, turning the back of her hand to Morgana and waggling the stump. "Of course you must. You're so wise in these subjects with all your studies and writing. It means I took a mortal lover. I was drugged by the pleasures of the flesh and forgot my love of the Light Bringer. I freely admit it was a mistake. It proves the need of women to mix with the company of women and use men only as instruments. To attempt to bring them to our level is a fruitless, barren enterprise."

Moving back into the living room, Faith smiled her dreamy smile and drew Morgana behind her with deep, all-knowing eyes. *I want you,* her voice said in Morgana's brain. *I need you. Follow me.*

Morgana fought it, but she was powerless. She drifted step by step behind her. Even when the green-eyed gaze shifted elsewhere and the pressure was slightly lifted, Morgana was still drawn as surely as the tides are drawn by the moon.

On the porch, Faith pulled her gloves back on as she

looked admiringly up at the moon, which was just a bit past full. "I've bought two tickets on Amtrak," she said aloud. "It's such a pleasant way to travel. I really regret the passing of the train in history. It was so civilized in its day."

Morgana tried to lean back, but felt she was trying to fall backward through a wall. A solid force was behind her that kept propelling her forward. She tried to go limp, to simply drop to the ground. Pressure built around her nose and throat, leaving her gasping for air. She lurched a step forward in panic at not being able to breathe. Her air passages opened slightly, then closed again. Only by following Faith could she breathe normally. She walked behind her down the flagstone walk.

Oglethorpe Street was still covered with silt and sticks and dried mud from the flooding. Faith picked her way carefully to where the church station wagon was parked against the curb.

From out of the night shadows stepped a tiny figure. Faith turned toward him and, in that moment, the pressure swept away from Morgana like a moving wave. She knew the man. It was Squirt Crawford. His appearance was altered, but she knew him just the same.

Backing up a step, Faith pointed a gloved finger at Squirt. "You get away from me!" she said, raising her voice for the first time. "You can't kill me, you know. I'm immortal. And I'll hurt you! You know I will!" She stared hard at him, her eyes glittering in the dark, her mouth twisting into a snarl.

There was a sharp click and a knife blade flashed. Faith didn't move another step. She seemed paralyzed under Squirt's stony eyes. His face was the face of death.

Squirt moved into her as if he were taking her in his arms to dance. His hand jabbed three, four, five times into her stomach, and then as she slumped, two, three, four times into her chest. She dropped to the street without a sound and lay in the mud. Blood formed in a pool around her and ran down both corners of her open mouth. It looked jet black in the darkness.

Squirt wiped the blade on her skirt, then folded it back into the hilt. Without any indication that he had even seen

Morgana, he crossed the street, got into a Toyota Corolla where Cerise sat waiting, and drove away into the night. Morgana stumbled back into the house, shaking and stunned.

The phone rang and Morgana picked it up. Her eyes did not focus, instead staring ahead of her into space. She heard Brian Murchison's voice, but it seemed far away.

"Morgana," he said slowly, "I finally got something decent from that private eye I had in Tennessee looking for information on Chris Dixon. Listen closely: Faith Dixon is dead. She died twenty years ago."

Morgana couldn't seem to speak for a long time. Finally, she heard herself say weakly, "I know."

"Look, Morgana," Murchison began again, "did you hear me? According to my information, Faith Dixon is an impostor. She's not really Chris Dixon's mother."

"I know," Morgana whispered. "She wasn't his mother because she was his lover—a witch for a lover." Had Squirt Crawford really killed her, or did she still exist in another place or time?

Morgana looked out the window to where the body lay sprawled in the street. Squirt Crawford had killed her. She was really dead.

"Are you there?" said Murchison anxiously. "Morgana?"

"Yes, I'm still here," she whispered. "I'll always be here."